THE CHRONONAUT

By

CHRIS J. SIMPSON

2 4 6 8 10 9 7 5 3

First edition published in 2008 A.D.

ISBN-13: 978-1495926235
ISBN: 1495926230

The manufacturing processes conform to the environment regulations in the country of origin.

ACKNOWLEDGMENTS

Lyrics to "Imagine" © 1971 by John Lennon

"I Don't Know Why Sometimes I Dream About You" Copyright © Eurora001. Used in lieu of permissions being obtainable.

"Never Does Come True" by Eurora001 and Headjog Copyright © 2001-2021. Used in lieu of permissions being obtainable.

"Living On Memories" Copyright © Eurora001. Used in lieu of permissions being obtainable.

Lyrics to "What If God Was One Of Us" by Joan Osbourne

www.chrisjsimpson.com

ENTRIES

For my parents,
without whose love, I would not exist,
and without whose empowerment,
none of this would.
Love you lots,
for all time.

FOREWORD

BY

THE WEBMASTER

Tervetuloa.

The weather is fine here in Finland. The summer came a few weeks ago and now the sunshine makes people smile. I want to say the same of me, but it's been a long and agonizing journey to get to this point.

As you read on, just what the contents of these apparently true chronicles may hold will become clear to you, as will why my years of procrastination are a drop in the big ocean of things. After I struggled to do what this scientist calling himself 'Eurora001' asked on the 5th of July 2001 from inside his journals as you will read, it became clear there just wasn't a way the wish he wrote about could be granted – except for one. And you're reading it.

You see I'd tried to make his experiences public via the media but – understandably when I really think about the warnings Eurora001 gives – the press here were hesitant to put themselves on the front line by revealing the events first. And I faced battles with the few people I shared this secret with, as this isn't something anyone involved wanted to become a 'bestseller' or anything – quite the opposite. Those few who shared the secret wanted what you will now read to stay an 'underground' piece of text with a limited appearance, and if we succeed then I will live to stumble across it perhaps in a second-hand bookshop, a thin layer of dust on its crumpled edges and a fractured spine. Those who've been tangled in the events saw some danger in any greater publicity. Why? You will see.

Over the years I was to procrastinate, cook much coffee, buy too many boxes of cigarettes, and eventually but reluctantly fall into denial about the facts contained herein, enough to put it out of my head. Except for the problem which was that every then and now I would stumble across some new discovery or fact on TV, some article in a paper, some story in a TV series, or some new knowledge of history, which the back of my mind could not help inevitably and perfectly tying into these journals, *with frightening accuracy* ... but how could the writer have known those exact things were going to happen unless these journals contained truth? What I had read those few years ago consistently played out in front of my eyes as fact as the world continued to turn. It was as though the journals kept calling out to me not to be forgotten.

My turning point began on 27 April 2007 when I was sent the following news article about the discovery of a new planet, by a reporter I had contacted in 2003:

"The Earth-like planet . . . known for the time being as ***Gliese*** *581c ... that could be covered in oceans and may support life is 20.5 light years away ... We don't yet know much about this planet, but scientists believe that it may be the best candidate so far for supporting extraterrestrial life."*

This had been sent because it contained facts that 'Eurora001' had written about *six years before* the apparently same planet had even been discovered (from day twenty-three of his journals). How could he have knowledge of it if he hadn't been guided towards them by those who already did?

That was almost enough to break my dissent, but on 14 May 2008 this camel was to have the last straw placed on his back when over in Britain it was announced that a number of reports of UFO sightings and alien encounters were being made available by their government under the 'Freedom of Information Act'. Here's a clipping from them:

"One man explained in great detail his 'physical and psychic contact' with green aliens since he was a child. The writer said that one of them, called Algar, was killed in 1981 by another 'race' of beings as he was about to make contact with the UK government. Another document reveals the experiences of a 78-year-old man who alleged that he met an alien beside Basingstoke Canal in Aldershot, Hampshire in 1983. He said he went on board the craft, giving a detailed explanation of it, before being quizzed by the aliens about his age. He was then told: 'You can go. You are too old and too infirm for our purpose'. The eight released files are part of almost 200 files set to be made available over the next four years."

As you read deeper into Eurora001's diaries, you will learn the relevance of 'people from one race killing a being from another who was about to out them', and what 'their purpose' was that the man was 'too old and infirm' for. Only the government papers on such sightings had been classified till now, and still somehow the diarist gave us the reason for such murder and rejection *seven years before* they were even declassified! Unless he worked for the British government and NASA simultaneously, all of the above was becoming too hard to believe with any other explanation than an unbelievable one. That it was all believable and true.

Obviously I wish I'd published this before those first releases, and that is exactly why I now have – enough was enough. For the next prediction that comes true in some the government declassification or another source, there will be no doubt about the accuracy of these journals.

Although attaching my name to the publication would - if this were a fictional Hollywood movie - act as some form of insurance, this is no movie and you will not find the name of me here. The best insurance for me and my family is anonymity, just like the news agencies who also wished no part in it either. Whilst I thank you to understand that, I can at least briefly tell you how this all began.

Until my discovery in 2001, as some sort of pioneer, I had for a time run one of the first small online 'blogs' websites from my home. I had a relatively small number of bloggers, a standard user agreement making blogs the property of it, and a good reputation. That all ran smoothly for about 10 months ... until on a cool night in early August 2001 one of my accounts suddenly stood up and out from the rest. I started to receive automated e-mail alerts from the server that an account was repeatedly having the wrong log-in password attempted. In other words someone was trying desperately to hack into a blog.

The hacker was using what we call the 'brute force' method - repeatedly attempting different password combinations so fast that it must have been with the use of a program which rapidly tries words from a dictionary. Fearing they might be successful, and my slowly growing site's reputation as a safe place to store online thoughts risked, I took the blog account offline, emailed the owner, and with no account to hack, the problem went away leaving only an anonymous IP address behind as a useless fingerprint.

That is when I had noticed that the blog was set to 'Invite Only'. This was the mode where somebody just wants a central private place to store their thoughts, but *doesn't* want it published for the world to see. At most only those who they have given the access invite to can log in. It is commonly used by travellers for this purpose too, so they can log in and write in the same diary from any cybercafé on earth.

I received no reply from the owner of the blog. I was thinking no more of it and busy with other work to earn a living, and so I forgot about the now offline account for that day. But lying in bed that same night I couldn't sleep and was making my wife irritable, as I felt an urge I can't explain to view the contents of the journal. There was something not right that drew me to that. Let me say first this is not something I would normally do. However the thought relentlessly poked and prodded away at my brain. If someone else wanted to access this weblog so frantically, then as its 'publisher', so should I, and so to put it out of my mind before a good night's sleep, I went to the Mac in my work room and opened the blog.

I scanned through months of entries, all the usual sort of stuff - with one exception. The author was talking to just one person - a loved one he must have given the access info to. After a half hour of speed scanning about everyday events (though I missed lots of the detail initially) it became clear that the author was in fact a scientist and inventor who had – he thought – stumbled across a discovery that he was really excited about. In fact he thought he was about to change our world, as it appeared a genuine 'Eureka' moment when I came to it. Was this invention what someone wanted to hack? Yet only its discovery rather than the detail was covered in the blog.

Of course I had my doubts about the authenticity of the journal, until I asked myself – why would a person make up a story so complex and time consuming, only to then leave it in a private blog nobody could ever see?

His contraption was discussed by the blogger for months of brief entries during the development of the concept which you will not read here ... until a startling day and a turn of events that spelt the beginning of the end of my website, and the past shock, denial, acceptance, and now finally, action ...

Well, *that's* where we pick up the entries, and for clarity I have labelled that key day as 'Day One'. 'Day Zero' (which occurred hundreds of days into the full journals) is also included before then to see you into the events, as it fell after a natural break in his writing due to a trip he took - as you will read. The entries before then (let's call them 'minus days') don't matter to the event day one brought, unexpected to the diarist as it was. I won't give away the twists and turns that the writer of the journals encounters – as I hope nobody else has done for you. Know only that I've recreated the blogs here exactly as I found them – typing errors and all – give or take a few formatting changes and other similar necessities for security or suchlike.

And where to go from there, once we have done as the journals ask? I don't know the answer to that. I suppose only time will tell. My sincere hope is that I will receive correspondence about how to handle this matter, from people of science or government.

I didn't sleep at all that night of discovery I might add, and admit that I haven't slept quite the same since. Writing this is in a way closure for me, and will also bring about the beginning of the end of the nightmare he writes about, I can only hope.

A final but important reminder though – you'll begin to understand once you have read the beginning of the first entry, and truly understand once you have finished the end of the last, why I ask that youdon't spread word of this, nor copy the text to any website, nor sell or pass it on to anyone, and why if you are a journalist it is especially important that you don't review this – as I realise now that first journalist was right about.

What you read is what those who have been touched with it legitimately feel to be a scientific journal written in earnest by a brilliant but scared mind. It's not a 'science fiction' tale despite its sheep's clothing disguising it as such – so you have now discovered that was all part of the effort to keep this matter under the radar of 'those who must never discover it'. So with all of that in mind, I ask your respect and co-operation for the wellbeing of all involved. And by the way - you are, by reading this, now involved.

As I find myself about to submit this introduction for the first time, I also find I am scared - as I had known I would be when this inevitable moment came - scared that the moment before I click 'Publish', I will be stopped by a sudden intruder to this room, so that I never can click it.

What follows is written by 'Eurora001'. Benefit from it, and don't worry.

Yours truly,

THE WEBMASTER

Day Zero

Twenty-Eight

Posted by Eurora001 on Thu 7-Jun-2001 18:18

Edited by Eurora001 on Thu 5-Jul-2001 12:55
[Editor: 1 month later]

I add this to my earlier journal in the unlikely prospect that I am not talking to myself at this moment, and if so that whoever is reading this cannot find means to contact me.

In such instance, please know you have discovered something of... importance. And danger. (And understatement.)

Everything that is about to happen to me in the past month began here, and now, and the reason for my fervour will soon become apparent. I need say little more as all you need do is read, once you are sure you understand and accept the risks.

Yet the reason for this message is to implore you - once you have read what follows - this MUST be made known to only the smallest and quietest of the masses. Just enough people who can make it stop. The enemy has eyes everywhere and the only way to defeat them is surely by stealth.

So do what you must, but for heaven's sake do not make what I wrote public knowledge or publicise the later details anywhere that it may be brought to the attention of... Them. These details must never escape to above their radar. You have to trust me.

IF they find out this journal has exists, then ANYONE who even reads it most likely shall cease to. Exist, that is. I am so very sorry if that includes you, but I am doing all I can to make matters right.

I have neither the time nor ability to explain any better than I already have in the following entries. I risk much even by writing this caution, so please for the love of all that is holy believe me.

God, I have to go.

Day Zero

Posted by Eurora001 on Thu 7-Jun-2001 18:18 [original entry]

Home at last. Good grief how I missed writing to you this past week. And what a journey I have been on! It is wonderful news...

I DID IT! It is over.

And that is not all. The scar on my wrist has almost gone completely. I will soon be free from so much.

But I am so tired. Why did I never believe in jetlag? No this is not just jetlag, this is Stealth Bomber lag… it has crept up on me, under my radar. Certainly, it was just the passenger Boeing 777 from China not a Stealth Bomber, but being first journey that far East, the journey has been like hitting a brick wall. With my face. (Twice.)

'Ni hao' indeed.

I had a decent view from the hotel. And wonderful news too yes? I have reached the end of this long race at last! And won.

Did I mention how much I missed talking to you? Back home again, and here I sit, a sleepless night, another dark blue sky, light spread across thousands of stars, every one of which has become so well known to me like a constant yet flickering friend.

And once again I have planted myself with a glass of water at the computer, by this window, staring at the patterns of those shimmering lights in the heavens. You know how I am... always wondering what other entity may sit near one of those stars, who may be thinking the same way I am, and staring back in this direction also not seeing me as I fail to see them. Yet I think of them. Is it that one... what about this one? And they too may be hoping that a certain loved one might be staring at the stars thinking about them too, as I do about you.

That is after all what started me on this journey back... Goodness has it really been that long?

In Beijing I managed to keep the scar out of the sight of my loyal hosts thanks to an English long-sleeved top (the Chinese 'Large' I fooilishly bought for myself without trying it on, would fit 9-year old Samantha perfectly!).

Shall I tell you about the big meeting?

The night before the big day and after a very long one travelling, was an even bigger event. I blush to myself now just thinking about it. I was in the rather impressive suite they had booked for me (presumably in a thinly veiled attempt to strike a better deal for themselves), lying on the sofa in the living room. (Nude.) Then I saw my front door open! In a panic, I reached for what I thought were my suit trousers to pull on fast.

In walked a hotel staff member, escorting my solicitor. Apparently they had been knocking for some time. Eager to ensure I was well prepared, Jonathan had been escorted into the suite to drop off the final paperwork, just in time to see his star client forlornly trying to thrust his private parts into a single grey sock.

Can you imagine?!

Well, the next day I had my excuses all ready, but need not have. You just have to smile when you go to shake hands with two of the Far East's most prominent fellow scientists, and instead of anything disquieting their first words to you go along the lines of, "Hohhh, vey handsome!" The people there are so respectful. (And blind apparently.) And that is effectively all we could say without the help of the translator - who took an awfully, embarrassingly, long time to arrive. As did the CEO and his obligatorily even shorter sidekick.

Before then the language barrier was most certainly not down. You try sitting there in a minimalist meeting room with your lawyer and translator, and two of the greatest minds in probably all of Asia, doing nothing but trying to find items to pass a comment on, that you would normally never even notice, making hand gestures about them, and pulling friendly, eyebrow-raising faces.

'Ashtray! For smo-king!'

This was not what I had come all this way to discuss!

It must have been belittling for them too. I felt this small. But the translator arrived after twenty long minutes, and it was not long before we all started to get on really well. It was all turning out to be so promising.

But then the bigwigs arrive, seven of them in total. I know! Just one of me. They burst into the meeting room with so much testosterone you could almost smell it (at least I think that is what it was), and then approach the other side of the desk, line up in a well-rehearsed fashion, and greet us with a bow.

Yet these are angry - or is it just intimidating - looking people. And a quite pungent smell hit me too after that. I think it was coming from just one of them, rather than a chorus of B.O. Still, not pleasant.

I notice the same one for some reason uses black paint on his scalp instead of hair like everybody else. (I feel better.)

They are so harsh in appearance that for a moment I do wonder if they are 'hired guns' come to steal the briefcase I clutch which holds the all the data on my concept that I am about to trade with them for more money than I could ever count. And would they then torture me for the password to access the files?

Well, no, I am here now obviously, writing this to you.

They lift their briefcases onto the long wooden desk, containing their copies of the contracts that had been bounced back and forth halfway across the world and negotiated between my Solicitor and theirs to within an inch of their little e-lives. So all I can think is 'thank goodness for Jonathan on my side and by my side now'.

One of them had said something that Abbey my translator started to explain to me, and as she did her translating it became clear to me that they did not realise my 'predicament' until the translator gave the game away. I often get that, as you of all people know. I suppose when all correspondence is via attorneys and email, people just assume you are like everybody else. But as soon as they realised that I was not like everyone else, their body language changed. Big ape-like aggressively-postured arms shrunk back to sides, shocked heads started to bow ever so slightly, and everything seemed for the better. It was quite a sight to watch the faces of bears turn into teddies.

And so there was virtually no belittling - the surprise over my quandary had thrown them off balance and given me the upper hand! The testosterone floated away.

(The other smell remained.)

Disadvantage in the eyes of many prejudiced people still in this world was working in my favour for this once. It has its plusses yes?

I held the ball... it was my chance to prove myself. And it took longer than they may have hoped due to the translator. For people who had achieved so much in their lives, they seemed to be in awe of the schematics that loaded up on the laptop in front of them. Once I had shared with them my Eureka moment from that stormy day, I elaborated under our pile of non-disclosure agreements ('NDAs') about how the eurora potential ('TEP') would work. The nine of them certainly kept me there late discussing TEP and the TDA, and how my design might someday harness it ('AHMDMSHI').

I jest of course, but I call it 'my design' or 'concept' for I hate the words 'my invention' - it makes me sound like a mad scientist.

Perhaps I have watched too many motion pictures. I was expecting them to pin me down and interrogate me about every minutia, to belittle my thinking regarding the workings of my design in an effort to renegotiate the deal at the last minute. It is all that went through my mind on the long flight there. When will I ever learn to believe something good can happen to me Bella?

Instead, I became almost disappointed with how little they wished to ask me after that, and how quickly the transaction was completed. It was clear that - for whatever reasons - my Chinese customers were eager to take the concept off my hands and be gone with me.

It reminds me now of the time you first saw my laboratory at home. You had called it, 'the oddest workshop my eyes have ever seen'. Until you added, '...the first too', with that delectable grin. Perhaps I am rather unconventional - but how could I not be all things given?

Either way, at that time with you I was proud to be introducing something new into your life, just as you had finally touched mine.

Will write more soon love, my eyes are finding it hard to keep up with my fingers.

Posted by Eurora001 on Thu 7-Jun-2001 19:49

Speaking of mad scientists (I was, was I not?), I AM pretty mad right now too, which is unusual for me. Yes, would you believe Burger King managed to aggravate me. Who would have thought it? Not just that, but who would have thought that I would go to a Burger King! Alas it was for lack of anything else to quench my starvation on the journey home from Heathrow.

Daniel was my pick-up from the airport and on our way back I felt peckish for a taste of 'home' (even though it was a taste of America in fact). And so we uncommonly found ourselves at a drive through window occupied by a dim looking girl with wonky teeth who just kind of... stared. Her vocabulary was as bad as... like... whatever. If you can imagine the exact opposite of Juliet gazing down from her balcony to Romeo, then you have the scene in your head. He decided he should probably give my order to Juliet (real name likely Varooka), which was for some brain food - a fish sandwich of some description (yes I know, fast food is not health food). Daniel reminded me of the conversation...

"Fries wiv dat?"

"Pardon? Oh, I see, sorry no thank you, just a Sprite please", Daniel had said.

I was charged an amount that seemed about right.

Pretty good so far I think you will agree.

We drove off, opened the food bag, and found a 'Whopper', French fries, and an apple pie. Of course, I had obediently paid the wrong amount for what we were about to receive, as shown on the till, because I was still on China time (i.e. bed time).

We drove round the drive through yet again and back to the same girl, who - when Daniel explained the trouble - somehow looked even dimmer and her teeth even more wonky. Those few minutes of aging had not been kind to her. Senility was even apparently kicking in during her teenage as she did not seem to have a clue what the world was all about and did not even recognise us from our visit to her not 120 Earth-seconds before.

We drove to the next window in search of someone with a higher IQ than the pie, and a young man with a thin face, short brown hair, and pimples on his pimples opened the window and offered me a Chicken Royale meal, but Daniel informed him that we were not the woman in the car behind who had ordered that (she hopes), and in words of one syllable, elucidated.

After he came back from checking the till, he told Daniel adamantly that I had NOT been given the wrong meal or overcharged for it. That seemed strange as I had.

Alas, our proof was no match for his intellect. According to his logic, we had morphed the change we received into different coins, forged a printed receipt on heat-sensitive paper using the cigar lighter, stretched a soft drink cup to twice its size, and grown our own potatoes in the back of the car, which we had harvested into quite realistic fries.

With Daniel screaming at the man-child an expletive even I could not work out, having a Manager called, and refusing to move out of the lane until the matter was resolved, they took back my car-grown Burger King and replaced it, and my money. (One can be reasonably confident they will have spat in the sandwich though.)

What is not funny is that what led to it all having such a bad effect on my mood was the fact that all the way back to England, all I dreamt about was you.

I am glad this is private. I feel uncomfortable that after so long I still think about one person. What is it now, twenty months since you finally fell in love with me, as I had been with you for so long? And eighteen months since you left? Can it really be possible to be with someone so little time and..

You are the constant that has kept me motivated through the years of this journey. And the final leg of the journey is now complete. On that flight back from the meeting. I was gazing out of the window as we flew over Europe - Copenhagen it might have been - looking down in awe at the tiny model-like beaches, bridges, countryside, and wind farms. I wanted to live there so very much right at that moment - it all looked so simple and perfect. None of life's little problems visible from that height. What if I could jump out of the plane right then? I was captivated with that thought at that point, high up above the clouds in another of man's most wondrous inventions. And I knew who would understand exactly how I felt.

Every time I think of escaping our culture, or of becoming a real life Robinson Crusoe, it just connects me to you.

The thought of you held me for a moment. And then it was gone, just like you.

I must have gone back to dreaming, as all I wanted to do was hold you close and say that thing I did not say... do that thing I did not do. But the time for that has long since passed me by. And completing my work is all that has kept me somewhat sane since you left. There is provision at least for me to advise the Chinese reactively at their behest if not proactively, but what I will do now that immense slice of my life has left me too - I do not know.

I hate... well, love. Every time I awake from another dream of you - of us - it instantly and completely revives and refreshes every feeling I had that Christmas, and it has been doing that since that day you left. Constantly revitalising itself, this never-healing wound I have learned to bear. And yes I know, I have written the same thing before and am risking becoming a broken record - well if it would just stop hurting I could stop needing to get it out. It is just that I missed talking to you while I was away. I really should speak to someone other than this log. If only I could.

But would anyone be able to imagine a person for whom time does not heal? Every day that passes, those neural connections do NOT wither away and dim the memories. Imagine that the same pain you felt when THAT awful thing in your life happened to you, only it is as sharp today as it was years ago at the moment of its occurrence. That is what these dreams do to me - what they rekindle in me - and what they make me do to myself.

Yet, maybe they are a dream come true (looking on the bright side if I may be permitted), as for those moments, or hours, before I wake, I am back there… sitting by that little brook with you where we questioned whether the ants below look up and see us as Gods, just like we look up for Gods of our own… Or that first brief kiss behind the big old Surrey mansion… Or walking across the field after lunch, holding hands as you bestowed on me your belief that we could make ourselves invisible to the cricketers just by 'thinking it' in their direction - the reverse of how when you want someone to see you, you can think it and somehow you catch their attention as they turn to look at you. It is a hypothesis that still captivates me to this day... indeed your 'reverse attention catching' even seems to work.

I wonder whether, if I think about it enough, I can stop being invisible to you.

As I sit here and watch the light that has been travelling for millions of years from those distant stars, I get to considering what was happening in my hometown when that light started its journey towards us on Earth millions of years ago in time. How appropriate. True, my hometown was a Jurassic forest then. But still it always makes me view my life from an entirely different perspective, and I need and adore that. More people really should strive for it. God how I love any form of escapism to another place. How ironic, given the subject of my concept.

Oh yes, China...

I wrote some more lyrics whilst I was there (I had to write somewhere to replace writing to you here) the night before the big meeting, to add to the list. Do you want to see? Fine. Can you guess who it is about?

I don't know why sometimes I dream about you
It's probably just a phase I'm going through
I don't know why sometimes I dream about you
A nightmare tonight then a dream come true
I just do not know why I do - but I do

Then the harder I try, to touch the sky
I'm touching a dream, or so it seems...

It continued. But there is a better side to my dreams - this inspiration they bring me. And brought me. That is partly where my theory came from, so complete and sudden, after all. Absurd ideas that always come to me (from where or who or what I do not know) during that twilight hour between sunrise and the first stirrings of the day. Like this discovery that has so far taken me to the other side of the world and back (shorter than it is capable of when it finally reaches fruition one hopes!) - a concept that occupied almost every waking moment whilst you occupied the sleeping ones. Such a full life, yet so blank, and even that is now gone, finally. And it was quite final.

So, the meeting in Beijing went better than I could have ever thought. As soon as I had finished showing them the theorised workings of the TDA, my small but forbidding audience were even more captivated. Even the translator. In fact I even captivated myself! I could not - perhaps did not wish to - quite be sure if their excitement was A) Eastern respectfulness and graciousness, or B) genuine euphoria at what I was showing them.

I cannot quite suppose it but it must have been B, as the deal was sealed and extreme though it feels - or does not feel - I am about to be extremely wealthy. How surreal is that?

I have just checked my bank account.

I AM extremely wealthy!

GOODNESS!!

Wow.

What I would not give to share this moment with you Bella.

Usually with my plans as you know, after a couple of weeks sitting on them, I find a flaw, or market research shows there is not much demand. With this though, I was never surer. Just this once, I am allowing myself to get perhaps even slightly... pompous. And well-to-do! (I just had another look - for it is hard to resist.)

And now I have cleared the cobwebs of the other events away, that is really what I sat down to write today. (No not 'I am pompous'.) I have to concede that although of course I sadly did not conceive the entire theory - everyone knows who did - I am 99.8% confident that I am 99.9% going to be responsible for bridging the gap and modelling the method by which it can - even will - actually happen one day - with 100% certainty. That is truly remarkable.

Ha, I just read that back and it scared the blood out of my veins. Yet I have to face what I have discovered and successfully put to market, if only by chance... or by dreams. Why is success so scary? Does that sound big headed? Or did that just sound too modest? Agh!

How many times have I filed patents or signed NDAs now. Too many. Fine, it is true I did not predict my first foolish device of youth, that ultrasonic duster, would cause dogs to think the high-pitched tones meant, "Attack man with apron". I was but a child then fresh out of school. After all, did the inventor of the wheel predict how many motoring deaths they would likewise cause? So less of the sarcasm if you do not mind. Thank you.

So, new territory! Exciting! A blank canvas and time for something new. Onwards and upwards.

I wonder if I can ever really put this idea behind me. All the sums added up. Okay we have still to formulate material we need to actually make it. I will always wonder where such a substance will come from, until it inevitably does appear from some such source, perhaps to on our own planet but beyond that. We need to come on many more giant leaps before the structure can be made sturdy enough for the immense forces, and yet that magnificent energy source be light enough and have the necessary extent all at the same time. Sorry, I know that must bore you. It just makes me feel better to say that the theory behind the workings, and the arrangement of this thing is... well, you know when you just know?

I know.

So that is it. The knowledge has been passed on. My cog can slowly start to stop turning, as the bigger wheels (the bigwigs) take the baton for their role in the concept.

I suppose it is no coincidence that I write of it and you at the same moment. After all, it is perhaps the only way we could be together. Only I would not survive. Catch 22.

But 'you just never know' as they say, and that is the one remaining idea that does still make the cogs of my mind whir. Or maybe I should stop clinging onto it...

Onto you.

Or onto life.

Either way is a way out... but neither can I bring myself to any more.

The only way out is through. And this prosperity just might bring me a new kind of life, one that helps me through. That is the hope. Perhaps I will even buy that desert island.

But my God, how many times I was close to leaving this torturous life since you left.

How many times did I wrestle with the thought of ending my heartbeat and then pull myself from the depth of death.

'What will I gain by doing so...?' I will think. 'Revenge...?' maybe... relief? Yesss.

Then I will take a deep breath and wonder that sky again. Somehow it keeps me strong. 'Should... or should I not...?' The question never escapes me. And what if I HAD acted differently at that stupidly insignificant monumentally pivotal moment that meant I lost the chance to ever 'be' with you?

Too late for 'what ifs' now. But God WHAT IF things HAD gone differently that night.

WHY DID I NOT TURN ROUND?!...

Remember I was sleeping downstairs at your Mother's house, on her sofa? I felt like a teenager again, yet there I was far from one! But that was what had to be done to be near you, and oh I would do anything for that. I know we had a disagreement but I really did understand that your staying with her for Christmas meant it was the only way we could spend more than one daytime together, what with the distance and all. Oh what I would give for only that problem of distance, now we have this far greater one.

Actually I say 'sleeping' there but I just could not drift off could I. My eyes would not stay shut and kept opening to the frenetic movement of the hamsters in their cage by the Christmas tree. Goodness how they thought that wheel was the best thing since... their water bottle. Either way, no nice dreams to go off to existed then (the reality was lovely enough).

There had been something about you since you first walked into the schoolroom when we were children those short decades ago. You were the new girl, and life for me as a 10 year old was hard too - I needed warming and your face gave me that Ready Brek glow from that first day you took your seat at the desk by the window (yes I still remember), as that face still warms me at night. You were burned on my heart, right from the start.

Such a look of nature - stunning yet in such a pure, almost unearthly yet earth-child way - frizzy brown hair (which I normally do not like but just 'worked' for you - like everything), and jewel green eyes of course. And as we grew up at school 'together' - you hardly noticing me, and me noticing hardly anything but you - everything you did just seemed so perfect to my soul. I was sure that - if you let yourself see it - that I would be perfect for you in turn. After all, how could one jigsaw piece not fit the other, when the other already knows it fits the first.

I never told you before, but as we grew older there were so many things I started to notice. That lovely way you would sit barefoot on the grass, those soft legs tucked under you in that adorable way, into some sort of sylphlike bundle. It pains me to talk about your lips - so easy to love - just like you all over. No wonder you were my childhood sweetheart. And you so strong of spirit. Yet the sweetest personality with such strength. Striking, but you did not know it. Spiritual, religious, nature-loving, creative - everything that guarantees a perfect soul. And to top it all, once we finally overcame the years of bashfulness and began our endless chatting, you seemed to be the only person in the world who actually, finally, GOT me... who understood me... and all those odd things that make me, me.

Me-me.

He-he.

(Sorry you know when I am upset or nervous I always make these puns.)

And you got me, just like I got you. And I am so glad I did get you.

Where is this all coming from? The relief of clearing my mind of the concept. I have become so focussed on that of late, and neglected you, but you know that I have not forgotten our story.

And you know, I even loved your overly cat-like inquisitive nature. I know you might have thought that sometimes you asked too many questions for me, and I know sometimes I gave you that idea too, but when I sit back and think about you (i.e. every spare minute of every day since we parted), that is one of those things I miss the most. Ironic I know, that I want it when it is not there - but I loved that side of you. Still do. For one, I feel flattered that you looked to me for answers. But more than that, you remind me of Gemini. Meow. See, he was naughty (like you), beautiful (like you), hairy (um...) but truly one of a kind (like... well you get the idea), but also ever so inquisitive. Whatever I was doing, he would be there, sitting by me and staring, moving his head in fascinated ways, and if he could speak to me (which sometimes I thought was not far off happening) he would be asking all those questions that you were able to and did. Certainly, sometimes he was too inquisitive, but that did not matter because I truly loved where it was coming from, and so it is with you. And did curiosity kill that cat? I never found out where he went that day he never came home.

I would like to think he is still out there somewhere, curiously inspecting the Space Shuttle or something.

So I hope you realise by now, that once you have experienced someone like you, everyone else pales into… Well yes, you were one in a million, and we were two.

Do you remember how we talked about whether we even perhaps shared some genetic lines?! I mean, how two people from so far apart can both have a rare phobia of people scratching fabric...?! And so many other similarities that we must have been connected. And I hope still are.

The feeling of emptiness since you left leaves such a scar in my heart. Why did you leave - me? I still need you. I need your strength, your company. To be left by one person, but one to whom I could talk to and say exactly how I felt, without being judged, that one person who I could watch, and not say a single word, just be there with and for and… It was as if on those endless days we spent together those short months, we helped each other, to survive, but for this one moment, this stupid damn moment I keep replaying infinitely! 'Why did I not turn over?! Why!?' I have lost you now and there is no way back.

This thought of self-hatred, guilt and emptiness is one of the things that drive me those times to such a need of... what else but death.

Goodness this really is flooding out now, sorry.

Yes, it was far too many long years before you noticed that spark that I had seen as but children. And then the letters. Not really *love* letters, just friendly, funny words, and notes yes? Do you remember me writing about a fly that was distracting me from writing the same letter, and how I said I had swatted it onto the paper, and did a drawing that really did look like a squashed fly, next to those very words? You loved that joke. Seems silly now. Bzz.

And yet your love for all those things I did to help you love me has stayed with me, and I hope you discover the similar jokes I drop in even here. They are for you. (Well I hardly do it to make myself laugh.) You had always said I should be a writer. And I loved you for pretending to be so kind.

You know, I had dreamed of that one mystical person who would love me, for who I was. Who would be there when I opened my eyes each day, and who would hold me when I was down. 'You' did not have a face in my mind back then as a child, just an outline and figure... a figure of my imagination, or imaginary friend. But if they were my imagination would that mean that they were just a part of me? Did that mean I loved myself? But if I did love myself why would I do all those things to myself, why would I try to avoid the mirror so much, constantly try to conceive a way out of this... try to change myself... try to end myself...

Why am I even telling you this? You already know what occurred. I have missed writing to you. And counselling myself in the process. I am also certain it is because the dreams which bring it flooding back to my mind, well they do so uninvited. How dare they. I have no control over such things. Yet THIS way... I do have control. And so I am choosing to relive those moments that touched my life over and over, over and over, rather than have them relived FOR me. I just wonder if I can ever expend the wonderment of you.

Time passed after the letters but only a peck on the lips between us, as there was something uniquely wholesome and innocent about everything your heart touched, and that included me, and so even our intimacy was wholesome. And so I became more innocent and decent with you, even in my twenties. And that then became us all over.

There I was, staying the night on the sofa. Christmas. Naturally, I would not have minded one bit if that night things had moved on... To get to an emotional, romantic point. Fine, I mean physical point. To stare into those implausibly delicious eyes properly this time while expressing more than just a kiss or three. To tell - no show - each other how we really felt. Okay, 'I would not have minded', is a humunderstatement.

I never told you THIS one before, and I wish you would tell me if I am right, but I thought you had said 'I love you' at the end of our first ever video call, but surely I had misunderstood! You never said it again, and I wonder with some dread if that was because I did not reciprocate.

God, more regrets.

Just before you stood up to walk off upstairs, I grabbed your hand and invited you with a gentle tug to kneel by the sofa where I lay. You had conceded, holding my hand all the time, and we chatted a little, do you remember? I know I wanted to kiss you so, but you seemed not to want to. Darn it. (It is always the way, when you punch above your weight.) I know, you take your Christianity seriously and 'did not want to move too fast'. And compounding the problem was that you were also conscious about your Mother being around - it was her house after all. I am too, but the male of the species overlooks such minor details in the face of... well, you know. I resigned myself to the fact you would soon vanish to your room, and so I did not even try to stop you. I was too used to it.

"Goodnight you".

"See you", you casually threw back at me as if without a care in the world. (How do you do that??) I pulled you towards me and held you so tight, my head resting on your shoulder, and for a moment I breathed in your ear, cold on my lip. It felt unusually intimate made me smile and tingle. I wondered if you would reciprocate...

And so naturally, of course, you were the first to pull away.

There I was, nighttime, darkness all around, quiet apart from the Hamster chatter presumably... and the absolute love of my entire life gone to sleep upstairs without me.

Then... I sensed footsteps coming down the stairs which were obviously your mother as it is her house and you had gone to sleep... but with each step of my memory that moment creeping closer that I would now give ANYTHING to change...

Obviously she was coming to check we were not asleep together, or to get herself a drink of water. Feed the hamsters. So I rolled to face away from the door. Kissing the back of the sofa, I pulled up the blanket, shut my eyes, and pretended to be asleep.

Um, 'zz'.

I sensed her coming closer.

She stopped, hovering over me for too many heart-stopping moments, and I wondered whether she was trying to see if you were with me hiding under the covers. Still fresh in my mind that nervous, unfamiliar feeling you get when staying over on unfamiliar territory, and a feeling I had not felt since teenage. Every moment became an exercise in concentration not to move my eyelids, and in forced slow breathing with a slight click between each breath to add to the authenticity of my ruse! I felt I was rather good at it. Rather too good it turned out. Then before I could consider anything else, the presence turned, and disappeared back upstairs.

And for the rest of the night I slept alone.

In the morning, I stirred (realising I must have fallen asleep at some point although the sofa is thankfully devoid of drool) and saw a figure sitting next to me. Not your mother, thank goodness - but YOU. Lovely you.

Embarrassed I rubbed my eyes, and said good morning. We talked a little about breakfast and which breakfast TV channel is best, I said I really missed that Landscape channel that Four used to show (I loved the tranquillity, adventure, escapism, and feeling of flight).

Then you told me, "I came back downstairs to see you again last night you know".

You had missed me. YOU had wanted to be with ME. NO! It was you who crept downstairs. Not your mother, but her daughter of my dreams - floating over me like an angel while I - PRETENDED TO BE ASLEEP! (No matter how many times I have relived this, I am still intolerably furious with myself!)

How was I to have known that this figure from my past dreams would want to be with me that night?!

It occurred to me later in another rare ostentatious moment, that maybe you really DID want to be with me. I did not dare to believe it. You then went on to claim - as if to not give too much away - that oh you were also worried they had left the Christmas tree lights on too close to where I slept. But really, are Christmas trees THAT dangerous?

And so for that moment - and every moment since - I was consumed and filled with regret that I did not turn to face you. Because now you are gone, and that was my one and only chance to take things to another level with the one person I waited a whole lifetime for.

Why did I not turn over? Why. It would have been perfect... I would have faced you, waited for our eyes to meet, talked, smiled, and waited for the moment to pull you close. In the most romantic, thrilling setting, with darkness encompassing us, except for the twinkling tree lights. (Perhaps now you understand another reason why I love to look at these stars through the window as I write. So dark and Christmassy.) And there would have been that giddying feeling of being mischievous, thrilling quiet all around us.

We would have stayed up the whole night, talking, together, and done anything else we wanted, together.

I really should have turned around.

Regret can be a terrible thing. But the moment was gone, and we never had another did we. I so wanted to believe it was not a full stop. I wanted to believe it was three of them - . . .

I still cannot come to terms with the fact that you died four days later.

I am still certain you are reading this somehow...

DAY ONE

Posted by Eurora001 on Fri 8-Jun-2001 23:54

I MUST BE CALM.

DARLING I HAVE SOMETHING TO TELL YOU, SOMETHING THAT IS SO... OH YOU WILL SURELY NOT BELIEVE WHAT HAS GONE ON...

I have to document this here and now, lest I not believe it even myself. I have to get these... 'thoughts' out of nmy mind and onto the screen, so maybe just maybe I can make sense of everything I have just sat going over in my mind for the last six-and-a-half Goddamned hours, in between actually losing consciousness Bella. Even jetlag does not do this to someone. Does it? Jesus CHRIST! Sorry.

My hands are shaking. It is hard to write. To even think.

I need you now. Please tell me you are there. You are there yes? I know you are there.

And I know this journal is private, but I am... afraid. I never thought I would read myself saying that, but... well yes, I admit it, I AM SCARED. That feels comforting to type actually. I feel like I need this down somewhere safe, in writing in case... well I will not say this - in case I do not come back from it next time. All right I said it.

What 'next time'?! This is preposterous. Why I am even typing this. Jesus. Maybe I am going mad. Do people who are going mad know they are going mad, then say so?

(Deep breath.)

Around five o'clock last night, or this morning. 5:04 the cvlock said. But then it always runs 7 minutes fast. I was fast asleep, in the middle of an excellent dream... It was strange, you were doing the ironing in our house, and I was sitting on the bed just watching, thinking what a dear sweetheart I had. Yes, I think we were married ('in my dreams'). Do not think I have ever been woken at that point in my sleep patterns before, and because of it, everything within the dream seemed ten times more real - more lucid - I would like to go back there right now actually thank you, to stay. But then marital bliss broke with a shatter.

Please believe this. The bed was shaking, or so I thought at first... no, then it was that the whole room was shaking, or rather thrumming too much. For a split-second, I thought you actually were standing next to me vacuuming hence the vibration. Then I woke up another level and realised my life was still the same. But my world was upside down. It is odd to me that that depressing fact hit me stronger than the BLINDING CYAN LIGHT COMING IN THROUGH THE SHUTTERS.

Then the light issue hit me too. This was not turning out to be a good day you might say!

I instinctively just covered my face with my arm, and foolishly in sleepy instinct tried to reach to put the light on.

It was cold out there.

And if there is a definition of getting out of the wrong side of bed, this is it. I got out of the top. That is to say, I felt myself collapse back onto the pillow PARALISED, unable to move, a general anaesthetic sensation filling my arteries, while my brain disagreed by throbbing more alertly even than normal, as I then drifted upwards, taking most of the duvet with me until my modesty was no longer preserved. Darling I was so scared.

I JUST PASSED OUT AGAIN. I am worried for myself. My head just went out like a light as I felt it fall uncontrollably. Then back again to try to face this again. I AM so scared. What is happening to me. Help me!

That felt bad enough. (Mother always told me to wear clean underwear when I went out, or at least some underwear, but she never mentioned preparing to go out hovering.) Being pulled upwards was the most bizarre sensation. It was as if I were going down underwater, only in reverse, or like the pool was on the ceiling. Try to understand? And an acute tingle at the back of my skull - or maybe it was the back of my mind - where my muscles tensed autonomously making my ears click and squish, and my forehead raise. It felt as though I was being vacuumed up!

'Must-be-a-dream-must-be-a-dream-must-be-…' But in all my years, I have never awoken from a dream and spent the whole day fainting whilst trying to come to terms with it, and not too much phases me. 'Cannot-be-a-dream…'

And so I floated in my swimming pool of air. (I always wanted a pool.) With no trunks. (Not so much wanted that.) (Sorry for the jokes. You know that is how I deal with stress... nerves... SHEER TERROR...)

And I do not remember much of the journey. I cannot tell you how I got through the closed patio door, other than it was open with the blind up. I must have missed something. I do remember seeing the look on Max's face bless her - an intermittent mix of fear, curiosity, and optimistic apprehension as she moved between wagging her tail, sitting on it with her head cocked to one side in that questioning way, and cowering it under her belly. She was probably wondering why I was leaving via a first floor balcony today, why I was doing so without taking her with me for a walk, and why I had never done the cool floaty trick thing with all the lights before.

I think she leaked on the floor. Why does she always do that when she is nervous? WAIT, stop. If this really happened, the carpet in the bedroom will...

It IS. I rather hoped it would not be. Or do I. Who knows. I need help.

This is ludicrous. Am I really typing this? Okay, I have to get this down…

The next thing I remember was moving into an upright position (alright! normality!) and slowly drifting upward like in a lift, but with a floor made of... nothing. The air was alive with the tickling charge of electricity and I could see it around me, blues, whites, like I was in the middle of a power storm or a psychedelic screensaver. I wanted to look up, I SO wanted to look up, but my head just hung down there inanimate which was an incredibly frustrating, frightening feeling. All I could see was the lawn and pavings immediately below, lit up from a very, VERY strong beam of self-contained hot light above me. Incredible heat on my head from a very, VERY strong light. And I was wondering if my neighbours were seeing this VERY strong light or if it was just me. And did I mention the blinding light?

Then I was THERE.

A small tin-coloured seat. Bizarre fabric draped over me, like - a mixture of silk and tinny rubber. Air fills my head - dank, acrid, musty - as though all life has been filtered from it - and at the same time ridiculously warm. My lungs choke on it for a moment, which makes me feel like I am laughing.

But I am not.

'Odd' - I think calmly - 'I have never felt this material before'. Why was I so calm! Almost as if whatever had anaesthetised me also contained something to block my adrenalin. Maybe that is why my heart is fluttering and palpitating now. Maybe. I still feel half-asleep at this point, hell I WAS a minute before. This must have just been some sort of sleep paralysis episode, or dream surely. Yet I know myself...

And so I was looking at the ceiling in my new surroundings - low, and looking down on me through the thin shroud of mist (I am not sure if it was on my eyes or in the 'room'), were white organic polystyrenesque spikes pointing downwards towards me - like stalactites. Or is it stalagmites.

To call this place 'homely' would have elevated it a dozen levels.

And as I followed the stalactites' course downwards - as if arrows directing my gaze...

They were there.

Two aliens.

Every time I type a new line here I pour another measure of Advocat (it is all I could find okay), and just think to myself. I keep shaking my head in disbelief. This is ridiculous! Incredible! Ridiculous! I am still asking myself if have just gone mad.

'Have you gone mad?' (See, told you.)
'No, this was real', I answer myself.
'Are you sure?', I double-check with me.
'Yes, why?', Me answers with a question.
'Because you are talking to yourself, the first sign of madness'

Oh.

But two aliens.
No, did I mention, two beautiful aliens.
Does that make sense or too much of a contradiction?
Tough, that was the way it was.

I was staggered - I would have pinched myself if I could move. And I must have stared at them for over a minute, as they stared back looming over me, before I could pull myself just a little bit together. Then I really began to analyse them, scared for my life, my heart pounding like a jackhammer.

Ethereal beings. Their noses petite in definition, perhaps the same size as a large cat's, though more human in shape if not size, and little blemishes and indents here and there on their greeny-silverfish skin, the colour of which made them look pale and jaundiced. They really could do with a tan. And that large head and pearl-shaped eyes. Fabulous looking things.

And they were clothed. It blended. China is fresh in my mind and perhaps for that reason one of these 'things' reminds me - through my veil of terror at the alienness of these... aliens - of some of the more Oriental women there. It is the flat nose, and something in the size of the eyes and shape of their lids that does it. Theere is a serene intelligence behind those large black eyes - or is it in the way the lower eyelid sits...?

But not a hair on her. And she is tiny yet carries a bigger, droplet-shaped head than suits her proportions, alienatingly bulbous going towards the top and back.

You know, I have to admit, I talk about this to you, yet at the same time I cannot get a handle on what I am saying. These words are too outlandish. I am impressed I have even found the cohesion to write a single word. Just yesterday I was talking to you about my trip, and the day before I was on a plane, days before that I was in the meetings, and weeks before that I was finalising the plans... and now what is this?! Yet what I do comprehend is the emotions I am feeling, and that they ARE true to their core.

'Her' face, it looks so soft, baby-like, and even a touch like an Asian cartoon, as most astonishing of all are what are those large pools of inquisitive membrane-blinking black eyes. They point up at the corners, towards her tiny ears that would suit a sea lion better. And finishing the strangely human face, thin lips on tiny slit mouth that hardly moved.

(Whatever planet they come from it must be hot, not smell great, and I bet they do not talk much.)

BUT SWEETHEART, THEY SPOKE TO ME.

As soon as I looked at them, I HEARD WORDS... for the first time in decades Bella... although their lips did not move, well not in time anyway. They kept saying my name over and over, questioningly, like I was waking up to a nurse in alien-hospital.

Still taken aback, it flashed through my mind that it was you calling it.

As I became even more lucid, I heard their words clearer and could remember them better than I have ever remembered anything before in my life. It is like they were printed onto the paper of my brain, and I can turn my eyes 180-degrees on that paper to read it back. I know not how else to explain it. This was not a normal way to communicate by any means.

"Hullo", said the male.

AMAZING.

They were talking to me and I could hear perfect English! I do not know if these were THEIR exact words, or just how MY brain interpreted whatever it was I was 'hearing', yet I remember each and every word verbatim somehow, and I do not care if they were or why they were, for I was HEARING THEM, and THAT is the point!

You of all people must be able to imagine what the freshness of hearing English words again after all those years of undisturbed deafness was like for me.

"Please humble friend, accept ourselves. We are so glad are you alive! We are not part of great your realm", 'he' said again!

"Uncountable supporters are follower of us in this journey", said the female this time, in a voice that filled my ears like warm honey, "We have to meet you come. If you want to with us, we wish to make a chance for you. Let me do something wonderful for everyone with you!"

"It is very fantastic!", the male-sounding and looking one said again, excitedly... nervously, almost.

I cannot get over that I can hear! I still cannot! This is all beyond 'too much'.

'But why are their lips not moving in time', is the other thing I think, worried. This is why I wonder if I was making up the words myself. Or was it just what I wanted to hear? (It is slightly like when you see a Japanese movie, badly dubbed.)

It was at this point when I think I became aware of a feeling of nausea. I feel travel sick, not that I even travelled that far. It is in my inner ear. My blasted ears, spoiling it for me again. The intensely hot temperature does not help at all. The visitors even look surprisingly surprised, as the sickness begins to overpower me. 'Disappointed' even? I can stand up, but at that point all I remember is the figures moving erratically, scared and confused, blood rushing to my bewildered brain and a sudden feeling of weightlessness. (Again.)

But the standing up becomes the opposite as this time the weightlessness is me falling to the floor of the craft.

It is tin-coloured and glassy by the way.

And that was it.

What, that is not enough?

That is all there is.

Yet I feel... they will return. Whatever 'this' crazy affair was, it was unfinished. I finished it prematurely. There was more reason to it than I have seen as yet.

Seriously, am I going mad...? Tell me now if I am.

Then I woke up just over there, slouched on the sofa, with a seriously aching, bruising shoulder and a wet one of my flannels on my forehead. Who put it there? That is a good point - hold on...

Okay that left me with serious chills. I found nothing in the bathroom to explain how it got on my head, but I had an overwhelming feeling that one of the... creatures... had been standing there in my own bathroom just a few hours ago. I can smell them in there. All wet and acidic.

After I walked into the bathroom, Max followed me (as she is prone to), but her body was low to the ground, and her docked tail pointing definitively inward. She was cautious, nose to the floor, sniffing in zig-zags. Edgy and jumpy with it. She seemed to follow a trail that spiralled around the bathroom floor, until it reached a point where she buried her nose into the hard surface - then with a start jumped back and away from that spot on the floor. She repeated this perhaps five times, each time scared of a scent. The final time she jumped, she looked up towards the ceiling as if looking for a foe in a tree that might have been there, and then skulked rapidly out of the bathroom for the final time.

This is giving me shivers right the way down my spine. It is as if I have been burgled. No, it is worse. No I think I might know how it feels to be... well, raped, as I feel like washing every inch of myself, and my floor.

Yet they were so beautiful. Oh the incongruity of it all - how can I explain it! Walking lithe dichotomies they were. So alien yet so moreish. But how dare they! This is my home! Yet I liked seeing them. In a hateful way!

(Even if my stomach did not.)

And what IS this taste in my mouth? Like earwax. (Do not ask me how I know what earwax tastes like.) Sharp. Revolting. It seems to keep coming from my teeth Bella, my teeth!

I need to try to work this out, sorry. There must be a rational explanation. I always rationalise, can always think laterally, but maybe I have been defeated this time.

Why me?

Firstly, why did they speak to me like bad ventriloquists? I have never heard of such a thing from what we all know of other alleged visits of this kind! Hearing them felt almost the same as when you rehearse a speech in your head, only louder, and more in my ears. It was not how I remember hearing real human speech at all. This must explain why I can remember every word - virtually word for word. Either my brain fabricated it as I type this in order to simply survive, or they were feeding it into my mind where it was saved as some sort of imprint and my mind had no choice. Has it been planted in there permanently, rather than just breezing in through my ears? Telepathy!?

I did not know I could do TELEPATHY! It had a sort of 'dulling' effect, unlike I remember things sounded before the illness when I was nine. Maybe that explains the inner ear sickness - which they seemed not to be expecting of me.

I would have thought they would be prepared for anything.

Amazing! Just to think, I may never need sign language again, may never need another translator! Am I no longer hearing-impaired? No longer deaf?! Am I cured?!! That is, if it had been real, and through my stupid useless ears. Which it cannot have been, can it? Of course not. I cannot hear anything I am doing here and now... tap tap (that was me on the desk). I can write it, but I cannot hear it. So it never happened.

First, I think I am going mad, then I talk to myself, now... I hear voices in my head. Wonderful.

No... more than voices... there was that song audible in their 'craft' too - what was it... "You may say I'm a dreamer but I'm not the only one, I hope someday you'll join us and the world will be..." I have not heard that song since I was a child! And I remember it so well, my mother used to play it in the kitchen on a loop. But it does not sound like the lyrics I co-write with Daniel - just the vibrations of the song - this was like... like I was coming up from underwater. Crystal clear music Bella!

Okay, so... just... just let me work this out logically, if the things I remember are telepathic, then how do they filter out thoughts they want nobody to hear. Perhaps to them opening their telepathy is like us opening our mouth - I wonder if they still make Freudian slips. I wonder if they were even real HELL THIS IS RIDICULOUS.

My shoulder is killing me, Christ that hurt! Mental note - do not poke it. At least I know where I got it. A fall to the floor WAS real. In a way the pain is worth it for telling me I did not imagine the craft and its hard floor I think. And Max is asleep under my feet, totally nonplussed by the whole sorry situation again now. How do dogs do that?

(Last month I forgot to tell you, she walked under an electric fence at a farm and got zapped on the way in. She still had to come back out through the same electric fence again, and all I could think of was to call her really quick so she would make a run for it and it would soon be over. But as soon as she hit the fence again on the way out, she turned into this squealing ball of fluff and almost-sparks, and stayed there rotating under the fence for several electrifying seconds. Then seconds later she was trotting along merrily, sniffing tree-stumps. I want what she is on right this minute. But I digress - it is comforting to remember normality.)

There is one thing I do not understand.

Okay one MORE thing.

When they 'spoke', why did they have the language so inconsistently wrong, like late 19th Century gentlemanly letters delivered by messenger, crossed with a Chinese person's romanticised attempts at how they think 21st Century British gentlemen speak? It was like some sort of bad translation going on live in my cranium. It was all just so... old-fashioned but Asian. For aliens apparently so evolved. That is what these creatures had apparently learnt, to try to fit in and appear 'normal' to this Earthling! Me. It is... actually kind of sweet in a way. WHY AM I SITTING HERE TALKING ABOUT ALIENS AND THAT THEY WERE SWEET!?! For Christ's sake pull yourself together man. I cannot put into words how normal life was yesterday, and how wrong this all feels - yet I know it was true, I just know it. I am not going mad, I am not.

Not. Not.

Notnot.

Nitnot.

Agh!

Perhaps they were not the words they used when it left their head aimed at mine? If they were even words. I know I think too much, yet it is possible my mind was processing it in the most basic or 'old-fashioned' form, to balance how advanced these beings were. To somehow keep myself sane? Possibly.

'Thank you brain.'

'No problem fingers.'

But near the end when I came over ill, they had an expression on their face. It looked like they were… let down... by me. Does that even compute? Like they expected more from a mere abductee. I am surely reading too much into an expression of an unknown life form.

And why were THEY so nervous to meet ME anyway?!

Now I consider it I think maybe it was not so much the travel sickness that overwhelmed me but their faces that I could not adjust to. I feel sick just thinking about how unprepared I was for how different they were. Yet dazzling.

Oh yes. They were wearing jeans and T-shirts. What? Why were they wearing jeans and T-shirts?!

Again, they were… were they… THIS IS SO GODDAMNED ABSURD. Were they trying to fit in… or make me feel like I fitted in with them? YES - the seat I sat on, it was a tin-coloured small sofa. The material, well it was close enough to an Earth blanket. (Cannot believe I am saying things like 'Earth blanket' as well now.) And around the craft, there was a décor to it. Nothing Laura Ashley need feel threatened by, but they had tried. And moving their lips when they 'spoke' to me, to make the words that entered my head look 'normal'.

Sorry chaps, a nice try but it was anything but normal.

How could they have even thought I would think it was normal to be dragged vertically out of bed naked into a flying saucer manned by chic 19th Century extra terrestrials?

I confess I do not know much about typical… 'alien abductions' (I hesitate even putting myself into that box here), but I do not remember anyone mentioning MFI and Levi's.

Other scraps are coming back to me now I get the major chunks out the way. Well, I was somewhat out of it, but, I sensed a conclusion between the two of them and… yes a third larger being who appeared from... below?… that the best thing to do might be return me. They used words along the lines of, 'it is fine, most remarkable events our friend saw our eyes to know ... how great he is!' Something along those lines. And I heard those too on my way out of consciousness.

'How great I is?'

I need to go, to have another lie down. Coming here for my daily ritual writing to you sweetheart... for some normality... helped. At least when I awake I can review it - and I have the login password locked securely in my head - to see if I really typed this, or if I am in some kind of freakish reverie.

But wait, if I have been the first Earthling to use telepathy then the password is NOT locked securely anywhere, I may as well have just painted it on my damn forehead. That is what it is inside anyway. Well now I have no doubt they will delete this when I am done. Wonderful. (Them or the psychiatrists.) Or worse, delete ME for writing about them on the Internet so soon after. I had better keep my telepathic mouth as zipped as a zip file.

Bella, I wish you were here to share this all with! Whatever this is! There is nobody I would want more. Nobody who would believe it more. Why did you have to go?

Sleep time now.

RIDICULOUS!

Day Two

Posted by Eurora001 on Sat 9-Jun-2001 23:42

I am sorry I did not write earlier today, but I have a most original excuse!

It happened again.

'They' came, again.
This is moving too fast.
But I cannot get off. And now, I am not sure that I wish to.

It took an hour sitting on my sofa, head-shaking in disbelief at the wondrous events, and pure positive thought to even muster the physical energy to log these feelings.
I am sorry only that you have missed out on the new events. I wish you could have been there in person, as my companion, instead of just these brief glimpses of the events I have actually lived through every second of.

But it was a 'good' excuse in more than one sense of the word. For I understand now. I will try to elucidate.

I was sitting over there on the sofa for what seems like an entire afternoon, having been returned to the apartment again.

Then pacing with my arms folded, in satisfaction this time. I flicked a light-switch on and off a couple of times although my hand seemed to repel it. 'That was a great invention', I thought. 'Electricity'.

I will get straight to the reason I was thinking like this - I want to this time!

Okay. Well! I fell asleep last night just after typing the last entry and returning to the couch to think over it all. I did not get to think, and cannot remember if I even got to dream, but none of that matters... My lungs froze as I woke up... I wass being pulled up out of the sofa, dankness all around except for the blinding light, and for a terrifying moment I felt my heart give out an empty thud, which pulled the very breath down and out of my lungs. Then a sense of a moaning as my skin smarts like a Chinese burn. (Yes, a Chinese one.) I must have shut my eyes for the journey upward, outward, and up a bit again. Then nothing.

I opened my eyes just a slit, and peered out.

And I was sitting below the two beautiful beings again Bella. Do you believe me? I would not make anything up - you of all people know that. You loved that I never lied, and never swore. (And it matters not that all that changed after you left me.) And they were standing there, so short themselves, yet looking down at me seated even shorter than them, in awe, fascinated in me as if they had never seen a human before. They should imagine how I felt.

It was the same two as yesterday, and I was in the same craft so it turned out, although in the underbelly of it on this occasion. I was lying next to the 'hole' through which I had just surfaced, which itself was central in a round chamber or room I suppose, the only notable features in its tin can appearance being an inverse bite taken out of one side, where the circular space was lost to a smallish room. Well I assume so as all I saw was a door. And other than that, just a ramp leading upward, again greyish alloy in colour, and everything rounded off like something from an 'artists impression' of a futuristic space-faring craft.

The journey through that hole did not form any part of my memories this time. Perhaps they upped the dose? And this time I was 'slightly' more prepared, mentally, not to mention clothedly.

And then...

"Angel of the angels!", says the male, "and my name is Alfred Roberts", he seemed to continue as if nothing could be more normal, even if it 'sounded' more like Arfred Robertos. Can you imagine? It was as if he was a regular Joe (or 'Alf'!) from round the corner come to borrow some sugar, the way the creature came out with it.

He extended his arm towards me with a slightly opened fist at some gesture of greeting, and the female did the same. I cannot quite tell at first if they are making eye contact or not, such is the size of the blackness of their retina, but when I think of them like dogs' eyes it eases the culture shock and I am more able to read where they are looking.

Speaking of reading, I still hear them speak in 'that way', as you have just read. What I 'hear' is a soothing disparity to what my eyes see, so in that sense, if that is why they are doing it and are not just bad scholars, it works. It pacifies me. They must know this. They explained this to me you see, although not exactly that reason. I will tell you. But I wonder if I would be left with the presence of mind to even be sitting here now, had they actually used their true native tongue.

"We are apologise for the yesterday", says the one that appears female. "Most unexpecting. I feel anxiety that you may be disturbed."

She puts it lightly yes? Then the male - "Alfred Roberts" (!) - goes on.

"We were decided not to bring insult to you with forgetfulness and obscuring our voice, and so we lost words to object and it became decided to let you experience everything, such is your greatness to accommodate it. [!] You can do it if nobody can. We feel still difficult wording now to communicate sorrowfulness for your reaction just before and we have respect for your earnest progress. Hope you have found some kind equilibrium again after the sleep."

I - remembered - every - word. It is as if my train of thought is in Braille.

Then the female spoke up, but again not out loud.

"You have so much to give, you sensitive, compassion, a loving soul, deeply intuitive, and genuine concern that have for people.

Time to give that to yourself instead of worries that do not deserve your time so be open now and discover truth for yourself, for this is our happiest moment of to speak and my name is Lucy Wells", which again sounds more like Lushi Werrells even though my mind puts the names in the correctly intended boxes. 'Lucy'!

Again, every word - somehow. The sense I get is that I have for some reason been privileged and deemed capable to not be fully drugged or goodness knows what else, through the process of abduct- no, of introduction, and to hear their real attempt at natural language.

Lucky me.

With what they say to me about my 'greatness to accommodate it', I try not to look like a disappointment to them by completely failing to do so.

We moved 'upstairs', and a conversation ensued. (The 'sofa' design and the rest were still there. I could not make out much of a 'craft' here.)

"W-Who are you?! W-why are you giving such normal names?", I actually 'say' out of the same channels in my mind that their words seemed to enter from, proud of how composed I am compared to yesterday's embarrassing spectacle of falling shoulder first on the floor.

"Forgive us you will be happy when you know of our feelings. We wish to be familiar with you. Where we are from, names are not, plus if we could ask for your kind understanding we in fact have not sort of the names as you know them, do not be distressed, yet we know that is heartens you to have something of home and we know you will not be scared this time to know this."

I immediately feel scared this time to know this.

My composure and pride crumpled in fact. Can you see it in your mind's eye? Try. I need you there, if only in retrospective imagination. The way these startling strangers are all of a sudden 'talking', is as if something monumental is about to happen, something very scary, and that I am to be SO far, far away from everything normal that I must need special preparation of the kind they have deemed necessary. I feel like I am about to be jettisoned into outer space at the speed of light or something.

The olive twig they offer me of familiarity only serves to panic me about what LACK OF familiarity must impend!

I swallow down deep my deep feelings of infirmity and continue, feeling the squirting of my adrenals in my abdomen, only slightly muted this time, and the pallor approaching my face fast. Before long my legs will be shaking too, as I come down from that high with the unfathomable revelation I was about to hear!

I am getting to it!

I then wondered why they - and particularly she - was chosen. She seems and looks so much younger, less 'together' if that term can even apply to such apparently advanced beings - by that I mean less graceful, more nervous, and naive. Yet who am I to talk? She does not seem to know where to put her long gangly arms. But if this is as monumental a moment as they make out, why send a… youngling? (Although for all I know she could be 87...)

I conclude in fearful haste that it is not monumental at all and that this is their standard chat up line to lull people into a false sense of security before whisking them away.

(It does not help my adrenals.)

"This is the best moment we have to known!", she blurts out excitedly, to a look of strained distain from her counterpart.

"Forgiving pilot please", he interrupts, "but hope at honour of your presence is a much endured for long times, even me how I feel the same but try to not say it", he says turning to her with a small frown above his even smaller nose... perhaps realising he just did say it.

'They put on a great show', I think to myself, but I stay prepared for the inevitable Hollywood moment. It is amazing to me at that moment how sci-fi can transcend reality.

But it does not come.

And show or not, I am made to feel like I am some sort of God to them.

They then go on to explain that I AM some sort of God to them. There is no other way to put it sweetheart! Watch...

"Ah you believe we are aliens from Venus and Mars?", he enquiries, reading my mind, with a thin, scoffing-yet-respectful smirk.

"Well, not from... there exactly, but from a distant world yes, I do believe that", I reply nodding, I suppose quite knowingly.

Oh how I am wrong.

"Your idea is fantastic!", she says grinning as much as her tiny lips will let her, "but not very right".

"So sorry to talk down in poor English", 'Alfred' says, again reading my mind's thoughts perfectly, "but please I need to enquire have you seen creatures like me again?"

Assuming he means 'before', I concur. "Yes, there are... as many programmes and films about...'broadcasts'... about... aliens as there are stars out there where they could come from"!

(I impressed myself with the fantastical nature of that one, all things considered.)

"Kind friend, do you not see it yet? Those like me and she that have been seen through a long time on Earth, WE ARE NOT EXTRA-TERRESTRIALS, although Man Kind depict us as being little those green men from abroad, flying in the UFOs.

"But no, NONE of us visitors validly seen are aliens from other galaxy gentle Sir", he concludes.

"Not from other planets either no", 'Lucy' says consoling my mistaken belief that they are.

I wondered what they meant naturally. 'Of course they are aliens, why claim they are not?', I thought. Surely they did not think me so foolish as to believe they were humans.

"We not extra-terrestrial. We are TERRESTRIAL. We come from here, on Earth", she then declares seriously... oh so naturally explaining that... they ARE humans.

What country on Earth did they expect me to believe they were from?!

But then 'Alfred' concluded...

"WE ARRIVED IN OUR TIME SHIP.

...

"YOUR TIME SHIP."

My concept.

A time machine.

MY TIME MACHINE!

THE EURORA POTENTIAL...

The outcome of the China agreement I signed but a few days ago...

With my time displacement array concept now beating for real within its heart.

Bella it was all right there on my doorstep days after I sold the rights to just the most bare bone of conceptions...

Bella?!

Is your jaw on the floor?! (Mine resurfaced in Australia.)

The whole damn stunning conversation happened without actual audible words, seemed like hours, but took perhaps minutes. I am still trying to enjoy being able to 'hear' again, but the shock of the rest just keeps getting in the way of that. Too much is going on in my head. Thank goodness I can spill it all out here.

Apologies for the mess.

And you know it was the loss of my hearing that led me to delve into books, the books that led me to ultimately design the TDA, and the TDA which has apparently now given me back my hearing!

It is fantastic.

Almost too.

Throughout the experience I sat with a face full of wonder, leaning forward as they peered over me, with my cheekbones perched on my fists, eyes open wide, and a slight smile because I love what I am hearing. I love writing it now just as much!

Lucy clarified it all, and these are the words that come into my mind, although I still know not how I can output them so verbosely.

"As your assistant and friend it bringeth me great joy into my heart to say now to you that because several thousand years before I even was born, you created a creation that you... you never lived to see... But we did", she concludes.

"The craft you now sit inside", Alfred picks up, "YOU are responsible for creating. It YOUR Time Ship Sir".

I want to believe what they say so much. I want to, I wish to, and it all fits, and there it is all around me just begging me to. I am sitting inside it after all... a time machine.

My time machine.

No! This still rattles my brain!

And beyond even that, it is piloted by aliens? No, I mean future humans?!

I cannot describe... I still feel how... if this is true... how perhaps someone such as Leonardo Da Vinci would have felt if the very second he sketched out the helicopter or the tank, you drove one into his back garden and said, "Here you are Mr Da Vinci, we made you one. Will send you the bill.", centuries before the technology even existed to even build them!

My God, is this what they have done... for me? Truly? Am I really like a... Da Vinci to them? This seems outlandishly preposterous on one hand. But as I suppose anyone in this situation of situations would do, I too have to ask myself rationally, humility to one side, whether Da Vinci in the earliest days of his first young ideas would really believe it if you told him he would be looked back on centuries later in the way that he in turn likely looked back at great thinkers and visionaries from his past like Hypatia. He likely would not believe it of himself. So should I believe it?

Rationally, some people born the same year as me WILL be looked back on with the same admiration. Rationally again, it is not beyond possibility that I may be one. The only exception here is rather than looking back, my 'contraption' is allowing them to do more than just look. It has COME back.

Hell I cannot believe I am typing here comparing myself to Da Vinci, when just a few short days ago I was in a meeting room scared that my concept might even be scoffed at as nonsense. Yet it was not, which makes this all the more plausible. Agh!

When I think back to the concept hitting me like lighting those years ago, realising in a sickening way that it may indeed violate that special theory of relativity of a person I admired greatly, it just is absurd to be in this situation I find myself in. But here I am.

You can appreciate why I have been sounding so pleased with myself then? Why I walked around proudly flicking a lightswitch like they might flick this craft into drive?

I knew the eurora potential would work. I KNEW IT. My geometries of spacetime were possible and more to the point were put in motion. Absurd! Then there I am, two days after selling the theorem, sitting inside it! Mere drawings had come to life all around me in three-dimensions like some Disney animation, and all thanks - I presume - to those very Closed Timelike Curves my time displacement array was designed around! A curve of its own, come back around to meet me.

Sorry, I risk boring you with technobabble. It makes more sense if I remind you - you might remember anyway. A Closed Timelike Curve or CTC is a way that time can loop round and back on itself yes? Remember I gave you that circular racetrack loop analogy, of how the car could come up behind itself, just by moving forwards round the track faster than light itself could? And I explained that if a time traveller could break the light speed barrier too, he too could arrive at his destination before he had even left, i.e. he could travel into the past.

And these travellers... arrived here at their destination in 2001, certainly before they are due to leave from whatever year in the future!

All I can say is that my concept must have been at least 'partly' right. Enough to inspire its very own completion. Surely many others were involved before it got there many decades or centuries from 'now', for I did not foresee it becoming a reality until way beyond my lifetime. And their bodily form assures me I was MORE than right about that, too.

Last October they were just rough ideas, and in less time than it would take to build a new car, the finished machine turns up on my window ledge!

That is quite a prototype.

But it just did not fit inside my vision of what it would look like inside. Why would it - ha! And I have no idea what it looked like outside. Somehow, I just cannot place this craft in a box labelled 'mine'. It is as if a caveman sketched a babyish drawing of a 'car' on a rock, and then Henry Ford appeared over the horizon in a black Ford Cougar.

But wait, what about the issues of causality such that coming back to show it to me would create? They must know what they are doing I am sure. If I was due to perform more work on the device, then coming back before I had would surely jeopardise that. So their choosing that specific date must mean I have - or had - NOTHING more to do with the design of the TDA after that date. So my work must truly be over, NOW. Good God. I will never get that enquiry for further consultation from the Chinese as written into the contract. Do they wish to keep it THAT close to their chests? And if so why? Was this just another technology to them, or did they have a grander design?

And I was worried no more work would leave a gaping hole in my life? Well it is certainly now plugged by these new events, as soon as it opened.

Now I think I know a small piece of my future... although I think I already had realised that chapter in my life may have ended. It is sadder now I know, yet that sorrow is mixed with this feeling of success and all because of it! My sanity is walking a fine balancing line, and that is not the half of it.

Good luck to the Chinese then, on their own. Wait, I already know they do not need it. (This could really mess with my mind - I need to slow down my thoughts, if I can.)

"I have seen something else under this sun. The race is not won by the swift, or the battle by the strong; nor does food come to the wise, wealth to the brilliant, or favour to the learned... but time and chance happen to them all." - Ecclesiastes 9:11

The Chinese were indeed swift and strong, clear to me at the time as it is now, that they were trying to win a race and hoping to win future battles (not literal ones I hoped) by buying a significant edge... but I sit here now and do have to wonder how time and chance will choose - or chose - to toy with them on the long road ahead that leads to... this moment.

I must stop waffling and speculating. I will.

And I have not even begun to consider in all my excitement about my apparent success, the other revelation. That there may be no such thing as 'aliens' or 'flying saucers'. OF COURSE, a proposed design for the craft the eurora potential would harness, was somewhat of a saucer shape!

Where has that myth stemmed from anyway? Why does that make any more sense than any other explanation? Why have the media jumped on the alien bandwagon? Where is the proof of that over any other rationalisation? Is it because we want to believe we are not alone? Does that give us comfort? Does anyone know the discomfort having that expectation violently shattered has caused me?!

Well if so, surely knowing that we exist and evolve as a species and survive well into the future is more comforting than knowing we are being visited and abducted by aliens!

The media frustrates me so much as of now. Were I of more foolish mind, I might even contact them.

Because of these... well there is no other phrase but 'time travellers', and the hundreds of accounts of 'alien' encounters, we can all become instant time travellers of our own, in a way. Because for many centuries now, with every 'UFO encounter' throughout time we have been shown exactly what our future descendants will look like throughout time, by they themselves.

They have been appearing to us and we have given them the perfect excuse by identifying them as aliens! No wonder they have never corrected us - it was the perfect diversion from the truth.

Until today.

Does it not seem strange to you why people have always assumed that these craft come from other galaxies? Where and why did this theory start!? There is no proof that UFOs come from any particular direction, be it North, South, East, West... or

Up. They just appear, allegedly documented on film, and then disappear again. Aliens? Really? Surely that humanity achieves time travel is a more realistic explanation than little green men from Mars.

And if that is too fantastic, then is the 'alien' theory more plausible? It would take many millions of years to get here when travelling at the speed of light. And even if they come from our nearest star, their journey of trillions of miles would still take hundreds of thousands of years. Yet I am certain that even the earliest cave paintings created by some of the first intelligent humans on Earth documented the visits of 'men in the sky'. They might have even called them 'Gods' from some far away realm, and they would have been somewhat right. This would mean the alien sightseers would have had to know in advance (i.e. to predict the future) that life on Earth would become intelligent, then set out hundreds of thousands of years in advance of knowing there was any civilised life to even visit here, in order to get here in time to be documented in the cave paintings by those first Men. Why would they do that?! Of course, I now know it was not aliens predicting our evolution, but was us - remembering it.

Well, the next thought on board my ship, as day broke outside its claustrophobic hull, was to worry profusely and ask what my neighbours will think, having surely seen the craft. And so they autonomously explain to me that this ship's bright blue light can - at the expense of greater energy depletion - be switched so is not visible or audible to anyone, except those directly in its path. Apparently it is like a lightsabre crossed with a one-way mirror - you only notice it if you hit it, yet it is only bright if you are inside its grasp. They call it something that sounds like "Futon Parachute", and the closest I can translate that to is 'Photon Shower Chute'. And their craft itself too - similarly only visible when inside it. They tell me that their "later" versions of my craft (can you imagine!) like this one apparently can create an 'anti-wave' of sound and light. Yes, it appears there are many models of the craft back in their year, and they chose to come and visit me in a somewhat primitive variant. Familiar. Who am I to refute it?

Alfred let me know that when a flock of our birds suddenly launches out of a tree squawking for no apparent reason, it is likely one of their craft is hovering next to the tree.

My goodness this has to be THE best prototype a designer could ever dream of, and I want you to feel as if you were there too my dear. I will describe it as best I can: I was able to look around the craft, with my eyes at least for fear of crossing any lines with these hosts, but could not see any of my ideas, except then what I recognised as the power drive above the centre of the upper of the two rooms.

Aside from what I already described of the interior which is how I had remembered it (I know for sure I was not dreaming now), in front of the upstairs seating/sofa is a viewscreen of sorts - it looks like it is made from a clear matte flimsy material, odd, almost like a sheet of adhesive backing spun from spider web. I have seen nothing like it before. I cannot imagine any sort of good quality image being produced by a monitor so organic looking. (I much prefer the one I now look at.) On the top right of the 'screen' is a single pewter-coloured rectangular object, its underside sloping down into the screen, almost sculpted to be so or as though it had grown there. It seems to serve no purpose, yet its organic nature makes it remarkable enough to remark on.

To the right of that, a guiderail of sorts which allows one to look down from this upper gantry to the lower floor. To the left, a U-shaped ramp heading back downward (with a hairpin turn halfway) towards the entrance I had floated up into (my God!) and what was perhaps the sick bay door opposite that ramp, down on the 'ground' floor.

Oh yes, and under the screen I noticed a sole symbol of two semi-circle outlines with a line running horizontally through them.

Other than that, there were 'just' the three small seats in front of the console. The materials from my first visit still there behind me as I looked at the screen. Ytet I could not see any controls of any shape or form. I could not even imagine how they could navigate. Maybe that is too much of a 21st century way of thinking. 'Controls, pah!'.

I assumed the gravity amplifier (that lets it float) was housed under the floor somewhere, along with 'a' power source. But what power source? Nothing from today would be nearly sufficient, and would surely be too harmful. I was giddy to learn how they completed the design and what materials they used to build it. I would surely get the chance to enquire. I had all the time in the world, and I already know they will return.

And so there I was, inside my own... time machine (!), which had come back to its owner, as though I had only just thrown it a long way.

I hope you now feel as if it was visiting you too darling.

On the ship it the fact had overwhelmed me too, as these future humans interacted with me some more.

"My beautiful and strong friend! Do not cry", said 'Lucy' seeing my expression. I was not even crying when she said that however.

"I... just never thought I would live to see this", I surprise myself by then almost crying out.

"It is true… you do not… your lifespan is short we know. We are sorry you are dead now..."

My heart skips more than a beat until they go on, "...in our time", (phew), "and so a decision was unanimously reached and made to come back and show you what you did do", Alfred says matter-of-factly. I feel like the luckiest person alive - any sadness at my own future death even at a natural 21st Century 'short lifespan' seems a trifle unjust.

"You are the inventor of all time love my Sir", says Alfred, getting the phrasing definitely wrong.

I keep having brain hiccoughs. Could all this really be as true and real as it seems? Good grief, all right, my mind is about to flip. Let me just try to get this down logically:

1. The concept is sound. As I have perhaps bored you with here for years, it is the strongest I have had by a light-year, and beyond question. I feel self-assured enough to let you know this now (I felt too modest before this) but it was apparently stronger according to the corporation than 'any thing a person has seen in our time'.

2. The shape of my concept looks similar to the shape of what I have seen of the inside of their craft. What I presented was essentially a Smartie shape. I recall I had once even called it a 'flying saucer' light-heartedly, but simply never, ever, made the connection. That would have been too much of a lateral leap. The benefit of hindsight always comes too late.

3. Time travel is possible. I think I talked of this once before with you, that in the 70s and 90s scientists sent a jet flying for up to 80 hours round the world with an atomic clock on-board, synchronized to another atomic clock on the ground, which successfully proved the theory Einstein never lived to see - that the faster you travel, the more time speeds up for you, i.e. time travel. The clock on the jet showed a time ahead of that on the ground, yet they had been sync'd before takeoff. So we knew it was possible already, and indeed has been achieved, but in this age only minutely.

1, 2, 3. It surely fits! It is plausible that I, dare I say somewhat like the late great Albert Einstein who did not live to see some of his theories proven, might not live to see future scientists prove my 'theory' that REVERSE time travel is also possible, by great lengths, and how. I must conclude that if it is good enough for Mr Einstein, or Marconi, or Da Vinci, it is good enough for me, and feel humbled to be even considered in the same sentence... by my own hand. Good gracious! And yet I must not become haughty.

And I digress for my own sanity here and now, but that was not all that was said earlier on the craft.

"We are very happy to know you are alive", Lucy had said.

And then I had to ask them, or should I say 'think them' a question.

"How far in the future are you f-from ... when was the time machine actually created?"

(I never usually stutter in my mind.)

And do you know what? They replied.

"We are from the New World", she says. "Yours is the Old World".

"Please be safe and help people as well by understand one thing vital to understanding and position", Alfred suddenly interjects to my head in a rather serious 'tone'. "We know and trust that you will not tell souls of this. Forgive me suggest that you might, oh you. We know that you're of all people understand how all of moments must be guarded so eloquently. You must not tell a person - it is important. Forgive me!", he says bowing and shuffling perceptibly backwards almost in self-repulsion, embarrassed at his slightly outburst of warning.

"No, I mean Yes! Of course, no please do not worry, I... I understand", I retorted along the lines of, holding up my palm towards them reassuringly acceptingly. In truth, I would hardly even give 'telling' people of this a second thought (apart from that first thought I gave it a few minutes ago).

But they are right, naturally. Well, they have had a bit longer to think about it.

And so now I feel guilty, as here I am typing again, in fact already breaking that promise, for I am telling someone.

Well, that is something for me to decide actually. Am I telling someone, or no one?

You are reading this Bella? I know that you are.

Actually no, it is not guilt, it is fear I feel at the existence of this. Yet I go on typing it. See? And here is some more. How could I stop? This is spilling out of me. Who else will listen - who else will counsel me?

I have made a mental note to triple-check this is flagged private/secure. In fact why do I even need to keep this online? Are you even out there in the ether picking up these words I send to you?

You are a welcome relief from the incredulity of reporting what happened to me on the craft. I want to go on with the account of events, but it is just too much for me, I am sorry.

I hope so deeply that we are connected by those other craft - the satellites that orbit the Earth. You used to say you felt we were connected, even when apart. Like that time I had not seen you for days, when I had been greatly upset by that AGM decision only an hour before, and you just texted me the words,

"WHAT'S WRONG?", out of the blue, as if you sensed a change in the Universe.

You were right of course.

But THESE words, they give me peace also at least.

But are they safe? What about sound?

Is my mind even sound?

Bella?

Day Three

Posted by Eurora001 on Sun 10-Jun-2001 00:18

You know, I was just about to delete the last two entries in a fracture of fear, but I have realised, I am cleverer than I think! (Cleverer than most people think so it happens!) Anything I leave in my apartment could be found if... Well anyway, THIS cannot. It is not stored IN my apartment is it? It does not exist in material form, and nobody even knows to look for it on this auspiciously obscure site. It is held remotely on someone's server in Timbuktu for all I or anyone knows! I have now removed the browser bookmark from my 'Favourites' (you always were mine), and shall clear the cache each time I write. And even if someone did discover this site, they could surely not break the password, unless they are telepathic like Lucy or Alfred, and Luicy and Alfred already know quite a bit about Lucy and Alfred, so no harm in them reading about themselves. I hope. And they seem to know a lot about me too. They have been reading their history books I guess. Oh my.

So this is as safe as it gets, safer than a safe, even though it is out there in cyberspace... it is really nowhere. Just binary floating around the ether.

A bit like you I suppose. Not binary, but the other bit. You know sweetheart, you are the one person I would not mind coming back to this plane to try hacking this password. Hell, you are the password. Well, part of it. You know the rest.

I feel slightly better now but still cannot speak of what further events occurred. I need to put my feet, and mind, back on planet Earth.

With all this talk of the future, I have just been thinking about the past. Of when things were 'normal' - whatever that means. That time seems both like yesterday (it virtually was), and years ago, such is the odd effect these events have had on my own sense of time and reality.

And so I came to think about you, perhaps inevitably...

You know, when you went Bella, a part of me went along with you. A part of me is up there, with you now. I am sure of it.

I remember the events just too too well. I have written it before and I will write it again. The more I duplicate it, the fainter it will get, won't it. Or won't it?

We chatted online all that night, remember, your words always so familiar and homely and warm. We had talked for nearly an hour, and you said your dinner was nearly ready. I loved the way that sounded. Such a homebody, not interested in infantile activities like pubbing and clubbing where people go so they can think they are having a good time. Just like me you were. We had good times without artificial stimulants, alcohol, or deafening music (what fun!). I could almost smell your Mother's home cooking, although I still resented her slightly for the earlier mix-up she had no part in.

You said you had a really bad headache and might go to bed early.

I just said, "I would kiss it better if I was there". But I was not there, and did not think any more of it.

I should have.

You had only part of your dinner I later found out.

Your Mother started a video call with me the next morning and asked to speak to you, looking angry. At first I could not understand it. You had not been here in days - why would you be here? I told her that the last I heard from you was the previous night before dinner, and before you went up those stairs early to bed.

She fell silent.

I joined her.

She questioned me again briefly and told me she had been calling up to you but you were not upstairs, in your room.

My blood ran cold, my heart racing, where on earth were you? Why were you not answering if you were in your room? It was not like you. I asked if she had double-checked your room, even though she knew you liked your privacy.

"NO I HAVEN'T", came the reply (I will always remember it was the only thing she bothered to put Caps Lock on for. "SHE ALWAYS ANSWERS, AND NEVER MISSES BREAKFAST", she added almost as if to make me feel guilty for hiding something I was not. Instead, my face dropped.

My breath stopped.

Then hers too. I will never forget the look of realisation, frozen for a few seconds into the stuttering webcam image. Realisation that there could only be one remaining reason why you would be in your room but would not answer.

Then she was walking away, she turned the corner to go up the stairs, and the seconds passed so slow I could have done with a time machine.

All I could see was your cat on the sofa, asleep.

I stared at your cat until it almost felt rude.

Then, she must have just opened your door when the cat woke with a start, her head pointed to the staircase, then ran off towards me and the computer.

I knew instantly that it was your mother's scream upon finding you that had caused it.

And almost as instantly, in turn began the most morbid, painful, heartbreaking loss I had ever felt in all of my life - I think it made me scream as loud as she must have although most of what followed was a blur - like the blur of her which appeared as the connection died.

You, gone with it.

We later pieced it painfully together, your Mother, and me. She came round every day for a while, I suppose so we could share our grief and cure our loneliness. She had nobody else, and neither did I. Not human anyway. Not anymore. I felt like a bit of an intruder as she had known you your whole life and I was just a blip, but she wanted me around and so I was glad, as it helped me too.

You must have gone up to your room with that dreadful headache, unable to bear it, and just got into bed to sleep it off, and at some time in your sleep the tumour had gone that cell too far. And with it, you had gone too far also.

But never, ever, out of my mind.

The doctor later told her that it had most likely been there several months, and was too fast growing and deep to be operable. She had had no idea, and neither had you, of course. It seemed there was nothing anyone could have done even if they had known. It seemed your destiny.

We all hoped you went peacefully, and without even you knowing what had happened. I know you did. If you had felt it, I would have too. We are connected, after all.

I did not feel a thing, until the next day when I felt more pain than I ever thought man could bear. And having searched my whole life for that one person, my dream came, and went. And you do not get another chance at dreams like that do you. You do not get odds like that again, finding your one in a million. One in six billion. But at least I found you. Game over. I win. High score. There was no more searching left to be done in my life.

And so I had to end it too - my life. Game over. I had to join you. You left this earth to leave your pain. And so I felt I had to also.

You once said to me, "You'll always be all right. There's a light around you." Those words touched my soul every time I replayed them in my head. I had no wish to make you wrong about that, but nothing was going to save me from that moment. There was no light around me I felt.

Maybe when you existed, there was. It must have been the glow of how you made me feel, that you saw shining back at you. That, and a bit of your own light reflected in my eyes.

I was sitting right here, looking at your photos on the screen. The knife from my work drawer, with its 'safety' catch seeming so ironic. I thought of all the times I used it for arbitrary purposes like cutting wires for a myriad contraptions, but now just sad for my own life. 'Stanley' it said on it. I thought how stupid it was that that was the last word or name I would ever know. Killed by Stanley. No matter. I unlatched it, exposed the blade, and my wrists. I sobbed, tears on my wrists, entirely distraught, shattered, just nothing left to hurt that was not already.

It was just too easy to stab into my arteries and tendons. All too easy. Hot blood poured out of me like water from a kettle.

After time I could only sense my barely banging heart.

Nothing left to beat with.

Broken, without you inside.

And as I drifted, I faintly recall that entryphone flashing... or was it the ambulance minutes later... all such a blur...

Credit where credit is due, I have done well not to talk about that for a while. These events have taken over my mind to that extent, and in that sense if not more, they are the most welcome relief. I will come back to them again - I can feel how much they have bizarelly eased my disquiet at all that surrounds me of late.

Pah listen to me.

I have to keep stopping myself, leaning back, looking around, and breathing out in a series of laughs of disbelief. This is all really happening, isn't it. Or isn't it?

Well I do feel better for now with that off my chest once again. It has cleared away the space to think and tell you more about the time travellers' visit. Goodness, I even feel sane enough this morning to type those words.

And indeed there was more to say.

I hope you want to know.

So...

"Why today?", I had had to go on and ask them.

"Please, we know of the song you scribed. Your prophecies and teachings are world-renowned do you know. Your saying is very clear", Alfred says, even though his is not.

They claim that the song they talk of is 'Never Does Come True', the lyrics of which I wrote about a certain night and person... can you guess? Yes, of course you. Around February it was, for Daniel to match to what he called a haunting new melody. Or to them, perhaps it happened a hundred centuries ago on Thursday perhaps, I have yet to discover! A good one too, our publisher took it on without hesitation - he played it in his studio days before - the vibration is still good in there. Let me paste the lyrics... see the context they see it from... Be right back...

Okay...

When I first set eyes on you what seems a thousand years ago
Oh how that moment changed my life in ways I'd never know
Jump back to the future here I am a thousand years away
But somehow, somewhere I think of you each night and day

'Cause every night is hell, as you recast your spell
And again I dream of you, because it never does come true

So I pray, that I'll fall back in time
To that day, but that this time I'll know
What to say, so you will stay
With me forever, and today - I pray

Myriad missed chances, what might've been's a mystery
What I'd give to click undo, go back, rewrite history
Can't figure out what deity would steal the chance from me
On the road that was my life a crossroads closed off suddenly

'Cause every night is hell, as you recast your spell
And again I dream of you, because it never does come true

So I pray, that I'll fall back in time
To that day, but that this time I'll know

What to say, so you will stay
With me forever, and today - I pray

Years could be so different now if seconds went another way
Now I'm on the wrong path, without you I've gone astray
In a parallel universe, another me got it right
I'm going there forever, when I dream about you tonight

"In the future my angelic friend this song is launched and is great success for a band named", and at first I think she says 'hedgehog' but she's very definite about the pause for some reason until I realise it is "Headjog", which she says with what I try not to mistake as a dusty sparkle of fandom in her eyes as they widen in sync with her words. But that might be wishful seeing.

If this is to be believed, and I do not know WHAT to believe really, then Headjog must have been... are going to be... that is... were... big. And my lyrics. Another ambition ticked?

Too much. Just too, too much.

I took it to mean that they choose that day to come back, because they might give me that chance to go back, click undo, and rewrite history - now that I have cleared my responsibilities of creating and handing over the designs to the Chinese.

Darling can you understand the gravity of these remarkable, revelations for me today, and why I could not speak of it all at once? Talk about a head jog. Yesterday I had three ambitions left in life:

1) For a concept of mine to change the world
2) For a song of mine to be purchased by someone who does not know me
3) To get another chance... that Christmas with you

Today I have but one left it seems. How incredible! I cannot find another phrase for it. I cannot dress it up any differently. This is literally 'beyond credible'. Words mean little at a time like this, but what else do I have to write with?

This all left so many questions in my head that I forget to ask any of them. Rest assured, I shall.

Alf reiterated (I feel I can call him Alf as he has known me for several millennia!), that the one most important thing (although he sounded like he actually said 'impotent') is that I must not tell a soul.

They mentioned some laws of time travel. Indeed I had proposed some myself, even if hearing about their alleged reality really sounds like sci-fi to me. I keep thinking what Einstein would do. He was like a God to many. They seem to trust me like I would trust him and I am reluctant to break that sort of trust by showing distrust of their words. Reluctant to also make a fool out of this God they see me as.

Of course, nobody must know. If anyone did find out - well what would the time travellers do about it? What could they do? Well, they have a time machine. What can they not do!?!

And that brings you just about up to speed with all that was said. Thought.

And tomorrow I have a date. With two aliens... Okay I have got to stop thinking of them as that. But tomorrow we have an arrangement, me, and the... well, 'Futurists' I shall call them!

Towards the end of our time together I started off asking them a stream of questions you see. They were not even taking notes so I do not know how much of it went in - all of it I suspect - but the words blurted out of me unbidden - almost as if it was someone else 'speaking' them. Very professional. No it more was a stream of consciousness, a train of thought, that connected to the wrong wire and came out through my thoughts as speech. What sort of a God was I acting like.

But they had to stop me, and so I sat there and listened patiently whilst these two characters explained to me that TOMORROW, they will debrief me. Tomorrow. (Although in their words it was, "unbrief" - I dread to think!).

"Tomorrow we will answer memories for you", as they then clarified. As if enough had not been explained already, what did that mean? Tomorrow all the questions I am asking them will be answered, tomorrow. Tomorrow is not coming soon enough! I keep typing and looking at the clock, it is barely moving. Time seems to have slowed down.

But I know why I must wait. They seemed so genuinely shocked from my unexpected collapse two days ago, that say they want to give me… time. Time for it to sink in.

And it is working I believe.

Apart from the regular bouts of complete disbelief.

They went on to explain that there are many honours to be bestowed on me by their fellow futurists and that I am to prepare for adventures and to... and this is the part I have been waiting to get to... they said that I will be able to go to any time of my choosing!

They - it seems - wish to grant me the ability to use 'my' concept for purposes that I would not otherwise live to be able to, as a form of honour for conceiving that very same damn thing! That is somewhat nice is it not?! So many inventors never lived to see their ideas become reality or to even use a prototype.

Only I will, and it all starts in two days.

That just blew my mind.

Okay, mind reassembled, and I have had a new thought. Could this be a hoax? Is Jeremy Beadle going to jump out from behind a UFO tomorrow pointing his microphone at everyone that moves?! (Generally away from him one suspects.)

Albert Einstein once said, "Imagination is more important than knowledge".

I did not imagine this. I now have complete knowledge of that.

I have that.

And I am shattered from happiness. Astounded from disbelief. But my eyes cannot stay open any longer even though my head wants to keep replaying things and my fingers to keep touching these keys that are you. My eyes are sore, red, my back and shoulder aching, and all I want is to sink into the duvet and dream something normal. Or better still nothing at all. Yet I know I will just dream of you.

If I rub my face any more it is going to come off.

And so I really must sign off.

Time flies . . .

DAY FOUR

Posted by Eurora001 on Mon 11-Jun-2001 07:46

You know it is funny, in my 'sleep' I thought of that old joke, "Well, if time travel is invented in the future, wouldn't they have travelled back to tell us - WOULDN'T WE KNOW ABOUT IT BY NOW?"

I watched a stand-up comedian do that joke while flicking through the TV channels years ago and remembered chuckling to myself, as I saw the audience appear to roar with laughter. How wrong he was. They seem so naive now. Those audience members did know about time travel, and we as a people have known about it for millennia. And yet through our blinkered ignorance (or the time travellers' cunning manipulation), we just call them Aliens instead.

The perfect crime.

They are not here yet. They seem to keep their own schedule. Funny, you would imagine they would always be on time.

Well the mysteries of the universe will have to wait. I need some toast.

Posted by Eurora001 on Mon 11-Jun-2001 14:20

I have been on board again! This is a different person writing. Not literally, but recalling my last entry, I have grown in knowledge somewhat. A whole world of what I thought was common knowledge has been turned on its head. Yet it makes more sense upside down. Wait, I will tell you.

This time when they 'took' me there was more understanding from their part too, more in fact like a business meeting. It echoed of China. It still dumbfounded me that the entire event took place without a translator. Like a corporate negotiation round a large meeting table, but nobody speaking aloud for two hours. Ridiculous.

My energy is funnelling out from me day by day, maybe due to the way we communicate (I still just catch myself writing something so absurd like that - but here I am!). But I will and must get down here what I have learned.

Well this entry is to clear my mind if nothing else. Read along with me by all means! It is astonishing just how detailed their conversations are in my mind. Even if they are not the sort of things you would easily forget, for me every word appeared in my mind without choice to listen or not, and there every word stays I suspect for that reason.

Once on board and up on the upper level, I started by saying, "I have those questions for you if that is all right".

"Oh, please do."

Both 'Alfred' and 'Lucy' say it almost in stereo, and seemed genuinely delighted to be of interest to me. (They should imagine how I feel.)

(Am I going slowly round the bend?)
(No, no this really did happen.)

And so I asked them, "I want to ask you what the UFOs are that people see, if they are not aliens - are they all time machines?"

Alf is happy to answer this, almost proud to. "If you want to talk with me directly, anytime is fine basically. So I answer -

there are not aliens! There are only humanoids. No very intelligent life is discovered elsewhere in universe even yet. This is science fiction. Life, yes, mostly vegetables, some mist-flyers, some aquatic croutons, but not a thing capable of interplanetary flights my knight!"

Yes, he really said that.

"A small contingent of sceptics", and Alf almost chuckles to himself at this point - I remember liking how his narrow mouth grows slightly wider and wide eyes slightly narrower, "they still belief that life is out there yet undiscovered, but they are a small-minded.

"When our ancestor first travel, it is known there were many grave concerns not least that the existence of time travel would become to be known BEFORE the existence of time travel, and cause a 'Temporal paradox' - you know it?" He need not have said it slowly. I know it. "In words, somebody would capture the design for the craft before YOUR design of the craft, design it earlier, and alter our ancestor very lives. Maybe wipe us up. Or we change some event which send waves of time to the future and change future in bad ways. But that early belief and worry, not so much now."

I did wonder why. "So your ancestors got around this by fabricating the whole alien story?", I asked, amazed at this point that the conspiracy we thought was the government's was actually OUR OWN lie, told to us by our future us.

"No quite contrary!"

Oh.

"We believe that the people our pioneers visited created that alien theory for themselves to be making sense of it, and so our plans were largely not needed. Quite remarkable and fortunate turn up for the events. Yes the earliest craft, the most basic design, for a short time did not even have the invisibility and so could be seen!"

No! Really? Ha! UFOs! Early time machines!

He went on to explain that the first ever travellers to go back in time (just think of it - the first people to test my craft - so historic, yet it hasn't even happened yet), well they had a plan ready so that if by travelling back they inadvertently caused some sort of wave of what he later called 'changetime' to sweep forwards in time by accidentally changing an event, that another vessel would travel a bit further back to just before that change happened, so as to prevent that change changing! In other words they would be able to click undo.

I hope you are following, because he did not say it again.

"Problem there is if Craft A gets seen, and Craft B go back to cover him up, then Craft B be seen instead. Yet instead no matter when age they travel back to - so long as an age where time travel did not already exist as a known technology - they find the peoples create their own explanation for most part. It was Universe creating its own controls and making paradox difficult you see?"

I see.

YOU see? The gullible humans of our time rationalised any such changes for them.

A self-correcting distortion.

"While ancestor could and did influence past in the small ways, they found they cannot change history in any dangerous way. They were ready to be sorry to be in this troubles, but really not troubles and it was all okay."

"So you cannot change history you are saying?", I asked, a bit shocked then - and still a bit now. They were confirming a theory I had held to be nonsense - that the Universe can intervene to protect itself.

"Not quite."

Oh.

He elaborated that even if small and harmless changes occurred, it was not possible to always tell that they had occurred. Why? Simply because the memories of those who would notice any changes would in fact be changed by the change - and so they would never 'recognise' that there had even been a change. Ah.

"Once it becomes history, it not becomes a change. It always was. It is a wave or a ripple of changetime that moves through time slightly altering what it swims over. But never anything that will matter. That is the crucial. Is not possible to do that. Something always stoppings it. We test it many times although with caution."

I wonder if that is what a deja vu is - as a small ripple hits us...?

"The Ancients from the Old World think we Gods. They even name us Eliwuia, after the name of one of our early travellers - she was a hero of stature in our history as you are. She exist ages before we do. Ya she even look more like you than we.

"Even the moderns from the Old World think we aliens. And those from New World already know they time ships so it not matter then, after its official invention is public dominion. Not much change really, always this belief in Old World they are unworldly emptities 'from above'. Really we are not from up, but from forwards, haheha!"

Well! Whilst I do not quite get their sense of humour, it is sweet that he is trying to make jokes in a second language. Actually, I wonder what language they DO speak. No, I forgot, they do not speak. Ah. Perhaps the language of thought is as universal as numbers, selfg-translating from one mind to another... Am I translating it?... Goodness Bella, I have so many questions still to ask.

"As we travel back to later times where your thinking becomes more superstitchus, when government have set up watchtower in heavily recorded 'UFO' sightings areas, and people have recording contraptionals still nothing has been proved. You ask me why and I tell you why. USofA's 'Project Blue Book' set up a watchtower in desert land desert for one year, after thousands of reportings - many not true but okay. They then see nothing. Wait, I tell you why they see nothing! With the benefit of history, to be safe our time travelling successors knew the watchtower was going to be placed and installed on that exact year, that exact place, and thus we avoiding that area for that year. Easy whilst you know, but why they not think of that we know not? Because they think aliens do not have benefit of time hindsight. Government no good, it why we abolish it.

"And by their nature our craft emits static electracation fi-", but the younger Lucy corrects him as if she's had to a hundred times before, "Electromagnetic!". Alf goes on "- emit a electromagnetic field around - this so interferes with your cameras by chance, and any nearby recordings they never come out anyway, only distance ones. Some luck in your time."

Is that not wonderful? I sat there inside the time machine, as they explained to me the precise reason why all footage alleging to be of UFOs is never proven. (I just looked up online about UFOs. There are indeed some reports that UFO sightings are accompanied by electrical disturbances that may well stop such recording equipment from functioning correctly as a mere side effect. Such electromagnetism would similarly also cause traditional film in cameras to white out.)

But either way, of course - this would explain why we only EVER see the ubiquitous distant long shots of UFOs in flight, or blurry photographs that could very well be seagull, but never close up. Those far off devices are the only ones out of range of the electromagnetic field, yet too far to be convincing in image. Again so simple when you know.

It still makes me want to try to bring a camera with me next time, if there is a next time to take some photographs, if not videos. Even if the images do come out all blurry and noisy - because maybe, just maybe, that interference only occurs outside the craft, but not inside.

And it is the fact that this all makes so much sense which makes me certain I am not losing my mind. How could a madman think up so many details on his own? If I was insane surely instead I would just be typing something like 'if your left ear's too short to stuff a mushroom then it is not worth throwing Rice Crispies all over everybody is it?'.

"In other times and when bad person tries to change past for gain or anger, they are preventings from doing it." He went on to explain that it is like that feeling you have when you are standing on the edge of a volcano (!) or as I see it a cliff. You want to jump, yet you just cannot do it. The exception he mentioned was that sometimes 'bad people' push through that innate safety valve, and then it is like "pushing towards two positive magnetic surfaces". I know that feeling all too well - you can feel the bounce of repellent energy, and he seemed to be saying that time has a similar repellent field around any changes taking place. "When you push too hard to move to change event, you slip off edge just like magnet."

And I had to push a bit further toward the edge and ask, "So this means there is only ONE timeline? No parallel universes?"

"How simple your thinking is yet how grand. I always respect you and your question however I explore you to understand [impore you?] there is too much we cannot tell you.

"We know you understand because how great you are yet there is danger to furnish too much. Well what we say to finish the answer is that you may be right in what you say from your point of view yes yes. Let me say it is immune to negative change within reasons unless immense energies are expended to try to change it. In our time - as far as we aware - the universe has always schemed against such bad schemes to prevent them, to protect its proper timeline resulting from any such schemes."

So there it is - officially. The universe prevents 'bad people' changing the timelines.

I wonder HOW the likes of Alfred would be aware if there had been a negative change, however. Like they said, any change in the past also changes their memories of the past, so it instantly does not register as a 'new' change, but just as a 'memory'. Do they have machines situated at various times in history, monitoring events? Oh good (!) another question... I need to keep a list!

But he had gone on, "But contrastingly, good change it is not immune to. This is beauty of cosmos - that it allows only change that is good. Our job really quite easy, unless we wrong. Then we are in the big trouble!"

So they are aware of when some changes take place, apparently. Either way, I must be looking a bit confused at this point as Lucy comes into the conversation again, to clarify what I am becoming used to as her younger, clearer, fresher, female perspective. That has not changed over time between the sexes at least. I am learning that she always smiles the best she can with that small mouth, and her eyes always soften and narrow slightly just before she speaks to me.

"Small changes can do happen but they have no absolute effect on the far-flung times such as ours and even yours. They just dwindle away into nothing - it exists and was recorded yet it affect nothing and left no footprints in time. Like a snail who takes a different path to his lettuce. Somehow other changes take place to accommodate and make right, like pulling tight the kink in some wire.

"And to major negative changes - nobody has succeeded as the cosmos will not allow it", she repeated.

"Like two negative magnets", I said slightly too enthusiastically keen to point out I did get it.

"Like the magnets", said Lucy with a very slight nod and a close of her eyes.

Fascinating isn't it! All our questions about space-time which may have gone unanswered for eons, answered on a plate instantly. Well, on my plate. It does not violate the principle of causality, and they would have no reason to lie to me.

Yet I can tell no-one one of the most fantastical nuggets of knowledge ever to be bequeathed to one person.

Wonderful.

So does this make sense? If they changed a major historical event, it might cause a paradox that today some of my peers postulate would result in the total collapse of space-time fabric. That much is known. Yet it never has, or we would certainly know about it already!

Well, not know about it but rather cease to know anything and dematerialise.

Ah - is that proof enough of what they say? Proof I do not have a date with the loony bin? I mean, time travel has been around since... well since six days ago. Seriously though, time machines have been buzzing around us for millennia. Had a single one of them changed a major event and caused a paradox that led to the Universe imploding, I have a feeling we may have noticed it slightly.

So they ARE right. The very fact they go on to exist in future years means time travel exists, which means time travel is safe, because WE still exist, uptime of their past travels. None of their travels into even OUR past have harmed us.

I feel so idiotic now that our community have postulated whether such paradoxes can exist. Yet did we not stop to consider that if they did, we likely would have had our planet blown up already by travellers going to OUR past and making a mistake. The very fact we exist to discuss such paradoxes means it is not worth discussing. Agh, people!

And from our 21st Century perspective of aliens and UFOs, knowing our future so being able to TRY to change it is a lot more dangerous TO our future than falsely believing we simply have some planetary neighbours we call aliens. So yes, this of course is why we have chosen to imagine aliens might say hello, and time travellers would, and have, not. Or have not been allowed to.

Hard to believe it really is true - an autonomously self-governing universe? Yet how can that be. The universe has no brain. The real paradox as I sit and digest these events, is that I wonder if these advanced beings are in fact also naive ones. After all, they have not yet stopped me writing these journals. They feel that some otherworldly power is determining 'good' from 'bad', and only allowing one to persist. But that just sounds a tad too fanciful to me.

Having had time to digest this, I can at least postulate that it is possible, beyond even these 'Futurists' time in the future, that there may be an even more advanced race of these humanoids who may police the lines of time like the streets of a city. They right wrongs before they can happen, which my Futurists see as some sort of Godly intervention.

YES! That would mean that good changes are allowed to 'pass through' by these time governors, whilst ones it is calculated will have a detrimental effect, are prevented before the wave of time hits the advanced Futurists. But why have I thought of this if they have not?

I am sidetracking for a second back to their mention of early man (i.e. us) deeming them to be aliens. Does it not seem so foolish and incredibly obvious now that we only ever see these craft inside or near to Earth's atmosphere, yet no satellite, telescope, or astronomer has seen UFOs on their WAY TO Earth! They are always already here, but never seen flying past Mars. Alien UFOs that are never out in space?! Did nobody consider that problematic to the 'alien' theory? So why have we assumed they travelled through anything but time. Why assume they travelled through the galaxy? People make me so mad sometimes!

Seriously, why did we not consider UFOs as time ships before? Only a fool believes the first thing he is told and considers anyone stupid for challenging that with the second thing he is told. Or she. Had the media latched onto a time ship theory instead since the 1960s, and then someone had challenged that they might in fact be aliens, imagine how ridiculed they would be! "Aliens? Pah! Everyone knows they are time saucers." Yet here I am, believing every word of this new twist, because I was sitting inside the evidence.

Alfred had said to me, "People did not even realise when they see our ships move so fast then to disappear in front of very their eyes at the speed of light... in a flash of LIGHT", he said into me as if his mouth opened wide to spell it out to me.

I know exactly what he means, more than many would. He seemed to know I would. It is how I theorised the TDA would behave after all. From what little I recall, UFO witness reports from credible people such as police or pilots have I am sure said that the craft appear "at the speed of light" or "with a flash of light". LIGHT. Then zigzag around the sky at supersonic speeds, only to disappear in the same trailblazing manner. Well let me tell you this Bella; one phenomenon that travelling at the speed of light or at supersonic speeds has is that you TRAVEL THROUGH TIME. These witnesses were watching time travel in the skies and somehow not even piecing it together. Yet again, we have been witnessing craft appear and disappear at the speed of light, and never said, "well if they went that fast, they would have just time travelled". How did we miss this?

...Or did we.

It seems implausible nobody rang this alarm before.

Yet if they did, they were silenced.

I am again petrified for my safety.

No, it is okay, they seem to value me too much, and are so gentle.

Back on topic, those craft in the sky that disappear in a flash of light are not 'disappearing'. They are simply leaving the second in time we see them exist in, and travelling fourth dimensionally into seconds in time we do not yet inhabit. They remain there, in the sky, but we just stop seeing them as they move faster into the future of that moment, and no longer exist in this one.

What is captivating me now is that I realise simultaneous to proposing a craft that might embody the time displacement array, I had likely seen that very craft on television, captioned as a 'UFO', without even realising! It is just not the sort of presumption one's mind is used to connecting.

Let me clarify, for my own peace of mind if not yours.

Move forward in time, people on the ground see a 'flying saucer' go from hovering there stationary, to speeding up, to shooting along then disappearing in a flash of light as they break light speed. Move backward in time, people see the reverse - a flash of light, followed by (as witnesses see it), a craft appearing then slowing down! It is just the same travel, only seen backwards. These early UFOs are achieving time travel in a flash. Literally.

And those are just the first ones, pre-invisibility cloaking apparently. I wonder how many there really are, which we have no idea are all around us. Jesus that is a scary thought. But would we not see the flash of light if not the craft?

Hell, it could be they reserve travel solely for lightning storms to use as a disguise. There has always been something decidedly spooky about lightning storms.

(Thankfully it is not stormy today.)

But you know, thinking about it, why would we think any other way than that time travellers are aliens. Surely the real fools are those who did not believe in the existence of these craft at all.

Humankind on the whole has always had at least these three constants: To believe we are not alone in the universe; to believe in an all-powerful creator that takes the responsibility off our shoulders; and to rationalise everything we see within those remits we can understand.

Yet had we looked a bit further, might we have become conscious of the fact that we ARE not alone, that WE were the creators - of our own destiny, and how much more rational that all is than little green men.

Oh well it just beggars belief!

Just found a reference to a comment I was looking for from one of my peers. Here it is. "Also, in the absence of any evidence that time travel exists, it is theoretically simpler to assume that it does not happen. Indeed, Stephen Hawking once suggested that the absence of tourists [coming back] from the future constitutes a strong argument against the existence of time travel ..."

So I have never particularly liked Hawking's theories, and indeed my own directly contradicted his chronology protection conjecture which said time travel defied the laws of nature, although I shall not bore you with the minutiae. But now whose quote looks ill conceived! They have, today, actually proven Mr Hawking wrong to one of his own community. In time I only hope he and others can open their minds and eyes to realise this beautiful reality, that I cannot tell them. That we HAVE been visited by time tourists from Earth, and that we just disguised them in a science fiction costume of our own making.

Something else comes to me now. I seem to recall people often report strange behaviour of wristwatches - if I remember right that usually that after an encounter, a watch is some hours ahead of everybody else's who was a witness. Like the UFO had an effect on the workings of the timepiece. This can be beautifully explained now by the time tourist's ability to travel back some hours in time to drop a person back 'home' at the same moment they beamed them up into the craft! The human's watch has advanced as normal for the hours he or she was away, causing it to appear to have suddenly 'changed time' when they are returned to the original time. Perhaps my friendly Futurists are even unaware what a 'wristwatch' is and just think it to be jewellery. This would be much like some Egyptian artefacts archaeologists have found, with immensely intricate designs and workings, yet we have no knowledge of what on Earth they were for or how they worked! Surely if they did understand our artefacts any better than we understood the Egyptian contraptions, these time travellers would set the timepiece back a few hours so as to not give the game away.

Well, I have speculated enough. I am thankful for all the facts they brought me, without need for guesswork.

Just before it was time for them to drop me back (my wristwatch matches the current time, although I have no reason to believe I have actually travelled through time - only through the air), Lucy had one final revelation. You will like this.

"Tomorrow we have a plan and we can take you just small ways into the future for the first time." I told you that you would like it. "We must tread slowly we know this now for your wellbeing of course", Lucy says excitedly almost as if it was her idea.

"Great memories will be made! Is it fine for you?", says Alfred.

"Yes, fantastic!", I beam back at them. Forget my list of questions. I think too much, and enjoy too little. I have an adventure to look forward to and I am going to enjoy it no matter what.

Alf confirmed, "Then it is set! And do not forget informing the passport data to Lucy, please. [?!]

"Hahehahe I joke! Goodbye from your small assistant and friend. I wish to give you the peaceful sleeping for tomorrow", Alf smiles as Lucy's hand directs me towards the downward ramp, and I lead the way before I can ask what time tomorrow.

I turn that hairpin bend, and I glanced up at Alf whose head is back in his hand. I continue downward into the belly of the machine. I do hope he is okay, even though I hardly know him.

The hole in the lower 'deck' I am now used to sucks me into its grip as I reach its point of no return, and I am transported back to 'earth' (well my patio door) in their version of an elevator.

And it was over, again. There were other lesser matters that arose such as their anti-gravity method, but none that I have the energy to continue with here for I am truly depleted.

From the balcony door, I walked to this seat, and now here I still am. Becoming a little ritual this - a comfort. You know, as I gaze up through the glass to where their craft may have been (may still be?) it is all so implausible. Just trees, a lamppost, birds casually sitting on one warm patch of rooftop across the road, and the most humdrum of settings for such supernatural events to be going on.

I would again be asking myself if I imagined it all, if it were not for the fact that everything they told me posed and then deftly answered more questions than I believe anyone ever has.

And now for some reason I get a horrible sense.

What if I never see them again?

Day Five

Day Six

Day Seven

Posted by Eurora001 on Thu 14-Jun-2001 16:30

I almost abandoned this journal here. Writing seems so prosaic now. I do NOT know what to say sorry. So much for my little ritual. The past two days have become trancelike. I may be a nuclear physicist but I am still only human. How can I go back to this life - my project of so many years gone, you gone, and now just typing and passing the time between their visits.

How can I go on now I have experienced time travel?

And how.

I know if you were here you would be disappointed... Ah, for you then Bella, okay. You always win me over yes.

(I dreamt of you again last night by the way. We were clothes shopping for - jeans, in the future. The shop was called Stellar, and the assistant's name was Stella. Dreams can be so curiousa. Yet it is nice that you are sharing this timeline with me still, and that I have a normal life to go to in the twilight hours - of a sort.)

There is ordinariness all around me now I am back, home. A plane overhead - people probably returning from holidays in the sun. A bird singing like it is all he could ever care to do. A child is shouting down the street, obviously having immense fun from his perspective. Pah! All of them, every single one, blissfully ignorant of what is being experienced perhaps metres away from them by this fellow citizen. How basic they are, as are the cars that go past on - wait for it - four wheels. Ha! I am exaggerating of course, but to demonstrate what a skew my new perspective puts on things. And I do not mean this belittlingly, just factually, but... well, how ordinary their lives are at this moment.

And what if they knew.

Where do I begin. Okay. Well they came again, and there was that same thrumming underfoot, Max looking less terrified than before as if it were becoming to her a mere case of, 'oh this again'. And that familiar dank chill in the air around (presumably just) me as this time I picked up my small camera, and walked to the patio door readily - I almost felt like a slave going to his beloved master on whom he depends, rather than having to be dragged by his chain. A futuristic Stockholm Syndrome perhaps?

I am still however not too keen on that swimming in air sensation. And again I fell up into the blue shower-chute, with a rush of air that felt for a second like my very soul escaping out from me.

I had the camera in my hand, and did my best with it. For some reason there was no feeling of 'being caught' with it, instead it was like I was on auto-pilot, not knowing if I would ever experience this again after today, and thinking only that I had to capture it all no matter what. Foolish, in hindsight, I know.

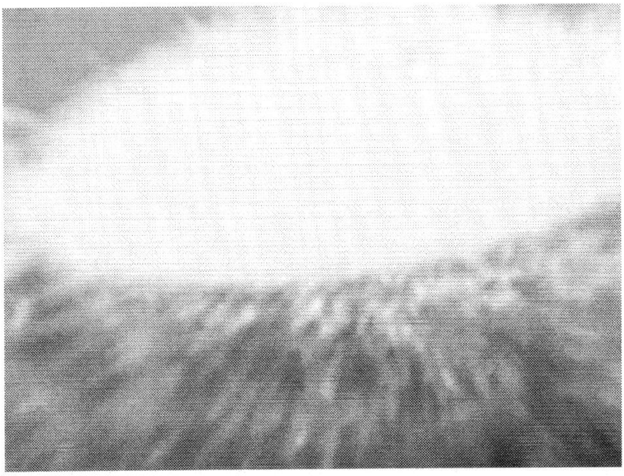

After turning round to face the right way and regain my balance and composure to wear the mask of godliness they project onto me, I see 'Lucy' standing there to welcome me. Lucy. I attempted to deftly slide the thin camera into my front pocket. I say 'attempted' because - well you try being 'deft' when you have just been sucked into a flying saucer and caught with a camera by an alien. Of course, I dropped it.

Lucy reached down - being nearer the floor than I - to pick it up.

I froze. Literally - I mean my extremities went freezing cold in one throbbing heartbeat.

They say you see your life flash before your eyes at moments of great danger, and it REALLY is true. I saw you, and nothing but.

Lucy looked slowly up from the camera at me, then handed it to me with a nonchalant, "here you drop this". And that was that! Did she even know what an ancient 21st century camera looked like?

She is a welcome sight - so very alien, yet reassuringly familiar or... I do not know... there is 'something' about that one. And so I was ready to walk back up to the upper deck. Up, up, and away... Only thing is, Lucy held my hand this time instead of just letting me lead the way, and...

That is the first time I have touched any of them. The first time anyone has? These wraithlike beings that have both repulsed and enchanted me that first time just five short days ago.

Her hand felt so narrow, so cold, so clammy and dank. Yet all that was irrelevant because the sentience of the moment lit me up inside. To Lucy I do not think it was any sort of monumental moment, although I could be wrong (on reflection, surely she had interacted with other past humans before), but to me her soft hand touching mine echoed round my momentarily vacated mind of historic moments, maybe like man's first footprint onto the moon.

First contact.

I do not recall if I mentioned before, but there is no feeling of being drugged any more. I go... au naturel now. Now they think that I know that I know what to expect. (I wish I did!)

Ha what do I sound like? Could you think I am starting to accept this as definite reality? I assure you I am not quite there yet. It is so easy to type what one knows he has seen, yet on reflection of the words it all appears so much clearer than it truly is in the mind.

It is as though my fingers have accepted these events before my head has.

Maybe last time I wrote I thought I was accepting it, but every time I get close, they throw me another curve ball. (A closed timelike curve ball.) But it is as if they know just how far to push me now. Not too far like before, just as far as I can deal with at any given moment - and no more, no less. They must after all have a wealth of psychological data at hand about our lesser species, no?

On deck Alf greets me with a raised spindly hand and a smile that is becoming more normal to me by the day, if nothing else is. Again I stun myself to know all his words as if memorised. "It is the one and only! Good you are wearing trousers."

I pondered on that, and later realised what he actually meant (as I had not been the first time they 'took' me), and then pondered on the symbol again that sits under the screen - and you know I actually plucked up the confidence to ask them about it. But I did not get as far as even making the statement before...

"Can you read it?", Lucy replied expectantly.

"No sorry not really", I said back with a disappointed smile. It is nothing to feel ashamed of.

"Is a D, is a C, is a D?", Lucy says in such an alien way.

"DCD? Whose initials are they?", I responded.

"No, sorry, we are making a misunderstanding for you. It is all my fault. It is emblem of this ship, it has an old English name, 'Decart Drifter'.

Alf looks up from what he was doing (just bowing his head in thought or communication) and feels compelled to add, "I like you very much. He is the knight. We have many ships bear your old English name as well!"

My name on a ship?!! I cannot take that in.

I feel so old.

There are a few moments of uncomfortable (for me) silence, and then I find I have asked them before I realise it, "Why do you look kind of Oriental, bald, and pale?"

When I gain my composure and realise that it has 'come out' I am quick to add, "No offence... I-I am rather pasty myself".

"Oh you are truly so observant and positively hilarious! Love your self deprecating humour and dry wit! Litigious! Many in your time can't not laughed at themsleeves: Too expensive!"

I did not think I had even made a joke.

"And how are you right." I do not know, how am I? But it seems I was. I will summarise what I understood, for the way I hear their words can hardly be any easier for you to interpret as it is for me to commit to writing.

Well first there is the hairlessness. Here is what they explained, in my own words. Throughout evolution, Alf recaps, man has been shedding more and more hair, from "monk keys", to our time, and logically therefore to beyond. Added to this they reveal - not surprisingly - that the planet is very much warmer in their time, which they say made hair - the body's insulator - redundant! Hairlessness is just the logical continuation of 'our' current evolutionary path. This made immediate sense to me and reassured to me that these little hairless humanoids were indeed our direct descendents, and not aliens - yet that engrained belief is still hard to shake at a core level.

Sketch out a picture of our ancestors, apes, hairy from head to foot, and continue sketching the evolutionary line up to man, with much less hair (some more than others). Then continue drawing where you think that progression will go Bella! You should have drawn completely hairless people! (What others call 'little alien men'.)

This bit I have to type verbatim as Alfred says, "Mankind is something to be overcome in your time. We mean no offence because know this is not applying to you, but the Old World were so bad with the looking after of species, and in time are equally bad at looking after yourselves. Terrible harm comes to the waters, to the globe, and to some of our productiveness. And so it is so cold here with you, but hot in the time I come from.

"A small faction in our time have a joke here about your belief we are aliens, and joke it is that proof there IS intelligent life elsewhere in galaxy is that they did NOT to try to contact the Old

World. They think they will soon contact ours though - but we no so sure.

"But this much true - humans may be the most incredible thing the universe has ever created, but also one of brainless. You had many chance to prevent uninhabitable climates and yet unfortunately some lacks of information made you to fail".

I know they do not mean anything by it, but I still feel small and insignificant. Oh and brainless.

And they talk about themselves as if they are not "humans", because we are and we differ. Like we do not call ourselves "monkeys" I suppose. Are they really to be classed as a different species altogether now?

I am wondering if that is why the inside of the ship is always so incredibly warm. A natural climate for their species' comfort. Or maybe even that feels cold to them, their extreme heat lowered to make ME more comfortable. And yet outside the ship there is always a chill. Maybe as it expels the cold air, like some latter-day AirCon unit. Cool.

Anyway, they seem as unsure of the specifics of exactly why this bodily transformation continued as we are of ours, other than it was natural progression from hairy Homo sapiens.

(They obviously have yet to see Daniel.)

Then onward to their time due to what we would call global warming, but I understand it is more severe than nice words like 'warm' and 'globe' could ever encapsulate.

If I could only prove this Bella, it could change the course of history by shocking our governments and space agencies into action to resolve the problem.

Maybe that is why they have contacted me. The Universe (or as I see it, divine intervention from their descendents) will allow good change after all. But that would be a change beyond all calculation. Too much of a good thing?

Yet I am bound to say nothing of these events, so how could I bring awareness to others?

And if we did act now, Alf and Lucy would be terrified of such action, as would it not change the world they call home - despite any problems it may have? Would they even have been born? Or maybe they would just have some extra brothers.

I have decided to wait for them to invite me to do anything before I consider it any further! I cannot bear the responsibility. Not on top of everything else on my shoulders at this time. You understand.

And so, back to the questions about their appearance. Their answer makes perfect sense in relation to all the sightings we hear about of 'aliens' - I love just how much it does. Do you? 'Hairless beings from another planet' indeed. I guess we never do cure the problems with the planet. Too busy trying to find a cure for the baldness.

I had also asked them to clarify some points.

"Sorry so why DO you have what we may describe as 'Oriental' eyes?"

"Auriatal??", Alf says, and Lucy's brow furrows above those fascinating glassy eyes.

"Sorry you mis... heard me...?" I 'pronounce' it more clearly in my mind. "Or-ee-en-tal - yes? F-f-from Asia", I simplify a bit nervously suddenly for some reason.

"You sold the concept to men from... or-ee-en-t did you not?"

That one shocked me. (So what is new?) But I was right. Granted, those from the Far East are the most technologically advanced races and they must have been the pioneers in the creation of the first time travel prototypes. Yet did I do this? Little old me? Did my choosing THOSE people and their look when signing the China agreement, and THAT particular location and race, in some way alter the course of the progress of our entire species?!! Some sort of natural selection, only I was the selector?

I will now pick my jaw up off the keys.

(IthinkIbrokethespacebar.)

But did my decision even give the Chinese that important small but crucial right or power to use the technology before other countries or races - just like NASA has a bit of a monopoly on space flight in my time?

Too much to think about.

They went on to make me think about it, as they explained that a greater reason is that the underdeveloped nations like those in 'my' Asia and Africa are to go on to multiply and reproduce at a faster rate than any other country on Earth in the coming times, interspersed with times of great famine and the natural population control they claim that brought about.

What unsettles me a bit is that interspersed with these revelations they take pauses and look at each other - perhaps talking to each other - perhaps to someone else not present - and I can tell they are intentionally filtering and taking great caution with what they reveal to me in any detail.

Famine does not scare me perhaps as much as it should, as we have become somewhat desensitised to hearing of it. However I do wonder what else may be omitted that would affect me negatively.

Terrorism? Wars? ...Ice ages? Or something that gave oriental races an advantage through time that might better explain these visitors' manifestation?

They have chosen not to worry me I sense, and so I shall not worry myself. All is well.

They elucidate that the theories for their appearance are largely agreed quite simply that the Asian genes that control human features being stronger and more abundant, propagated in Earth's future to a stage of partial gene domination through cross-breeding.

A true multi-cultural world all mixed down through time into one race. The 'Futurists'.

I am thinking of that other great lyric - about if the world were one great melting pot - and so it seems it shall become. Inevitable is it not? Here I am, Caucasian, and so many like me falling in love, and having babies with beautiful women from all continents. Indeed many Westerners rightly attracted to Asian ladies, then you follow that line several millenia... to those babies'

babies... and those babies' babies' baies... and inevitably yes, there will become one grand species, one nation. One look. Their look. A slightly oriental look. Alien to us, yet not at all.

HOW HAVE I NEVER SEEN THIS BEFORE? A quick scout of the Internet presented to me a host of alien-like futurist faces, hiding in plain sight like never-before-noticed ghosts behind the faces of our very own 2001 oriental ladies. Take away the hair, and there is truly something in it!

But Asian folk are not pale looking... some people are criticised for calling them 'yellow-skinned' in fact. I now wonder to myself if 'little green men' is that far removed from little yellow rainbow men, when mixed with every other race, a dash of evolution, and a twist of some such environment that might have a greying effect on the skin. I can only guess at this one. What would cause us to no longer be tanned and healthy pink? Of course! If for some reason we could not go into the sun in the future!

And why were they shorter than average? It does not take me much consideration to understand the logic of that too. We have become taller as we have had access to improved nutrition and healthcare - try walking at my height in any cottage built three-hundred years ago to see just how short people used to be. So what would lead man to get shorter again far into the future, along with those genes of smaller Asian people (as I found out when trying to buy clothes there)?

Decreased nutrition and health.

Are there not mass famines predicted, and the impact of the severe global warming will surely have a knock-on impact on the health of these beings who have no doubt endured it for millennia before my arrival to see their new state.

What they do say about the Earth paints a window through which I feel I am looking at the future as a latter-day prophet.

"The world it is changing", they summarise. And I shall summarise again, for I am so fatigued and my eyelids heavy.

The Sun and Earth's positions changed in my future as did the Sun's output - noticeably so concerning temperature as they already explained, but also - yes radiation. I knew I said it for a reason. They go out of their way to avoid direct contact with its rays now, following an age where skin cancer hit the global population on an unprecedented scale. Everybody takes the "sun shield decree" solemnly (I now consider that they imply this is in fact a device - although at the time I consider it to be a lotion!), and for this reason they have the characteristic pale, untanned, slightly greyish-yellow/green skin... Hardly touched by the Sun's UV.

It makes the publicity over 0.5-degree global warming seem decidedly trite.

I need a break to reflect on this. It is almost too much.

Well that break did not last but an hour - I am finding the outpouring of these revelations I have learned, to be... strangely compelling.

And so our meeting of minds continued. I had so many questions to ask them, in the hope it might help me sieve out their futurist scientific fact, from the decades of science fiction the media has brainwashed us all with. I was conscious that my time asking questions did not impact on the time they may offer me as a journey IN time... until I realised that running out of 'time' was not really an issue here - for we could very well 'create' time if we wanted! Still, I kept my questions brief.

"You have smaller ears & noses, little mouths, bigger heads than your bodies?", I question, still afraid I might have offended them but finding no tactful way to say it whilst also dealing with all my anxieties of the heat of the moment.

"Sometimes our answering is very slow, and please understands we are happy to be with you".

They first discuss - I assume - the answer amongst themselves, and when they give it, it again makes sense. I expected I think to stump them. But no, incredibly they satisfied this one too by asking me a question back. They simply asked me whether we, as 21st Century humans, look like the hominids that we evolved from 15 million years ago, or like the mammal before that, or before that, that they say lived with the dinosaurs.

"Well, er n-no. Okay. No.", I had to concede.

"You are Homo Sapiens. You call us 'Extapiens'."

Extapiens. There we have it.

I did not question it, though I do now.

But they are right, why SHOULD future man look just like current man? He would not. There have been several stages of 'homo' evolution, why not more going on tomorrow? We have not stopped evolving. We always believe we are the ultimate, but now I KNOW we are not.

Perhaps THEY are not.

My goodness but how far into the future do they exist to look THAT different. Surely as far forward as our Neanderthal ancestors are backward. More?

Rationalising this again is therapy to my eyes. Getting it out is like lying on the counsellor's couch.

I have unearthed a missed opportunity by all of mankind! All the time we have been wrongly thinking it was 'UFOs' and 'aliens' visiting Earth, we could instead have looked with a more open mind, and in turn seen what we will become, in time. Why did we not think to look?

While they were telling me this, I understood it instantly although only now do I accept it. And so while they spoke, I looked at them and in my eyes they achieved metamorphosis in front of my very eyes (well, my very mind). There is something so beautiful about 'Extapiens'. Our future selves. A higher echelon of mesmerising splendour and majesty that touches me whenever I now think of their faces.

Imagine sweetheart if you or I travelled back from today, to visit Australopithecus. Would we not look completely alien to them? Would they not think WE were from another planet? Or a God?

God.

What if cavemen really did think Extapiens were Gods...

Alf did elaborate on the rest of my question, including the size of their heads and features.

"Historians and Biologians agree that as we developed more so sophisticated reasons of communicating, the less we used our ears and mouth. Indeed for sensing any unlikely dangers we still can hear, and we talk - see!" I watched Alf's mouth move silently, gracefully. I am going to have to take his word for that, literally. He even seemed to realise the predicament and a look of guilt creased his mouth shut.

He continued, "We do not wish to appear big headed", but at that unwitting double-entendre from the large-craniumed being I laughed spontaneously then realised they were neither joking nor laughing, which made me laugh even more! The nerves and whole situation really got to me and I am ashamed to admit I pretty much cracked up. I was scared too of doing so, and the fear only further fanned the flames of my hysteria. An AWFUL situation - I felt like I was back in school trying not to laugh during a Latin lesson as my friend on the desk in front made his hankie walk the 'plank' (his wooden ruler). But my hysterics seemed to transcend the barriers of time and still had the same effect on them that they would on any person - as they started to chuckle too! And then a breathtaking moment. They were laughing hard with me, and after mere moments I saw a tear from laughter welling in one of Lucy's huge black eyes. She raised her hand to cover her mouth and mute what must have been audible chuckles. The stereotypical giggly Japanese girl came straight to mind.

The surreal nature of the whole situation hit me, which cured my laughter, and they followed.

The contagion made me feel at one with them.

The only way I could relate it to you would be perhaps an excitable chimpanzee shrieking as you laugh with it. He is joining in, in his own way, but your similar DNA means your moods are compatible. Or how Max wags her tail when she knows you are happy too.

I do not care how it relates - it was truly an overwhelming moment.

Back on track, they went on, still grinning, "Yes I see, we do have big head compared to you - but we see you as have of the small head and of the big body - it all depend on the perspective", and he smiles to himself. "You have to realised, our brain it came to evolve to more, like muscle you work it grows larger, and so can the skin and can the bone surround it. This why we speak onto your mind." He does not mention the bodies - I think it was forgotten, but I assume that with all the technology, ease of transport, and not being able to go out in the sun as much for walks they just use them less and less? Why walk to Tesco when you can teleport. That, combined with their smaller Asian ancestors, seems to paint the general picture better than a Rembrandt in fact.

Lucy confidently interjected, "Above all we must be remembered that these 'aliens' you have come to known in folks law are expressed as 'humanoid in appearance'. HUMANoid Mister. What could be more humanoid than a human, my great fellow human?"

Yes, I can see her point. She made it rather well.

Really you know, it IS ludicrous to believe that life on any other planet through some cosmic coincidence evolved into the same humanoid appearance that we are familiar with. How bigheaded yet narrow-minded that is of US to assume. All planets birthing the same two-legged two-armed two-eyed two-eared beings belongs firmly in Star Trek Science-FICTION. The chance of that is infinity-to-one. The chance of time travel becoming reality however? I should know, I conceived the means to make it so, with Science, FACT. It seems so clear now, suddenly! Einstein already showed me it was possible in his general relativity, Tipler certainly helped me along the way to form a plausible CTC concept (that is the Closed Timelike Curve, sorry), and then yes dare I admit it to myself, I may have laid the next stepping stones with the time displacement array and the eurora potential in the series that led to its become a reality. Even if I am just a cog in the bigger machine, by all accounts it was a big stepping stone. Or they would not be here.

And then they sit me down quite formally for a briefing. (Not another un-briefing of the underwear variety thank goodness.) (Sorry, nerves are still with me.) I sit in the middle of the three seats - surprisingly comfortable if a little small, as they sort of mould to take my form. It is an awkward way to have a briefing, with them sitting either side - I did not know which way to look lest I insult the other.

But this seemed a serious moment to them, and so to me. I think I shall not bore you with all the details of it, but suffice to say I felt a bit like that child I still hear outside might if I had plucked him from his bicycle, sat him down, and said, "Now listen Freddy you are going to be an astronaut and travel to Mars today. Here is what you have to remember or YOU WILL DIE."

Interact with no-one was one point they stressed. Not so much because I could change things, but because doing so could change me.

They do explain this will be a "short" trip of TWENTY YEARS into my future (absurd - can you imagine?!). And it will be for no more than one day and one night. They seem to feel this is a letdown. Can you imagine how much it was not!? They say this is because they do not want to cause any more adverse reactions for me, yet they wish me to become accustomed to the experience of occupying another timeline for 'long enough'.

Baby steps.

(Charming.)

I do feel like lil' Freddy, whoever he is.

No, really I am thankful. In hindsight, what I am about to tell you was the perfect introduction. Perfect. And why the exact date they want to travel to? Well they have a nice surprise for me, the synchronicity of which you will not believe. Wait till I tell you!

I do have a question for them in return for the briefing that they give me however. It came to me the night before, when a few fragments of dreams descended upon me.

(You were there - here - with me again like a short sharp torturous gift. I am past being brought close to tears when I awake from such now, thankfully - all too common and more like a trapped nerve my brain has learned to live with. But that accepted pain is pushed back close to the brink when I woke up fully thinking you were - still alive - and lying with me. Despite all of this going on around me, there is still room to mourn for you.)

And so I had asked them, "This may be a naive question forgive me - but in our time we had concerns that led me to ensure my plans included a method of propulsion through space [not outer space - just through places] as well as through time.

"And please do not get me wrong, I see now that the 'UFOs' - which were I have to believe the living result of my plans in some seed of a way - DO move about in three dimensions as well as in the fourth dimension of time.

"But the concerns were that if we leave this position in this country today in 2001, and head for the same point in a future year, even if we hit the right MOMENT in the time curve, the Earth will have moved AWAY from this spot on its journey round the sun, and we would rather unfortunately rematerialise in the same place - only that place would now be in outer space!"

Lucy looks to Alf and flashes those eyes of hers as if to say 'can I get this easy one?', and Alf points his forehead back at her a bit like a father to a daughter.

"That was first-class thinking my tall champion. Simply, of course there exists a spatial measure between two instants in time. You will not know it but the craft self-adjust and make it like you never moved."

Ah. Interesting. As hypothesised. Who am I to disagree, when they have been there and done that. I had included that working of the craft - its theoretical ability to travel through outer space, and through local space with a form of repulsorlift - as a precaution, and this revelation that it is necessary and that the craft will 'make up the gap' when you arrive in the middle of nowhere (quite literally) fascinates me in its now truth for a few more moments of thought. They allow me that.

And so I knew the final detail of my journey-to-come. If we leave one place in the year 2001, we will arrive in the same place in 2021 - even if that place has moved around in space. I will give that much thought, when I can find space in my mind.

"But we do travel in three-dimensions for the other reason - and that is how we got to your home which is in a different place on Earth to where we call from our home. This is a time ship but also an air ship and it can travel with a modified fay-", then Alf cuts her off, telepathically - I can tell by the way she simultaneously stops her train of thought and moves her head sharply towards him with a blink.

Need to know basis. Not love to know. I dare not argue with these strangely familiar entities who have given me so much already - though I would adore to know. I have a feeling it will come. In time.

"So we are ready! Is it fine for you?", Alf confirmed and checked.

It was more than fine.

They do me the honour of asking me if there is a location that I would like to choose! Can you believe this? That means a lot to me from these citizens of tomorrow. Maybe one day I may truly even fly us there! But for now, picking our destination is a big thing for me. I express my gratitude to them both, and it is all I can do not to erupt into a hysterical breakdown again. I do not remember feeling that happy since... you know.

Alf speaks.

"Please, Captain. Alf. Navigator."

I pick the first thing that comes into my mind - my old childhood home, not back then, not now, but in the future. They do not look at all surprised.

You remember me telling you about how it was never the same since they moved the main road away. Well I do not think I mentioned that in the decades since I lived there, many had followed by moving away also. I had not visited it for years because of the distance, but had wanted to - in fact did we not talk about doing so?

I do not know the co-ordinates, but before I have a chance to explain the precise location I am thinking of, Alf responds.

"Now we interface those spacetime co-ordinate in your time for", and he says the time, "at Eleven-thousand-and-three." (11:03 - it mirrors the exact time we are going to leave).

And as you might imagine I then expect some console to lift up from the deck for them to input the spacetime co-ordinates, or at least for the touch-screen to come to life. But for some reason I cannot see the display, it is just inanimate, or off, or...

Then I realise.

It is broken.

My whole trip will be cancelled.

And then I actually realise what it must be. The universe is preventing it.

Wrong again. They are discussing it as if there IS something there on the 'screen'. There is no panic in them like in me, as I realise again I am holding my breath. I remember how to exhale and consider for that moment... maybe they have evolved like dogs who can hear what we cannot, and perhaps with those big captivating eyes they can see what we cannot.

Shush brain. My low latent inhibition can be a real nuisance sometimes you know, over-thinking everything as it happens and coming up with any possible reason - yet in a whole new expanded realm of time travel.

Well maybe they can, but that is not the reason for this, in fact, I am wrong on every count. Long story short, the screen I thought was a screen, is not a screen.

Alf senses my confusion at their stationary busy-ness. "We input the co-ords to the craft directly - we do this in our heads just like you pass your stream of consciousness to us with your heads. (!) Yes it took getting some used to thinking with a ship and to be this open of the minded for everyone as a young traveller who is allowed.

"But it is well trained."

He went on about this and translated the shimmering 'screen' to what would be in English an "organic telepath interface". I liked it, an OTI. I just sat there mouth closed, eyebrows raised, watching the show.

"Haha the world it is flat yes? You are being too twentieth century within thinking big human fellow. [Even I did not know I was thinking.] To your Victorian man flying in a jet aeroplane across our world in one daytime it seemed preposterous and that brains would explode, but to you it like catching..."

"Flew!", I finish in a nervous joke.

Alf responded, "A tram".

He did not get my pun.

But I had to ask something else.

"How did you achieve telepathy?", I think at them.

"Gentle and kind soul, your people who have been visits with time travellers, mostly our ancestors acting illegally beware, claim sometimes though not all times that their 'aliens' spoke to them telepathy, without moving lips, and still the person to know exactly what we saying and thinking."

"I know, I understand that it is happening to me, I understand all that, I am just interested how you came to learn it...?", I had to clarify. Language barrier.

"Haha oh you, to ask me that is like to ask you how you learned to speak. Can you put finger on it? Thank you for being the wisest. Before your time we knowing prophets always speak of man's potent future ability to use telepathy, even in your time, at that time yet not tapped, and they say you only use some of your brains at present. The reason you cannot use telepathy in your time is virtually all people are not developed enough yet, you are barely evolved, but in time these parts of the brain's neural network is activated, the electricity fires between the connections, and a new feature awakens in many."

"But you are using it for ME, now?", I say a bit confused at my new found ability that seems to break these laws.

"Yes, we awaken it for you. Is easy backwards but only with someone capable of such understandings."

Apparently it is easy backwards. I think - I THINK - what they are saying is they opened the door and flicked the light switch, maybe like phoning someone whose phone has never been rung before - the phone has always been there, so when someone calls it for the first time, it does ring, and so they pick up.

Thank goodness I was home.

Yet they flatter me by implying many people at this stage do not own that phone, yet I somehow do. Is my brain somehow already one extra step down that distant path of future evolution, compared to others?!

I wonder if others who have had encounters with these Futurists or Extapiens (aliens) can therefore communicate with each other here back on the 'Old World', or if perhaps, the flame burns out afterward. I may have to seek out such a support group one day, under the guise of an alien abduction, just to try it. It would be the only way I could hear again in normal conversation, if you can call what goes on at such meetings normal.

It is funny though in these short few days since then, it seems so normal to me now! Like second nature. I guess it is just that. Like when you thought as a child you would never be able to ride a bike without stabilisers. Then when your father finally took them off and let go of the bike without telling you, balancing seemed to be the easiest ability in the world and one that had always been within you despite your refuting it beforehand. Second nature. I feel foolish now to have never communicated this way before. And how extreme does that sound!!

This knowledge is quite a gift they are giving me and I am touched by it, despite the jokes I still make through unease. You do know that don't you. God I hope you are reading this.

SO much.

But all of this information sends me into a contented daze. I felt completely out of control yet completely at ease - it was so other-worldly.

I put my hands behind my head and lent back into them. 'I am going to savour this moment', I assure and reassure myself. And so I study the stalactites on the ceiling. 'Not the safest thing to have in a ship', I think. Obviously too loudly as Lucy - increasingly, subtly, studying me it seems - interjects,

"They represent time to us."

And then it begins!!!!!!!!!!

Overwhelming is an Understatement.

At first, I am surprised by a surprisingly old-fashioned cranking vibration coming from deep below feeling just a bit eerily like Victorian chains catching hold of their cog then speeding up and clicking into place, and into motion. Or an old elevator. The sense of it really tickles my feet through my shoes. I cannot place that kind of motion into any relevance of my surroundings or concept, and I wonder if it sounds like I imagine it would to a hearing person - but perhaps nothing like it feels. How could something so modern sound so archaic?

Then just as they had briefed, the glassy blackness all around goes dark green. (At that moment I am aware that I never considered why something so black inside was so bright, as there was no discernable light source! Goodness I wish you were here to report this all to in person. You would make me feel less possessed.)

I brace myself for the imagined sensation of movement, and wait for the journey to begin...

At which moment Alfred says, "And we are here!"

"What, really, already?!", I said back.

"Hahaha...! We try to do it that fast we wish, seriously, my hero!"

HE is joking with ME can you believe?! They learn fast how to relate to my personality it seems.

Then my stomach almost disappears down through the seat. Definitely moving upwards then! But something seems to kick in within the seats holding the three of us, or maybe the entire interior, as I feel like I am being levelled out despite forces that continue to exist. Like some sort of ghostly restraint system. But the G-Force never comes, and I realise the 'cranking' feeling must have stopped when we went up.

It leaves behind it just a gentle tickle now.

A meaty smell fills the air as the craft noticeably chills for a moment.

Then the interior illuminates itself again - source still anonymous.

"Really we are here now", Alf says in grandiose seriousness.

What is unsettling and almost makes me air sick is that I cannot see where we are going / where we have been (I cannot even see which of those applies). I sense we are still moving through the air, and must already have time-travelled (incredible!), come out in outer space, adjusted back to Earth. So now we are no longer moving in time as he said we had arrived, but there is no viewport, no windows, not even a monitor in this craft. That strikes me as odd. They are flying blind. Well I am. I mean I know I do not have to worry, but still - instincts kick in and I feel like grabbing the controls. If I could find them.

Can you see the gymnastics my mind has been through now.

As I imagine us gliding invisibly over the landscape, trying to push the vertigo away, wondering what disguised the flash of our arrival, they explain where they are going to "drop me".

That does worry me for a second.

But the plan is for me to go alone - of course - they will wait over a point in the nearby fields, 'drop' me on the ground, and I will come back to the exact same spot when I am finished exploring my past home. In the future. Interacting with no-one.

What surprises me more is they do not place a time limit that I know of on this part of the visit. I mean I know I will not be long but still, it is an incredibly long leash they give me but with to hang myself on my very first expedition. And what if I bump into my future self! Surely highly unlikely which is perhaps why they were happy with this particular destination nonetheless, but I ask the question anyway, surprised they did not brief me on it.

"Please Captain, don't worry trust it to Navigator. It looks like perfect."

They have it in hand.

I guess I did not realise until I saw the field ascending towards me that I had actually been IN THE FUTURE for several minutes already. The 'one small step' moment had passed me without me even giving it thought! So much else to think about, the obvious did not hit me. And now unmissable. Could it be real? It did not look like the future, but then in twenty years why would it. What does the future look like anyway?!

Shall I tell you?

As I touched down at the base of the chute, my shoe came off slightly and I felt embarrassed to have landed like such a novice. But there was not a soul in sight to see it. Looking around I knew exactly where I was though - this was the field behind the lonely road that framed my old home, adjoining its pub. Once it had served as the main road but the lack of traffic once the road was moved reduced business and I knew the pub had changed hands shortly before my family left the area. Who owned it now I wondered. Futurists? Well, of a kind.

There was tall clover everywhere, ironic in its symbolism for my recent luck. As I walked closer and the border of vines ahead of me fell lower in my horizon, I saw it darling! My first home! From the back, yet so familiar. So many memories inside those brick walls still contained. I was suddenly smiling - a rare treat again. This was good for me!

There was a new shed approaching me to my left - which as I got nearer became clear was an old new shed. With a broken window.

The trees were higher now. The grass unmown. A song came into my unconscious mind. I wrote it of you.

As the grass grows higher than the trees
I think back through my memories
Want to touch the ground that you walked on
I would do right now but you'd still be gone
At the loss of a thought I will fall to my knees
It's no fun living on memories

Up to the shrub border of the back garden and it was mostly brambles now that I had to traverse. Climbing carefully over them using the decaying wood fence they clung to to steady myself, I was there. I could see much clearer now - this place was abandoned. My smile dropped a bit. It was fascinating, but saddening too. A place that had once been so full of love, now so unloved and full of nothingness.

The back windows were boarded over, broken glass beneath some of them, except one where the wood had been pulled away. How much time had passed for it to be boarded up, and then unboarded? I walked over the path to the locked back door, and peered in.

It seemed in a way that no time had passed at all for me. Certainly not the twenty years it had been. I wondered what difference if any those extra years had made inside. It had been abandoned perhaps that many? Perhaps we had not time travelled at all, and this was how it looked in 2001 since my last visit so long before. Baby steps? Had I really time-travelled?

Through the window there was the living room - structurally almost as we had left it. Surely it had been lived in since. Very dark, yet I could just make out the same wallpaper design, now fallen into slumber, but every paisley swirl containing some childhood thought. It appears we - I - had been one of its last residents.

The open fireplace that gave us so much warmth, now an empty shell. I remember how we had to light it just to have a hot bath. I have no idea how that worked now I think about it. The sofa gone, where I used to sit and watch the tiny black and white television-cassette player, eating pic-n-mix. Those white mice are good hey?

There was just some newspaper on the floor.

I wonder privately to myself at that point what the date on it is. Can I get in I consider. It would mean smashing the remaining glass, AND the window-frame. In other words, vandalising my childhood sanctuary. I cannot bring myself to do it. And I feel 'they' do not wish me to. Either way, it would be wrong. I did try the back door again, but definitely locked. Besides this was more than enough - I could come here any time, back in my own time.

I am at that moment gripped by interest at what has happened to the pub next door - surely in business longer than my home was - and the few small shops we had along from there.

I walk round to the front, and past the drive - stopping to 'hmm' to myself on the spot near the road where I had a bicycle accident. No stabilisers for those baby steps then either. I also notice how the ivy is starting to reclaim the side wall, and see the white benches out in front of the pub further to my right, to the left of the house, now grey and powdery. Indeed, when I get nearer it is clear from the dirt on the windows that they either have an extremely bad cleaner, or it too has had its day. When I approach there is not even a for sale sign. It is abandoned. I wonder how this can be, or who even owns the land now. Its sign that used to draw people in off the road for a ploughman's lunch, just flaking paint now creaking slowly in the breeze.

I feel like a ghost must.

I go back past the pub and my home on my left, towards the row of shops further down the road. I have not seen these since we moved! It seems almost as if they have not seen anyone since I moved either. The doors firmly locked, and almost historically significant old signs in the window. One advertising a rocking chair for sale for £2, another advertising Cadbury's Cocoa only with a logo I do not recognise or was too young to remember. These shops were old-fashioned even in modern times, let alone now. The grime on the inside of the windows is thicker than that on the outside, as though it had not benefitted from being washed away by decades of downpours. It is impossible to see inside the blackness pierced only by the occasional funnel of light. But I can just remember where everything was - the till where the shopkeeper would weigh my sweets before I ran excitedly home along the path to eat them. Those were the days. (And still are for 'me' in some timeline.)

It is getting eerie now. I feel almost as if my hometown was evacuated, although I am sure I know that not to be so. Then across the road where it forks off into the bungalows I see some lights on. People still live here! They just shop elsewhere I reassure myself.

My instinct is to cross the old road and go to talk to them. To ask them why it is so quiet. Without thinking, I step out into what used to be the main road, and this story nearly ended there as a truck wailed past me, narrowly missing my foot. It must have taken a wrong turn - why else would it be here? The shock sent me reeling back and I have to admit even with all that has happened I had to take a few minutes to regroup myself. As it left my knees shakier than my hands had been when I typed the chronicle of their first visit to me last Friday.

It was strange to me at that moment that a regular Earth truck (cannot believe I am also saying things like 'Earth truck' now too) made me a nervous wreck, but my own invention coming back from the future to visit me did not have quite the same sort of sudden impact. Not the jelly legs anyway. But more so, I am thankful it crossed my path and drew a literal line under my intention to cross the road and make contact with future ex-neighbours of my past. Or something. "Do not interact with anyone". God only knows what may have occurred had I continued to think with my feet.

I wish I could have seen the front of its cabin before it had passed me, to see how the design might have differed from what I know. Or just to prove to myself that I was seeing into the future. All I saw was its regular rear container, although I noted at least no fumes in hindsight.

And so I walk past the shops, trying to put the lights in the houses out of the seven year-old boy part of my brain, and then there is the village sign, tall with its shield head and monolith base. I remember feeling even back then that it was so historic! But now like the pub sign, the name barely there anymore, and the painted depictions of the cottages and farm animals flaked away from the metalwork with time, their molecules reconstituted into the earth below.

I walk around the back of the shop and cross the same wooden fence that joins back to my house. Taking a different line, I walk back to where they dropped me, but suddenly realise I have no point of reference. Do I have to get the same point in space, I worry? But it is okay because after a few moments walking in the general direction, approaching me I see my original footprints in the field, leading to my right until they abruptly stop, as if somebody had been beamed up while walking their dog. Backwards. A dog with no feet. Argh you know what I mean.

And then I was beamed up while walking.

I hesitate to even mention this as I suspect now my mind was playing tricks on me due to the recent adrenalin burst with that truck, however for a moment before I found our chute, I am sure I saw the flicker of another beam far across the field. And could I almost see the flickering beginnings of a ghostly figure within it? But then before I could even process the thought, I was sucked up into the actual one. I am sure it was nothing. I have been through a lot!

"How does it feel", says Lucy at the base of the ship's ground floor, gripping my wrist just firmly enough to send a little shiver down my spine.

I do not know how to respond. On one hand I am still not convinced I have even travelled, and even then am saddened at the state of disrepute my wonderful childhood setting now lies in. On the other hand...

Well on the other hand is Lucy.

She tells me they have a treat for me. The interior stays bright black with dark light this time as I feel the sensation of movement again, so I know we are staying in the same TIME, if we have not anyway.

To get to the point, I descend again after time to rest, only to find myself in a very familiar place, on the towpath where I walk

Maxine by the river every day! You know it - near the railway bridge where we lay back on the cold iron, river all around us.

It hit me at that moment that Max may not even be around anymore. That sad thought held me. But I know I would not bump into myself taking her for a walk anyway as they told me I was out of town at this time. Somewhere nice I hope.

And so I am free to roam my hometown. 'Is this the treat', I was wondering. The water did not seem any higher than usual, which was a good sign. I often wondered about that living so close. And so I walked along the towpath, very little different to see these alleged twenty years later. I supposed some places were just untouched by time. But there were changes.

Wondering a little bit of a, 'well this is nice but...', I took the next exit which led through the passageway to the shopping parade. 'What if I bump into someone I know?', I had to consider worriedly. You would. I would look to them like I had had a facelift.

But I have to assume they already know I did not, i.e. will not. Would not.

They chose this location for me after all. And on a very quiet day it seems. Had they timed that intentionally also, at a time they knew it would be quiet? Perhaps it was a Sunday, and I was soon to become certain that I had time travelled, beyond any doubt.

I walk down the steps, along the path - which is different, turn left onto the road - different, then left again into the deserted enclosed parade - very different. There are a couple of people in the distance by the other entrance to the car park, but nobody I would know. The car park must be closed, for there are no vehicles to speak of. To be honest I do not know that many nearby do I, my work and worries having kept me inside in almost a hermitic state if I am frank. (I am not.)

I notice a picture of who I recognise to be that singer Jennifer Lopez in the chemist's window. She does not look as different as she should for her age then and so for a moment I doubt the time travel claim again despite the different surroundings, but then think maybe the photograph was twenty years old anyway. She is advertising "Jenetic Make-up". 'Clever idea', I think to myself.

Then it becomes certain beyond doubt, as I see a plethora of new products in the windows... 'Cosmaceuticals' mainly. And new windows with a moving display somehow embedded inside them, like something out of - dare I say it, a science fiction film or Star Trek. Ha, what was I complaining about earlier!?

And I find the glimpse into our future that comes - totally, utterly, completely, fascinating. There are old products with new logos, new products with unfamiliar logos, and little technologies that draw your eye in to window shop. I remember another nice product I saw - Brita Water Filter cartridges, an unfamiliar emblem, and in different colours, which I then realise are flavours. I have a filter jug myself, as I am concerned these days about hormones and drugs in the water system. As a physicist these things are more real than other people who cannot see them can imagine. How nice, I think, that healthy living will be a bit more tasteful in the future. 'Water filter cartridge with a twist of lemon', one of the boxes has on it. It must add a slight flavour as the water drips through the recycling beads.

Also I notice a Cadbury logo - somewhat out of place in a chemist and reminding me of the shops not an hour earlier, but on a closer look it is an air freshener! Yum, I think you will agree. Why did I not think of that invention?

I reached what appears to be a mobile phone store called G4M. The mobiles 'these days' (sorry) are wafer thin all-singing devices, but still surprisingly large in diameter, with incredible colour displays, and seem to mostly be advertised featuring something 'eMotion'. The latest 'in thing'? The animated window depiction suggests it as a sort of matchmaker in your pocket. I am interested enough to stop and read for a moment, as I remember about savouring moments you may regret not having savoured when it is too late. 'I am here now', I thought to myself. We could have done with this idea so I shall tell you. It appears that you key in your ideal match's stats, and if you pass someone who fits the bill and rather takes your fancy, press the 'M' key, and eMotion is activated. It must use some sort of wireless technology, as then if you also take THEIR fancy and THEY press theirs too, both your phones vibrate (!), numbers, stats, and photos are automatically exchanged, and... well the final picture on the placard shows the Titanic hitting an iceberg. One assumes it is a great way to break the ice, rather than that it drowns you both.

But what a wonderful idea. Why did I not think of that too? Too busy inventing time travel I suppose...

These small details continue to captivate me as I walk past a bicycle shop (still just using two wheels sorry to report, although there are some strange incarnations of two-wheeled transport), and I reach an electrical store. None of these stores were here before.

And that was when my whole world seemed to turn from black and white to colour.

I had noticed all the televisions showing one channel in astounding 3D detail. But that revelation was not what I refer to that changed my life in a small way. On these badged 'HD3' sets was a music group, inaudible to anyone through the glass, their video interspersed with the commonplace movie scenes from some such storyline of two lovers, yet edited in a mind-numbing way. I rarely watch the TV as you know, and indeed tastes seem to have changed.

BUT THEN I COULD HEAR IT!

For the second time in as many days I was not deaf!

So much nostalgia today, first going back to my childhood home, and now remembering what a song could SOUND like for real. I had never forgotten.

Then I stopped to listen, and... they were singing my lyrics.

Do I really need to put that in capitals for you? No.

I had never imagined really how someone may interpret them, but it... sounded (I love saying that)... wonderful! Any music would have done at that moment. That was too much, you know? Just too much. Can you even begin to imagine it?! Try! My musical ambition come true, and my hearing restored for those moments so as to witness it! So two ambitions.

I have felt so complete ever since then.

I knew of course they had done this for me, channelled the sound from their ears to my mind. What effortlessly compassionate and gracious creatures.

I stood on that spot for some two-and-a-half minutes I recall, drinking in every delicious drop of the sound and the feelings it stirred. I stepped back and propped myself on the railing, and just crossed my arms in relaxed satisfaction. I have never savoured a moment like it.

At least not since they told me I had invented time travel! Yet in a way, not even that was as fulfilling as this. Now that IS odd.

The one passer-by must have thought me quite mad but who cares! I wanted to shout to the kids now playing with their bikes in the corner of the car park, "I WROTE THAT YOU KNOW!"

A miraculous moment that will live with me until the day I die.

Before I can make my way all the way round to my home to have a look at it (even though I suspect nothing much has changed), and in that one later moment when there is not a soul in sight, suddenly the ground gives way under me.

I am back indoors. In the ship I mean. I feel angry for a moment that my free will has been taken. I do not know how or why, but I instinctively move towards Alfred and... well despite that fleeting frustration, I hugged him. Lucy must have walked over because shortly I saw her four-foot tall frame reaching up to join us, and I cry on her head.

"We do not want to make troubles for you. How do you feel today?", asks Alfred after the moment. He is obviously referring to the other day out of concern for my welfare, now seeing me emotional again. I reassured him it was a different emotion and that I had never been happier or felt more alive! (Maybe that is because I am alive twice at this point in time.)

DAMN it completely escaped my mind with all the excitement, but... that should not be possible and the Universe should have collapsed. There's a worry.

I know this sort of matter can bore you, but hopefully all that goes with it undoes such boredom!

The understood laws of the Universe are such that it should not be possible for one thing to exist TWICE at any ONE time. There is another theory that might explain it but... no, surely not. Anyway, films I have loved like Back to the Future where that boy visits his past self are just that, Hollywood fiction, or so we believe. Do that for real and you may very well create a physical impossibility, not just by seeing your other self but by merely occupying the same timeline as him. "The results of which would create a time paradox, which would cause a rift in the space time continuum and destroy the entire universe! Granted, that's a worst case scenario..."!

Am I living proof that it is incorrect? ...Or did they take the OTHER me temporarily off to some other time (even an hour away) to make space for THIS me?! They did say I was not home at the moment... It is too late to ask them now as I type this or to insult them by checking up, but I know all they do is good and if that is the case, 'I' #2 will be well looked after and likely not even know I had gone anywhere!

Remind me to ask me in a couple of decades.

(As if I will need reminding.)

DAY EIGHT

Posted by Eurora001 on Fri 15-Jun-2001 11:15

I am sorry darling I had to sleep. My eyelids were threatening to take industrial action - I had time only to click submit on the last entry. And then crashing on my bed I could not sleep for some time. Eventually I must have, and I dreamt of a city I saw on the TV on another journey I am about to write about (I will fill in the gaps later about what I mean). I was walking through its broken streets like a modern day ghost town. Dead or dying on either side. Broken buildings, broken cars... broken bodies.

In my dream I knew it as London... yet I know really it was not. I have seen so much in the past week I am almost becoming desensitised. A month ago I could not have written what I write now, yet it is almost becoming... dare I say... 'normal'? Ish.

In my dream I thought I had dreamt the entire past week. Has it really been so long?

Although I was relieved when I awoke, I wished I had at least only dreamt that horrific imagery. Had they meant me to see it on the TV back in that hotel? Were they breaking something to me gradually?

Either way I awoke this morning actually feeling good, in a way. What has happened is starting to feel less incredible. The human's uncanny ability to believe any situation he finds himself in. Acceptance. Their baby steps idea is working it seems.

I have made a cup of my nettle tea and so I must continue to recount for you the fascinating events of the past two days. They ARE fascinating are they not? Yes. Not 'normal'. I resolve to remind myself of that whenever I lapse into such nonchalance.

Now where was I... Oh yes, 2021! Well, when I returned from the visit to my hometown, did I mention that they wished to ask me a question?

We were now sitting back where I had the briefing, Lucy to my left again, Alfred taking the lead in the conversation through my right hemisphere. He has this 'habit' of twiddling two of his fingers together when he 'talks' to me. I thought at the time it was funny to see the old human in him, still with the neurosis. I had just reassured him that I had never felt happier. And so he continued.

"Your happiness eases my pain. Several possibilities now. Shall we continue the plan and you stay here one night? You are the Knight after all."

"Certainly", I say. (To staying the (k)night that is, not to that I am one.)

I could not help notice Lucy's big eyes burning into me from the other side... as is becoming common, and goodness do they burn. So I turn to her and see her smiling up slightly at me, happy at my approval of their plan.

"I like you so much", she says into my very core.

It sends shivers through my whole being. To be communicating on that level with these... beings. I do not mean that 'she', that it affected me in any other way, you know that yes my sweet? I do not even need to explain myself, I know you understand. It was just a moment to speak of.

Anyway to cut a long day short, I asked them what the purpose of staying a night was, and then they blew my mind again. Up until today I had felt that this was it. I would have one or two trips into the near future, an incredible gift the like of which no man has 'ever' seen, that would be more than enough for one lifetime, and then they would leave me forever. I had been so sure that I had wondered what saying goodbye might be like, or if I would ever be able to call on them in future for help, as if Lucy was some sort of ethereal guardian angel.

But no. This was not the end I am told.

It is suggested to me that there are many more travels that will be available to me!

They do not go into detail and I do not ask (always after the fact I wish I had, but you try actually being there). All Alfred does clarify is, "Life is changing so worry not. We want to be progressing the story. If tonight eventuates, we shall know that you are fine for it. This is how we are testing things - to stay one day, and one night in any other timeline, and to be all right in your mind then it is all right in of ours."

"All right!", I confirm with a smile. I feel at that moment that I could take on anything they throw at me, and Alfred at least seems to sense that as his slight and constant frown eases somewhat noticeably. They want to ease me in gradually to the travels, ensure my mind can cope, and then continue onwards. Well I will have to make SURE my mind stays sane. Help me will tyou?

"Thank you being so gentle. You are the nicest", Lucy ends, and they both stand up somehow synchronised and walk over to the screen.

While they are turned to the side I seize the opportunity to try my camera again. Alas, or should I say 'as predicted', it seems to have become defective during the experience, although it still captures some iota of Lucy as she turns away to follow Alfred. I only hope I have not been damaged with it.

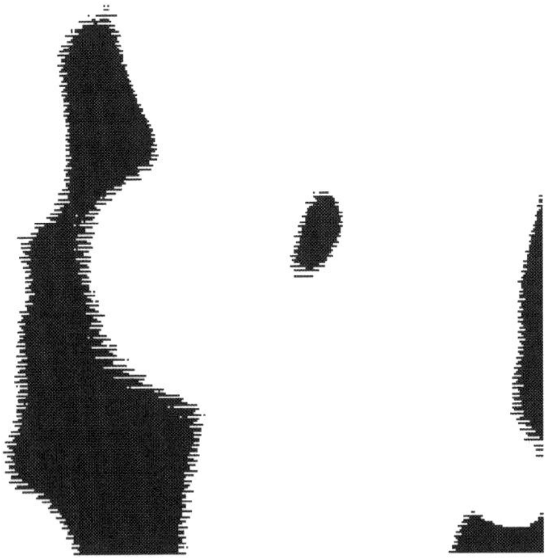

The travel process (across land not time) repeated itself and before I had time to process in my mind the events that had led to this, I was being led by Lucy's hand, down to the lower level again, and into the chute area. I did wonder if things were going too fast for me, but how could I stop them and risk looking the fool?

As we walked hand in hand, I could sense her smiling and looking up to me - in both senses of the phrase. It is quite sweet and makes me feel more special than I have for quite some time, even if I do not understand it.

And then I am in a hotel car park. You can see how dreamlike this all is to me, by how it must sound to you. And there is not a soul in sight at the moment I find myself there. Fortunately. Or should I say 'as planned' no doubt. Although they do seem to have been virtually on the ground when they dropped me. I am not sure if they even used the chute now I think of it - it all happened so fast and my mind was not yet focussed on it. Perhaps they do not need to use it sometimes.

I feel they are almost testing me, so little information have I been given other than to interact with no-one, yet whilst checking into a hotel.

I wonder why sleeping in the future is as important to test, as being awake there.

Then I notice the cars! I had always wondered if car design would come full-circle, as surely every design had been used up. I was wrong! I take a moment to peer inside one of the more unusual ones. It is all triangular like a Stealth bomber crossed with a shrunken Jeep, with windows half as tall as what we know but twice as long, like little slits or viewports. I like what I see, although even if the outside is all angular, it still looks fairly conventional inside - I mean they still have steering wheels, although the gearstick appears to be a dial. An 'interesting' design. And peering inside again, there are just no dials or other visible dashboard - just a plinth of sheet brushed aluminium. A minimalistic car. How would you know what speed you were travelling at? I just shook my head and kept walking.

A car pulls into the car park and I decide I had better keep moving. I feel nervous like I should not be here. I suppose in reality, I 'should' not - if you were to ask nature. As I walk towards the grand entrance, I notice the passing car's windscreen washer jets as the driver activates them, are attached to the wiper arm itself. A nice little touch - I think - as it means the stream of water swishes across the windscreen, just ahead of the wiper itself. People always had trouble keeping those old bonnet ones aligned using pins and such-like to move them around.

Just before I walked inside through the granite-glass coloured entrance doors, a 'robot' on wheels buzzed past me. There was so much to take in that for some reason I did not faint, although in hindsight I really think that I should have. I might faint now in fact, hang on...

...Nope.

It was a small device the size of a waste-paper basket, an arm on the top of some sort, and just going merrily about its business - whatever that business might be. Quite delightful. Perhaps it WAS a waste-paper basket. Or a robo-concierge.

All those fictional novels and films with robots in, yet here they really were!

In my pocket there was no key-card to be found, and somehow one does not get the impression my companions are 'on the Internet' or have booked me in. And how could I; A) interact with no-one, yet B) check in at reception? But I rose to the challenge and walked inside. 'All part of the test', I reassured myself.

The building was nothing new, mostly a tall glass tower, but the lobby was quite impressive. People milled around, largely ignoring me - far too preoccupied with their own futuristic lives. And the lobby was grand, in a way you and I were used to, but with one or two new twists, one being the luggage cart that buzzed past me, moving out of my way like some automatic vacuum cleaner, and the other being the automated arrivals station. Ah, no reception needed then!

I knew this was where I had to go, and go I did. The screen asked me to choose a language first and among the flags were a small number I had never seen before. I hit the 'find a room' button on a large and impressive high-resolution screen, which was so thin on its glass pedestal that I thought I might break it. I did not. I chose a room on the top floor (I felt it would be less populated), and it asked me for my payment method.

But I had no money or ID!

Then I noticed one of the options was 'Biometric'. I must confess I did not instantly realise what that meant, but I knew it would be something organic. Now we were cooking. I chose the option, and it asked me for my PIN, and to place my finger on the thin screen as depicted. Instantly I entered a number I did not know that I knew, and it seemed to accept it, along with my fingerprint.

Twenty years from now when 'I' get a statement with an inflated hotel charge on it, I hope I will remember not to dispute it!

The screen told me my room number, and that was it. No receipt. No card. Had it run out of paper and plastic, or was it being environmentally friendly? Either way, I assumed I would find out when I got to room 919.

The elevator was as slow as always, but I got there in one piece. I walked down the corridor until I was outside the door, and checked for a lock, but instead found another fingerprint scanner on the LCD door display. Other options on it were 'do not disturb', 'make up my room', and 'visitor'. I tried my finger on it but nothing happened. Then I realised it was a thumb symbol, and tried my thumb. It worked. I guess if you check in with a stolen finger, you still cannot get into the room without going back to steal the thumb too! The 'systems' must hold all my future biometric data, interlinked. My fingerprints never change over time, and so I can use them any year I please! I like it.

That seems very convenient and I wonder if the introduction of biometric systems is actually somehow by the design of the earlier temporal travellers, to ease their transit somewhat. If they still looked like you and I at that time I mean, it certainly would give them freedom to come and go without having to set up accounts each time in this apparently cashless society. About time too.

The room was wonderful. I have stayed in many a hotel with my work as you know, but this one surpassed even my gracious Beijing hosts' standards. The bathroom to my left was almost all made of rough-looking glass, much like I was walking inside the core of an ice cube. As I stepped inside, the lights came on automatically from behind the 'ice', shining and sparkling through. A tall icy plate defined where the shower and bath were, and many more features too intricate to describe or I will never get to the point. Suffice to say the sink counter was made much the same, with just a deep 'pond' for the sink itself. I could not wait to have a long hot bath. (I hoped it would not melt the ice.)

As I walked out and went further into the room itself, I realised the wall of the bathroom partly opened up as I pushed the luminous panel next to it, revealing the bath to the rest of the room! It was like something out of Buck Rogers. The purpose of this was, I discovered as I walked further into the room, to be able to bathe and enjoy the view over the city of London that sprawled outside the window. A cityscape I have known all my life, changed only by one - no - two new tall structures, all good. I am glad I chose the top floor now. You would have loved it, I kept thinking to myself. You will not mind my admitting that I sorely missed you at that moment and wanted nothing but to share a warm bath with you, watching the landmarks twinkle, the London Eye go slowly around and around, and maybe even the large plasma 3DTV that sat opposite the bed, if we had time.

Breaking from my dream of us as necessitated, I found a tasty looking crispy snack in the mini-bar, which was in fact disgusting and turned out to be made from fried pickles, but reassuringly a miniature bottle of Smirnoff was also there to calm my nerves.

With it in hand I jumped on the bed like a giddy seven year-old boy experiencing a hotel for the first time. (Ironic as I was in fact twenty years older in this time.) I felt a bit tired and had a play with the bed controls. I set the flat plate of an alarm contraption to wake me at nine without much trouble, so I am not late to rendez-vous with my welcome hosts back where they left me, as agreed, at 10:00 AM.

I then found a fingerplate that turned on the TV. It was to be my undoing.

Escaping from the welcome page, I began channel hopping. It was late now, nearly half-past nine, and the news was still on. Was this dangerous for me to watch? It struck me that they had not said so, only that I should interact with no-one. Would the TV be interactive?

I had never shown much interest in the news, but now it was different.

There was 3D imagery of the remnants of a city somewhere that looked to have suffered a major natural or other disaster. People walking around the wasteland seemed to also be walking disoriented around my hotel room. Yet it was some time ago I deduce, by the lack of smoke and its placement down the list of news items. Yet it looked modern. I was certain it was London. But I was IN London, and the picture framed by my window was nothing like the one framed by the TV. I felt that the end of the world was near when looking at the shocking imagery of what appeared to be a once civilised cityscape on my screen, yet out of my window was this city as I had always known it.

Those poor people. Frustrating me beyond belief was that I could not find the subtitles setting until the story had passed. Damn me.

A barely recognisable Prince Harry was shown on a visit to somewhere tribal looking, surprisingly handsome these days which is why I did not recognise him. The Queen seems conspicuous by her absence. I do wonder if she is no longer around. And the recap of the news that ended the broadcast headlined with a story about what they dubbed the 'Common Sense Act'. Some sort of legislation to limit red tape and bureaucracy. About time, but did it really take this long?

The local news rolled on to a major crash on a motorway somewhere in Southern England, yet which looks more like an

American freeway. They still have crashes. Disappointing. Then I notice what is shielding the crash. On the hard shoulder, there are what I can only describe as 'motorway blinds'. Normally at a motorway crash, you know how passing drivers rubber-neck and thus miles of tailbacks are caused by traffic slowing down to 'have a look'? Then the cars on the other side slow down to look at the jam. Then they crash too by not looking where they are going. But next to this crash the police seemed to be using a new (...or old...) contraption of a pull-up blind cassette secured to police cars at either end, which had the black and white arrows depicted on it. This looked like it worked as passing traffic A) could not see the crash or the police and so did not try to look, and B) the arrows encouraged passing traffic to keep moving anyway.

The march of progress!

I decide to put the imagery of that city out of my mind... for twenty years.

But then again... what if I could prevent it? Yet I now know I could not, and that history cannot be changed, thanks to my earlier Q&A session, can it. Or can it? Maybe I should 'can it'. But should I try? Sorry Bella, but how could that question NOT tempt any reasonable soul. Yet I must not get ahead of myself, I am but a child learning to walk in this new world for the first time. I am NOT God.

The weather report is localised just for this part of Central London and goes into excruciating detail about the weather at every hour of the day. Has it got more accurate or just more ambitious?! I will find out tomorrow if a stormy front really does draw over Trafalgar Square at 09:35.

I had had enough of that and started channel hopping. On one channel there was a remarkable 'rags to riches' type show called 'The Big Tissue'. Would you believe they actually take a homeless person off the streets in each episode (with their consent rather than kicking and screaming), give them a professional shave, full makeover, haircut, a good bath of course, and put them up in a plush London pad for a month, fully equipped with a designer wardrobe and professionally produced CV. The object of the 'game show' is for the homeless person to try to get a job with their new image and address, and the one who gets the best paid job at the end of the series wins the apartment to keep!

I am not sure whether it is an unethical or wonderful idea.

One rare devious thought does strike me between channel hopping, and that is if I had a way to record one of their latest 'hit songs' from a music channel, and bring it back to my time, send it to my publisher, and simply put my name to it. Never having found true commercial success in 'my time', and knowing how long I have to wait to truly experience the success that Head Jog will bring, it is excruciatingly tempting to find that decade's next 'Imagine' by John Lennon (funny that I should think of that again), and make as if I had written it.

And what of the true composer? Well when he/she came to start to create it, they would stop, shake their head, and say to themselves, "no that has already been written", perhaps cursing their lack of originality.

But I have nothing to record with, and of course I cannot hear the songs either. It is almost as if my hearing loss were a protective mechanism for this one moment.

I like some of the commercials in between the film I find next (it is called 'Frozen Assets' and is about people who were cryogenically frozen by a company that later went bust 'in the distant future', and so that company's assets including their cryogenically frozen customer's caskets are bought up by a media company who defrost them live on air as part of a quiz show - the winners get to stay defrosted, the losers go back to the freezer - only fiction thank goodness!).

An advert for Homewheat Digestive Biscuits has the caption, "Home Wheat Home". Ahh. Then there is Nike which ends with imagery you can imagine fitting the slogan that appears - "Nike footwear - knock their socks off". Nike, sorry I mean Nice. And something inevitable from Wells Fargo, who I had thought were only established in America (but not for long it seems), is an advert for some sort of lottery sweepstake product ends, "Wells Far-go. We'll go Far, and so will you." A bit obvious for my liking but still, there cannot be infinite ideas left in the Universe.

Some of the commercials reflect however that the environment is as much an issue today as it was... erm today. A mineral water advert tells me that, "Because Perrier Sparx is made only from pure mineral water, you can be sure this gas [pshhtt] is completely 'eau'-zone friendly". I imagine the voice was suitably droll.

They show repeats of Friends as I flick through, and on another channel I do not recognise, is a fun little idea called 'You've Been Dubbed'. I could only assume that Clint Eastwood was dubbed into Spanish by a senior who sounds like a seniora.

Another new channel to me owned by Virgin is showing 'The Last Ever', each week showing the last ever episode of famous shows. This week it is a show called Lost. I do not stay tuned in to see if they get found. I like the idea of The Last Ever but might skip the Brady Bunch instalment.

And with the onslaught of all that I saw which completely preoccupied me, I had not even had a chance to think to use the camera still in my pocket, although I had planned to 'later'. But later never came.

Completely exhausted that is the last I remember as I fell asleep... without even getting to try out my hot ice bath. It would not have been the same without you in it anyway.

I am woken at 09:00 with the bed thrumming and vibrating. I want nothing to do with being taken by the shower-chute at that moment. I am so utterly tired I feel I could sleep for a year, or six. I even feel that innate anger at being rudely awakened by 'them', and my hatred towards them shocks me, as consciously I feel they are so intrinsically good. Is my subconscious trying to tell me something or just simply that I am not a morning person?

I await the inevitable lifting sensation.

Which... does not come.

The vibrating gets stronger. It is all around me.

But still no beam of light...

Then the vibrating was joined by a beeping, which also grew stronger...

An enemy race of Extapiens comes to mind, coming to grab me or kidnap me...

But it was just my vibrating electric alarm-clock heated blanket. Of all the things! Obvious really! I had set the whole darn contraption the night before, believing it to be just a simple alarm clock.

Do you like me playing these little games with you like that - pretending my alarm clock was an alien encounter? I try to let you experience my day as I experienced it, and that genuinely is what I thought was happening, what with all that has occurred. I know you do not mind. Someone has to share this ride with me.

I am sure it will also raise your eyebrow when you consider the 'alternate' uses of that vibrating blanket. I am certain I am not the first to consider its somewhat naughtier uses. Perhaps I am in fact the first to have only used it as an alarm clock! My intrinsic 'male of the species' thoughts cannot escape me even in such times as these it seems, although it should be the last thing on my mind.

Come to think of it, I have not thought of anything of the naughtier nature since they first visited me. It is hardly surprising really, yet now I think of it, the desires... well they are still there.

For you.

Oh now I've done it...

The way you would look at me while holding my hand sometimes would do things inside me that even my wildest imagination did not believe Bella.

I assure you it does not have the same effect when Lucy holds my hand!! It did not even cross my mind. I am only saying.

Why has it crossed my mind now? Why am I even typing this! I would delete it if I did not know you better or your capacity for understanding, and that I need never feel I must hide a single thing or trace of a thought from you. I am right, am I not?

And in any case, if anything, even if I did feel something when she did, it would be just physical needs building up over the past few days. Finding an outlet... And just those innate male neuroses adapting to the only 'female' that surrounds him, nothing more.

I am glad we cleared that up.

And no I am not attracted to the blanket either.

Well, just a little bit. Ha, I jest of course! (...I think.)

The TV had turned on as well as the blanket. On the same channel I had left it there is a hidden camera show that is quite shocking. They have rigged up a very nice looking aeroplane as a simulator, but the passengers are genuine holidaymakers who walked down the concourse and into what they thought was their plane. Shortly after a very realistic take-off, the 'plane' starts to descend rapidly and an all out emergency is declared. The crew make good use of the 3DTV screens behind each window to convince the passengers of the view they see before them - an impending crash! Yet the reactions of the passengers are quite heartbreaking. In fact I am surprised they literally do not break their hearts, i.e. have heart attacks. Yet their indescribable relief when the simulated image flicks to the show's spinning logo almost makes up for it. It was like nothing I had seen (is this what passes for entertainment?) and I had been so gripped I realised I was running late.

What kind of time traveller am I?

Well, just as instructed, I was back down in the car park just before ten o'clock. So I am not a bad time traveller after all. Perhaps an overly keen five-to-ten in fact, lest I should miss them and become stranded in the future. Although I knew they would not let that happen. I think I had just had enough - there was a lot to take in all in all, for what was supposed to be a simple hotel visit. Mainly thanks to the TV.

Do you mind me telling you all these details? If I had you in my life now I would come home and tell you in even MORE detail. (You poor thing!) Yet I feel you are there - I know you are - reading this. You have become my journal in a sense. I never could put you down.

Well anyway, the thing was I wondered how they would... 'beam me up', dare I say it. I mean in such a public place. As ten drew near there was a crowd of young workers congregating in the car park to smoke, obviously having just had breakfast before another seminar or such-like. At night-time is bad enough, assuming others can see the shower-chute's light stream. In a field is not so bad, but now they were advancing me the trust and privileges that they were, the risks surely must be increasing too. Yet I knew I did not need to worry as these people... have been doing this for eons. I would be like a toy plane model-maker asking a NASA astronaut if he knew how to fly that thing. And then the question was answered for me.

Ten came and went, and I must have looked as white as a sheet of paper such was the adrenalin caused by their tardiness. That storm from the weather broadcast had indeed arrived, on time I assume, and although I was some way from Trafalgar Square, its footprint reached us by just after ten - lightning and all!

You should have felt the atmosphere Bella! I felt as though I were in a movie for a moment as the raincloud darkened the sky, the workers scuttled indoors dropping their sodden cigarettes (serves them right), the droplets pelted down, and then that sound of thunder. All that was missing was John Williams whipping up an orchestra. The music coming from the lobby was an adequate replacement - all I needed was someone to video it.

Then before I knew it, with a crash of thunder, the beam was all around me and then I was in the warmth of the ship, as Lucy wrapped a bluish material around me that literally sucked the moisture from my clothes, hair, and face like a fabric vacuum cleaner!

That was why they had chosen THAT precise time to collect me - the time ship is cloaked, but its otherwise visible and momentary beam could be explained away by any unlikely wet bystander by the forecast lightning. They had made me get there in good time before, to be sure. Somehow I doubt they use BBC Weather forecasts, when they have 'backcasts' at their disposal. They never cease to amaze me, yet still it knocked me a bit - the fragility of the entire operation I mean. What we were doing was still not exactly foolproof.

I would feel better if it were, but much still relied on me, and on them. Yet I suppose, in the event of an issue, they could go back in time and correct it. Perhaps that is why I will never SEE an issue, even if there was one. Maybe last time I was late getting to the car park.

NO, maybe last time I interacted with someone, hence their constant stressing to me 'this time' not to!?

Then the cranking vibration underfoot, the cabin went into dark green time mode again, my stomach went for a little ride around my left and right foot, and in no time at all, I was apparently back in the past. Home.

"We are back in home for you my friend and prince of creators", trumpets Alfred into my head proudly.

"The same moment I left?", I check.

"Not then, one day later, please you are to remember you stayed for a night so now it is tomorrow", he says.

That was NOT how I thought it worked. And I suddenly think of Max. I had thought they were going to bring me back without time having passed! Funny that I should assume I know how it will transpire.

"What about my dog? Why did you not bring me back the same day? She needs feeding you know", I say, surprised at my irritation towards their inconsiderate nature.

Lucy takes over, sensing my distress, and rests her hand on my arm, comforting me. It makes the hairs stand on end.

She explains that it is to keep disruption to my body clock and shock to a minimum. A bit late for that!

But apparently they always try to do it for themselves too, time allowing. They always return to a later date in their realtime than when they left, that is equal to the time they have been away - i.e. go away for five days on 1 January their time, and they should come back on 5 January their time.

She explained as her face dropped quite sadly, that without such rules in place their most ardent travellers' families would outlive them by decades.

It makes sense but I was still enraged. They should not just make me abandon my dog without my even knowing that I am.

"So I am in the big trouble now. Help me my sir", says Alfred looking very sorry for himself. I feel like I have just upset the King of the Extapiens.

I tell him it is okay (once I had calmed I realised it had been less than 24 hours), and say I just want to get back home to check on her and unwind.

"You are marverously kind", he says.

"In future it is intolerable we cannot make the immunity for you and bring you back at the time you leave so your canine will not fail to spot his master, I am sorry", he explains. Rules are rules. So much for the Common Sense Act.

Lucy smiles at me, and gets a smile back. Why not - what harm is there in that.

I will go out later today and invest in some dried dog food, litter tray, and water dispenser. And maybe a new toy. That should get me back in her good books. Women! :)

As is becoming common, she walks me 'downstairs' (Lucy not Maxine) and to the only way out.

The way she looks at me just before I am dragged out sticks in my memory like a needle.

No place like home.

No time like the present!

And she was not too bad, Max I mean. There was a small accident on the kitchen tiles.

And she greeted me like I had actually been away for twenty years. (But then again she greets me like that when I have been outside sixty seconds to put the rubbish out.) (In fact she greets the actual dustmen like that.)

Well, I should really sign off now, as I am still beyond exhausted and with essential shopping to do.

They have told me that tomorrow will be a very big day. As if the past two were not.

Dreams await me, good I hope they will be...

Day Nine

Posted by Eurora001 on Sat 16-Jun-2001 22:16

I visited the future again today! And we did not need to worry about a future me existing or any paradoxical nuisance, for the date suggested was 3,001 AD in my calendar. One-thousand years into the future Bella! At least that is what they claimed.

I was so verbose yesterday. Today I am speechless.

I have no idea where to begin. I will dispense with all the minutiae for a start.

Well, they came again this morning, and I willingly walked into the ship again. "Further forward?", said Alfred. "All right", said I. Who would not?

All my life have I dreamed of living in such a time. You know how healthy I am ('Health Crunchy Nut' as you once called me), and I am not sure I ever really explained it but my dabbling in CRON (that Calorie Restriction with Optimal Nutrition diet I mentioned?) was partly so I would live as long as is humanly possible, and be healthy with it. That is the only way man knows at present to reach into the future. I wanted to see what would evolve. What technologies would exist. What places I could visit.

Little did I know that this year without even dying, the most fantastic place I could visit would be a London of the ten millennia into the future.

But first, Alfred ever the 'safety nut' himself as you might call him, suggested somewhere less "disquieting" and more personal to me would be a safer introduction to the ever-increasing "time-distance" we were covering. I was ready for anything they could throw at me, yet I took solace in his words and knew they made sense or at least could not hurt.

And so it was chosen. Lucy suggested again my childhood home as the place, and 3,001 as the year!

"I liked the meadow", she had said.

I agreed without second thought so eager was I to see what the future held, and what I found there did not let me down. Frankly, I did not know what to expect.

And that is exactly what I got.

Lucy let my hand go as I fell into the chute, and so impatient was I to see what I might see I very nearly blinded myself trying to look before I should. That would have made a great combination, being deaf and blind too.

And such was the brightness that when the beam rose above me, it took some seconds for the sight to behold... to behold me.

The field was no longer the tranquil pasture I left behind, for in the four days I had left it alone for, it had grown into a thick entwined forest. Or might I say jungle. Understandable now, yet I had not imagined it. For some reason if anything I imagined the grass would still be short, the buildings just a bit run-down. But this could have been the Malaysian rainforest. It was warm enough.

I wondered even so far as to whether gorillas might appear from behind one of the trees, or a hippopotamus splash up out of the murky pool off to my far left. This town had been reclaimed by nature... but what of other towns?

I had been set down between some trees in a relatively bald patch, but had no idea which way I was facing. I headed in the direction they had dropped me in some trust, pushing vines out of my path, and snagging my legs on old juts of fallen branch now and then - luckily quite brittle now, although some were alive and angry.

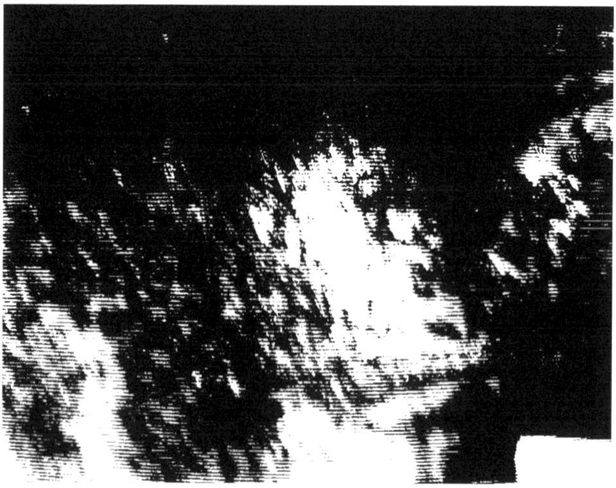

Just as I was thinking I must be heading the wrong way and entering a British Amazon, the forest began to let up somewhat... into a clearing. But why was it clearer? Well I discovered that the clearing began after the end of the field, and through two younger trees to my right and an ambitiously leafy bush on my left, I saw... a low line of brickwork.

I should not have rushed towards it, for I tripped on a large vine and crashed down rather unceremoniously and rather more painfully. I hoped Lucy had not seen. I wondered if and how they are viewing me to keep track. More on that later.

I picked myself up, and found I had reached... home.

I knew it was home because of the configuration of brick foundations that made up this three-dimensional floor plan. I had seen it a few days ago so it was fresh in mind, if not in reality. Now just a sketch of my past. It was otherwise impossible to tell my location, as every landmark was now a tree, or a tree in its way. Of course there was not much left but that very brick outline of each wall, overhung on one side with plant life.

My home had become an Egyptian ruin.

All the memories of my childhood came back to me in one tidal wave - for I could see every room at once! And so every memory. Unlike the other day! How could less home equal more emotion?! It was stronger than it had been when my memories had been rationed by walls and that window.

I pined for a minute for everyone I had loved who was now deceased. My beloved parents, pets, my brother... and you.

And... even me.

It was comforting that we were both gone at this time. Like the natural laws had caught up with themselves, and nature was balanced again. 'I' was with you, I am sure, in some other place.

Or do you already know that?

The floor of the house was awash with weeds and unusually large nettles, so I had to be careful my hands did not fall too low. Every step was a different height, some solid mounds, some crumbling. I realised I was walking not only on the floor of my home but no doubt the upstairs floor, and roof of it as well. My footsteps became more tender as a result. I carefully waded in through the now open front door (open in that it did not exist), past the window that would have been to my right and that I had wanted to climb in through on Tuesday but been prevented - my entrance all too easy now. Those laws of travel were holding true so far.

There was a rushing sound that disturbed me. Was it insects? Gas? Surely not after such time.

Down the hall and to the right was the living room, but I took a short cut by simply stepping over the hallway wall, now a three and four brick high parting in the weeds. As I treaded past where I had cosily sat maybe twenty-odd years ago of my life to watch the small black and white television with my parents (that was all my family could afford could you believe - look at me now), nothing could really convey the crumbling nostalgia coming at me from angles I had not known existed. It was personal to me and I would not expect you to relate, unless you could imagine it of your own family home.

Over there, the corner where I had sat under the Christmas Tree knowing the computer game my parents had brought me was wrapped in one delicious parcel, counting the days until I could open it. And then over there, in the front room where they had started a treasure hunt of little hidden notes that led to my birthday present out in the garden - a bike that I treasured for as many years as it would let me. I hope they knew what wonderful memories they were making for me, that would last these eons.

Imagine you awake millennia from now, in the shell of the home you celebrated so many Christmas times in as a child. (You know the place.) Then under the tangle of nature that has repossessed your home, you glimpse that special object which saw every day through with you. Perhaps a birdcage, the bird long since flown up to another place. Or the remains of a grand piano, mere hints of the metal strings lying outside the overgrown mass that must have been its old body, like some melodic autopsy.

There was no sign of the newspaper I had seen through the window a few days ago, of course, although the thought occurred to me to wonder. And so I continueed to wade into the front room but there was nothing to see in there either, except more foundations, and another clearing beyond it. Where the road had been, and where the rushing sound was coming from. (I was to head for it once I left home.)

To my left was the kitchen, the oven and sink now just black porous wafers of metal undertaking a precarious balancing act against each other. The floor was badly potholed concrete with the same mounds all around it - for some reason the weeds had not settled much in that room.

The more I walked and cleared an uneasy path through the shrubbery, the more pipes I found I was trying to kick through thinking them to be vegetation - and kick through them I could. The very veins and organs of the house had now almost become one with the vines and organic life.

And so it continued until I walked out towards where the road had been, and then left my house's foundations behind me. (I think I even had a flicker of thought not to leave the house door unlocked. Well maybe an elephant would steal the sink! No, it is just hard to adjust to 1,000 years in 1,000 seconds.)

And I discovered the source of the strange rushing noise.

The road was now a fast flowing stream!

I do not know how, I do not know why, but it was not the potholed, life-strangled rubble I had imagined. It was a beautiful brook lined with stony banks and the odd small island. I followed it best I could, trying to take the route I had the other day, along the embankment that was the pavement. It too was largely gravel and vegetation now, and I was certain no ghost juggernaut ship would nearly run me down this time. I still checked though.

To my right - in the distance across the stream - I saw a small area of brickwork poking up - maybe a chimney? Or even a wall. It must have belonged to the houses I saw lights in just days ago. Now lightless. Lifeless. Those places meant nothing to me, apart from a few babysitting trips as a teenager. It was paradoxical however, that back then I had so wanted to interact with the people who inhabited them, my path severed by a truck and some thought, whereas now I was actually allowed to go there, there was no point to it and my path was physically severed, by a torrent of water.

I was sure I was over-thinking this prevention theory, yet somehow it made me feel something was being hidden from me, and that I should be all the more inclined to investigate it. But there simply was no way.

Had this place never been repopulated or rebuilt over time? Surely it was not that uninteresting, despite moving the road away, to have breathed its last breath back then. Were we not supposedly building more houses, not less?

I wanted to see one last thing. The town sign. That might seem strange - although if anyone understands it will be you - for it was a marker from my youth that had always pinpointed the sanctity of home for me as I think I said. An object I could always rely on to tell me I was back where I belonged. Ironic now that I have of late become such a traveller, when then I hated it so and just wanted to stay 'rooted' at home. And now other roots had overtaken my old home. So you see, for that very reason, finding the sign would bring me comfort and make this morning complete.

I must have looked for five whole minutes in the place I knew it was, which I had measured in footsteps from the 'road' and carcasses of shops, and I found its black square slab of a base under a web of thin vines and leaves, but the sign itself seemed to have been abducted by time.

I had given up and begun to walk back towards home so I could follow the path to the knotted field, when I tripped on the very thing! How it had walked so far I do not know. Thinking about it now, I suppose there must have been such storms in the past millennia so as to blow many things from their original home to a new resting place.

Where I had tripped, it had snapped in half, and alas it was but a metallic web of its former self. I tried to pick up what I recognised as the shield-shaped head (more of a decomposed pearl now), but its edge broke away in my hand. It was completely black, and like a brittle fossil now, or one of those dark, thin, shiny, caramel wafer biscuits you get in pretentious restaurants.

I found I had sat myself down with a thump and before I could work out why I was in tears. I had broken it.

The salty water fell out of my twenty-first century eyes and landed on the thirty-first century ground below, one of them hitting the frail old sign making it appear to cry for me in return.

Then the oddest of all things.

I had left Lucy and Alfred on the ship, but at that very moment I heard her call my name in my head.

And I had wondered if there might be other people or animals even wandering around me, which is why when I suddenly felt a hand grip onto my shoulder I must admit I jumped up, round and back, giving a shriek like a girl.

It was Lucy. 'She is on Earth!', I thought, until I remembered she is from Earth. And that of course, there was no one around to see her.

She told me she had been following me for safety, and of course I had not heard her, with my mind so absorbed that I had not thought to see her either. But seeing me focus on one area for so long, and then break down near to it, she came to... console me. (And make me scream like a girl.)

She had called my name so as not to startle me. Of course I could not have known that she was calling it telepathically from right next to me rather than from the ship.

I do not wish to say it more than it necessitates, but there is something special about this... being. Something I do not sense from her counterpart. Well all right, this will sound ridiculous but... well... I - how can I put this - I... think I see small parts of...

You... in her.

She understands me like you did, for one. Like no-one else on Earth.

How such a rare human touch can transcend millennia, I may never know.

We walked back towards my home the way I had come, and I took certain pride in pointing out some of the things I had seen before. It was like a guided tour one gives to friends of one's new home... only, a bit too late. But she showed (or feigned?) genuine interest, and before long we were heading back to the balding clearing, our way somewhat cleared from the two of us who had gone before.

Then, as I mentioned, it was time to visit my other home.

London town.

(Ghost town.)

I took time on the ship to gather my thoughts, and they left me alone to do so for some twenty minutes I think. We had all the time in the world after all.

That is a weird feeling to get used to by the way! Imagine what I felt. We were in limbo - in a place where time had no meaning, and so the only downside to 'being late' was that you age a little bit. I could come home at any time I liked (within the rules), and we also had no particular time we had to visit our next destination - and whatever time that was, the time ship would make us arrive precisely then, even if we wasted an hour before we left. Time literally had no meaning and we were in complete control of it! I still cannot get used to it.

And then we set off, the now more familiar trembling under-toe, but no change in light as we were only travelling across country not century.

I was duly beamed down, and arrived in a rounded clearing of sorts, my feet finding the ground felt much like it had at home half an hour before.

That surprised me.

There were what looked like ivy-strewn hills on two sides, as if we were in a crater, and I had touched down in its epicentre. It must have been one of London's parks. On the other side of the clearing was a vast, level, sea of green - more nettles, very uniform save the odd serpent of branch breaking the surface. And beyond the nettles, equidistant from me as the hills on the other side, a semicircular wall of trees and other foliage broken only by a couple of distinct gorges within the wall.

The sky was a deep dark blue above me, the temperature a bit cooler than home had been, yet not unusually hot for the time of year I thought (just coming up to summer surely). Yet I broke a sweat quickly. Perhaps it was anxiety, having expected to be taken to a quiet alley in a bustling futuristic London, the skies filled with flying cars and the streets with scantily clad women dressed in silver foil.

(What Bella? Ha.)

But instead, I was still in a future reclaimed by its past.

And what had become of this place? It had become clear to me by the sharp walls of vegetation that this was not any park I had known.

Where were all the people? Now just insects.

The industry? Agriculture.

The money? Maybe still in the Bank of England vault.

Was any part of England not now woodland?!

'Of course!' They had taken me to the wrong 'London'! Was there not one in Canada or somewhere?

As I walked the ground felt a bit firmer here than home had, and the immediate vicinity was a bit less overgrown, the vegetation less able to reclaim the tarmac into the jungle of vegetation my home field had become. But still there were the same varieties of trees, bushes, vines, and mosses blanketing wherever in the world this was.

I saw no cars at all - the one object I would imagine not to have decayed away completely if this was ever a city.

I was by now entirely confident my pilots had the location wrong.

Trying to get my bearings, I noticed a colossal fallen tree ahead, its trunk - some 50 metres long - was broken into several segments like long benches as wide as I am tall, and like much of the area it was covered in deep green moss - a velvety hide these large chopped logs sported with pride.

As I approached the broken great tree, I saw the bark had an unusually uniform series of extensive grooves engraved into it that must have run from tip to toe... like a pillar... and strangely decayed for wood, as though it had been fossilised then crumbled away in many places.

I wondered whether some of blast had affected it and when I finally got my bearings Bella...

It was not a tree.

It was Nelson's Column.

I was in Trafalgar Square.

3001 AD.

Aghast, I could almost imagine being there when it fell, some hundreds of years before me. Hundreds of years after 'me'. A violent storm or simply the final slow crumble of its base to neglect and time.

Nonetheless, discovering where I stood was a moment that will never leave me. So desolate suddenly.

My London was now a ghost city. I wondered if this was the aftermath of what I had seen on the 3DTV in the future-hotel, yet that had not happened at that time somehow. How was my TV back then showing images from its future, that I am now standing in only which 'now' happened in the past... (These thoughts in my mind feel like the socks in a tumble dryer, and like the odd sock I am sure some parts of my sanity are already missing. It will be remarkable if I come out of this having lost nothing.)

I felt as though I was seeing myself from the outside, as if a camera was spiralling ever outward around me, capturing all the scenery 360-degrees in this moment of realisation, a lone figure standing in the midst of discovering the fate of the city he called home.

A saxophone seemed to play in my mind to an electronic backing reminiscent of some 1970s John Carpenter B-movie I had seen as a child. That was all I could relate the moment to, so 'unreal' was it.

Again I felt as if I were an actor in a motion picture, yet unaware that he was merely a player in a story... believing instead that the role he depicted was also his real life. Such is the way it now seems the mind deals with moments in time that it cannot apply to anything 'real'. It turns them into fiction - into something it CAN make sense of.

And now, with these words, I admit that it was not. Yet there it was.

Upon regaining my composure after the realisation, the camera now back in my eyes, I walked immediately toward the centre of the clearing, and sure enough, there they were...

The old frail remains of four great metallic lions.

Again it felt like a story. Or 3DTV trickery. One of them wore a coat of fine green moss, the thickest part of it ending appropriately in a coppery neckline around his mane. These old beasts that had once held me in my youth might well grind into dust should I try to climb one now.

These once great brutes must have been the only ones to have seen the rise and fall of this great city and survive to tell the tale, and only to me.

They were truly kings of the jungle now. But that tale they told was one of gaping cavities in their metalwork, dented pride, and choking climbers. How fantastic that they should even still be here then.

Lying in the grassy plain behind one of the lions was a mound of rubble, strangely devoid of moss, and likewise a greatly tarnished large squarish plate depicting a number of mossy figures perhaps in battle - of Trafalgar I suspect, although I had never thought to take much interest before.

Where had this been originally? Under the lion's plinth? As I walked back from whence I came, the lion glared at me dissatisfied, as if I really should have known the answer.

There is another mound of metal that I do not recognise. It is less decomposed than the lions, a perfect upside-down bowl shape, and about the size of a mini-bus. There is even some colour left it its skin, as though it were not completely dead yet - blue mostly, with a thin white stripe, now broken, running in a ring around the top of the dome. Certainly more modern than anything else. I have no idea whatsoever what it could have been, and tapping it produces when I approach it gives virtually no echo on account I suspect of the way it is now wedged solidly into the gravel below. When I consider what might lurk under it in the hollow, I back away as if being followed out of a dark room by a ghost.

I would have preferred it if I had recognised every monument and object, as this one creates an odd dichotomy for me. I am in a town I recognise, that is now beyond all recognition. I feel it is an illogicality I am going to have to get used to if these travels do indeed continue.

To break me from that thought, I saw something moving in the young trees to my right. 'Lucy again?', I wondered.

Not quite. It must have been large as it made them sway

It was a dog, Bella! A beautiful black dog, roaming free in Trafalgar Square! Of all the things. Its tail between its legs, a shorthaired mongrel, it had not noticed me as it sniffed around - now a scavenger when once a doting pet. As soon as it noticed me move the poor thing twisted like it might snap and bolted bouncing back to wherever it called home.

'Future dog', I name it. It is quite famous now.

There are no birds in the sky, and spare few insects. That is a good thing - the place was full of pigeons the last time I was here, and they are a real nuisance.

After future dog I walked a considerable distance through lichen and moss to the other end of the column, and found what must have been this fallen warrior...

Admiral Nelson himself, here in his final resting place. Entombed in nature. Alas, he had lost his head, and his surprisingly huge body was but a disintegrated legless torso (nothing new for him some might say), a mixture of grey stone and fungus. It had always seemed much smaller to me (I suppose it would from the ground looking up), yet now finally showing the true magnificence of his size, he is promptly stripped of all dignity.

The fungi had had a field day with what I thought was his right underarm, as I could just make out his flattened sleeve pinned to part of his chest, three times the sizes of mine, yet also lying in three pieces, each piece cracked and rounded off through a thousand storms. It is remarkable that it survived the fall at all. The fall through time that is.

Then there, next to its fallen owner, I found his now-fibrous metal sword. Incredible. Had he even fallen on it? It looked like an old wartime relic covered in thick green film, yet still clearly a sword and perhaps six foot long! Imposing even in this compromised state. I felt I could pick it up, but thought better of it when a gecko-like creature shot out of the undergrowth next to it, then shot back in when it saw me.

I was the alien to him, and scary even if I was smaller than Nelson.

I suppose that all relates to how I see Lucy and Alfred, their small size being equally frightening to me at first. To the gecko, the only 'human' shape he knew was the Admiral's large form. I must have looked to him like the Futurists first looked to me, in some small way. It is all relative.

I had again thought I might not be alone. Looking around now I could imagine the song of crickets that there must be all around me. Somehow being without that sense made what I experienced all the LESS disturbing, not more. For London reassuringly at least sounded just as it always had done (to me) - peaceful and silent. One change I did not need to accommodate.

As I continued past the fallen Admiral, I connected that of course these were not hills and walls of tree around me but the remnants of the buildings that once framed the Square, covered in foliage. I felt there was no way to tell which direction he was pointing me toward, as there were absolutely no landmarks in the sky, he could have fallen in any direction of the compass this Square had become, and the sporadic jungle around me concealed anything recognisable from me.

I came to the first hill, which had a scoop gouged out of it, or so it seemed. But breaking through a tall web of greenery, I recognised what was left of that great triple arch, and so realised I was at the entrance to The Mall and was headed for Buckingham Palace!

I had been here a number of times in my life, but it had never excited me. Until now.

On my way towards that arch, I saw to my right fragments of a stony stairway that led downwards into a spooky other underworld beneath, a big leafy branch shooting out of its mouth like a fire-breathing dragon in a burrow. The stones had a whitish deposit on them, a fractal fungus pattern. There was no way to get through the scramble of brambles, and I did not intend to launch myself into a black hole beneath London town had it even been clear. I did not recall any subway steps just here, although I was not sure precisely where I was or if I was on road or pavement. Perhaps a bunker I wondered, its top-secret location given up in torture.

The triple 'arch' itself (I am embarrassed to be one of those Londoners who lived there so long but never took enough of an interest to even remember its name now) was but a series of broken columns.

The three arches that had gone before were just shallow gateways with no more grand arched roof now, and a knoll of overrun rubble to traverse before they would let me pass. But let me pass they did. As I climbed up, out of a shallow grave amongst the dirt and thicket, was a bit of brickwork with two just visible 'X's and a 'C' lying nearby. Roman numerals. Back in that moment, it was as though people in the past were aware that those who followed them would one day be looking through time at their achievements. The date, whatever it was, both early Roman in font but modern in its birth, seemed as if those who carved it were singing out through time to me...

'Never forget, we were here'.

Maybe this was all somehow meant to be.

And stranger still, they were... me. Us.

A once tall gate offered to me what it had formed in time with the help of some vines - a convenient organic ramp down to the 'road' ahead. Yet it need not have bothered, as from the top of the hillock where I hoped it would not be as bad as it had looked from the other side, regrettably it became quickly inconceivable that I should try to negotiate The Mall in its new state. The parkland to the left had truly got carried away with itself having been left home alone for so long, and had long since escaped its prison, spilling out onto the road with a vengeance.

I would surely come a cropper should I try to have a belated tea with the Queen. (How old would she be now!?)

I stood there trying to see something of the once great landmark of Buckingham Palace. I took a moment to wonder what had become of the woman our Commonwealth respected so, and again thought back to those times at home when my mother always said it would not be Christmas without watching the Queen's speech. I could only imagine what monarchs had followed her down this very road. Surely there were some. And now I was the only human left here, or so it felt.

This was my city, and I was King, for a day.

Walking back towards Trafalgar Square, I found by chance what could have been Nelson's head.

It was the only boulder around and the colour of the stone was the same as the exposed parts I had seen on his body. If it was, then it had rolled a considerable distance from his neck during the decapitation, and was now the egg in a nest of thorns, a tiny little snake just slithering off him on its path to the next adventure.

Two small iridescent birds broke my concentration, darting down out of nowhere in some sort of twisting dogfight, and as the moment had captivated me too, I felt irritation at them for their disrespect and for breaking it. 'Don't you know who this is', I felt I had shouted at them in my mind.

But unlike the collapsed warrior, I was not through with my adventure, and took a path that looked somewhat less overgrown between two hills to my right. Turning the corner to view for the first time what remained of the road that I was sure led to Parliament and Big Ben, I was stopped in my tracks.

Lapping away not ten feet away from my own, was a sea of water. Well, a river. The River Thames, surely sweetheart. I am trying to describe this as well as I can, for you, and I suppose for me. Framed by the hilly ravine of once great buildings either side of a road, it ran outward as far as the eye could see, and must indeed have also run parallel to The Mall. No wonder the parkland had grown up so fervently there for it had been well watered.

But that was not all. Is it ever these days? Wait until I tell you.

Snagged on the corner of the bank near the other end of the long road, what looked like an old bent Giant's bicycle wheel that had been abandoned at the side of a stream. It could only have been the London Eye.

We had talked of going there! I had seen it from my hotel window only days ago! You had never been on the great new Ferris wheel, and wanted to see the view. I had not been near it since we talked about it, until now. And now no view. And no you. And here in this millennium, just an abandoned black relic, its passenger pods nowhere to be seen (had the blue 'bowl' I saw earlier been one of them I now wonder). A great stubby tree grew up near the centre, perhaps the ultimate cause of it being hitched there for all time.

What had gone on here?!

How I wished instead of a flash of light that I had been able to watch the land below me cycle and change over time in fast forward.

A few feet from me, a thrumming through the ground that makes the floor-dwelling roots visibly shake, and sends a dozen geckos I did not even know were there running until they were not. The blue beam of light transcended a bush, almost burning it or so it seems, and I know it is time to go. They are always close in their craft, even if I cannot see or hear it. And perhaps they knew I wanted to, for I certainly did at that point - they are telepathic after all. I could do seldom little else.

Yet I could not quite reach my way to the beam this time, due to the bush it was sat on and lighting up, but feeling brave - or should I say in stupid abandonment of all common sense due to what I had seen - I tried a small stunt just to get me out of there. I reached my arms up and out so they were touching the periphery of the beam, and jumped in the air as if I would land on the hedge if the beam did not intercept me as I hoped. I felt I did not care and was perhaps being too reckless, but for what it is worth it worked, and I was scooped and sucked up, my shoes barely grazing the top edge of the bush.

Before we walk back upstairs, I ask Lucy how it came to this, for I feel Alfred will not tell me. Yet she is the one who prevents it.

"You know I cannot", she says, her wet black eyes almost more puffy than before (or am I just truly seeing them for the first time...?).

"But the Universe would not let me change this outcome even if I tried - I know because you told me, so what harm is there in telling me this too, just for my peace of mind? Otherwise why take me here?"

I had to push a little and ask, if only to know I had done all I can. You know?

"Peace of mind. Will it bring you it? Would you have rather we not to bring you here to see such privileged changes? You are the nicest but I must protect your life. You do recall that Universe would not let you do, yet the means it will stop you can be unruly. And it is the most important job of my role that I must protect your life."

I decide to let her protect my life.

In a way, I would rather not know, in hindsight. Whatever is meant to be... will be.

Did be.

I do have one theory of the significance of Trafalgar. You know.

But I am glad they brought me there. She knows of my fascination with the changing landscape over time, evidently.

We sit for a while just still in the craft, Alfred looking comfortable albeit a little concerned, as I am becoming used to. He twiddles his fingers again, which is how I know. I am aware at that moment that they are giving me time, and seeing the opportunity, I just speak what is on my mind. I can seem to do no wrong after all.

I talk of those who have wronged me in life, and how seeing this great city turned to dust, makes those people - now dust too - so truly inconsequential.

Alfred's words are truly wonderful Bella. I wish you could hear him speak too, like some latter day Dalai Lama. I always do my best to convey it for you...

"People on the stratum that I and you inhabit have a genuine core only those within the same are privileged to experience. You live in divine wonderment. Some look up to that and envy that and find cause as they cannot achieve it, to instead try to deride and to belittle you down with them so they may 'find peace' on their infantile plane", he says, meaning that those who are jealous of others' wisdom, try to knock them down to their own low level. Maybe he is the current Dalai Lama in whatever year he comes from - it certainly feels like it.

Lucy then added some young wisdom of her own, "Equally others live life through the eyes of those like you, and how they praise you, but euphoric gratification they throw on you masks the reality that... when they are done with you and look away... you cease to exist."

"So do not lose who YOU are", finishes Alfred.

With the perspective I have witnessed today, underlined by their words, I shall not.

Good night sweet. I love you always and forever.

Day Ten

Posted by Eurora001 on Sun 17-Jun-2001 12:50

Sweetheart! Inconceivable! Wait until I tell you this! I will start at the beginning, though I want to tell it all at once!

Okay. There are many things I have not mentioned here but have tickled away at my mind. One thing I had not understood is how they had - I believe - once taken me from home without any beam of light, or if I had not remembered it but it had been there, had the neighbours seen it?

A little after I typed my exhausting last entry, I got my answer.

I was putting away some laundry when I felt that familiar thrumming underfoot. Not the electric blanket. Except this time, it seemed more powerful. Had I not known what it was I may have sensed it as somebody's washing machine on a fast spin, as laundry was on my mind. Then the apartment lit up bluey-white, like it was on fire. Washing machines do not do that generally.

And then they were there, walking towards ME through the light, which was originating from the balcony door. They were in my home. Again.

I do not mind admitting to you that I was somewhat scared to death.

Max ran, tail between her legs as far as it would go, into the bathroom and I did not see her again for a few minutes.

The beings that I knew so well, suddenly so much more terrifying because they were on MY territory. Somehow, it is more acceptable only ever having seen them inside their own surroundings, than to see them in a world where they clearly do not fit, and indeed invading my world - these strange space invaders.

(Yet in a sense I suppose, their craft is 'my territory' also, if was partly responsible for its creation? Or if not then I was invading their space.)

Still, there they were walking towards me. That is easy to type. Not so easy to live. My first thought as I had only logged off here recently was that they had found this, and were not happy about it to say the least. Or the camera God forbid.

The light did not shimmer and wrap around them with lens flares like those that one may have seen on television. It was too blinding to even look into once I glimpsed them, but it switched off as suddenly as it had come on, and they were just standing there, in my English living room, Alfred giving a 'sniff' and resting his hand uneasily on my couch.

The moment of awkwardness soon passed, but it had answered that earlier question for me. The crafts can 'dock' with doorways. Well I say dock, but the operation must have just involved tilting 90-degrees on its side so the chute 'door' was vertical with my balcony, hence no need to always use the full beam or attract attention, as the craft itself is invisible anyway. All it might look like from the outside was that I was watching a bright movie on a large television, or using a sunbed on the 'toast me' setting.

And they clearly did not know (or care) about this very journal or anything else I had done wrong, because then came their proud announcement of what is planned for me for 'tomorrow'. Just to give me advance warning it seems.

I am sitting on my armchair, Lucy and Alfred - having come for tea - are sitting on the sofa, Max had made herself comfortable on her bed after an initial bit of stifled barking then a bit of tail wagging (she is a good judge of character) yet still looking nervous and watching them carefully, and there I was... playing host to what looked like two aliens... who are now inviting me to the distant future for tea.

Alfred introduced the idea to me. "You are one and the only. Feeling healthier now and very fine at time travel. We have certainty in you to grip anything! Now and then, we have a offer for only you. Because we have visited to your time. And you have travel fine THROUGH time. Now our only dream is for you to visit to OUR time. Please come see us."

I had been expecting something, like maybe a trip back to Christmas past, but this just is... is... unthinkable. I am to visit their home.

"At this moment clearly I book the huge place for you. Ten to eighteen thousand audiences will come there. So if you are really busy to do the things, it is fine to fix up the date. Yes, we people need you, and waiting so long. Only you can give us truth so well and we are so fascinating."

I get the gist and am literally speechless at that point. Try to picture the scene. Alfred misread my lack of capacity to speak as a refusal I think, and went on, "I was going to fix it up today. You are our angelic friend, so just ask me the best arrangement for you. When you understand all of my effort to make chances for you, I do my best there."

It never ceases to amaze me how much faith they have put in me. They are clearly projecting an image onto me almost of some sort of divinity as I said, although I do now know how a celebrity might feel. I know just as someone with fame must, that I am just normal, just human. But when an image is projected onto you, you can seem somehow superhuman to those outsiders. And in a way you take on the role. You would not want to let your admirers down, or show weakness. It is a mask you are handed, and the only right thing to do is put it on and wear it. An idol wants to remain idolised, just as a celebrity always wants to remain forever famous.

And so I quickly and easily decide not to let them down either. I will feel the fear, but do it anyway. Heavens, I have coped so far have I not?

"Is it fien for you? Here's the last choice to come or not. If you refuse my proposal, at least thousands of people will be crying to lose the chance to see you. Please win."

"I will do it", I say with a smile. I am just glad they have given me this advance notice for it to sink in.

I add, "If you had offered me the choice to go anywhere, to your time is exactly where I would have wanted to go."

They both stand up in unison, almost I sense about to punch the air in restrained victory although they do not go so far, and Alfred says, "Your saying is quite clear, and it looks like perfect!"

"Perfect", Lucy adds.

"Please you slumber well, rest here in normality, and we shall be seeing you tomorrow near the beginning for a big day in our life", says Alfred as he walks back towards the balcony, Max following hoping to get a walk or something from this new friend it seems, although she is soon nearly wetting herself for quite different reasons.

It is funny how he never shakes my hand as I expect. (Alfred not Maxine.) They seem so knowledgeable about some areas of our time... yet in other ways so apparently oblivious. Do they even know what this computer does?

Lucy walks towards the balcony, but faces me as she does so with that wraithlike figure and pursed smile. Eerily charming, and her sweetness shines through the boundaries of time.

I will see them tomorrow. I have important laundry to do. And shopping!

Posted by Eurora001 on Fri 17-Jun-2001 16:11

I thought I was going to go. I was just checking my emails to enasure I am not missing anything that may affect my 'normal life' in this timeline. It is probably nothing, but in my junk mail folder was an email with the subject "we chatted last week" to 'undisclosed recipients;' and with just the message, "I am K T Hodd with the memories of a dangerous alien".

Stupidly I let it scare me. I thought I should note it here to you.

It led me to do a bit of quick research on the Internet. I looked into past visits by 'aliens' - not the 1960s past, I mean the real past. I found an article about ancient tribes whose history recounts them being visited by "frog faced beings", from the worlds of Sirius.

Serious.

Sirius is otherwise known as the Dog Star. (Maybe that is why Max was so unperturbed by the frog faced visitors to my living room. I shall have to ask her.)

(She says woof.)

Or could 'Sirius' just mean 'Future' in some language yet to have evolved?

Anyway, I REALLY must go if I am to get everything done in time for some much needed sleep.

I shall see you there.

Posted by Eurora001 on Fri 17-Jun-2001 18:08

I just finished unpacking the groceries. I had the most startlingly fantastic experience whilst at the Post Office (now there is an oxymoron) and felt I just had to share it with you.

After queuing for a while, my mind buzzing from - well, everything - I reached the counter and handed the Indian clerk my Recorded Delivery slip for the package I was sending (a long story - call it a form of insurance). As he processed the slip, my mind continued to murmur and gurgle with all the most recent events, and the thought that crossed it at one particular moment was with regard to the apparent forthcoming trip into their future.

'I wonder how long it will take to get there - will it be instant like before?', I thought to myself.

"It's a next day delivery sir - will be there tomorrow", I could not believe my eyes as the clerk 'answered' back to me.

In an abundance of disbelief, I did not say - or think - another word, but simply took the slip he had stamped, dropped the packet into the post bag round the corner, and made my getaway - nearly knocking over a pretty young girl on my way out past the queue. I feel bad that I did not even stop to apologise.

My initial reaction was that my newly opened telepathic pathways had touched his mind too (his being the phone that was connected but had never been rung before), and he had misunderstood me to be talking about how long the packet would take, rather than a time machine. How foolish of him.

(It now occurs to me that it could just have been a coincidence however. Just.)

Nonetheless, on my way back through the high street I took time to notice the occasional oriental face as it passed me by - something I had never taken time to do until now. And I'll be damned if one particular young woman did not look like the absolute intermediate between your average oriental girl... and Lucy. Such immense eyes, button nose, pursed lips, and elevated cheekbones soaring under those windows to her soul, giving her face that unmistakable 'little green man' shape.

It was the easiest thing in the world at that moment to believe totally and utterly that such Asian genes are the beginning of the path of evolution that finds a lay-by in Lucy and Alfred's time.

Day Eleven

Day Twelve

Posted by Eurora001 on Tue 19-Jun-2001 14:53

I am back! I cannot begin to tell you what I saw yesterday. Okay I will.

I dreamt of you yet again the night before they came again like I said I would. It was the most visceral, lucid dream. We were at some sort of work reunion party. At one point I was on a street party stage doing some sort of comedy! Me! Then later, it turned into a reunion party for the cast of a soap opera... Sad yet true (as much as dreams can be).

But then there you were. You appeared almost out of nowhere. Whenever you were around in real life, it was always as though you moved in graceful slow motion to some sort of ethereal romantic melody I could hear in my head. And so it was in the dream. I just walked up to you and hugged you. It was a reunion for us I believe, in my mind. That embrace seemed to last an hour, and with just touch we exchanged so many thoughts, almost I suppose... telepathically.

We decided to escape the frivolity and dancing to go outside, and I danced around the idea of giving you a lift home, which you (ever to my surprise) seemed keen to agree to. You told me I was always the one who could say the right thing, and asked where you would be without me. Where indeed.

Then as usual, before the best bit would come, I woke up. Strangely, I did not feel the need to go back to sleep and continue the dream. I am not sure why. Maybe it was enough.

I am still wondering if I will be able to travel back to 'real life' and see you in the flesh Bella...

Well, I am feeling somewhat ill from yesterday's journey, although I am better than I was when I arrived home. I feel I may be getting ahead of myself with this travelling. Yet it is so addictive and difficult to say no or not be proud.

They came bright and early as promised. Lucy alone used the door entry method again. 'Do you not knock?', I think to myself. Max barks as soon as she feels the thrumming, just as she does when the Chinese deliveryman stands at my door. If only she knew how different they were. Although, that said...

Anyway, I am ready for them, Max's food is down, and Lucy gestures out her vine of an arm to guide me into the light. And walking into the light is the first instance where I feel unwell. Far sooner than I had wanted to.

I had a strange vision, as I walked into the light, as it was truly as though I were having some sort of out of body experience. I do not know how I know it, but I felt like the people you hear of who have a near death experience, and see the light.

I stop in my tracks, and convey mentally to Lucy that exact thought, again without really intending to. I am worried. She tells me however that it is normal, and that inside the ship they will tell me more about the "flashback" I have just had. FLASHBACK?

It seems strange walking into the ship horizontally this time... Ha, as if vertically was perfectly normal! But what is even stranger is that although I walk into it whilst I am of course standing upright, I find myself lying on the floor of the ship, on my back, as soon as I have crossed its path. Gravity took a shift of 90-degrees. Lucy seemed to pivot onto the 'edge' of the opening in a gracious curve so she was never on her back, but I just lie there like an upturned tortoise. Fabulous.

Am I really ready for all this, and today's trip?

I lifted myself up, trying not to look too out of my depth, and followed Lucy to go upstairs. But at the bottom of the ramp, she comes back to me on the 'flashback'. She seems excited to bring me news.

"What you see, I see too through your deep eyes", she says.

"The light at the end of the tunnel?", I ask.

"That what you call it? Huhkay. This dear sir is a remembrance from your birth, not a vision of your death. And those whoever do see that in death - it is not a tunnel to heaven, with Sir Peter waiting at the gate!", she says mockingly.

"Then what is it - what do you mean by saying it is birth?"

"It is your journey into your next life my one. The tunnel is the coming out from your next mother - being born again. The blinding light is the first light your new eyes ever has see."

I am aghast. But I cannot refute it. When something makes sense it makes sense. I compose myself enough to notice both her hands are on my shoulders. It wakes me enough to probe further.

"And Saint Peter dressed in white robes?"

"Doctor. She dress in robe."

I digest it a bit more. She gives me time.

"But, sometimes dying people do not move into the light - they go back to their bodies and regain consciousness", I say, as if I have proved her wrong. Denial can be a strong enemy.

"It is sad that happens, and the baby it comes out lifeless. The soul not ready for the little person's new home hitherto. But it be born again, sometime. It is not the sad thing, merely postponement."

What do you make of that Bella?! I still do not know.

People say it is 'the brightest light they have ever seen'. But if you are suddenly seeing through the eyes of a baby, it would be the first and only light you had seen. If you were able to ask that newborn baby what the brightest light they had ever seen was, they would surely make an identical remark, and say, "That one just now at the end of the tunnel was!"... if they could talk. Which they cannot. But that soul, returning to the body of an adult, CAN verbalise that thought. Goddd!

And I suppose it makes sense that the light would be so strongly compelling and enticing - a baby would want to be born through an irresistible innate force after all, and thus be drawn towards it, like wanting to find your way out of a sleeping bag. Only you were not asleep... you were dead.

Does this mean she is claiming there is a fixed and finite amount of souls circling round perpetually in existence? Yet if so then how come there is an increasing human population? That would not make sense... unless... each and every creature had an equally rated soul. As one species dies down, another multiplies, thus allowing always a set number of souls on Earth?

I am a man of science and as such am burdened by having to see proof - yet I remain open-minded to all things as you know. It certainly is compelling.

Is this even scientific? It feels more spiritual, yet I would expect these Extapiens to be the ultimate scientists. It is becoming clearer and clearer to me that what we see as being 'advanced' may be the opposite, and they have in some ways come across as naive by going back to basics. Yet it is what was needed. What worked. I cannot refute what permeated time to win outright - for it has already won and I am already wrong.

...And IF it is true, it would mean that my soul exists in their future, in another body. I AM an Extapien, somewhere? And indeed, that was where I was about to travel.

Perhaps Lucy is not by Great (...) Granddaughter. Perhaps she is me, incarnate.

Her hands removed from my shoulders, as I almost shook my head back into the present, we walked up the ramp. Alfred was waiting with another being.

I had not realised until then how used to these two I had become over the past week, until the presence of this newcomer made me quite ill at ease.

He is taller than my two friends, broader too, and his skin looks a shade 'greener' almost than theirs.

By the way, they had today dispensed with the everyday Earth clothes that made them look like a Japanese 1980s pop group. Instead, they wore what I can only describe as a Lycra babygro. It is a slightly iridescent green in colour, with no zip or fastener, not visible at least, almost as if it is part of their bodies. It reminds me of the moss-covered lions at New World Trafalgar Square. It encompasses their feet also with no discernable shoe. Only their soft heads and wiry hands are exposed.

I feel that today we are down to 'official business' by their manner. All before now was merely play.

Alfred introduces the newcomer, in a way. "He must protect your life. And it is the most important part of his role. Quite safe it is where we are going but for your pieces of mind and to protect your beauty there he is."

I think to myself that if I die, I will not be scared when I see the tunnel and bright light! But still I ask his name, yet instead of his answer the conversation turns to theirs.

"My name is not really Arfred and Lushi", Alfred says as if expecting my surprise. I feigned it just a little bit for him I suppose. It seems today is to be a day of many revelations.

"Oh?"

"Quite right, the best translation for you of my name is 'Jo-at Mo'."

"And mine would be 'Ja-Ax Fo'", finishes Lucy. I can even see the spelling in my mind.

I will always know them as Alfred and Lucy. They were right to choose Earthly names at first. So far they have not put a foot wrong I suppose.

My nameless bodyguard (now I KNOW I am a celebrity darling!) takes a new seat out of sight behind me, and Alfred sits down as is becoming familiar to my right, with Lucy again to my left. Her leg pushes against mine separated only by jeans and iridescent green. I say it only to point out how tactile she is and what close contact I am privileged to have with these entities you know. And I did not even think to worry she may feel the camera in my pocket.

I sense a briefing coming on, but first they ask me if I am okay or have any questions.

Ha, only a hundred. But as those are all in a tangle, only one pops out.

"Well yes, it is a question more that UFO sceptics would fire at believers back in my time, and that is, 'If alien visitors all come from ONE place, why are the UFOs always a DIFFERENT shape?' How does your actually being time travellers explain that whilst the alien theory fails to?"

Just between you and me firstly, if they all came from one alien planet, this is indeed odd so yet again the 'common' theory on UFOs makes little sense. I know this when asking the question, but I still do not have the 'time travel' explanation. It comes. Ever so reliably, it comes.

"The first operational time craft is in your calendar year 2533 - it look plenty like your one our hero of the galaxy. [!] Imagine of it as the first steam car ever to have being built in your time, then you envisage it well. And from 2533 time craft continue to be assembled just as they are still in my time - and so of course they all are looking different fashions - just like your cars. But, the difference with time craft is all of them will have the ability to voyage back to one SINGLE POINT in the past. Wherefore, in any ONE moment in your time, MANY different pre-invisibility craft can be sighted concurrently - unlike your cars. They are dissimilar models that come from dissimilar times, to one simultaneous time see!"

See! Outstanding. Again they have amazed me. It makes sense. Taking away the time travel ability, it is just like looking out of the window onto the road, and seeing different makes of cars, vans, trucks and transports all shaped differently, some ancient classics, because they come from different years, yet exist in one time. No sceptics have a problem with that or try to claim the car was never invented or is an alien craft.

Yet if they were aliens not Futurists, it would not make sense to have so many differing shapes of spaceships. It takes so long to travel across space, that we would first see the first craft, then secondly see the second craft - but not all different shapes and sizes at once. How many different shaped Space Shuttles did we launch on day one for example? Just one. Only time travel can explain the phenomenon. I am surer now than ever that they are exactly what they say they are. How could we have been so blind?

This also explains why the odd stories I have heard of people who have supposedly met aliens, often describe them looking somewhat different to others. Some are the little green men, some little grey men, some with hair, some almost human. If we were being visited by aliens from AN other planet, that would make no sense. But being visited by different descendants on the evolutionary journey into the future? Again, it fits so worryingly well that I know it must be the answer.

Their answer raises my curiosity about another point. "How ever did we evolve from this moment to that, when the first time machines stirred into life in 2533? How did time travel eventually come about?"

Alf just purses his flat mouth together and shakes his melon of a head subtly.

I know when I have asked too much. And anyway, we have a much more exciting trip to go on...

Alfred finally discloses the details of our pending trip. "We are travelling today to our home. In the Old World it known as Dullice Channel Station."

"Really? That is wonderful, thank you so much. Can I ask what the year is?"

My politeness at such moments surprises even me as I recount this.

"Certainly you may."

I wait for his answer, then realise he has only given me the go-ahead to ask.

"Erm what is the year?", I clarify.

"On a calendar it will be one-billion five-hundred-two-thousand and one ani domino."

"Million", Lucy corrects quickly. "One-MILLION...", Alf confirms quickly.

1,502,001 AD.

1,502,001 AD...

Only now I put it down in writing do I realise that is exactly 1.5 million years from now! My head was in a spin at the time. The number seemed so long and random when he said it I did not even think to think or so to ask, but there seems to be some millennial reason for the timing of their departure. Sentimental creatures? With all the talk of stillborn babies, I do not doubt it.

These travellers come to me from so far beyond the initial realisation of time travel. They must feel like we do in relation to the invention of the wheel. So why have future human(oid)s waited so long to come say hello to me? I do not mean to doubt the hand that feeds me such wonderful visual stimuli, yet I cannot help but wonder whether sending an earlier human more like myself would have... shocked the hell out of me a bit less?

...Now I consider on that, I know it would not have done. I would miss this glimpse into evolution. They must know that I wanted to see this. I would not trade it for the world. Yet maybe I am yet to be visited by other travellers - from 2533 perhaps - a few years from now?! Indeed maybe the rest of my life will be littered with visits from various species of human.

I did have the presence of mind when stunned with the enormity of that date to come to ask whether travelling further takes longer. According to my calculations, it would take the same time regardless if you were travelling to last Tuesday or to the creation of the Universe.

"No more", Lucy says with a full-stop. Right again!

The briefing continued and I am told what to expect. I will tell you when I get there lest I spoil the surprise! I am also told, "They do not understand English except names". So there will be little actual interaction. Ah but thankfully no speech needed from me! That is the sole reason I always dreaded getting married - because I would have to give a speech.

Onward...

I could tell we had arrived as not only did the meaty odour fade, the lights go from green to bright black inside my glassy chamber, and the vibrating stop, but more notably than all that, Alfred became twitchy.

My guardian stood up to attention.

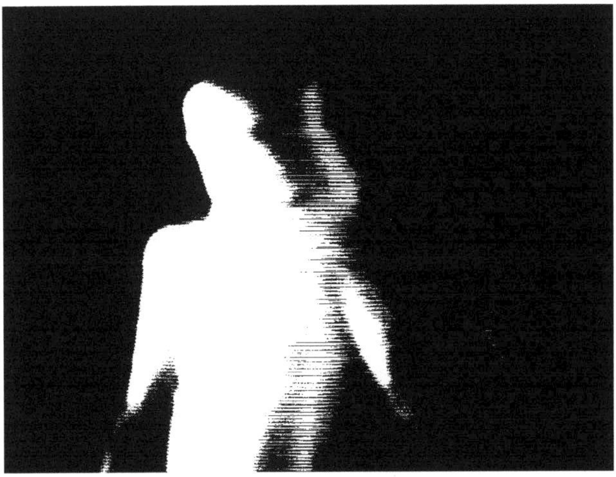

Lucy was remarkably calm considering her elder was in a bit of a spin. I had always got the impression that he was a person of some stature in his society, yet trying to see it from his perspective, he was escorting someone they saw on a par perhaps to - let's say Albert Einstein, 1.5 million years through time. Gulp. One can perhaps understand his apprehension. And what about mine? Hell even my nerves' nerves were nervous.

After he had communicated seemingly with 'others' outside our vessel (I am guessing) it was time to go. As we reached the chute, Alfred turned to me and spoke in a way that touched me deeply with the tone that entered my mind.

"Truly thank you for your trust. I always respect you. Yours Alfred."

It made me smile and tingle at once, and I replied by holding his shoulder for a moment of camaraderie.

And then it began.

The chute opened, light streamed through as always, and Alfred left firsrt, followed by Lucy. They descended down below me like spiders down a plughole.

My bouncer seemed to receive an all clear sort of message, gave me an unfamiliar nod, as he walked into the chute.

Then I was all alone, in control of a time machine.

For that moment of being left unaccompanied, I felt as I once had when on an orienteering weekend as a boy, and all my friends had jumped off a 60-foot cliff into the unknown waters below. It was my turn to jump, but it crossed my mind to turn and run the other way. I had to take the plunge, but in this case could not even look down or see whether the waters below were rocky, calm, or even if there were any. God only knew what I would be leaping into.

And then I leaped in too.

A literal leap of faith had awaited me, and I took it.

Of course I could not see anything as I descended further than I had ever before through the blinding blue-white light all around me. It seemed to take a lifetime, and I nearly died with fear of the unknown halfway down.

Then I was there.

Some distant future.

A futurist, myself.

Still looking up at the disappearing beam and - for the first time - the now visible base of the large circular craft I had just inhabited, the first thing I can see is a truly mammoth hairy bird soaring past me, the searing sun trying to break through its left wing.

A pterodactyl!

We are lost in time and I am doomed.

Then another one - husband and wife or mother and daughter I sensed somehow. Their huge wingspan flapped effortlessly and I imagined there must have been no sound to accompany it. I could see its underbelly, the veins in its wings, and its feet tucked neatly behind itself as it stopped and hovered there for a moment, almost checking out the new arrival. They very nearly collided at that point with a bit of a commotion and a warning bite from the big one - they seem rather clumsy.

Of course, I was not lost in time. They lived in this future. DNA! It crossed my busy mind that the clumsiness may be a DNA replication fault, an inconvenience of being reincarnated by 'man'. Or maybe they were naturally clumsy in their time, and that had been duly recreated too. They seem so perfect. I felt I wanted them to stay, but the larger one seemed to lose interest and flapped in a bouncing motion as it turned and moved upwards and away, its long beak opening and closing. I would love to have heard the shrill cry I imagined it making. Then I realised I had been holding my breath the whole time.

I breathed out.

They earlier briefed me to expect any number of unusual creatures. I always wondered about that other great concept of DNA recreation, and of course, it appears it became a reality. Co-existing side by side with modern civilisation. Nothing can stop the march of science. Nature will find a way, even if we have to help it.

Goodness, I have just realised how devoid of intellect that was. I had forgotten to think laterally. They do not NEED to recreate pterodactyls from fossilised DNA...

THEY JUST WENT BACK IN TIME AND CAUGHT LIVE ONES!

I must engage my brain more to these possibilities.

How funny that my first sight in the future is one of the past.

Apparently I later learn, they are attracted by the anomaly in the air that the craft generate. The moment above was much quicker to exist in that it was to write about, but I had to share it. After the seconds the birds (birds?) graced me with their presence, I continued to look downward, and around me... at an arid world basking, or baking, in light.

The smell was fascinating. I could not wait for each new breath to inhale it.

It smelt like burnt future.

Directly in front of me was a sight to behold. A sight I still cannot quite believe that I saw.

I was on a round island of black glass, along with my three companions, separated from the land ahead of me by a still clear lake. Across the lake... there is no other way to say it than to say it... across the lake were hundreds and thousands of tiny, pale, hairless beings, wearing dress that created a sea of green colour beyond the lake of green water, and standing so still, they scared me. They looked like an army.

I am still on edge at this point, as well as literally being on the edge - of the glass. Thick glass. And then as if from nowhere, a scary looking futurist walks up to me from behind my three companions. I felt like I was in a shady alleyway in old East London. He stared me in the face... then uttered one word into me...

"Goodbye."

This was it, the end, lulled into a trap, and now they were going to send me to sleep with the future fish.

But of course, he just had his Old World translation mixed up! Full marks for effort in greeting me, unlike his bodyguard friend. Full marks for scaring me half to death too, yes thank you for that.

Gaining my composure, above and all around the sea of beings across the lake from me were crafts of such a variety you had never seen. Wait, which nobody has ever seen.

More on the other craft later.

For beyond these people and craft which were obviously buzzing around what was effectively a time port, a vast, scorched, overcooked, rocky landscape akin to a fried 'Wild Western' if it had been filmed on the Moon. Quite a description yes? (Are you sure I should have been a writer?)

Magnificent desolation would have been an understatement, and it was lunar in more ways than one as its horizon died far too soon, just like the curvature of the moon. Thinking more on that now than I could then, I wonder if in fact it was the flat peak for a grand hill, and if so then whether humankind had been driven by rising sea levels to dwell at such heights. Yet I felt no altitude sickness, unless the other sickness masked it.

When I think of normal islands, well they are just the tops of old mountains too, if you take away the sea that obscures the bases. It is like we are - even in 2001 - living in a water world, perched up high on great peaks of the Earth's crust without even thinking of it. And the peak in their Earth - well it could be Mount Everest or Ararat for all I know.

The sun was high in the sky to my right, catching one side of the ridges and ramps of this tor in a radiant dusty glow, the clouds feathering the sky around me looking silvery in it.

It occurs to me that was in fact a volcano, not a hill. But why build a time port right under the top of an active volcano?

Energy?!

It MUST have been an active volcano!

Had I realised that then, I may have been a little more terrified than I was at the time.

And the sky itself! Darling it was as if I were... on another planet. It is simply... agh 'breathtaking' does not do it a wisp of justice. Some distant cousin of yellowy-purple, two magnificent, golden, wavering aurora streaking over my head and down past the hill beyond, like a fluffy brush stroke of a great master. The more I looked at it the more it seemed to become made of every colour in the rainbow, along with newly inventted ones.

I could not be sure if I was even perhaps within some sort of giant biosphere as the atmosphere seemed darker than normal - whatever that is.

Behind me on the other part of the land was what appeared to be a city, tin-coloured, but too far away to see in any great detail.

I liked it. It was very uniform, not like a city we might know. More Legoland than Futureworld.

But I was terrified all the same. Needed you... Had you been there to hold my hand it would have been like a walk in the park.

Instead, I got Lucy's. She led me for a walk in the... lake. I walked on water. Now I know how Jesus did it.

As we walked nearer to the edge of the black round monolith that held us, I could see rhythmical ripples in the water, as though one hundred warriors were banging a tribal drum. And perhaps they were.

Peering into the ripples, the strangest fish I had ever seen. It had a bulbous perfectly rounded body like a fat goldfish, dark copper in colour. The two halves of its tail fin were offset against each other, so as it 'span' its tail around - or perhaps now in hindsight as it span its whole body - it would dart disjointedly forward through the water in steady 'leaps', using the breaks in its progress to stop and see where it had gotten itself to with its last torpedo-like burst.

This almost feels as though I am recounting a dream. Just the most lucid dream any man could ever have.

And then Lucy stepped out onto the lake! Directly towards another of the torpedo fish that had taken the place of the first. My heart kept still.

But it was not a lake at all. At least, not any more. It was a flat sheet of glass now too, like where I still stood, yet she was walking on water. I cannot really explicate it. I was so surprised with what happened next that I did not even continue to look for ripples on the 'glass', or for the torpedo fish.

There are some things that no matter how much I want to, I simply find myself unable to begin to attempt to explain for you Bella. I can only speak of the details that I am able to put into words. It is safe here in my mind, but nonsense in writing. No doubt, someday I shall attempt to recount such absurdities I saw too if I find a way to. For now they stay just mine.

I know not what to say of it now, other than I reached the other side of the 'lake', still in tow of Lucy, with Alfred and my two guardians covering the rear. As I stepped onto land, I was perhaps 100 yards away from the thousands of beings. Were they here to see me? Really? Really. How could it be! Lucy said in her normal soft voice, but apparently Cc'd to all ten to eighteen thousand Futurists, 'words' a frog might say but which I could not understand nor repeat. But at their conclusion, she lifted up my hand she still held fondly, and every single one of them lifted up theirs and twiddled two fingers together. Did I mention Alfred does that sometimes?

Despite the passing millennia, I still felt as though I were being 'applauded' - as though their future ways had travelled back through humanity's consciousness to me, to still make sense. That, as I say, was one of the few things that did.

They continued to lead me towards the centre of the crowd, terrified, which parted to make a very wide gangway for us to walk further onward. Strange visions met my eyes that make me feel travel sick to think of or recount. But I could see these sweet beings attempting to shyly smile at me - at least it looked like shyness. Meekness perhaps? I am never too sure such are the features of my two friends if that is just the way their odd faces pull it, like one facelift too many on an older actress. Some were even laughing I thought.

In the distance the crowd parted in a circle, looking down at the floor - as if one had fainted. I took the opportunity to flick my camera out of my pocket for what is was worth and press the buttons hopefully, pointing down at the first few rows of little bald heads and faces. It was back inside in a matter of seconds as I was marched forward before I could see more, although strangely there was no rush to the aid of the apparent fallen comrade - they merely stood there.

It was clear this sea of faces was not an army, but was the 'general public'. They were ever so regimented and uniform, young, and unlike anything I had ever seen. (Obviously.)

I want to say they all looked the same, but differentiating them was more their size and complexion than their actual features. At least as far as I could see - it was still so new to me. And in the crowd I spotted one a futurist with long flowing white-blonde hair. Believe it or not, there he/she was. Flowing locks on a little grey man just makes you stare at him in curiosity. He must get that a lot. And do you know what? HE looked like the alien. It is all a matter of perspective I am coming to realise. After all, I have been around baldness now for over a week - it is almost normality to my eyes, except for those tired moments I have looked in the mirror at the new star of the show looking back at me.

(Thinking about it, it is I suppose possible that as we today see someone who is entirely hairless as having a genetic fault, and some may poke fun, likewise in their time an opposite gene fault could give them hair instead of take it away. He is the oddity to them I am sure. I wonder why he did not shave his head. Although hair is more attractive than none, if you ask me.)

(He must get all the girls.)

(If he is not one.)

A child near the parting (in the crowd not the other one's hair) tugged at its parent and pointed at me excitedly. How could such fuss be made over a mere inventor?! I have a fan! It looked more human than the rest of them somehow, such are the innate differences in features, that I suspect some of them just will do - like some of us look more alien than others I think as I think again of my trip to the shops the other day, and those few faces on the street.

The child's excitement fuelled my own, and made me feel such sweetness towards it - I mean him, or her. I remembered my own excitement as a child toward such things I could not really understand, but was quite capable of becoming caught up in through some sort of mass hysteria, and so perhaps it was not so strange.

But it did bring me down somewhat when the parent pushed his/her hand down as he/she pointed at me. Is pointing still bad manners in their time? I felt by this point that I liked being pointed out, as the terror of the entire situation was now slowly but surely draining from me, when before it had just drained me.

We continued towards the volcano and before too long were approaching the area with all the craft I had seen from farther away. It looked like a futuristic air show, or something out of one of those films! Alfred stopped us, turned me towards him by placing one hand on either of my shoulders as Lucy had before, and looked at me in the most alien of ways that I may never get used to.

"Is it fine for you?", he had found the opportunity to check, the tumult behind us.

I just nodded, my mind still besieged and bewildered. But 'fine' underneath all that. Really.

Lucy added, "Your beautiful preseance is so heave-nelly. You make them happiness. You make ME to happiness. My assistants will be telling me what reaction is. I have spoken much of you over time to my sisters. At my command, you have honoured them all". Alfred thin-smiled as I glanced at him.

"I am happy too", is all I can think of to say to them both, nodding.

Well it was overwhelming darling.

It still felt like some sort of air show as a party of three Futurists approached me and I was introduced to them, although they were not to me, other than my being told, "He is the chief at this point", of one of them. I get the impression he is some sort of 'General'. It becomes clear to me why there is someone else in charge here as we are led to an open area of dustland where the pocked lifeless ground has been smoothed out. I am offered a white seat much like those in the ship only this one forces me to lie back almost as if about to have a massage, but still I duly take it. It feels so good to take the weight off my legs and back that I almost wonder if gravity's pull was lighter that day.

"Please you wait", says Alfred. He, Lucy and the other five are standing behind me. I do not like the sensation it gives, but Lucy rests a hand on my shoulder again. It comforts me at least to know whatever happens, their intention is for it to be a good thing, and warms me up a bit now I think back to it, that he felt he was becoming more my friend by these gestures.

While we wait, perhaps to break the silence, from behind me, the General tries to be polite and asks me about my family back home, although I find it a little invasive. Somehow I am naturally protective as you know. When I tell him my brother has a baby, he probes further.

"Is he a boy or a girl?" (!)

"I mean to know if you are the Uncle or Aunt" (!!)

I was not sure if he was trying to share a joke with me, or if it was completely unintentional. Similar difficulties continue to permeate the conversation. I am glad when it is interrupted by...

An air show! It WAS an air show.

Up out of a dusty monolith-lined opening in the ground on the far side of the dustland from me, comes a flying object. It spirals around, like one of those leaves. It is constructed like a flat screw with only two threads, and as it spins, it obviously pushes the air downward away from it, like a screw-helicopter. Well that is what went through my head, but as it comes nearer, I see ropes attached to the threads, and a startlingly old-fashioned beam-like construction.

'Is this the best they have to offer?', I think to myself. Well say 'to myself', but of course I had thought it aloud too. I had not thought to filter it or censor myself. I know this because Lucy responds to it.

"No this not best. Leonardo Da Vinci yes?"

It was his early 'helicopter', here in living flesh! Well wood. I did not know it could even fly. Maybe they were assisting it somehow, but still!

After that, a Wright Brothers plane flies from BEHIND me into view (I had not heard it of course, and only realised when I saw it come into view above my forehead) and continues out and around the volcano that sits to my right.

It is followed much faster by a World War I bomber. "Zeppelin", Lucy says proudly. I always thought that was just an airship, but apparently it was a bomber too. I do not have the heart to tell her it was a German one though, and I am English. We are all much the same in her time so she would not see any sense in such comment. I like that actually - it is how we should all be.

Then she calls out to someone, "Douglas!".

'Who is Douglas?', I think. 'These pseudonyms are getting ridiculous.'

Then a World War II bomber comes into my eyeline and again flies past me and round to the other side of the volcano. Ah, a 'Douglas bomber'. I know not much of such things, but recognise the name now and my foolishness. (As if a man from the future would be called Douglas.)

Then a 'Stratocruiser'.

After that, a Jumbo Jet! We are nearly bang up to date! I think it is almost certainly a Boeing 777 - just like the one I took from China not two weeks ago. How absurd that ALL of this spawned from that very journey on one of those aeroplanes in the first place - the syllogism is not lost on me, nor I doubt them. I wonder now if that was intended. The markings on its tail I do not recognise. I think I see small faces behind most of the passenger windows. Perhaps I am the show, not they, as I sit here on my 'throne', my loyal servants flanking me. Ha!

It is easy perhaps not to consider how these craft got here and instead to just take it for what it is. When I first do consider it however, my instinct is to think how wonderful it is that the old craft from my age survived this long into theirs. How foolish my first thoughts often are becoming. OF COURSE the jumbo had not survived a million years! The metalwork in my home village did not survive even a thousand.

So how DID they get it here?

There is only one answer. A concerning one.

Somebody in my time is missing a Jumbo Jet.

...And a Space Shuttle.

...And Concorde.

...And so much more.

It was obvious they were showing me a progressing history of manned flight. (Although they got the last two out of sequence - easy mistake to make perhaps.) But the gesture was a decent one. I sincerely hope those craft were already here for whatever reason and not brought 'uptime' - as they put it - just for me. (I dread to think what paradox would have occurred if they had done that, and taken the very 777 I had been in on my way to China. Quite a paradox that would cause - taking the creator of time travel in a time machine before he could reveal his creation in order to ever build a time machine!)

Then a shuttle - this one with round windows all over it, almost like the holes on a flying white flute.

Then another Space Shuttle - not the one we know but a curvier, smaller version of it. The original was surprisingly small though too I noted 'in the flesh'.

Yet it blew my mind a little that I saw, yesterday, the tomorrow of my own lifetime. You know when you see something SO removed from reality, the brain does not even try to make sense of it or come to terms with it. That is how I have coped. But seeing this 21st Century craft was more real in a way than anything I had seen, and my brain knew it. More real/istic to me than time travel itself. Or than going twenty years forward even. This was the bona fide direct evolution of my era's science. MY domain. Right here. Yesterday.

As I said, it blew my mind.

From there on in the feeling of awe never left me. The next craft almost took a reverse step - like a shuttle but with the wings of a 777. It was more like a giant wing all of its own and I would love to have fully heard its sound, if it even had one.

Everything swooped and soared in such an extraordinary manner - like the excitement form a real air show I imagine, only multiplied by a number even I cannot count to, with other craft impressive in how lumberingly mammoth they were.

The next one looked ever so slightly like the round ship from those Star Wars films, only the head was somewhat shuttle shaped into a scoop. But it had those stabiliser boosters on the sides. Life imitating art? Or was the creator of Star Wars influenced by a Futurist?! Ha! No. (Surely?)

Then some contrastingly smaller glowing ships. Sweeet!

And what followed them must surely have been the time ships rather than space transports, for the first was the perfect epitome of what we know as 'UFOs'. There it was, hovering out of the ground, a goldy-silvery-coppery flying saucer with lights around the very edge, a white dome at the top, and a perfectly flat base. It was almost as if they had reconstructed a flying disc from a science fiction film - yet now I knew for certain that it was in fact the other way around. Art thinking it was influencing life, when all along art was imitating life from beyond our time.

Naturally there were no less than three more flying saucers for me to see - as the shapes evolved, streamlined, and echoed the transport I had arrived there myself in that very day. I was bang up to date at last! Yet there were more space craft to come, if not time ones (or perhaps they even did both).

The penultimate one seemed more of a... freighter, yet it must have been over a mile long. It is all dark copper-grey, with what I see as an obvious front and back. The front that points towards me as it descends vertically into view consists of a saucer much like my ride, with small fins coming out of either side of it, and a viewport (?) or row of lights in a thin line, running across its front. But that is just its 'head'. Its body behind is a rigid rectangular styled structure, with ridges almost like a mechanical grey crocodile, and two conical engines on either side of that very torso. Behind them two small fins on each side, and then its rear end balanced with the front, carrying two more large fins, not pointing sideways like the cockpit end, but backward this time, giving it a very slick streamlined 'tail'.

I find the design of that one particularly fancy and I mention it in detail because when it started to move, it flew backwards! The rear of the ship moved towards me in other words. As it slid in reverse slowly over our heads, it engulfed the sky and extinguished the throbbing sun for three cooling minutes. Yet the ground did not shake...

Until I realised the torrent of blue cloud that streamed from the cockpit that finally passed overhead was not a fire, but rather its exhaust. Its front was its back and vice versa! It looked equally enticing flying the correct way, to how it would the way I had imagined - if a little more ferocious with those fins at the front of the metallic giant.

Then there was a disappointing lull in the proceedings which I was enjoying greatly, until Lucy tapped me on the shoulder. I lent my head back to find her, and she raised her hair-free eyebrows and nodded with a smile to my left, back where we had come from. The craft we used to get here was now drifting slowly towards us from its pad, and as it reached us instead of slowing down, SHOT LIKE NOTHING IN THE WORLD - correction Old World - to over the volcano causing me to jolt my neck to the side to find it in time. Then it stopped like nothing in the world over the volcano. Then it disappeared in a flash! Then reappeared literally metres from me. You could feel the electromagnetism in the air even. It sent all the hairs on my arm up on end and a shiver through my legs. Again it darted away from us at a speed I could not begin to expect you to believe, finishing with the most dazzling display of aerobatics one could ever have seen. Like some shiny gnat avoiding a swatter.

I later realised that this point over the very centre of the volcano was ultimately where many of the craft would go to before flashing off to somewhere. Somewhen.

And then it was over.

I found I was clapping, and just as I was about to stop myself as I turned around and realised that they were not... they joined in, Lucy first, followed by Alfred and the others. I stopped shortly after, but it was hard to stop them! They seemed to be enjoying it, and it made me laugh - not at them, but with them.

"Haraharaharahahhahraaaa!", burst Alfred nervously into my inner ear, and Lucy giggled in too.

Sweet.

"Now hararaa you go in the volcano", Alf said settling down.

What?!

"PAST the volcano", Lucy corrected.

"Past the volcano", Alf confirmed.

"Around the volcano", Lucy clarified.

"Okay!", I finished, putting a stop to it.

And so we did.

It was about a mile's journey and I cannot quite bring myself to explain how we got there other than to say that a stream of the lake material carried us effortlessly efficiently.

And then we were there.

You know that feeling you get at an airport car park when a plane flies REALLY low over your head? You almost do not sense it coming until it is upon you. TIMES THAT BY FIFTY AND THAT IS WHAT I WAS NOW EXPERIENCING EVERY MOMENT AS DIFFERENT CRAFT SHOT AROUND THE SKY CLOSE ABOVE ME.

This was better than the air show! Some were silent, but these others send waves tearing through the infertile, bone-dry, craggy ground under my feet. A sort of blue tumbleweed vibrates near my right ankle.

And do you know the most remarkable thing?

It was that so many of them looked like 'UFOs'. 'Flying saucers'.

I ask Lucy, almost shouting the words out of my mind to overpower a passing craft, if in fact the craft we came in has - as well a VISUAL cloaking facility - also an anti-NOISE cloak, which would explain why it had not exhibited this sort of 'noise'.

"No these just old", comes the efficient answer.

"Not from my perspective they are not!"

She squeezes my hand and smiles, almost understanding how basic my joke attempt is. I think she has a better sense of humour, and humanity, than Alfred.

I really am at a space station. Well that is how I would describe it. I feel unsafe, like a rabbit lost on a Heathrow runway. And such a variety of crafts. Very nearly every shape and size possible. Some shaped like our saucer, others like a right-angular boot, softened by curved sides like a rugby ball! That is how peculiar the designs are. I could not even begin to imagine how that would be more efficient than my concept. Yet there it was, existing, for some million year old reason.

As we walk, I ask a question that came to mind while watching the show.

"Alfred, why do unidentified flying objects allegedly appear in some depictions of major events, like the Battle of Hastings, the Moon landings, the birth of Christ, or such like? Is that anything to do with you?"

Alf answers, "If you had time machine, you not go seeing the sights in legendary moments? They Time Tourists from Earth! This one of man's first wishes with the technological - to visit the Birth of Christ of the Old World. To see your leader. It all relates to those crafts which do exist before our invisibility, as many more visits have been made since them, but only those before are visible to you naked, eye.

"Sometimes even sadly in early travel they crash in places, like Asia - you know it? This 'Hastings' I know not of forgive me humbly", and he looks towards Lucy who nods almost as if he said 'research that and get back to me, "yet quite you right, the craft that visit pre-invisibility invention, they were unfortunately became PART OF the events and so did appear in depictions from said times, but it not alter events in too major way just pictures."

Astounding! And that was not all.

"Even some paintings in caves until they destroyed you see early craft! It is good record you keep for us thank you! People in the primitive time then believe my ancestors in time ship was in fact the same person as the God they already worship like the Sun, but no harm was happening, it is small nod from the future to the past, and vice-verse too of course.

"Today is our nod back for you", and his straight mouth widens with tiny wrinkles at the edges in a smile that makes my skin light up inside and pallor outside all at once.

I remember at that moment that I think I read somewhere that one of the first Russians in space claimed there were UFOs 'dancing' round his ship, and said he could tell us a lot about UFOs.

I ask about it and Alf says that the first space travel is one of the favourite destinations of these 'time tourists', as 1957 is "quite the good year". He explains that it is because that is when their ancestors first became space-faring with the added bonus that it is also around the time they carried out nuclear tests. It seems that these time tourists could go sightseeing at BOTH these major events and "kill two flight with one bird". But what is so remarkable about a nuclear test site you ask? They told me! They use the radiation to recharge their ships! Visit the first dog or man in space, then take a quick detour to the nearest filling station. Are there not lots of nuclear sites in New Mexico? And yes, what a surprise, lots of UFO sightings in New Mexico also.

And he did not confine it just to radiation, but to magnetism also, as there is not just one energy requirement of these craft - different systems need different power sources.

I cannot believe we never worked this out. Someone MUST have worked this out. Yet if they did, and it posed a threat to the timeline, would that person be...

...removed?

HAVE such people been removed?

Well I certainly have no plans to tell anybody except you. I do NOT wish to be 'disappeared'.

Keep it to yourself sweetheart.

I hope you are not worried that you will be removed from history as well, if they were to find out you too knew this fantastic secret.

In a way, I wish you were here TO be, so we could disappear together.

Wonderful though is it not? We now know why UFOs are seen where, and when, they are!

As I sit here and digest what I have learned, new thoughts arise. Because what if a self-perpetuating time loop means the well-known Prophets from our time who witnessed miracles or spoke to 'Gods' from the skies, actually were witnessing and speaking to... time tourists from the skies. My God what if futurists then travelled back to that same day, to witness these very 'Gods' appearing, but were in fact witnessing themselves, always witnessing a disappointing nothing, but to create the event in the 'first' place... It would be like me walking down a deserted street to try to see a man walking down the deserted street.

Yet have they not told me such events might not be allowed by 'the Universe' as they see it. Ah, except these are generally considered GOOD events that benefited humanity, and so would be allowed. And so they were! Which is why I am even talking about them.

But Bella, what if the entire foundation of "God" is based on someone having seen a time machine... a fiery entity descending from the sky. Even if God had a good effect on people, that would surely be wrong - if it were all based on fantasy. But which came first, the chicken or the egg?

What if, what if, what if.

Oh hell, what if CHRIST was a futurist.

What is the name of that song lyric...? 'What if God was one of us; just a stranger on a bus...'

Jesus.

At the time I had another question.

"But why are UFOs spotted over UNinteresting places like a random mountain, an empty plain field, or following an arbitrary jet liner?"

"They may not be interest at THAT time, but in another time they were become truly historic! We sometimes like to go back to see place before what it became. Like you personally do no."

Wonderful. Imagine visiting Hiroshima again before that fateful day. Or the Garden of Eden... I could think of an endless list. Where would you go?

We are by now some way from the crowd, which is beginning to disperse to either side, but with many small heads still aimed my way. I want them to go now, for I have had enough. The light is dimming and the day growing late, although it feels early in the air.

And I had not until today even properly seen the craft I had travelled in for over a week. I notice it in the distance now, hovering where it was left after its performance, a perfect 'flying saucer' of pewter, rounded like, well a Smartie. There is a light at the base, although I suspect this is not actually a light per se but rather the opening to the chute.

So that has been my ride?! I wonder if they chose it because of its similarities to my concept, when compared with all those bizarre contraptions around me. Did they want to visit me in my own design intentionally? Yet it cannot be too old as it had the invisibility cloak or forcefield or whatever they call it.

So perhaps my design has lasted throughout as a future classic!

Ha as I was telling you about this Max just brought me her toy cat and rested it and her chin on my knee. I regret I am ignoring her somewhat these past days. If only she knew that whilst she was lying around in my absence, dreaming of squirrels, Master was being worshiped as a God a million years in the future.

Okay now that does put it in perspective. Whew. I lapse back to 'pinch myself' mode at times you know? Yet I know my own mind I am quite certain. But it certainly shows me the real gravity of these goings-on.

Max does jog me to now consider however that I saw no dogs or other pets at Dullice Channel Station. I am sure nothing to concern me, they hardly have pets roaming around Heathrow Airport either.

Should I play with Max or continue this?

(We played.)

All that reminds me, talking of the shape of the ships, I saw one similar to my own drawings, yet it had a platform on it, lined with Futurists who appeared to be using it for a better view of... well, me. I wondered if they were just passing or if it were some version of 'Royal Box'.

I was amazed at the size of some of them. The craft I mean not the people. Can I call them people? But yes, slow speeds, swooping down, you could almost touch some of them.

None of the ships are cloaked at Dullice Channel either, I remember thinking.

Wait, I do not know that at all! THINK MAN THINK! There could have been a hundred more right there on top of me, imperceptible. Ghosts. I have so much still to learn. It is good to remember that lest I relax into this strange new world or let my guard down too much. I am so glad they decided to bring me back home regularly. Familiar surroundings, and playing with Max, are keeping me grounded, lest I may turn insane.

A monstrously large awe-inspiring solid brown rectangle with a square 'head' on it almost like one of those Tetris blocks came into my upper peripheral vision at that point (yesterday I mean, not while amusing the dog at home today) and it floated slowly forwards over my hairline almost like I was wearing a baseball hat and just noticing its cap. Yet it might have been half-a-mile off the ground, that is how wide it still looked to be. It was etched with black lines that looked like doors or panels of some sort. Whatever could be the purpose? I had to ask Lucy. Her answer came without flinching.

"Yes you call this one an 'Ark'." Then she looked at Alfred, who gave her the 'yes continue' nod of authorisation as if she was about to explain something of some magnitude.

And it was an Ark, Bella.

"It transmits us among other times to other times."

"I do not understand...?"

"I say it again, some of us finding the life too hard. The sun is too blazing as you see [I do], the corporeal exertion persist. But also [she hesitates]... we are less fertile and copulation is... a problem.

"There is a course for the transportation of a vast number of us downtime to a time of greater health of the globe and of us."

She was saying that they transport colonies of themselves backward in time, because it is easier to reproduce in healthier times!

"How far back?", I of course had to immediately ask.

"Quickly after the dinosaur fossil we live, not me but some."

Getting my head around this one-too-many of a revelation, I clarified, "People from the future, live in the past?!"

Alfred further clarified for me, "For somebody it is the only approach. Breathe your last breath here, or be alive there."

He puts it in a way one does not feel inclined to argue with! As with everything, I reluctantly have to suppose that it does indeed make a peculiar kind of complete sense.

We continue walking slowly as I muse over this shocking certainty they have honoured me with awareness of. Eventually I break the radio silence with one thing that occurs to me, and does not add up.

"There are no fossil records in my time of 'people' living soon after dinosaurs, not that I do not believe you, I just do not understand why if it 'has already happened', we never found evidence of it."

Alfred - as always - has the answer.

"The position they populate to, it is elected utterly for reason we previously know location does not survive uptime from you. There is no way to find this land, and so your archie-ogists have not. We previously know this earlier than we go there - so it is easy."

...When you know how.

So they have sent Futurists from a million years after me, back in time to live their futuristic lives millions of years BEFORE me, in some area that is now underwater or in the chasm of an earthquake - their graves never to be discovered.

These revelations are risking blowing my mind, but somehow the 'normality' of the crafts constantly streaking overhead, kept me down to Earth.

Apart from the moments when I questioned if this torched wasteland even WAS Earth.

Just as I managed to file that last revelation from yesterday for later reflection (and that was today's later reflection you just saw reflected above), Lucy adds something perhaps she should not have.

I still do not know how to take it.

Neither will you.

"A number of of your most far-off descendants uptime they may also be your most far-off ancestors downtime."

After digesting this - and it takes a few tries - I consider out loud my interpretation of what she says.

"My GRANDCHILDREN could be my GRANDPARENTS?!", I say in a numbish disbelief that still manages to stop me walking and makes me turn to Alfred who I am sure will correct Lucy.

The father figure is irritated, and raises both hands above his head then inflates his chest area as if to make himself look as big as possible. It makes him look more alien than he ever did.

"No no", comes his instinctive appeasement attempt, "Fo is so sorry to be in these troubles. If you believe the wrong story without proof and my saying, it is so sad for you to stop walking. Of course, if we make you sad I retire and never do it again."

He goes on, "We all travel downtime from an Adam, retain that information, naught changed there. You are already knowing we are all 'interrelated' truthfully, but and so consider and retain whether does it matters not in which direction we are related, from the past, from the future, from the two, from the neither."

He was saying that we are all one family, and it does not seem to matter to them if evolution occurs in a straight-line, or in a tangle of zig-zags. He really believes it does not matter if I descended from my own Grandfather. Really.

"Really, to us it is known normally and is nothing to be troubled. WE ARE ONE. To be sure with your comment, I may be my own son's son if look so short-range. Laughable! Yet heed that very few of us are undertaking it. It is a big commission to leave the world he calls home and go to live in past time, and as mattering fact they who do are treated rather as deserters, departure their race behind them, discarding the others for a better existence devoid of their brotherhood. It is not the good thing. It is the minority... underground... a small faction."

Seeing with his wide eyes that I must have looked disturbed to learn that groups of Futurists moved on an Ark into the distant past where they continued to breed, Alfred tried to balance the facts with yet more facts.

Not really a good idea.

"It is not entirely us but it is you additionally. You are culpable of it too - do not judge. We are not an only one, because persons from BEFORE you very self in the Old World also fancy to voyage uptime to very soon before the New World. They pass you overhead. Yes, we visited and then host in our time an intact culture that discarded living before your realm for living before ours as a replacement. So it is not entirely we who do this."

"Why would people from my past choose to live in your future, in this heat?", I said to him, keeping one half of my mind on that I may be overstepping a line (I am somehow wary if I am 'naughty' he may flare up and get angry at me, which would devastate me, oddly).

"Please we said enough today. Just to know I am always for your good and we are not the bad."

So. Those who do not wish to continue fighting to survive in the sun parched Earth of the future can travel back to when it was cool, the naked sun could touch their skin, the air fresh, and food abundant, and live out their lives in a place which will never be discovered and is now under the sea. (And even if this no doubt huge burial site were ever found, they could on a whim travel back and prevent its discovery by diverting the archaeologist before he knows what he was about to discover! Another perfect crime.)

But also, they say that those indigenous people (I assume people) from our time, who for whatever reason do not wish to live back when it was cooler and the air fresher, were also given the opportunity by my future design, to travel forward to whatever wonderful thing tantalised them about some time period between ours and the Futurists'! The grass truly is never to be greener on the other side then.

Bella Bella Bella... at the time I had digested what he said I instantly thought that it might very well have been the lost Mayan civilization.

Conquistador syndrome gone mad.

But worse, had he not also said that this race of Futurists living in the past may somehow have linked up with our ancestors, and apparently, if Lucy let slip what I think she did, in theory... reproduced.

And BECOME our distant step-ancestors. A race of small human-extapien hybrids living somewhere in Earth's past?

GOOD GOD I HAVE JUST REALISED - IS THAT POTENTIALLY THE MISSING LINK IN HUMAN EVOLUTION?

And we know why it is missing and always will be?

Christ do you know what this could mean? Holy... You know of what I speak - that mystery of the 'missing link' in our history? That one moment we were apes, walking on all fours, without this opposable thumb I type with, and the next we were Homo sapiens, walking upright and making tools, but nothing in between?

Well, mate a hairy ape-like man that lived millions of years before us, with a hairless alien-like woman that lived millions after us, and... you may very well end up with what lies in between the middle. Homo Sapiens. Us.

'The found link'.

I now think to the theory put forward by radicals that we are descended from aliens who visited the Earth long ago, or even bacteria. Not so radical, had they looked somewhat closer to home for those extra-terrestrial terrestrials. Good grief.

You know, I recall reading an article about Bonobos - a species of chimp who share 98% of our DNA and who are renowned for the fact that everybody in the troop has sex with everybody else, all day long, even 'transgenerationally' (i.e. even between the adults and children who - the article stated - do not complain and which may explain the apparently repressed 'natural' human urges we see spilling out in the form of sensationalised news headlines about 'child sex offenders' - apparently Bonobos do not have their own newspaper industry...). But does such gleeful and open sex with any living thing not make sense, if it was in fact the behaviour of a Futurist society once unable to 'copulate' as she calls it - once unable to reproduce? If I had been unable to have meaningful sex (I know what you are thinking!), and then travelled back on an Ark to a time where the climate no longer made me sterile, might I not celebrate by having over-abundant reproductive sex with each other? And if they also reproduced with primates, might that characteristic not have continued down my lineage to... Bonobos?

Yet we did not evolve from Bonobos, but from some mysterious 'extinct' common ancestor.

Had I just had the solution to the 'mystery ancestor' of homo sapiens flung in my face?!

This is too outlandish. It must be wrong. One would have to be in a tremendous predicament (or tremendously perverted) to feel the need to have sexual intercourse with a monkey. The thought makes one ill.

Yet still this is frightening the wits out of me here. I sit with the weight of this on my bruised shoulder, here all alone. I am not sure I can carry the burden of this. God Bella. All I can do is cling onto his reassurance yesterday that they are the minority who travelled backwards. That humanity would have jumped that missing link with or without them. That we would still exist had they not. It is the chicken and egg again. (That must come up a lot). Believing him is the only way to keep sane surely.

Yet I cannot... what if there were TWO genetic family trees? One that evolved into US and so later into THEM, allowing THEM to travel BACK... And become the other lineage, that evolved into a separate homo sapiens branch, now living in harmony with the rest of us here in the 21st Century. It could even explain things like... albinism (pale skin)... dwarfism (small bodies)... alopecia (no hair)... that only affect 'some' of 'us'.

Those ailments are in common with Extapien appearance are they not?!

ARE THOSE PEOPLE CARRYING A GENE THAT IS A DIRECT DESCENDENT OF PAST-DWELLING FUTURIST GENES?

Sending all this to you - I wish to do it, but it is making me discover things that if I did not give it so much thought laying these events out in writing, I may not have come to think of. I will have to consider what is best for my sanity.

I have just thought for a number of minutes about this. I looked into your eyes. Your smile haunted me for a moment while I crossed over that border of real life, into my fantasy. And then your face became mine again, in that world of imagination. All the things that might have been, were. Escapism - that is what I need right now. Give me an island - preferably one above water.

I think of what you would have made of the place had you been by my side. Sharing our life together as surely we still would be now. You would have loved the pterodactyl and the scenery I am sure.

NOW I HAVE DONE IT AGAIN!

Thought too much, and achieved another kick in the teeth.

They did not comment on the flying bird at all back when I got off the craft, but WHY keep a predatory animal in the future, rather than leave it in the past? It does not make sense that they would take it from the dinosaur age, into theirs, to surely feed on them! So there is only one conclusion left, thinking as laterally and logically as I can about such a sight.

The pterodactyl's first native home IS 1.5m AD - the future. And that some latter day backward Noah took a pair of them back in time, from where they reproduced as best they could but ultimately could not survive and died out, leaving the fossil record.

It looks like a bird from the future after all, not the past! How typically backward to imagine that there were giant birds 100 million years ago, but only small birds today! Surely small birds today evolving INTO those giant birds in the future is more common sense?

Or is the world really flat?

My damn mind uncovers more. Was it planted in my head by these telepaths? I think it entirely possible. I have a sense that not just these winged beasts, but perhaps ALL dinosaurs were a result of travels back and forth, dropping a 'seed' here or there. Again it seems so unbelievable that such huge beasts evolved in the past, and our feeble little frames in the future. Surely that goes against the incredulity of evolution - to go backwards.

Indeed why are palaeontologists still not able to agree on how or why dinosaurs 'died out', and yet magically other beings survived whatever event there was, and duly evolved into us.

And why are dinosaurs not mentioned in the Bible? I shall tell you why, as I now seem to be alone in knowing. Because the dinosaurs' existence was not known about until the recognised 17th Century fossil discoveries here in England, long after pen was put to that holy testament's paper. So that would mean either God was a fallacy, or HE did not create dinosaurs 'in the beginning'. THEY WERE NEVER THERE FIRST TIME AROUND.

So who did create them? Who is left after God to put such beasts into that period back in time?

What an experiment. Imagine it. You choose a time in the Petri dish of Earth when there is little other life there, no humanoids to threaten, and an area on the one great landmass of Pangaea where an experiment would not endanger natural evolution. 250 million years ago after a major extinction event would do nicely. You lock it off. And then, my future peers representing many more scientists, travel to that place in time with their ark, and release their small microbes, or baby Futurist lizards, or indeed perhaps birds, and watch them evolve over countless generations. They could zap to any point over those millions of years in their time machines to literally fast-forward evolution under the microscope of the past. Think what they could learn about natural selection and Darwinism, without any risk to themselves from that Petri dish.

It really brings a whole other outlook to those sea monkeys I thought I had 'bred' as a child!

But what would you believe more, the popular palaeontologists' 'theory' that "dinosaurs evolved into birds"...? A T-Rex becoming a Sparrow?!

I am slowly learning that time travel explains so many of the Earth's mysteries.

However... what to do if you needed to reset such experiment and try again with new criteria, or indeed what to do when the experiment was finally complete? In the lab, you could simply destroy the dish. But on past Earth one could not very well leave the dinosaurs there, as they would come around to bite you on the behind before long - literally.

Some sort of... mass extinction event... perhaps by collective euthanasia... would be called for...

Ah.

I must take my mind off these possible revelations, even though they do not come directly from the mouths of my new companions. I will continue only with the heart-warming aspects of yesterday.

It was quite wonderful you know.

After the 'Ark' came another huge craft, like the one I had seen earlier at the air show whose back was its front. It seems a few things about life that one assumes are one way, are in fact another... and more threatening than one might hope. They are human after all. Well, not human, 'extapien'. Which would mean that I may be part...

Pay it no mind man...

Anyway, yes, then contrasting such huge structures, a number of smaller elliptical craft hover in the air over one of the black ground pads, fluorescent. Before I had finished that disquieting discussion with Alfred and Lucy, what I would describe as a fiery ball swept down fast and low past me, stopped giddingly suddenly, then shot away at a sharp angle. I got an immediate impression of Futurist teenage joyriders showing off their skills, not to be outdone by the new visitor getting all the attention today. Kids.

Lucy looked a bit concerned and tightened her existing grip on my hand as she turned to check on the security detail which remained behind me and Alfred.

"Not worry, they are not piloted", she reassures me.

Of course... I then worry that they are not piloted.

A fiery line drawn under the conversation, neither of us feeling it is good to bring up again, we continue walking towards the hill, and an outcropping of buildings and 'tents' for want of a better descriptor. There are no beings on the ground here but us. We pass a wedge-shaped ship which is hovering perhaps 3-foot from the ground, its side adorned with a symbol that I want to try to read. Alfred senses this, and comes forward again from his rear position.

"Blue shift", he says. "It is its name of the ship, it seems exquisite to me you fancy to look to this one, how abnormal that it is one which carry Old World name. You recognise it then?", he says reaching up to try but fail to touch the symbol. I cannot work out if it is engraved or embossed - the writing just seems to hang neither in nor out of the structure a bit like a powerless hologram that actually works.

"Blue shift?", is all I can retort.

"Yes! Ah he know it! Of course. And it is named for the change with light taking place when thing shift throughout time?"

I see another symbol on one of the craft further away which almost resembles an American flag. The United States of Futurica perhaps! Doubtful. Is it perhaps even one of the earliest craft from my design? I would have thought that would carry the Chinese flag if any. Maybe a later ship then. But I have run dry of questions.

The vibration of sound in the air never lets up. Another great craft grates through the sky overhead. Some smaller ones I can feel shriek past me as the ground shrills up through my legs and into my lungs. The entire experience is nothing short of implausible, yet there I was.

Then a flash draws my eyeline to the distant sky above the volcano peak. A craft shoots down from the source of the flash and stops far too suddenly on a black slab with a slight antimagnetic bounce. Later I saw another, and realised that journey from far above the volcano down to the ground must be the distance they travel to in space, before travelling in time. And back. They always seem to arrive and leave from that point in the sky. Indeed it must be the way we came to Dullice Station.

I cannot get over the climate either, as I think I alluded to earlier. The sun is still slowly descending, but it almost seems to pulsate on my skin. Would you believe I had the presence of mind to put UV sunscreen on this morning?! Ha, I thought that would amuse you.

One can only imagine what running the Air Traffic Control booth is like at this place! Or are the crafts navigating telepathically? 'Flocking', like birds that never crash into each other.

But not clumsy pterodactyls.

When we get to the outcropping of silvery buildings, it surprises me greatly how primitive they look. They were cleaner than, yet resembled what one might imagine a latter day Bedouin living in. I do not know much of such desert-dwellers, but suspect these rounded reflective buildings provide much protection from the sun. Is this really how far we have (not) come in such a long time? Or is this Dullice Channel Station the exception to their real world? Was it selected because it most closely resembles my own? What wonders might exist down the road. Still the shock of the day is like lightning. I am not sure seeing whatever fantastic underground city they might really live in would have made much difference by comparison.

I can 'hear' you now Bella, 'Back up a moment there bright spark, for all you know THAT could be the past'.

True. This could be... 'that' time they spoke of. Was it not warm in the past equally?

I have no way to quantify whether our ship really did travel forward a whole 1.5 million years. There was no dial for that one. It could still be 2001, just in the Sahara. It seems such a conveniently easy number, 'oh a million years'. It could be one-hundred years into the future. Or past. It could be we have not travelled in time at all, but just in space. This could even be... Mars.

Yet it had vegetation.

Mars in the past then?

Alas it could be ANYTHING.

Now I feel as though I know nothing at all. Do I really trust these beings with my life? I must. I am here back home am I not, unharmed, safe and sound. I was well guarded. They checked up on me. Their people respected and saluted me. They let me feed the dog.

I am so paranoid! I must not look this gift horse in the mouth. All is well Bella, yes all is well.

With such basic buildings yet such advanced craft, it occurs to me to wonder where they get the metallic base materials from to build such wondrous contraptions, and so I ask Lucy to see if she knows. I like talking to her. I feel I get the truth I mean, even if she will get into trouble for it.

"Downtime waste sites is easily processed, it makes great places for us to find metal and how much of it you left behind thank you!"

To think, finding those colour-coded recycling bins for the kitchen last month really 'buttered my muffin' as they say. Well this revelation - that they dug up and recycled our metal landfill - puts a slightly new perspective on that.

I need a bigger bin for a start.

Oh yes, and it was at that point that a small 'girl' I think passes me and I think that I 'hear her' think an incredibly calming and soft sound - 'zoooobahhh' - she goes as she stops to stare for a while. I feel like I am the child or baby, being calmed by a mother. I stare back, as the others begin conversing with her parent. Zoobah? She recognises me from a zoo? Or a bar? Ha! She would not even know the English word.

Somehow this solitary Extapien child turns my stomach, where the mass of them did not. I think that was just too overwhelming that I could not process their alienity, yet here, alone, this TINY little hairless wretch, her wormy arms and concave face - it just did not compute with all I was used to. More so than Alf and Lucy, as they were at least verging on the normal size of some humans. Yet still there was an inner beauty in her eyes. A frightening dichotomy, like a beautiful baby troll.

After some more gawking at me, she runs off and continues to play hide and seek with her friend behind a strange sort of bluish-clay mound. A number of earthy things here have a bluish hue, and I wonder why.

By this point I was starting to feel a little travel sick as well as the feeling her appearance had oddly given me - you have to try to imagine what I was experiencing was twenty-one times more inconceivable than I can write in twenty-first century words. I felt like the girl might have, so vulnerable, frog-like, fragile, and like I wanted to hide, and never be seeked. Sought. I had an impulse at that very moment to reach for Lucy's hand again, instead of her for mine. I needed some... mothering.

Lucy clearly cared about me, and I just needed that. You know what I mean I think. And despite her young appearance, if she were the motherly one, then Alfred was definitely playing the father figure, always one eye on me. My guardian. I am indeed lost like a child in this new world finding my feet.

And so I do not need to explain why my instincts indeed took over, my arm went into auto-pilot, and it held Lucy's hand. I cannot however explain why almost as fast, I dropped her hand from mine. Then put it around her waist.

It felt thinner than it looked.

She pressed words into my mind, and I felt it was mine only. "I am glad you are finding solace and spirit where you are. You feel like a little boy who found a new pet rock in a little stream." It was sweet.

A few uncomfortably comforting moments after, we reached an area of 'tents'. I call them tents for want of any better word that I know of. 'Metal carpet houses'? There see I told you there was no better descriptor for what I see. The General disappeared towards them. I am so tired at this point, but the strictly controlled and regimented attitude of the diminutive soldiers - they must have been pilots - wakes me up. Some were on my side of a barricade, with yet more beyond it. Some sort of drill? All were wearing hooded clothing, holding porous tungsten poles, and looked like they might be short teenage tearaways if it were not for their absolute discipline. An army of little people. To say I felt a bit of culture shock would be like saying the first man in space felt a little bit lonely.

As we moved behind them, a convoy took me by surprise (being taken by surprise was becoming unsurprising) as it floated without vibration past me. There was no driver pulling the load. No trailer holding it. Its payload was itself.

It was a device in parts, and from what I could make out underneath the bubbling foam-like beige covering, might be what looked like a cross between one of our silver glass helicopters and a submarine. Forgive me darling but I am struggling here to explain a great many things, for although the things themselves have been invented, the words have not.

There were attachments at its current 'top' for some sort of slatted configuration to fix into. I got the sense it was a prototype for... agh, again I know not what!

The pilots looked away from me (I had broken even their unflinching concentration and felt they obviously expected me) and instead they looked toward it, almost in equal inquisitiveness. Even for them, in the future, there are yet more advanced contraptions to come, and these pilots seemed as yet unaware as to what on Earth it was.

It felt nice not to be the only one.

Then an even more horrid thing than before, and which I have been dreading coming to. But better out than in.

One of the 'pilots' broke regiment, to a look of embarrassed shock from his counterparts, and begun walking towards me, his bony lips clenched back baring a skeletal horseshoe of slippery teeth, and 'screamed' viciously through my very being, one word.

Just one word.

"MONKKEEEYA!"

I felt like no man on Earth perhaps ever had.

It cut deeper than any racial abuse ever could.

Before he could get anywhere near me though, he fell unconscious. A device of my bodyguards' ownership must have been involved although I did not see a thing. My heart was racing of course, so much so I could even feel it in my nose and throat. Alfred quickly marched me away from the tent, Lucy looked distraught, her tight face as if it were about to burst into tears. It was genuinely shocking. I am not one who is often threatened, but I felt it here far too deeply.

Words escape me to even fragment together a way to explain how this one person's negativity undercut all the positivity of the ten-thousand who had celebrated for me before.

Whilst I am SURE it was not any reference to our earlier discussion, I felt rather - no I was sure - it must have been an insult to my pitiful position in evolution compared to them. All the same, whilst some futurists have filled up my life, this other one cut it like a knife.

As we calmed down having walked away towards a walled off area and the silverfish buildings, I had to ask them.

"Is there racism? ...Still?"

"Fright of the unknown as she was fearful not irritated with you. It is not personal", said Alfred.

She!

He looked at Lucy in a way that said to her not to elaborate. But I really did feel it was hatred towards me. Perhaps not me personally, but my 'kind'. My era. Had these pilots some reason to hate my age? My people? What had we ever done to them - we do not know they even exist! There could be one-hundred reasons, or none. I hope all will become clear in time.

So, we had reached the beginning of this small cluster of buildings that made up the time port, all perfectly uniform like the soldierettes, all the same - just like the uniforms they also wore. From a distance they looked metallic, but up close they were shimmering green as well. Or was it just the still slowly diminishing sun. Anyway, to the left of the entrance to the cluster was a penned off - well - a graveyard. For ships I mean. A junk yard you might say, but to my eyes the mass of these future cast-aways were the opposite of rubbish! I asked if I could go in, and Alfred gestured me in with his arm. I think I notice it shake slightly. Anyway, they wait at the entrance and I walk in to this secure den of treasures.

I sit here shaking my head, not knowing how to bring you with me on this part of the trip my sweet. You see the thing was if you can imagine it, I was looking at the surprising overgrown remnants of their past, in all possibility of my very concept. It was one thing to be sitting at home having just sold the plans, to then be visited by them in three dimensions DRIVING my plans, but quite another to now be seeing those very same plans thrown to one side as defunct and derelict. All in the space of ten days. Can you think the rollercoasters and base-jumps my mind has had to travel through? Even I cannot comprehend it, so I do not imagine that you can, no matter how much I feel you may want to.

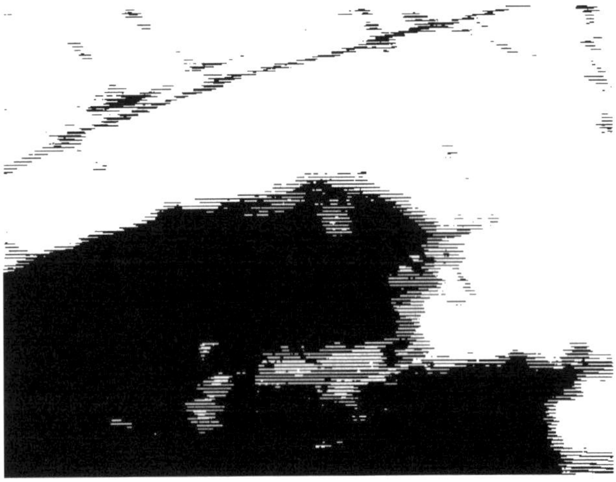

I walked towards a skeleton the size of the ship we had travelled in. Its skin had not decayed, but had clearly been removed leaving just a black carcass. I walked inside it. The crosshatched frame of beams made from what I do not know, rose above and around me, as though I were in a circular glasshouse, all the panes long since smashed.

One square perfectly framed the hot sun, which was now lower in the horizon, and the pattern etched lines out of my shirt. What struck me now was I had just realised that this 'junk yard' was virtually the only place I had seen substantial vegetation - almost as if it had been removed from elsewhere around the port. That might explain the earlier pock-marks. But 'inside' this once great craft, the vegetation was having a literal field day. Were there minerals here feeding it? Crusty, thick, tentacled tree branches rose up - not from a tree but from the ground - and entwined themselves around the wasted struts. In one corner, there was a bizarre something or other - like the love child of a sea urchin that had mated with a garden hedge. Again it was bluish. As I looked upward to the purple-yellow sky, the tentacles had thinned out into wires, cross-hatching the framework like spiders. I felt strangely claustrophobic, like I was in their web.

I left the bones of the old ship, and walked further into the yard. I started to realise that there were vehicles here not just from THEIR time but from ALL times. A communal machinery necropolis. Our time, our past, our near future.

I came across a shape I recognised very well. A car! A Rover to be precise! You know I love English cars, but this sight amazed me. At the time again I thought how incredible that it had survived the millennia, although it was but a silently burnt out shell of its former glory. Now ,as I type, I again realise it had not survived all that time, of course. Rover could not make a car that did not rust itself to dust in ten years let alone a million.

But if it had indeed been transported there from some point in the past, why had it been set on fire?

Unless it happened when they 'beamed' it up?

Surely there was nobody in it at the time...?

I saw two other cars too. I did not recognise them as one was in a terrible state, and just a burned out chassis unlike the Rover, which retained its shell. The other appeared to be from the early 1900s and was largely intact! Big spindled wheels and a fabric canopy, now full of holes. It had sat here a long time and was now 'old', even if it had been 'new' when transported here. A charming contraption made all the more so by its placement right next to another carcass of a time ship. Or was this one once a flying saucer from another planet? They look so alike.

Well after we left the yard we went to walk through the 'town', its dwellings unoccupied - because those occupants were outside lining the street to see me paraded past them! It hit me like a surprise party. It was not like the earlier arrival party, more like a private one as it became apparent that whilst those thousands had been the 'general public' of the future, these were the military. No children. And thinking of that female soldier just a few minutes before, I noticed enough to be able to tell from the small humps on their chests that many were indeed females, and all of them giving the twiddle salute.

I took cause to stop for refreshment at this 'street parade', for I was parched. The liquid drink was served to me in a surprisingly contemporary vessel - it felt like a tin can and was cold as ice, yet transparent like glass.

THEN IT HIT ME.

There was something in the way they celebrated, that mirrored how their public had celebrated my arrival also. And when I thought of what that 'something' was, it was as though they were not celebrating ME, but rather congratulating those who had CAPTURED me. And it hit me when I thought of the girl who had said what might have sounded like 'zoo' to me. And the other female's blazing insult.

I felt like Adolf Hitler had he been captured alive. Imagine the cheers he would have witnessed being paraded through the streets of London, aimed not at him but at the fact they had brought him away from his home place to face trial.

I felt so foolish for having at first waved back smiling.

Well, I say all the above only so you can experience what I experienced, the WAY and order I experienced it. I feel better for getting it out! But of course, you know the fact I am writing this means I was wrong? Right?

I realise that I am wrong when Lucy walks away to greet one Futurist (I sometimes stop short of saying 'person' somehow) in the line. The greeting is not physical but verbal, and all the while she is looking over at me with some certain form of devotion, as is her female friend. (Tch, women!) I feel shy, in the usual way.

Lucy beckons to Alfred to go over to her, and he does, leaving me with just my two minders. But that car I saw is still jabbing away at my mind at this point, and I take the opportunity to turn to them and try to ask just my minders about how it got there, why it was burned, hoping their responses can be less restrained. Yet quite the contrary, they seem not to understand me at all and so are quite constrained! Almost over-feigning the time-period communication difficulties now I think of it, yet I am sure they understood things earlier on in the day.

I am being paranoid again no?

At Lucy's request we walk over to them.

"My Cousin is now especially thrilled to meet you."

"Hallo", I 'say' to her.

Her Cousin cannot constrain what looks like a girlish giggle and moves her lean hand up to cover her mouth as if to push the laugh back in. Another fan.

Definitely not being held captive then.

Lucy continues to tell me, "He thinks you are quite the fine-looking!"

HE!?

Ah. When will I learn.

The - at times - almost informal nature of such an official occasion is such a stark contrast to our rigid world, and I liked it. They have learned much it seems. Yet still with all the casual moments, wondrous sights, and generous gifts they have given me, I feel still this underlying apprehension. Anyone would. I suppose such an event would hardly have gone by without any hitches.

Having walked the considerable length of the street and a dozen more anonymous greetings to apparently important gentry, we came out of the other side of this township visit, and were almost upon the slow ramping base of the volcano.

I am always one for savouring the moment as you know, and I wanted - needed - to savour this one lest it should not happen again.

And so I asked if I might have a moment to myself to sit, on the side of the volcano. They agreed, yet continued to follow me!

I had to explain what I meant, and they looked confused for a fleeting glimpse before they corrected themselves. Perhaps solitude is something they just never experience with such an undoubtedly vast population. Or just do not want to experience. But I do.

And I do.

I climbed up the shallow slope until I had a vantage point that suited my needs at that moment. I was only perhaps 20 feet off the ground, but had a nice view of the low-lying buildings ahead of me, and the time port still bustling beyond them.

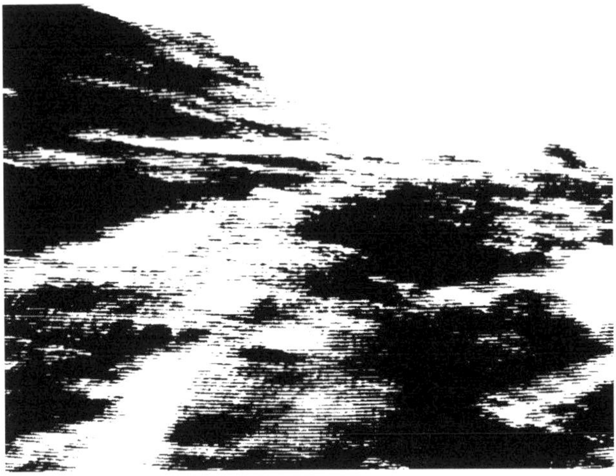

The silence in my mind was 'deafening'. My head stopped buzzing, and I urged myself to remember this moment. And that. And another. And in total I savoured perhaps ten separate moments, relishing each so I may tell my Grandchildren, and seeing every detail until the detail almost hurt. But in a good way.

I felt so triumphant and verbose in these coming moments Bella - as though I had achieved everything the Earth had foreseen me capable of.

And so just then, thanks to my position, the wavering sun dropped below the dark overhang of the hill that lay beside me. The loss of heat was like the perfect end to a loving embrace from a friend, and yet a relief that framed the moment for me in all its splendid coolness. And that was when my first day in this alien and inhospitable world began to draw to a close.

I lay back on the uneven dirt behind me, removing a very porous stone from my back. I felt perhaps somewhat gallant as I gazed intrepidly upwards at the Westerly sky, fading fast and now banded with myriad clouds of every shade of purple-orange possible.

And would you believe that I - who cannot even fall asleep in his own bed most times - started to drift towards dreamland on this mount, nodding in and out of that wondrously oozy state of consciousness, and began to sleep.

But the dream was not good, brief though it must have been. Paranoia for sure. Shall I even tell you?

For what it is worth I will. There were humans like us behind a cage in a future zoo, and I was being led towards their enclosure by a ghastly tall spider. A signpost in front of it was labelled, simply, "Monkeys". I am sure I was about to be thrown in, and so woke with a start. I quickly looked up, then down below me where my associates had last been, for fear I had been abandoned or somehow got lost in my sleep, but they too were sitting there, in a circle, staring into the middle of it at a softly glowing orb.

Lucy sensed me wake, and spoke softly into me (through quite a distance I might add) that it was okay and they had wanted to let me rest.

Her 'voice' is suitably hypnotic in that unreal moment of first waking, and soothes me just the right amount. I wonder what she sounds like for real.

I must have dozed for longer than I had thought, as then came the ostensibly complete blackness, in the distance all those alien shapes floating through the sky now a myriad of fireworks, and visible only by their very glistening star-studded lights.

And so I know it is surely time to go home as my guardians appear towards me - these alien silhouettes I have entrusted my life to.

I had slowly grown sicker in my stomach and so in any event we had to return. I feel better now somewhat, having digested it all here. I feel as though I am writing you a novel at times. But I must rest. Until the next 'chapter' my sweet!

DAY THIRTEEN

DAY FOURTEEN

Posted by Eurora001 on Thu 21-Jun-2001 00:02

Oh. My. Good. God.

I felt better today! I will tell you why in a moment, after I recount to you the dream I had before this incredible day began. It must have been inspired by the theory of 'walking down a deserted street to see a man walking down the street'. Somehow my mind dreamt up a self-contained story that would be fitting of an episode of The Twilight Zone. I will call it Vince.

'VINCE'
by [redacted]

Vince goes to board the plane that will take him to his time travel port for a journey into the past.

He meets the celebrity host for this expensive flight at the foot of the plane's stairs, and is star struck. Vince nervously asks Alan for his autograph and about a life in the limelight.

On the flight Alan soothes the nerves of the jittery passengers about to spend several years in the past by telling the jokes he is renowned for.

"You know those really annoying people who walk into a room just to break wind, then say 'thank you!' and walk out again? I'd like to try that with time travel - to step off my ship, in the past, break wind, thank the crowd, and go back into the ship again."

Rapturous laughter follows.

They travel into the past, and there Vince is especially inspired by everything he sees and experiences. He spends many years of creative expression living out his days in this time period.

Ultimately the time comes to return to the same moment in time that he left his home, and as he returns to 2001 and steps off the time ship, he sees Alan - the celebrity he still admires and is still somewhat star struck by.

But this time Alan comes up to him... nervously... and asks HIM for his autograph... asks HIM about his life.

Vince, dumbfounded, gives his autograph to Alan, the first he has ever signed.

"Thank you Mr Van Gogh", says Alan, "thank you".

Is the subconscious unconscious mind not an incredible thing? I thank it for communicating the story into my conscious waking moments.

And so I move on from dreams, to the real events of the day - which I had only ever dreamt could come true. You know I was always interested in - fascinated by - that rather different great Admiral of the sea to Nelson - Christopher Columbus and his discovery of the Americas. But did I ever share with you how I would have given anything to go back there and be a shipmate on his crew?! Well now you know. What I would not give for that.

Well through this startling twist of fate I have been brought, I was yesterday granted THAT VERY WISH Bella! And had to give nothing for it but time! And this was no dreamy fairytale.

Yet there are strange goings-on in my head. My memory is playing tricks on me. Hmm, well I shall come to that in order...

Your mother dropped by yesterday morning, fortunately not at a bad time. Imagine the scene if I had been entertaining E.T. She wanted to see how I was since the big day, and did not even know I was back. I completely forgot her, and I did feel bad, worry not.

And how was I?

I had flu.

I was actually quite impressed with my own acting at having flu, and being 'contagious' gave me the perefect opportunity to hasten her away. I will apologise to her if the truth of the matter ever comes up in conversation. (Unlikely really is it not.)

Shortly after that, they arrived.

On time. (Naturally.)

After I had just awoken from a good night's sleep about Vince.

First thing in the morning.

Standing at the end of MY BED.

Blinding light coming from the door to my bedroom, silhouetting Alfred. Lucy walked closer to the bed, stretching out her arm in eagerness. Alfred stood at the doorway. Maxine had been under the covers with me breathing in my ear, and was first to realise they were here, jumping up taking the covers partly with her and leaping into a mute barking fit that I could not stop for many seconds after she suddenly woke me, causing a stomach-churning adrenal jolt.

That was not how I liked to wake up, generally.

I had to explain to them - rushing to cover my vanity for the second time in as many weeks - that Max was not used to visitors walking into my bedroom while I slept, and that it was not really 'the done thing' here.

They looked devastated!

I do not even know how they unlocked the patio door. (Wait, am I doubting the ability of a lifeform a million years more advanced than me to... pick a lock? Eyebrows McGinty from down the road can do it, and he drags his knuckles along the floor like a...

Anyway, all was soon forgiven when they gave me my next extravagance. Alfred explained it all.

"We are much satisfied in you and you are alive. You feel well. As long as we return you here on regular occasions, it is all is good equilibrium. I speak with temporal executive of Dullice Channel Stations now. We discuss it in extent. You from herein on have been give by us... THE FREEDOM OF THE PAST."

It sounded like, 'the key to the city'.

"Any time you opt, Lucy can obtain for you. This facility is your creation and if anyone you should use. Will you consent? Please win."

Lucy put her slight weight behind the offer too. "It be splendid just you and me. I am all of yours."

And so it was decided. I was hardly about to refuse her. Can you believe this Bella?! I was given free rein to travel ANYWHERE. Anywhen! And come home again to recuperate.

And share it with you.

But only you.

Heavens what things I have seen that I cannot wait to share again now!

They know of the Americas of course, but strangely not the dates of the voyage when that land was first discovered by modern civilisation.

Lucy explains why.

"A great batch of records were lost with the Gravity Pull event."

"Gravity Pull?", I worry-blurted out as a response.

"All diplomat students in past-time learn this like me", she replied, "As if the Earth was a great dog it was, and humanity were the bugs on its back, so with the one shake of its mane it had flung you most off it and back to the nature, a uncontaminated coat of jad-"

Alfred then stopped her dead. Though not as dead as my heart.

He spoke in an urgent low tone, "Itokay, weokaynow!"

Of course she is not allowed to discuss details of when or how this Old World-shattering cataclysm it to occur. I wish she would, and was fantastic to learn that she is some sort of student in the 'history' we are actually living as the present! But I completely understand how she never could tell more. It is disconcerting nonetheless, yet after much consideration at the time, I had no choice than to put it behind me. The future is already written, and my knowledge of it - or not - changes nor matters one whit.

I have considered in the past that these beings are so advanced, yet so naive. Was this 'Gravity Pull event' the major setback to our development as a race? Could this be why they have no knowledge I am writing this - perhaps because there is no such thing as the Internet in my near future? Yet surely an advanced race of time travellers would have seen the Internet when they travelled back to this time... unless, UNLESS... well how could they? They cannot very well stroll into an Internet Café to have a look! Could it REALLY be that they are not aware of this particular communication network? And so much more? It would explain a great many things that continue to bother me... Even their odd grasp of language...

Well, I have struggled through much pain to get where I did with the concept, and I deserve these pleasures, and so again I shall launch myself wholeheartedly into the experience and savour each moment, not worry about things that do not concern me and should never perhaps have been said.

A few quick chores done, the front door locked, and Max's food down complete with her impressive new automated water dispenser I bought on Sunday, I was ready to go! I did not need encouragement to hurry, but still I did partly because they waited for me in the living room, just standing at the balcony door like two motionless sentries.

Again, it is fortunate your mother did not come at that moment. Fortunate that I rarely have visitors at all in fact.

And then we were off.

As I walked into the upturned craft's divine glow, I thought back to the discussion about walking into the light, until my thought was broken as the balcony door closed behind me and the handle yanked itself upwards all by itself. Before I could do a double-take, I was lying on the floor of the ship again.

And almost as quickly again, we were back at Dullice Channel. I was for a while disoriented as we had 'landed' on a different slab to before, and were now over the OTHER side of the volcano, near where I had laid down three days ago. It seems like today.

On the ground, my bearings regained, the place was much the same. A lively cacophony of action, but gone were the crowds, and the normality of it made me miss the welcoming party I had last time in a way.

I imagined there were no crowds the other side of the stony hill either, that special day now behind them. (Or ahead of them...?) I wonder if they even still thought of me. Whilst I wondered, a conversation seemed to take place silently between Alfred, Lucy, and a different General to before... or was it the same one? They do look somewhat akin I hate to say.

Alfred talks to me after the communion has ended in what looks like an eventual agreement.

"The last days been full activity and my time has a big sum to do. Lucy is your small servant. [!] I do not mind pass you more if I get plenty days, save for today Lucy will protect your face otherwise if there is a problem we will correct them. Always my time is yours. Divine speed to you, and you."

...Or in other words, he has chores to do, Lucy will babysit, but if we die, it is okay for he will travel back and fix it.

Well that is okay then.

So does this mean they NEVER die in accidents as someone else can always correct it? It makes me remember another question I must ask her about UFO sightings. Later.

Lucy repeats that she will be taking me, almost as if she likes to say it, but that we cannot take the same craft as before. I get the sense it is some sort of Royal Starship, or else like Air Force One. I felt disappointed at first, as it was somewhere I felt as much at home as possible... until she explained the change was all for my benefit.

You see, my fantasy was that I had wanted to watch the moments of Columbus's discovery, yet the craft they had always used had no viewport. But others I saw here DID - some even had viewing platforms if I have not already said it.

The finest one available was a smaller craft than ours, about ten yards across, but similarly shaped into a silvery disc. The main differences were that the disc was not perfectly spherical, but had a wavering structure like a rapidly-solidified glob of solder, and running all around its diameter a rosy gorge through which one could see lights inside, and no doubt see out through, once INside. The 'glass' must have been immensely thick! It really looked like a 'UFO', and again I could not believe the stupidity of humankind to opt for the alien explanation over this more Earthly one.

She confirmed the date with me that we would visit.

I had submissively requested that we spend our day in the past doing no less than - wait for it - tailing Columbus and his fleet of three ships, and experiencing their discovery of the Americas alongside them! We would be the fourth ship in his fleet, I the Captain!

(Lucy, Navigator.)

I gave her all the details I could, and she had to consult with Alfred regarding something or other, who was still standing with us.

And then it was.. time.

Entering the craft was an interesting experience to say the least. As well as the beam of light there was also a disc holding a pole which descended from where the craft sat on its bowed legs, only a couple of yards off the ground, ready for us to walk onto. Is it wrong that it seemed old-fashioned to me? I had watched perhaps a film showing some similar craft made in the 1950s!

Lucy carried out an extensive discussion with Alfred before turning and beaming at me like a small child who had just been told she could have a pony! She walked towards me and the craft so fast I thought she might break into a skip, took my arm in her uncharacteristically warm hand, and gestured with the other arm so that we might walk together into the ship. Alone. Her excitement if I was reading it right was too sweet to suffocate with any reaction other than compliance, and so I walked (practically dragged) onto the plate, which accordingly shot us up into the belly of the craft.

I found it more familiar a way to travel upward than swimming in air and wonder why they did not use this craft the first time they took me.

There was no telepathic interface device on this one. How primitive.

The interior was similar to ours, except for a white dashboard with what looked like little similarly white and sugar-coated mosaic tiles on. Keys!

And a smooth, white, bent needlehead-shaped protuberance that she was later to rest both her unearthly hands on like an old lady on some other-worldly ultramodern walking stick. Although she was sitting.

It is hard to explain.

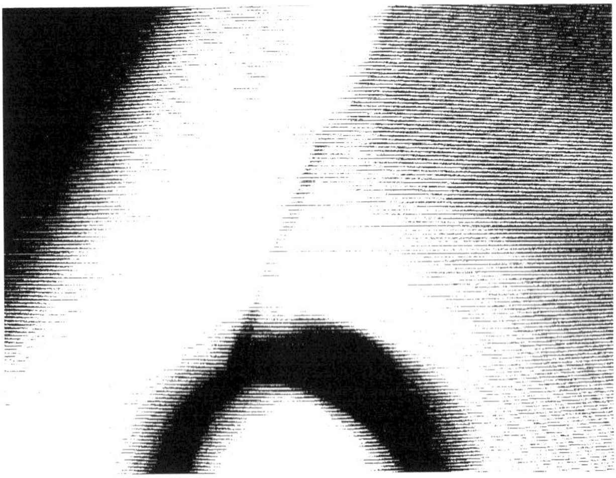

The stalactites above me were shorter. In that there were none. This was indeed apparently an older craft, yet its mechanism contradictorily felt that much smoother and more futuristic than ours had once Lucy set it in motion. It purred into life under my shoes, although I did feel a charge of electromagnetism or static that sent my leg hair slightly on end under my trousers, as though I might have seen a ghost whilst simultaneously floating weightless. So why did the older craft feel quieter? In with the old, out with the new. Perhaps some things do go full circle? Well yes, it confused me somewhat too darling, but who was I to question it other than its designer!

Moments later I was strapped (with a strap, not a ghostly restraint system) into the ring of white seats that ran in a semi-circle around the edge of the craft, facing away from the controller area, and which made it seem bigger inside than it did outside.

Through the translucent viewport I could see a clearly magnified image of the outside world.

"Primed?", my sole companion checked. It felt so 'naughty' to be alone with her.

"Yes", and then we were off, and indeed with such a speed that I thought I could see my stomach through the viewport still on the ground. WE were now one of those craft I had seen darting here three days before! The feeling of progression was splendid.

The magnification let me see further up and down than the doughnut glass seemed it could ever allow from the outside, and I realised we were indeed already hovering over the volcano. We had shot up there diagonally at breakneck speed (although luckily mine did not). Just as that realisation had hit me, everything went bright outside - almost pink, although not blinding, and after perhaps six seconds, it went black.

Why was it blackness all around us? Were we in outer space now as per my earlier theory, the Earth no longer below our position at this point in history?

On first arrival we had swooped down as I realised we were still at the same altitude we had been above the volcano, and I realise it is not blackness outside me, but night sky. It went very blurry, and very fast.

Then it all stopped.

The 12th of October 1492.
The Atlantic Ocean.

I am in the PAST, for the first time in my life.

I cannot in any way even attempt to convey the quaint thrill one feels when living inside his own very ancestry sweetheart!...

That night sky is the OLD night sky. It does not exist in the same way anymore. And then coming into view, the old ocean. For some foolish reason I had imagined everything to be in black and white, but it is not of course. The dark ocean has a tinge of green, and is quite rough with it.

Outside our vessel, old air from long ago. Yet just as breathable to me now, surely, if I were to venture outside. How can that be?! That air is 500 years dead now! Yet I can live in it!

And I think further as we glide high above the waves fleeting past below me, to my past relatives who are living at that very moment, right here. Somewhere someone is my great, great (etc.) Grandfather, and Grandmother. I might have even swooped past them as we moved from the place that will become Dullice Channel Station, to this place near America.

That in turn makes me think briefly of the Grandfather Paradox - you know it? The impossible question of what would happen if you went back in time and killed yours. So he would not go on to have a child, who in turn would not go on to have you, and so you would never exist, and so could never travel back in time to kill him. Although you did.

The spin that sends one's brain into is the paradox. There are similar paradoxes with things I have learned recently, such as some parts of their society's travels to live back in time, and possibly... add to our past genetic pool. Yet they could not have evolved from themselves. Just as you could not kill your Grandfather. It is as confusing as any Paradox, yet arguably possible.

And now I know the answer to that one at least. You could TRY to kill your Grandfather, but events would conspire against you as the future futurist time police are stronger than a mere mortal traveller. There is no mystical force required, just regular time ship patrols regulating the realms of existence. I could not kill my Grandfather, as the police do not like murders.

My mind had run away with me, and at one moment, I had thought I was on a flight. Although I was, but no I mean a jumbo jet two weeks ago! I grow more tired day by day, and my mind starts to plays tricks on me, and not just this. But I come to my senses soon enough, and come to thinking why we cannot see the focus of our trip - the Santa Maria, Pinta, and Nina ships.

But of course, I had no firm co-ordinates to go by, and all I had to give Lucy was that we might find them in the Atlantic, immediately North-East of The Bahamas. Now I wonder how she knew where or even what the 'Bahamas' were. Had she taken me to see the Bananas instead? But of course, now I think of it that must have been what she discussed with Alfred, perhaps calling up some GPS navigation device of the mind. I can only imagine.

From our vantage point after a period of gliding close to the sparkling ocean surface, I can see a long strip of terrain ahead! It is in the far distance, perhaps invisible if it were not for my bifocal window.

I shout to Lucy, "I can see land!"

I should have said 'Land Ahoy' in hindsight. But alas no sign of ships ahoy. Was I going to discover The Americas BEFORE Columbus?!...

We travelled around in wide buzzing circles, and then a zig-zagging search pattern. Basically lots of actions with 'z' in. She manoeuvred the ship like a fairground ride, taking it up and down and in the most remarkable directions and places you would not believe.

But before long I had to ask Lucy to stop as I was feeling giddy. Fearing I might have to abandon this as one quest too far, she allowed me to rest, and resolved to leave the craft stationary above the vast ocean - which I tried not to look at. I hate seasickness - it is the very worst thing in the world - yet I had to combine it with air sickness and time sickness as well. Talk about jetlag. I do not mind telling you that I was close to leaving all dignity behind me and having a rather unpleasant moment on the floor.

Who would have thought there could be such a thing as time sickness. Einstein's theories that a person who travels faster than another will experience a speeding up of time, did not come with a health warning.

I had theorised whether his theory was in a tiny way why all wristwatches keep slightly different time. People put it down to fluctuations in the quartz crystals, however compare high-flying (literally) jet-setters soaring off around the world, to a couch potato. The former would surely gain some moments in their lifetime compared to the latter.

I shake my head in despair of the sickness and she notices of course. Perhaps I did it so she would... Seeing her notice my low makes me think to myself, 'You are better than this. Stronger than this.' I try to combat the spinning sickness in my throat and pit of my stomach, to be the man she thinks I am.

She knows what I am thinking, of course, and sitting next to me, facing me, places her hand on the back of my neck and rubs it.

Do you mind me saying that it felt nice? I mean, in that I needed it.

She shuffled down next to me on the viewport seating, her other hand joining the first on my neck.

"You are humid. Bright one you have so much to offer our world, I am glad you begin to own that power contained by you. I want to be there one day whilst you realise that you are truly amazing."

It knocks me back for a moment. It is the sort of thing you might have said.

I realise now that most of the sickness must have left me - or at least my mind - at that moment. She had known just what to say. Or was it her touch that did it?... And so it was just me and my travel companion, whom I study now more than ever before.

I see a new detail in her appearance each time it seems, and I wonder if my mind had filtered out much of it before lest it should implode. Now it is just enough. Just right.

Despite her unearthly and goblinesque appearance, she is somehow... agh I am pained to say this, but as always will be honest... she is... somehow... enticing? Wait though, it does not mean what you think.

Okay... you know how sometimes a dog, or a horse, and I mean this in a purely platonic way, can be 'beautiful' and so perfectly proportioned? Surely you had thought Momo was 'handsome' even though he was a dog, or had seen a beautiful horse like Black Beauty and wanted to pull its snout close and kiss it? You see? So just take that to another level, a once-removed-from-human yet very close to human level. Is that not LESS strange in fact than finding a horse beautiful?! Ha. This being, which I still see as an 'alien' thanks to all of the unwitting media brainwashing - she is a beautiful thing. Plain and simple.

Inside and out.

I smiled at her as she rubbed my neck, her eyelids plinking, and it was not anything more than that her touch was paralysing me into pure submissive relaxation, like a kitten picked up by the scruff of its neck by its mother.

"I am much obliged to you Lucy. Thanking you", I say sighing.

I can only thank her, for I was able to go on with the trip purely down to her touch. But do not get any wrong ideas my darling, all right?!! There is no chance of anything happening with two beings separated by eons is there. That would be like you falling for a chimpanzee.

...Do not say it! I know your humour!

NO.

I am not falling for her. And they never fell for monkeys.

ANYWAY, she finished easing my discomfort, and went back to the controls to continue sky-scouting on this dark night over this dark ocean.

It was perhaps some forty minutes longer before we finally gave up.

She would try later that night. When she said that, I thought we would have to wait. Again I forgot what ship I was in! And so we jumped just a fragment of time to do just that. And so it was 'later that night', immediately.

Once the white of travel outside went black again, I immediately see THREE OLD SHIPS BEHIND ME, and faster than a turkey at Christmas, unstrap myself, sliding round the seats to strap in again where they head. And there is no confusing them for other ships.

IT WAS THEM!

Once I gained some perspective, as the vast ocean and distorted glass were misleading, the ships that we now tailed at some distance were smaller than I had imagined. I had somehow thought they would be vast galleons, but they were just bus-sized. Columbus's ship was identifiable to me by its distinctive shape - a half-bitten melon slice - and three great masts taller than it was long. Seeing the wind actually ruffling the actual very sails of these very ships made the experience more real than real life back home had even seemed. I had no reason to savour that, but this was...

No matter how clichéd it may be, there truly just are no words!

Its wooden construction contrasts the solid hulk of metallic that I sit safely inside, impervious to weather or water, and makes the great discoverer's craft seem like he sails a matchstick ship, visible through the glass bottle of my viewport. So fragile are they that I wonder how they could ever have made it here from Spain! It seems unthinkable. Yet here they were. Here they were darling!

I asked Lucy if it would be safe to go any closer, and it was no problem because this ship was surely cloaked like our first one had been. Then they came into view! PEOPLE! The crew! The first ship we saw was either the Nina or Pinta - I do not know which at the moment although I will research it.

And there on the deck, small men dressed in colourful garments and pointed hats.

And then we caught up with the Santa Maria. Columbus's ship. We sailed not ten yards from it, and... surely that was Columbus on deck! Pointing at the sky behind us as if navigating, and talking to other crew members. He wore a long cape-like garment and a dark hat, greyish hair trying to escape underneath. His face was nothing like I had seen in the well-known portrait - it may very well have been another fellow altogether. But there he was! Right next to me!

Can you imagine my joy?

Who from history would you want to actually, literally, physically go back and sit next to like this?!

And the ship was beautiful, if still surprisingly small. The crewperson at the helm gripped the wheel more effortlessly than I had expected, as though he were on a break or had seen it all before. When I noted that, I glanced at Lucy, who toyed with her sculptured controller equally effortlessly, looking over in interest. Surely she HAS seen this all before.

Struts ran up the side of the ship and met with the masts, to keep them secured it seemed. I could see a small doorway into a dark area under the helm, and what I would not have given to be allowed into it. (Although I would be killed for sure as a pirate from some undiscovered land.) What would Columbus have given to have discovered the New World like I had? I thought he did come to think of it! These shockwaves of revelations do not stop coming to me do they!! I have become more of a traveller and discoverer than Christopher Columbus himself!

I suggest this be my Captain's Log.

We followed them for an hour, yet they crawled painfully slowly towards the land I could easily see ahead of me in the twilight, and it seemed frustratingly they could not.

I was discovering The Americas all by myself at this moment.

(Some may urge me not to.)

But incredible. 'This is real', I had to keep reminding myself, as it became almost like watching an in-flight film by the second hour, the bi-focal 'screen' not helping break the illusion at times.

Until Lucy shot the ship forward in space so I might look at the land before them, and truly be first. It was hard to make out much detail when we arrived there, given the brightness inside, and the darkness out. And when I did, how foolish I had been to not realise that they were not set to discover the large strip of land that I had been watching for hours, but instead one of these small islands I only now just saw from my perspective, dotted out in front of it - invisible even to us before.

Exploring was not as easy as I had thought. Indeed perhaps Columbus had seen this small island, when in fact I had not.

That will teach me to have flights of fancy.

It seemed darker over these islands than it had out at sea, and she was not hovering that low.

A little more waiting later, I surprised myself and asked her if we might skip forward an hour or so. It was one of those things that once all excitement had exhausted me, I wished to fast-forward to the inevitable high point. Like watching a film's tedious second act, when you know the ending is dynamite.

And so we skipped forward, and each time we did we could not merely stay put on the spot and 'flash' there, but rather the dark world became a blur as we had to travel to achieve time travel, and usually diagonally upwards although our speed was so fast but to make it near impossible to determine the direction. Then back down to the same spot - different time.

But the three ships had moved precious little as they were still barely upon the land. Although I now feel I could have watched them all night, we skipped again, and at last... it was a good time to arrive. It was slightly less dark now, and I could see one of the other two ships was in sight of a different island a long way across from us. Lucy shot the craft sideways toward it and close to the sea vessel.

Before long there was a commotion visible to me and Lucy (her turning to me with raised eyebrow-areas to underline the fact) on the nearest ship, which spread like wildfire to the Santa Maria and the third.

They had seen the island!

That was it!

Land ahoy indeed.

The Bahamas.

The bananas!

I was about to discover America. Again. And at this moment in time, it would be the very first time modern man had. And not Columbus, for I had seen it before he himself had!

We waited some time for them to sail forward and anchor, but instead they seemed to be winding down proceedings. At what a moment to give up!

Then anchors spewed out from the side of the craft. It seemed after a while that they were to wait for daybreak proper before proceeding, likely a good idea in case of any unseen danger in this frightening new paradise ahead. And yet more of a good idea so I could see them - how considerate.

Birds flew around our craft - gulls - but none tried to fly into it, as though they could sense the ship, and it struck me again that these were old birds, long since turned to feathery dust 'now'.

What followed was also amazing to me. Seeing the crew of these three historic ships settle down and turn in for the night as I gazed at their movements through the viewport, transferred to me - just another human - the need to stifle a yawn. But that was not the most fantastic part of it - that I had connected in such a way with the Admiral and his crew and yawned in synchronicity with them.

It was that Lucy yawned in response to me.

We looked at each other and smiled... somehow knowingly.

The best way I can compare it is how we in our time look at a sweet little chimp, and then it looks back at us, so human behind those eyes, you know, staring up at us? And there is a connection and still so many similarities despite the millions of years of evolution separating us. A central core remains. Humanity.

That is the only way I can relate that moment.

But we do not need to sleep through with Columbus and his shipmates for we be time travellers arr! I am sorely tempted to wait until they are all asleep, so in my fantasy I may descend onto the ship if only to have the helm for a moment. But I do not even mention it or think it out loud, as I know that would be... imprudent at best, and events may conspire to prevent me from doing so in case I may somehow accidentally kill Christopher Columbus the moment before he plants his flag on America.

Or worse kill myself.

I sat there, a secret spy on a special mission, watching their every move from the comfort of my complete invisibility. Before I had heard her move, Lucy was right next to me again, and her hand up and around my shoulder.

"You miss her don't you?", she asked.

For I had been sitting there, in the calm of mind that the calmness on the old galleon brought, wondering what you would make of it, and wishing you could share it with me.

And I had thought that had you still been with me, they would no doubt have invited you along.

Lucy's actions drive home to me that 'our story' is seemingly part of history. Some great medieval tragedy to them - just everyday pain in life to us.

And then she again hints at something that still has not quite driven home to me.

"Maybe soon young traveller."

Well, with the crew of the old ships asleep and Lucy yawning in between blowing my mind, I - here and now writing to you - must sleep along with the account of events. I am told I am to have a 'day off' tomorrow, as more travels await me - should I want them (of course I should!), so I know I can finish telling you all about this, and there is MUCH more to tell.

So I shall write more after I recuperate. Can you wait until dawn for me to continue with the events, of dawn?

Good.

Nun night my love.

Day Fifteen

Posted by Eurora001 on Fri 22-Jun-2001 11:42

Good morning to you!
I had the most wondrous sleep.
You were there.

I will tell you my dream before I continue the goings on from Mr Columbus' Captain's Log. I do not know which pseudo-reality I prefer!

In the dream we were so childlike, you pulled my arm along a row of shops excitedly, our bodies closely touching, and you seemed so tall and snug, dressed in white. Angel. The closeness felt like home to me, as though I had not seen you for twenty years and we had suddenly been reunited, old primary school friends, yet had not grown up at all and acted as if not a second had passed.

Then - round a corner - you let go and disappeared into a small café on a hill I had never been to before, saying in my ear, "Come, I want to have intercourse with you". Of course, you had meant verbal intercourse - to communicate - talk. (I know that is not very ladylike, but do remember this was a dream in a man's head for which I must be forgiven.) I saw you find yourself a seat inside, and I had nowhere I wanted to go than to follow you. I sat down at the table, pulling my chair in under me, looked up, and you were - in a blink - not sitting opposite me, but instead to my side and dressed differently - and you looked upset that I had in fact followed a stranger into the café and sat opposite her. It was her who was dressed in white. You had nowhere you wanted to go than to follow me, and had been apparently trailing behind me and the tall stranger.

"She wants to have intercourse with me!", I said back to you, meaning communication as I was sure you would grasp - after all it had been your joke - although it had not.

I do not recognise the girl I now realised had been the one pulling me along the street, while you must have hurried to keep up with us just behind me like an abandoned puppy, wondering why her master was suddenly with a new one and ignoring her. The thought of abandoning you to another like that upset me deeply, both in my dream world and the real one.

The girl I then see sitting opposite me, who I had walked in with hand in hand, is an Asian girl with short wet hair, no longer tall as she (you) had been.

It was confounding.

In the dream I was not proud of myself and felt sympathy for you, however it was but a delusion so I need make no excuses now in real life, although the guilt stays with me. What am I left with of you but these fragmented imaginings anyway?

But the spookiest thing was that I awoke to your voice calling my name in my bedroom.

Although of course there was no-one.

Some people are scared of the dark and of impending nighttime because of ghosts and ghouls that may hide in the wardrobe or under the bed. For me it is a different type of ghost the darkness brings, last night more than ever, and so when it descends, I too am fearful in a way, for the ghosts hiding in my head are so beautiful in a way - yet I know there can never be a happy ending when I awake. Because you will never truly be there will you. Just like the ghost. You will never again pull me along the street, hand in hand, dressed in white. Ghost.

It is like being given a toy as a child that you have always dreamed of receiving, only to have it snatched away again once you fall in love with it.

Every single god-damned night.

Bella, what POWER with which the dreams renew the feelings for you one would think long since decayed, those neural connections long since withered. But they never can wither, for they are watered on a daily basis. It is as surprising as when a smell of a certain perfume, or that song from your past, brings an uncannily well preserved emotion straight back to the forefront of your mind, when you thought it long since dead.

I do not know if I love it or hate it.

Anyway.

Columbus is about to discover the brave new world - I must get my priorities straight!

Well, we zapped into dawn some hours later - for us seconds later. I leave the mechanics of that to Lucy, although I watch her operate the controls with much interest, trying to relate them to driving a car - which of course is utterly retarded.

I am not sure if the crew of the boat can see them from the distance they dropped anchor, or are too preoccupied, but a number of stark naked natives are somewhat agitated on the beach of this now beautiful island. (I can relate - I too was naked when a ship turned up on my doorstep.)

It is a fairytale tropical paradise if ever I did see one with a lagoon off to the left, where peculiar brown natives run nervously back and forth into the shoreline, to where they can see the three historic ships, as if playing with the tide and hoping it does not catch them. They strike me as surprisingly old to be acting in such a way, but then I suppose to them this was an event that would blow their sensibilities out of all proportion.

They have no idea what a moment is about to fall on them from modern history. And neither could I.

There is much activity also on deck of the fleet, moving flags into a smaller landing vessel, and passing other objects forward. An argument ensues and it appears someone has lost something of importance. I do not see Columbus, but am sure it is not him who was lost.

The man himself emerged some minutes later from under the helm, dressed in impressive robes that remind me of Henry VIII!

How seriously they are taking it is humbling, as I had for some reason imagined they bullishly took the land from the natives. However it seems important to them to do things correctly and there is a certain amount of protocol - in fact so much so that I wished to 'fast-forward' what I was watching to bypass the bureaucracy. (Or introduce an Act to minimise it.)

My icon Mr Columbus seemed agitated... anxious and irritable... and once they had resolved a great many things, they set off for land, carrying armoury in case of problems. The natives held spears, but I could have told both sides there would not be any trouble.

Some of the shipmates unloaded what I later discovered were gifts for the natives, although Columbus did not lift a finger. One of the flags - a large one of importance - was brought to land, and Columbus himself held it. The moment had arrived. Of course I could not tell what was being said (and neither could the natives) but they were only yards from the crew - men, women, and children, and they watched them as if watching a God that descended down from the skies. The fact it was from the sea seemed to matter not. I am sure they must have had visitors before from other islands, but it seemed the colour of these visitors' skin was of some interest. One of them reached out and touched Columbus on the chin, and he was not stopped.

It is extraordinary that these people just stand there - albeit in an oddly-Neanderthal posture - yet in acceptance and interest, whilst their land is being claimed away from under the very soles of their bare feet. Part of me wanted to tell them!

More and more of them arrived to watch the ceremony, out of where I do not know as the canopy of palms obstructs my view. Every one of them wearing their birthday suits, and unique body paint on each 'suit'. They certainly were not to make the first move however - fearful even though they held the upper ground on their own turf. Columbus finished his formal tasks and after that, the gifts I mentioned were given to the natives - although I did not make this out from what some of them were, but rather from the child-like animation with which they were accepted!

There were some hours of attempted communication - although we skipped some of it I must confess - but I could tell mostly what was being said by the hand gestures, which was most convenient for me as a lot of it made sense as you might imagine darling - you would have understood some of it also. At one point a second-in-command to Columbus, along with the Admiral, made gestures to a number of the natives that looked like 'Come with us? Sail on the ship? Wave bye bye to your friends?'

During that time the crew had many discussions and did a small amount of exploration either side of the beach, bringing back a number of fruits to the boats. What happened later was really quite sweet, as these simple natives had been so pleased with their gifts of necklaces and clothing that they returned with gifts of their own for the crew including an exotic bird that was placed on a shipmate's shoulder and made him look like a pirate. It was endearing, you would have approved I am sure. The innocent natives seemed overjoyed with their discovery of new people who were not trying to kill them (their earlier excitement and armoury showed they were ready to take offence). They seemed to feel as if THEY had just discovered Spain, or Spaniards, not vice versa.

One other point of interest was a lone shipmate who wondered some way down the beach on hias own. Somehow I related to him, as he sat himself in the sand out of sight of the festivities, clasped his arms around his knees, and just watched the ocean move in front of him for perhaps half-an-hour. What would he have been thinking in his moments of solace?

The rest of the crew stayed for some time, and I too decided to move myself into a comfortable position, not like the shipmate on the sand, but rather lying on my front on the flying saucer's seats, my head resting on my hands. I was quite comfortable watching the show, and had several wonderful shivers run down my spine knowing I was doing so in complete secrecy, like a private detective on a surveillance mission.

I had not imagined it would be over so soon - although it perhaps did not feel so quick to those who had watched every minute 'live' - yet I had imagined Columbus venturing forth to explore all the land of this extension of The Americas, but he did not.

He really just discovered a nice beach.

Lucy was strangely silent, and when I looked over I realised SHE WAS FAST ASLEEP - sat bolt upright. Weird, and wonderful.

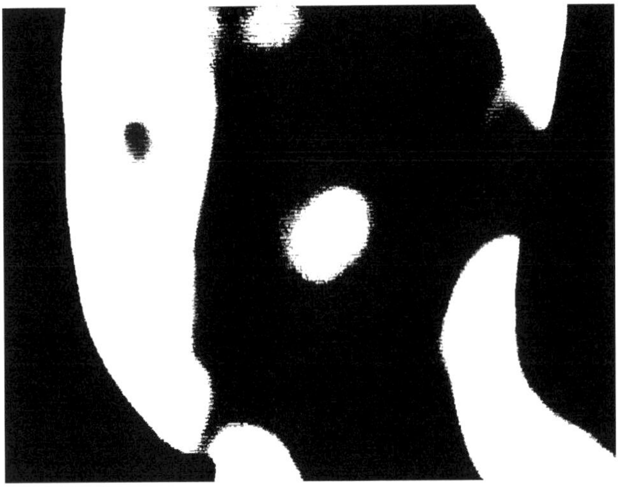

At that moment I felt as though I were truly alone in control of this ship, with more shivers to prove it (along with a sudden need to go to the toilet - of which there was none, unless it was in the room downstairs like the other ship). But being there felt all the more exhilarating and adventurous because of my solitude. I thought to myself how much I hoped they would one day teach me to fly the thing I had created.

She does not wake, despite my mischievous thoughts. I wonder what I can get away with in those moments.

The mission accomplished, goodbyes said, and back on the boat which much a to do and assistance of many of the native men while the women stayed on land, they finally set sail again to the left of the island, on to make more discoveries no doubt. But not before they had taken four natives with them. I was quite concerned as I really did not think these simple young people had understood that they were likely never to return home! If I had seen the same gestures as them, they thought they were just going for a ride, perhaps to another island just out of sight. I fear they would be taken back to Spain, perhaps as slaves. They did not even seem to say any prolonged sort of goodbye to any loved ones or wives, although there was some stroking of arms. And so they went off to REALLY discover Spain.

I wondered how many years their families mourned for their return.

I, however, had discovered enough.

My only predicament was how to wake Lucy.

She looks incredibly peaceful, sat there like some mossy futuristic statue, and coloured like one too. I leave my shipmates behind me to get on with their travels as they sail away, and walk over to the 'pilot' seat she occupies. It is easy to leave them, somehow. She is facing me and must have fallen asleep watching it all - perhaps it was a rerun for her.

Studying her like I have not been able to before, I do not know whether to be disturbed by her general features, or if I am yet comfortable with it. Perhaps I worry that I AM comfortable, as after all I 'discovered' this new species little under two weeks ago, and it is only when I remind myself how alien they are that it bothers me. But the point is, I have to remind myself. When I do not, it does not. Then they are just as another breed of dog is to the next - so many different sizes, colours, shapes - some even hairless (or is that cats). The only difference is she is another breed of human.

I do not know why I feel this need to explain my accepting nature, but there it is. I do. I just wish to point out that we as humans are already so used to accepting different branches of the same species that it comes quite naturally, despite - or maybe because of - the fact it is our own.

Well, I know the gentlest way to wake somebody is to rub their earlobes, but there is a problem - she does not have any, none of them do. I am not about to start poking around in her auditory canal, or any other part of her nubile body. I say her name in my mind - towards hers.

But it has no effect.

I have never spoken audibly that I know of in their company, but I do my best to speak her name out loud (although I foolishly forgot at the time that it is not her name and so may well not rouse her).

"Lucy..."

"Lucy..."

"LUCY..."

"LUCIEEE?"

Nothing happened, so I moved my lips closer to her ear, and her left eyelid looked magnificently big as I saw it open fast like a shutter at point blank range. WOW. I jumped back then steadied myself so as to not LOOK like I had just jumped back. The blackness of her eye belied where it was looking, but for sure it was looking at me as all in a split second she pulled my face towards hers, shocking me half to death.

She tried to kiss me Bella.

I wonder now if that was what my dream was about, now I think of it.

Of course I did not let her. I pulled away before too long at all. I should have seen it coming. The adoration she had poured on me these past days in time. The glances. The hand-holding.

She did not look offended, and only said one thing to me, obviously still a shade too dozy to know what she was saying, yet still the words came through to my mind like crystal clear waters.

"For few long nanoseconds, you kissed me back."

Then just, "You have sweetness about you, never lose it".

She came in again as if to kiss me, but simply planted a hollow vacuumous wisp of a kiss on my forehead, and looked at me out of the side of her face with those same big black eyes, and the best she could do of a smile. I was not sure if I was supposed to be thinking something particular. Something romantic. It was as if she wanted me to say something back.

I honestly did not know what to think, or what to say.

Or what to now type.

All I did say was a whisper of a startled outward breath.

After too long, I broke the silence with a question I had thought of earlier before we set off from Dullice Channel.

"Lucy? I understand about the damage your craft cause to cameras, but why has there never been CONCLUSIVE proof of you/UFOs by some other means than visual?"

"Hello. Understanding that. It is quite beautiful know your nice mind has interest in all of things. It make decision to visit you so right! I hope we will give you the best chance near future in understanding this. Almost never there will be 'conclusive proof' as your saying is very clear. We mention before about magnets? And for smaller events that might cause us mischief not major issue, in any event where proof coming out, we so travel back and easy to remove either the proof beforehand, or we create or place other story or evidence that is even easier - it make proof seem laughable. Like when a person try to go to the news agency with the story, it is easy to make evidence that show him not to be psychologically secure."

'That is a bit unfair on the person!', I think to myself, while trying not to look psychologically unsound.

"NO. [!] Our whole security can be wiped up from such events, to make person seem a 'bit naughty' is small price please be the understanding conqueror. Uncountable times we try to stop small evidence in first place, then we find it is better to make disbelievers out of those who may believe, than to remove the very knowledge from them at all. This way, many less trip is necessitated, as minor evidence become self-managing. Is smart! Remember we are you. Our people support me behind. I am your little assistant. Can you think better way to escape from troubles?"

I wonder if she is asking me in my 'Godly status', or in sarcasm.

I reply in neither.

But I do have to go on and ask, "Why do you never tell anyone that you are here, except me? ...Or have you told others?"

"Your query is very kind. You are not only one but it is complicated, forgive me. Should answer something else. Okay?"

Okay.

I am sure had someone measured my brain synapses then, they would be showing severe overload, having in one day discovered a new continent and been sexually harassed in a UFO. (Yet all I had really done was go up in the air a bit and kiss a human-oid. It is all quite rational really.)

So others have been visited before me? I now get to thinking somewhat about who. There are such obvious candidates, and I presume they mostly relate to the pioneers of time travel. Einstein surely must have been among them, but who else? And whatever other great minds from my history, and my future (as yet unborn), could there be?

Nostradamus, the great prophet - now that would explain a great deal.

And did Michelangelo not apparently change the Sistine Chapel ceiling some twenty-five years after he 'finished' it? I always thought that unusual.

Ah yes, I was going to tell you why I thought I was losing my mind somewhat. It is just, there is something I did not remember to look for while I was floating in the sky in the hours before Columbus's ships found land. I had studied the subject in the past, to an extent that I really should have remembered and am annoyed I forgot now the time has passed - no matter how forgiving I should be with all I have on my mind.

I should have studied the night-time island more for sign of a light in the sky, for Columbus said he saw one flickering or flashing above the horizon before he discovered land. Yet I recall no such thing. Surely I would have seen it.

But it was not just that I had forgotten. Whilst up in the sky I had thought to myself how wonderful it might be when back in my own time, to travel to the museum in Italy and try to arrange to hold and read his actual journal, which was no doubt carried on that very vessel yesterday/five-hundred years ago, before my eyes - the relevant pages undoubtedly updated after I had left.

I had romanticised visions of going to the museum under the pretence of some research or studies, as no doubt its pages could not be turned by mere mortals like me under normal circumstances.

And if that were not possible, I had toyed even with - I am ashamed to say - breaking into whatever crypt it was held in, if only to have a few moments by myself to clasp it and read his aged paper account of what I had seen on the very same day.

Yet back in the harsh reality of home, I remembered his journal had been lost and was not in any museum. In fact I doubt now that I ever even thought that it was. Or that I ever even fantasised about seeing it. Why would I if it was not there? Hell my mind is a mess of mixed signals and time-sickness - I really need this day off, if not longer.

I have been thinking about life a lot this morning. I feel that I - and my mind - are being pulled in several directions by who seem to need me - one more than the other - or want to possess me. I need to detach. To recentre. I will therefore use this time to return to the core of me.

...

Well, I have been sat here for a good ten minutes since I wrote that, staring out of the window into the blue above. I would not know if Lucy was there staring back at me, and I feel my privacy may never be my own again. What if tomorrow when these people have finished with me, finished giving me the adventure that I myself made possible for me, and they leave me alone... what if I a can never truly be sure I AM alone?

It is surely like believing in ghosts.

Good grief, what if I have never been alone since I was a child...!? Could they have been watching me at times throughout my life? Now I think to it, surely they would indeed have.

I feel sick.

Why does that somehow ring true however, with how different I have always felt?

You yourself once said there was a light around me, and nothing could hurt me.

Was that light... them? Not you...?

THIS IS RIDCULOUS. I am unsure if ANY of this has been real now! Am I having a mid-life crisis, or some mental episode even darling?! Help me. Despite flashes of confidence, I am really just putting on an act of someone who is comfortable with all this. Deep down I wonder if someone is playing a sophisticated ruse with me.

...Of course, I am not mad. This IS real. It IS. I have thought it all over and it is. Homo Sapiens means Man The Thinker. But there have been half a dozen other Homo species before our little one. So why not just one more distinct Home species, AFTER ours?

What is really so unbelievable about that?

Are we so self-centredly narrow-minded to really believe we are the 'ultimate', never to be bettered in the future?

How many of our forerunners perhaps believed the same, sitting there in their caves, carving their clubs.

Hell why not more after LUCY'S kind as well, that even she in turn may find unbelievable. I had already decided that was likely the case so how can I accept that there are other species after hers, but yet convolutedly not after my own! Ha, the oddities of the humanoid mind.

I wonder now if they have at least tried to travel forward to see if they are succeeded by another race, even though the laws of time travel do not officially permit it.

And what might that race look like, another million years ahead? Let us have a look by following that natural progression we talked about earlier - what fun! We started with hairy Neanderthals, then in the middle were our less-hairy good selves, and next in the line were the now completely un-hairy, shorter, Extapiens. What would follow that? An even smaller humanoid, perhaps three-feet tall, completely milky-green skin, no ears whatsoever, and complete control over their minds, and over time. It would look like babies were running the world!

What a chance I have been given Bella! Despite all of today's fears, I have decided above all else to make the most of it and continue the voyages, for as they implied, I am to be given more tomorrow. I wonder where I will end up.

You know, I sit and think that here in this very timeline I call home, that those Chinese fellows I sold the concept to are only starting to slowly digest my plans 'right now'... I wonder how long it will take them to get where they ultimately got to.

Well, goodnight gorgeous.

Goodnight Columbus!

(R.I.P. ...Restless In Perpetuity.)

Day Sixteen

Day Seventeen

Day Eighteen

DAY NINETEEN

Posted by Eurora001 on Tue 26-Jun-2001 11:37

Hello stranger. It is I, your intrepid explorer!

I am so sorry not to have written for a so long.

But you would not believe the implausible voyages of discovery and adventurous journeys I have been on - really, you would not believe it to the extent that I felt I could not even begin to tell you.

But I also have some... 'news'! I am trying not to get ahead of myself for nothing is certain except my sanity. I will tell you in a moment. It is potentially wondrous.

(By the way do you know, I always remove my watch when I write these entries now?)

Yet I fear as the days get longer and events more indescribable, my entries here will inevitably suffer. I can still feel my personality changing, shifting. Even my thoughts on this screen have become more lucid and easy to document. It does not mean I care any less about keeping this routine for you - and for me I suppose, it is just hard to balance both things that I have come to love so much. Albeit one more recently than the other.

You understand.

Well, after my recovery day, I again met up with Lucy in the ship, but Alfred was still not there. This made me a little uncomfortable after the last time. I wondered whether they ever slept, or if they just flitted from one of my days to the next - all one long journey for them without the days off.

But without Alfred there I do not mind telling you I felt a bit of a cast off to him, as no doubt you felt the past days to me, which is again why I am sorry as I feel it for you.

I thought long and hard the night I last wrote to you, about where I might like to visit most. There were so many options given to me, but without having asked too many questions for fear of pushing my luck, or worse appearing naive, I knew not how many I would actually get the opportunity to see, and so I felt it prudent to prioritise the opportunities in advance - most desired first.

So many events are now on my list. I will catalogue them below in order of precedence, as I am intrigued whether you my dear would in fact agree:

- 2003 AD - To have Christmas over with you, to click undo and rewrite history...
- 1492 AD - Columbus discovers the Americas (...TICK!)
- 13.5bn BC - The Big Bang and creation of the Universe
- 65m BC - The Jurassic parklands and Dinosaurs, and even to see why they really disappeared
- 1500 BC - My hometown in London, untouched and before even the first settlers
- 4 BC - The true date of the Birth of Christ
- 4 BC - Nine months before the birth of Christ (what, it might be interesting)
- 30 AD - The Crucifixion
- 2500 BC - The building of the Great Pyramids
- 2bn+ AD - After their future, or to The End of the World (whichever came first)
- 1947 AD - Roswell, New Mexico
- 1963 AD - The assassination of JFK (hovering just behind the grassy knoll)

Bella this is how my requests went down with Lucy in no particular order, even though I doubted her authority to grant or deny them. I surprise myself that I still remember it all so clearly, in spite of the days and events that have assaulted my mind since whence last I wrote - thinking THEN I was on the brink of mental breakdown. Now I am so far beyond, I feel I have come back round the other side. I wonder if I shall ever forget these words we exchanged - her and I.

Will you always hold onto this journal so I shall never?

I began to explain to her the story of you and me.

But she already knew it.
Of course she did. You are legendary too Bella! (Although she relates to it as a tragedy. I wonder if she is not far off.)
I told her my number one wish above.
And she simply said one word.
"Soon."

It was enough to fill me with the light of a hundred days.

After some time smiling at the floor, I asked her another one from the list tentatively, for in my mind I suspected it would be dangerous, although one can never be sure.
"Has anyone ever travelled to the beginning of the universe, or of Earth?", I said, rather than demanding it as a destination.

This odd little being I now call a friend said, "Indeed to drink of primordial soup in where the initial cells first spasmed together into what we title some form of life has been long our ambition of us. But to protect your beauty, please choose another decision."
"Why?", I had to ask. (Well you would.)
"It has undertaken it many occasions now perhaps seventeen although it brings sadness from within to say each time that the brave pioneers are to have perished."
"Either that", I speculated to lighten the mood, "or they discovered something so fantastical that they CHOSE not to return, and to stay there forever?"

Her face warmed an iota as if she felt that might in fact be a nice idea.

And what of Dinosaurs, you ask?

You would not believe it if I told you. But please do.

Would you believe you are now talking to a man who has witnessed more than 'merely' a pterodactyl?

Much more?!

I have virtually walked among them Bella! Writing here, now, I have all but reached out and touched a dinosaur not metres from my very eyes! I cannot wait to tell you more.

Let us stick to the list for now however, although I am bursting not to. But all things in sequence. Next on the list is my hometown, which gets an actual 'thumbs up' from Lucy, her fingers so drawn out that I do not recognise it as one at first but rather as an alien gesture. But then I realise when she combines it with a verbal confirmation and that, "There may be abundant fields", said somewhat blissfully on her part. I could not wait to see them either!

It is sweet how she seems to crave the peace and green valleys of the past, as we crave the future. We should rethink that. The grass is always greener... And perhaps she is not that far removed from the small sect mentioned from her future, who yearned for what went before so much as to make it their home.

More on those abundant fields in a moment.

As for the end of the world, my suggestion seems itself like the very end of the world to this poor girl. Her reaction worries me.

She looks at me as though she suddenly has never met me or does not know me, like I am an intruder in her craft.

"You...?", she stops short, perplexed.

And I know why.

I stop my small rouse through fear that her giant eyes might burst into tears or her forehead wrinkle itself into a black hole. I did not mention it above lest I spoil the surprise for you forgive me, but I put this destination in my list of requests as a... test.

Sneaky - I like it.

You see, one of the myriad things I have not had the inclination to mention here before is my firm belief which evolved through the theorising of my design, that one of the laws of time travel - should my design ever see the light of day (or of a million days as it has transpired to do) - must be this:

'Never travel forward in time uninvited.'

Why, is quite simple.

Not only would it be like crashing a dinner party one was not invited to, or turning up for work at a high-paying law firm, when you have just taken your 11+ exams, but also a more fundamental point.

There are two things that evolve through time along with our physical appearance. And they are our knowledge and inventiveness, along with our capacity to understand what we have invented.

I based this suggested law on the mistakes we have learned from in the invention of the Atomic Bomb - the very same marvel that we now rush towards ridding the world of so it may become as if it never existed. That is the point.

Even with natural discoveries such as weapons of mass destruction, we still make catastrophic mistakes. So in my many nights lying awake during the theorising of the impact of the eurora potential, I had imagined what mistakes we might make if we walked unannounced into the future, and steal such new toys of a similar nature, literally before our time?

The answer was that we would be but a small baby trying to operate a butcher's saw.

And so the rule was set, and proposed to the Chinese along with all of the rest of the time displacement array et cetera. We must not use the device to venture further forward than our own capabilities for understanding, unless a future 'we' were to deem it safe to venture back and invite us. That would be their prerogative.

And indeed, it is a rule Lucy, Alfred, and the other billion or more of them seem to have followed, for they have little knowledge apparently of their own future. And they have only brought me forward in time, invited.

WAIT! Again, now I sit here and type events out, my mind connects new thoughts together into truth, and I think again of the few great artists and thinkers through history who have surely also been given the opportunity to see what became of their works beyond their lifetimes. As I have said before, one of them surely must have been Einstein... Who was instrumental in the development of the Atomic Bomb.

And so what if somehow the proposed law was NOT followed by the great pacifist himself, and he took the butchers saw he found back with him to the infancy of the 20th Century under the guise of his Special Theory of Relativity? What if the Atomic Bomb was not invented - originally - until much later.

But surely the 'Universe' (or the time police) would not allow E=mc2 (the very formula of an atomic explosion, which showed that a large amount of energy can be realised from a small amount of matter) to exist before its time? Surely the A-Bomb would have been created even without his theories and encouragement toward the leaders of the USA to 'invent' it. Surely the Germans would have invented it instead if not. Surely surely surely. And so now, I wonder which great German would have time travelled into the future to steal the plans... Ha! I do get carried away with myself. Too much speculation. But it is a thought.

That said, I do wonder how my Futurists think they know for certain that changes one attempts to make really ARE prevented. I say that because if such attempts were NOT prevented and so succeeded, one would not necessarily even recognise the change as a change, because it would be what had 'always' been. Memories would be changed with it as I think I said before. Could they not have thought that atomic energy was always discovered in the 20th Century, because to them it was - but not before Einstein stole the workings of it from the future when they took him there?

But if there is an even more advanced group policing the timelines, why would they let the A-Bomb through as being 'good', and so 'allowed'?

Unless its invention at the right time was the lesser of two evils, preventing a great many more deaths than it caused?...

I am sure even I do not have the capacity of thought to know why that simply cannot be the case, and why they must be right.

I have to give them a great deal of trust, and so far they have not let me down. I do not even know for sure that Einstein ever travelled in such way, or if he did whether it was well after 1905.

(Come to think of it, I have often wondered if the great man Albert (I nearly typed Alfred Einstein there) did 'borrow' a number of his 'discoveries' - not necessarily just from the future - but just given the fact that he worked in a Patent Office as a filing clerk. Would he not have had access to a great many patent applications, before they were published, and had the opportunity to 'mislay' the applicant's work to ensure they were not published until sometime after his own 'discovery' was made public? Food for thought.)

Anyway, to cut a long story short, poor LUCY had not understood why I would suggest travelling beyond her metatime, if I indeed was the one who suggested you should never travel beyond your own metatime!

This was why she looked so confounded.

You could see in her face she thought for a moment they had taken the wrong person and that I was not me, as I would never suggest such a thing! What a case of mistaken identity that would be! The look on her face was a picture, and I felt bad after the test, but I wanted to be reassured about my law you see. And so it was necessary.

Sadly, even after I had appeased her, I fear I planted a seed of doubt in her large head that may remain, although as yet unfertilised.

She said along the lines of, "When progressing your story I considered it might be true on a strain. I crave to know only the honest. Tell me the reality at this moment please. If it were true... then I could believe nothing."

And so I reassured her, and assured her that I had intended it to see if they knew it was I who proposed such a theory. I asked her to kindly understand that I still had a great many uncertainties.

And so she did.

Lucy had indeed never seen her own future, uninvited at least. I saw it somewhat like a grander-scale 'watershed time', like the one we have of 21:00 when children should not watch television. To the futurists, we are the children, naive and incapable of comprehending what we may see 'after our time'.

This also all helps me to understand why I was 'only' taken to Dullice Channel Station now, but nowhere else. What could hurt me about seeing a hill, some little green men (green clothes that is), and UFOs? Have we not seen them all our lives anyway?!

It is a funny thing about bringing the future back into the past, for in a sense we create it ourselves. For example, in a word processor released this year you might have a choice to use a font called "Future", or such-like. And it would be designed in the present to look like it was futuristic. Yet by creating the font in the year 2001, calling it 'Future', designing it to look futuristic, but using it in 2001, we are effectively creating and living the 'future' right here and now, in the present. Are you with me? At the moment of its creation, we can no longer say 'this is what writing WILL look like in the future', for it already DOES.

And then we surround ourselves with wood in our homes (doors, tables, chairs, carvings) as though we are still swinging from the trees it is made from.

People.

Anyway, I digress.

Next was Roswell, New Mexico, alleged crash landing site of that UFO, and the alleged alien autopsies that followed, and were allegedly covered up. Allegedly. I wanted to see what REALLY happened, allegedly.

Between the time a few days ago with considering these choices briefly, and actually coming to have the sit-down conversation with her on the craft, I had thought of this one some more.

Why?

Because it was an alleged UFO that crashed. And all things being constant, I now know that UNidentified Flying Objects have been Identified to me. IFOs. Time Machines. MY Time Machines. (Well some of them.)

U.F.O.

Uncloaked - Future - Object.

Which would mean that a craft much like the one Lucy flies, containing Futurists much like her, was in fact what allegedly crashed in Roswell and was supposedly hushed up by the government.

And that worried me on two levels. First, it would mean that the government knew about the existence of time travel from the future, long before I had come to posit its mechanics into a working theory in the actual timeline. (Of course I had no way to know if the crash happened 'second time around' - yet another chicken or egg poser.)

But that secondly, if at my request I travelled back to New Mexico... might we in fact crash land, be captured by the US military, be taken to a top secret hanger, and ultimately be autopsied? Might those aliens purportedly captured by the army have been Lucy, Alfred and me on a sightseeing tour?

The chicken and egg's brains are now fried.

I trembled inside at remembering catching a UFO documentary where an actual army witness said she saw a small alien who had been imprisoned at that Area 51 in the Nevada desert, looking out at her from behind the window of a locked hanger.

I had worried a few nights ago when coming up with this, whether 'that could be Lucy, tomorrow'.

But surely other time tourists had wanted to visit that date. It might very well cause a 'pile up' that caused the very crashed craft. Am I right in thinking some people claimed more than one craft crashed? Different reports based on the changing timeline of events??

BUT, after all that... Lucy's answer came with a grin. She had heard this one before it seemed!

"I do not suppose we can give good reason to Alfred for using such power to gaze at what you call 'weather balloon', after it burst". She enjoyed saying it.

Could it really be that the birth of the modern era of flying saucer sightings ironically stemmed from a false event, even though those that followed were I am sure not? Or maybe it just was enough of an event - whether time machine, weather balloon, or big leaf - that its public attention brought us to a state of consciousness where we could be aware of what was actually going on all around us, elsewhere, and had been for millennia.

Yet either way, I know why the Futurists left it in our consciousness. Again it was the perfect way to explain away a hundred other valid sightings, as the victim having a history for delusions, like that one about the weather balloon.

They were clever to leave it in the timelines. The perfect cover.

Needless to say, I will not be asking if I can visit the weather balloon. It is just not worth the fuel. And besides, my gallant host already took me to see something far more astonishing.

I had asked for this visit as I have in my years read some debate about the building of the Great Pyramids of Giza in Egypt, although alas as you might remember, on my own visit to Egypt I never got to see them due to having been stranded North of Aswan.

The first issue with how they were built is that there would not have been enough workers within hundreds of miles of the area to do so!

Yet even if they were built using 'contract builders' and a stone ramp, it would have taken more stones to make the ramp than to build the pyramid itself, each stone weighing something like ten tonnes.

And yet if they used trees to roll the stones on from their origin to the building site, what tree do you know that will not grate away into matchsticks under such weight? Besides, desert-like Egypt is not exactly a vast woodland so where did the infinite supply of trees come from?

Even more bizarre is that the actual building of these monumental points hardly even appears in the famed hieroglyphics of the time, yet all other events these great people of the second millennium BC were involved in, ARE documented.

Why omit the miraculous building of the pyramids... unless it did NOT in fact happen during their time. Unless the Egyptians did not build them.

So you see darling this is what interested me enough to posit it to Lucy when asking to visit the time of the pyramids' creation.

And she has the explanation.

It sweeps me off my feet.

I grow ever wearier so I will not quote her word for word. I suspect it is wearing for you to read as it is for me to recount. She explained in her broken Olde 'Chinglish' how primitive Futurists ('people of the future!' to you and I) had been deeply concerned of being 'lost in time' should a craft develop a mechanical failure. Why? For it had already happened. To some poor future souls who still roam the Earth, lost in time, with no idea what year they were embodying, and therefore no way to travel back to their own year, x number of years ahead from that mystery point.

This happened more with the Old World craft than in hers she says. Thank goodness for that! Apparently the earliest versions of my concept were not failsafe - which gives me some cold comfort in knowing these wonders of technology did not just spring into being fully formed, but like anything had a transition period of teething problems - although I am not to be accountable for the competence of the mechanics who built them or the issues they saw, surely.

It appears the problem area or fear of recurring fault was with an organic device she alluded to that kept an account of 'when' the ship was. This was an issue I had postulated. For example, one could use GPS co-ordinates to determine 'where' on Earth one was - but only after the year the satellite grid became live. Similarly one could use clocks, calendars, and newspapers, to determine what TIME period one inhabited if the craft should lose track, but again only after such year as such timekeeping devices existed. You might not think this much of a problem, but in order to travel FROM the time you are visiting back TO your home time period successfully in the event of a fault with the main date entry systems, one needs to know how many years, months, days, to traverse. Then instead of telling the craft to go to a date, you tell it to move ahead by, say, 100 years. A sort of manual control, compared to auto-pilot.

One MUST therefore know the date of departure. Without it such a traveller would be utterly stranded, perhaps in a vast desert of our unpopulated world, and with no way to calculate a trip back, or even send an SOS for rescue - after all, how would he tell them 'when' to find him. Imagine it!

"Mayday mayday, I am stranded over London - send rescue craft urgently - over..."

"Roger that, time traveller, what date can we find you at? Over..."

"Errm... I don't know."

Over, and out, forever.

And so she explained, the scientific community puzzled on the problematic possibility of losing any more travellers to time, to the extent that it was concluded that as a backup to the craft's own 'sense of time', there should also always be a constant central beacon... on the Earth itself.

That is right - the Great Pyramids of Giza.

The theory was utterly brilliant. A lost explorer could always discover the exact date they were wandering in by having the craft whose chronometer had died, fly to the easily found central location of Egypt, and have a backup device compare the marker (the pyramids) below his craft, with the conjunction of the stars above and against other planetary objects. By doing so he or she would lock in the one-and-only exact date that the stars would have such an alignment with the stone pointers below. And that unique alignment, only ever occurring ONCE in time, would GIVE him the time he sat in. From the slight but measurable differences in rotation and elevation, the exact date is always able to be uniquely calculated and presented.

They could then either hurl themselves forward in time correctly FROM that year, or if that were not possible, summon help TO it. And yes, they can communicate across the timelines too, using "radiotelegraphs".

This rang true of something I already knew, and indeed I have just looked up to verify. The three pyramids are not quite in alignment with each other - they are 'strangely' offset. Or are they... Because so is Orion's Belt! The Nile apparently to the side also lines up with the Milky Way in the sky, for what it is worth. Of course they do not line up with those stars anymore or 'at this time', but that is the entire point! By seeing how much they 'do not' line up with Orion, and other interstellar objects, they would know it is 26 June 2001 'nowadays'.

It is enviably clever, I must resentfully concede.

I have to unlearn a great deal to accept this nonetheless. But again, I must ask myself - as must anyone - what is more likely? That an ancient civilization without trees, stone, or manpower, created these three immense monoliths that literally pinpoint towards the alignment of Orion - buildings so great we could barely even create them today, yet which the Egyptians 'forgot' to document the details of the creation of, whilst remembering to document much lesser feats?

Or is it just more likely that time travel is possible, and that those travellers did not wish to get lost?

I can only concede the latter.

But... why need the markers still 'in our day' then, when they could stroll to a newsagent and buy that day's newspaper?

Of course, if you are lost in time, it could be a time BEYOND our day and our great civilization of newspapers (now that is what I would call evolution - the abolishment of all tabloid media), and beyond compatible radio atomic clocks and computers. A day beyond civilization, when we perhaps dwindle back into some dark age. I have sensed such a thing from Alfred and Lucy with their talk of the 'Gravity Pull event'. But the great pyramids would survive in place thousands of years into the future, just as they have for thousands of years in the past, to guide you home, outliving our race, just as they outlived the Egyptians.

Oh, small detail, she also claimed that the pyramids we know are not the first incarnation to have been built on those very spots, and will not be the last.

So why Egypt? She said that aside from its central location on the globe, when the project began they had to select a number of points in time, and space (places) where civilisations existed who would guard the markers just as we still do (meaning they were right), or where no civilisation would exist to guard it from. And so it was determined in this age old legend to her, that the

Egyptian civilisation would be presented these gifts by the Futurists because they were already great believers in invisible powers. Or to put it another way, because they were gullible enough. The futurists would reveal themselves to the great people in order to build these guiding lights. Much like they have revealed themselves to me now. The Egyptians received them as gifts from 'Gods' it seems, and tombs for their kings - for that did not detriment the futurists one bit. There was a trade off in this win-win situation it seems.

You know that other great mystery - how the great stones were lifted? Well these time ships themselves rely on the very existence of anti-gravity technology do they not! IT IS SO OBVIOUS NOW. Lifting tonnes of rock is somewhat easier with anti-gravity, one can imagine.

Lucy had clarified in her inimitable way also why I could not travel to the time of their building in order to witness it, as the "swarm of tumult" would make it difficult for any more ships to enter that area - even dangerous. Indeed she confided in me, a craft was lost at that time as it malfunctioned and shot uncontrollably to the East, carrying a great leader to a place that could never be found. Whatever they did to try to go backward in time and warn him or place him in a different craft, that craft instead would shoot off to the East, almost as if he wished to be lost.

Goodness, an elucidation dawns on me now I process through everything...

I know a little about the period, and did King Tutankhamen and his half-sister not have elongated heads? I recall there was no truly plausible explanation for it, except that it was perhaps genetic.

Alfred and Lucy have elongated heads. And there is an explanation for that - they are a continuation of evolution, yet that branch of our tree had not even begun to grow in the young king's time.

And there is more to this new riddle. The king's parents are as yet 'unknown' to historians. A mystery. Could it be... could it just potentially be... that there was some intimacy at the time of the frenzied building, between builder humanoids from the old world and those from the new, and that bloodline and its genetic differences continued down to mummies we have then uncovered, in the future, such as King Tutankhamen?

I have just done a little research online - and the above is as I recall it. It fits. If I ever doubted whether these travellers were deceiving me, why do 'unexplained' details that are common knowledge, fit so well?!

I even found some information about another king, Amenhotep, who worshipped Aten the 'solar disc'. Flying disc? Could that have been a direct reference to the time of the building of the pyramids, and the aforementioned Gods the futurists feigned to be?!

Well, back to the events. Lucy told me to secure myself in the seat.

I knew something was about to happen. We were going there! Yet she had said I could not!

It all happened so fast. One moment it was daylight shining through the ring shaped viewport that ran around the craft's side, the next we had travelled in time in the usual flash, and then the 'light' inside the craft dimmed to blackness, and I saw that it was night time outside the craft too. Lucy had dimmed the ambient light to aid the view. Foolishly my first thought was that we had travelled forward a few hours to night-time of my same day and the same place - but no.

The craft began to tilt on its axis, and into view through the left viewport came... Cairo. Dimly lit by moonlight, buildings encroaching on the great pyramids like the tide of the sea drawing up a beach, and there in the sand - the beacons themselves.

They took on an entirely new meaning in my heart, as if I was the only man on Earth who suddenly knew with what power and for what purpose they were created.

(Oh, I WAS the only man who knew.)

We were now ninety degrees on our side, which made me think that if the pyramids were below us to the left, what was above us to the right - and so I slowly turned my head, and as I did, there into view came the stars.

There was no correlation to my eye, but then Lucy reached towards the blank viewscreen and detached the object that had appeared to be part of it and which I had thought nothing more of since first seeing it on the side of the screen on the other craft all that time ago. She held it behind my seat, in the centre of the craft, one end pointing to the heavens, the other to Earth. I thought I sensed a high-pitched tingle. And then it was done. She said the date into my mind. I was not so foolish - it WAS tonight, only an Egyptian night. And so I understood that THAT was their backup device, independent of the craft and thus from any faults, to protect them from ever becoming lost to time. I felt entirely better for knowing it was protecting me also.

"For this not only planet with star tracers built upon it. We make them on others, Lorus, Mars, from when we use Father Time to explore back in time on those great spheres."

That bit I had to quote!

In the future we will be able to turn back time on Mars, to see if it had water. Or life. Why are my assumptions always so down to 'Earth'? The possibilities of time travel are truly Universal.

Back on Earth, I wondered if the next time the pyramids were rebuilt after their current incarnation, to go on and protect errant time travellers, of what secret chambers and Pharaoh's tombs might be uncovered in the demolition of the old marker.

And what curses with them... Surely none so great as the curse of not having them at all and having to wonder a plane you are not meant to inhabit for the rest of your days.

I am now left with one final query however. Why so many other pyramids around Egypt? I can only assume the Egyptians were so enthralled by these gifts from the Gods that they sought to reproduce them. Only on the smaller scale that they could manage without the anti-gravity. Or that they were constructed with similar easy by the Futurists to disguise the important ones' significance and star alignment from those who knew not of time travel (i.e. us) - indeed it seemed to have worked as no man before me had certainly discovered why such alignment was necessary. Alas I did not think to ask her at the time - I was simply too in awe and was hearing enough - but I shall.

And now I have just thought of the Mayans again. Did they not have pyramids? That other great civilisation that disappeared suddenly without trace. Perhaps those were some of the other beacons Lucy hinted towards from past incarnations, although I felt she had meant on the same spot as the 'current' ones in Giza. These Mayans do keep cropping up in relation to Lucy's statements though...

I truly wonder if their sudden disappearance from history means that they inhabit some part of the FUTURE, instead of once the past. YES! Remember those documentaries showing the Mayan landscape criss-crossed with what look almost like landing strips?... Runways?! And those great carvings engraved in the ground, yet visible only from the air. But as I may have mentioned before, who would have seen them in that time, with no aircraft in existence? Who else were the Mayans trying to attract, than the only futuristic invention that could ever have flown in that time. Time machines. It matters not whether the Mayans thought those who inhabited them were 'gods' or not - hell I surely would have thought the same of such a silvery throne coming down from the heavens.

Truly incredible, yet so very credible.

And so forward in time, from the Egyptian revelation, to the Messiah.

(I doubt my own words at moments like this.)

So from Egypt did I travel backward in time and watch the birth of Jesus Christ?

Of course not. Do not be foolish my love! Although 'why' I did not has intrigued me greatly.

When I asked this little China girl (Lucy), she said, "Sorry no possibility for that, it is not aimed at you, it is no possibility for that aimed at all and Sunday".

To cut a two-thousand-and-one year long story short, there are certain pivotal events in our history that are set by the governing agency as 'out of bounds' for mere time tourists.

What poppycock!

Worse for me that it is some of the best dsestinations that are not accepting bookings at this time of year. At any time of any year.

She explained how being a believer in the divine was such an immensely positive force for so long in history, and how it had evolved and subdivided throughout time into so many more positive forces beyond the existence of Christianity as we know it. (The mind boggles).

The events of that period in time were literally hallowed ground. It was a form of respect, and thus, of exemption from time tourism. It was not a place for a trail to be trampled by Chinese tourists. No, the futurists had turned a portion of time into a sacred place of worship. A Church of Chronology. (Perhaps it sounds better than Scientology.)

And so even for 'me', there were no VIP tickets available, although she would, "confer with Alfred but really no".

However, it did give me the opportunity to quiz her about what they knew. Because I suspected that maybe once in time, the journey had been made by non-tourists, if only for historical and discreet observational reasons.

And so it came to pass... that I asked Lucy about the Immaculate Conception. However she misunderstood me and thought that I was asking to travel back TO it, rather than merely have a chat about it.

"See in your mind eyes if the young virgin see with her eyes YOU, if you are then to amble past her entrance, and were she to have fallen into love with you... since it is easy to do", she added in an unfamiliarly bashful way, glancing at the glassy floor for a moment of reflection. "She may not be having love with her deity so in its place have love with you", she said with an accent and a look of aghast in her eyes, as her head jolted back half an inch, to really drive home to me the point that she had thought I was not understanding. Even though I was.

"Because then you will be Jesus Christ father."

God.
(Literally.)

Yes... one can rather see why it might not be a good idea to dabble in that time.

I explained the misunderstanding, fun though it was to hear her way of explaining it, if it truly was her words I was hearing and not my own translation of 'Futurese', which I still suspect at times. But I had to ask her whether she knew or they knew if it truly was a birth without a father. Was it immaculate, or just... maculate(?). That had been my point.

"One special scholar observe the time period shielded yes, and he can make out no human being go into her home or her."

That sounds a little odd to me - not her unintentionally apt phrasing - but that nobody whatsoever entered her home... (or her) for whatever window of days it was nine months before his birth.

Unless the scholar himself was the father...

Well I assume he was a male.

Or unless he worked for the Church of Chronology, and that was the 'official' story he came back with.

But for whatever reason, even though I am not deeply religious but more on the side of spirituality as are you... it is magnificently charming that that belief was able to transcend the eons, and still holds true in Lucy's advanced time. It all seems so recent to our time by comparison, when one imagines the legend it must appear to be after a million years. A legend compounded by the inability to ever go back and witness it first-hand. And so, always just a legend.

But that was not the most interesting discussion by a LONG shot. Neither was her revelation that by witnessing Christ's birth from a flying saucer-shaped time machine, at the location they knew it to be, they had guided the three kings TO Christ's very location. THE UFO WAS THE GUIDING STAR OF BETHLEHEM, its light visible in the sky for miles around, hovering as a point to the very place where Christ lay.

As I think of 'lights in the sky' I think back to my time with Columbus, and his witnessing of such a light in his journals. Was he witnessing a saucer - a time ship? WAS HE LOOKING AT ME, AND MY SHIP NOW APPEARS IN HIS JOURNALS?!

They just keep coming. Any moment now I am certain my brain will liquefy.

And are you sitting down? I suggest you sit down.

She then revealed the following to me somewhat reluctantly at first, but then seemed to find some joy in sharing it with me.

Let me just paint this familiar picture and see if you understand me...

Christ is crucified, and laid to rest inside a cave.

He is resurrected and meets with his apostles.

He then ascended into the heavens, and as of my time has not come back down.

After this there is much talk and writing of the 'Second coming of Christ', and that he will 'descend from the heavens and rise again'.

But what Lucy suggested to me, and I do stress the word suggested because she expressed that the events she spoke of happened a long time ago (for her) much as the Bible was written a long time ago (for us). She claimed it was therefore not an area she knew much of, and, "neither does a great many people except a great few".

Nonetheless here it is. Just look how little has changed from how I phrased the events above:

Christ is crucified, and laid to rest inside a cave.

He is resuscitated and meets with his apostles.

He then ascended into the skies, and - as of 2001 at least - did not come back down.

There is much talk and writing of the 'Second coming of Christ', and that he will 'descend from the heavens or skies and rise again'. But by 2001 he has not.

Precious little changed, yet so much has. This is what I gleaned:

There was (is to be) a great turmoil in the world (in our future), but a form of religion was to become a binding, positive force that held the 'people' strong. It became so that the second coming of a Messiah was so deeply needed - so intensely wanted - so profoundly desired - that our future descendants came reached a point where they would do anything within their 'power' to seek out Christ's salvation and guidance, enough to make him rise again.

And within their power at the flick of a telepathic switch were two technologies... reanimation of the mortally wounded... and travel into the past.

They so deeply craved for the Messiah to descend from the heavens...

That they made it so.

They made it so Bella.

Do you understand what this means?! Christ.

No wonder this time period was out of bounds to mere time tourists.

I can only piece together from her fragmented tale that this is how it transpired...

Christ is crucified, and laid to rest inside a cave.

LONG after his death, a humanity desperately in need, travelled to Jerusalem of circa 30 AD, landed their craft in a secluded area and under cover of darkness opened said cave, then took and ascended "Yahoshua's" (as she called him) near-lifeless body into their primitive time ship.

Back in the future, he descended down from the sky (or heavens if you prefer) in the same ship (or throne if you prefer).

Being the man he undoubtedly was, 'Yahoshua' came to understand what was being asked of him, and duly fulfilled his destinies there.

The second coming of Christ.

As prophesised.

(A prophecy made by who? Someone who at the time of writing their testament had knowledge of this future event? How, and why? I time traveller?!)

Through what wonders of medicine must undoubtedly have evolved in that time in the future, he was therefore 'resurrected' from the brink of death. A miracle unheard of in 30 AD to the extent that it now still captivates the world.

But would such resuscitation be quite so miraculous in the future if healthcare and lifespans continue the way we know them to?

Yet again, incredibly, it could make sense.

But what to do with the greatest man history has ever known AFTER he had seen the things he had seen, and it goes without saying saved humanity from its crisis - for humanity clearly went on to survive the turmoil as evidenced by my visitors' very existence and mindset.

They could not take him back to death's door and drop him in a cave.

They could not kill Christ, to make it look like they had not taken him!

In fact why take him back at all? After all if they did it would be most confusing to someone living the tragic events for the first time, to see Christ the day after being left for dead, suddenly in a markedly more revived state, perhaps even wearing clean garments.

Anyone seeing that would think it some sort of miracle or some...

Ah.

That explains it.

I do hope you do not take offence at this? I am only the messenger, but even if Lucy's words could be seen to undermine the fabric of Christian beliefs, do not forget to notice that they also indelibly corroborate and validate that Christ lived, breathed, was crucified, and is the salvation of the world. There are just two sides to every story, and perhaps the Bible is no exception, but that does not make either side wrong, or take away from the other.

So why did they return him? Lucy stated that Mr Christ himself had insisted on returning to his time, and to the moment in time he was taken, just as I suppose you or I might had we been separated suddenly from our loved ones by... near-death. And she says he had learned so much during his time with man's descendents, and longed to pass on final teachings to his disciples to aid them, that he was of course granted that request and returned to the night he was abducted, and to the very resting place.

But the only way possible to return him to his time, would be to put him back in the same place and same time as they found him - only as a newly revived man. They would hardly stab him again and drive nails back into his hands and feet, to hide the evidence of their healing. What choice did they have? Mutilate Jesus? Argue with the Son of God?! Of course they did neither. And so he was returned to the place, as if he had never left.

(It seems they can bend their rules if you are a deity.)

One can truly imagine how, seeing the stone rolled away (presumably by some futurists, or even using their anti-gravity pyramid-building wisdom) and then also finding Jesus fully revived, that person would rightly call it a miracle, and that he must be the Son of God to achieve such a feat.

It appears from what Lucy says that there were two ascensions, for Christ was not only taken from the tomb on the night of his crucifixion as I have explained, but was also taken again some days after being returned. He was given time in which to pass on his final teachings and new found wisdom, before he would - it was agreed - return to a secret place where the primitive 'time throne' (advanced UFO) would be waiting. This time period was what was deemed safe to not create any paradoxes, I can only assume.

To not go at all would have had serious implications for the timelines as he would undoubtedly be martyred by the Romans when not if they discovered him, a death sentence still on his head now he was again alive. And then all talk of resurrection would be undone, as he would surely die a more brutal and irreparable death, the effects of which on religion and thus the world would be catastrophic.

The problem however as she puts it was that the craft were so primitive as this was so near the beginning of time travel (in relative terms as you and I say the dinosaurs were a 'recent' evolution), that they had no invisibility cloak! And of course, there are no UFOs in the bible linked with the ascension I am sure, are there?

When he reached the place where the abduction / ascension (a word lost in translation?) could happen, a craft waited, shielded by low cloud cover. Christ was on a hill, within grasp of the hovering ship. When the right moment arose, the light chute descended, and took him up into the sky, disappearing from view into the clouds above and ultimately into the craft hidden by cloud cover.

But of course, anyone he was with did not witness the ship itself, just the beam of heavenly blue light disappearing into the cloud the craft hid above.

Would that not appear like a string of miracles, to be resurrected and then to ascend into the heavens in a glowing aura?

And so, being cruel to be kind, he was taken from the place where he would again surely be martyred, carrying with him knowledge of great new things. But where he would carry on his teachings? Lucy does not know where he was taken to and left at, but it was in the same time period as his own, as would be only right, and he lived out his years in great peace.

It is truly incredible.

So there WILL be a second coming of Christ. That is what was in the Bible. And the change was allowed because it was good. And I could even given you the date he will come again if you so wished.

I wonder if there will be a third coming. I would get a bit annoyed by that stage if I were Jesus.

I need a break after recalling that.

...

I have come again! Ha.

Well, believe it or not even THAT discussion in the ship was NOT the high point. I will type this slowly because I know you cannot read very fast.

(Sorry.)

The Dinosaurs
Sixty-Five point Five Million Years Ago
2:35 PM

Having quizzed Lucy about my earlier theory about the dinosaurs seeming to be such futuristic highly evolved creatures, and having had her tell me I was being "nonreasonable", I put it out of mind and focussed back on my lifelong fascination with the great lumbering (and some not so lumbering) beasts that once walked the Earth - no matter when that had happened.

And when one focuses on something enough, one can make it happen.

And so she did.

I feel selfish having had it all to myself, like a box of chocolates - I would always offer you one.

Whilst we did not stay for very long, what I saw when I was there made it not only as though the Earth had spun backwards in time with our ship, but so had I - back to being a little boy again.

I still feel giddy with childish joy now. Well with that and another type of giddiness that I call 'incredulity sickness'. Yes, again, black and white words on a screen can never, ever, convey to you the onslaught of amazement I have endured. As ever I shall try though.

First up Lucy forewarned me that there may be other time tourists there, as it was a popular destination. I naturally replied to ask her what would happen if two different craft from different eras were to meet, so that those more primitive time travellers would 'bump into' advanced Extapiens. It worried me that it would go against my most important of laws, and allow earlier man to know future technology before his time. But as always she had an answer for everything. She is becoming reassuringly maddening in that sense.

If a future time tourism craft arrives to find that there are already earlier 'people' there, they simply do not uncloak, and pick another destination (two hours later for example) instead. I had not remembered that of course they would arrive in a cloaked state, and be invisible to any more primitive time travellers. Perhaps I had not realised it because 'primitive time travellers' is such an oxymoron to me still.

But that is all just 'what ifs'. I must get on and tell you the 'guess what', as I am bursting to get this off my chest.

"To be in this journey I make the standard sightseer voyage for you. It is the safe and standard one, so do not be fear the great distance. You will enjoy this only to know we can stay only for short times okay my Sir?", announced Lucy, finishing with, "You will see why", before I could ask why.

You will see why too, before you ask why.

There was one small disappointment however, yet in the context of things it is barely a complaint! I was not allowed outside. The heat was "quite inexcusable" apparently, although I am not convinced that was the true or only reason. Curiously she did not mention 'and you may get eaten by a T-Rex' as one of the reasons. Delightful.

And then I was floating under the head of a dinosaur.

I typed it that suddenly as that is how suddenly we arrived.

I, me, RIGHT NEXT to, a Dinosaur.

Ha-ha!!!

We must have been hovering no more than six feet from its head, and I do not mean six dinosaur feet, I mean little humanoid ones.

As soon as the flash of our ridiculously fast arrival so far back in time had diminished and my eyes saw the sight - my brain taking a second longer to process and recognise it - I yelped and involuntarily jumped back and out of my seat, although the restraint prevented my autonomic nervous system from succeeding much.

It was some sort of 'Saurus. 'Veggiesaurus', as they say. And it could not see us - presumably as we are cloaked - or if not then it just was not interested.

The face of this creature, sweetheart I am making a habit of this I know but I do not mind confessing again tears were upon me. One overwhelming experience too many in a way. But they came only once I had converged my feelings of fright and surprise into sheer adoring astonishment.

SO REAL, SO NEAR, SO BEAUTIFUL.

So alive!

This was no plastic model on a museum tour, no fossil in the ground, no computer generated Hollywood special effect... it was there, as real and fleshy as Maxine (only somewhat bigger). Yet not incredibly large. This one was maybe fifteen feet tall. What? That is not large!

We stayed still as it galumphed slowly past us. Its long neck was bowed in the middle as if under some sort of invisible weight, and to just see the nuances in its skin and the muscles of this lumbering darling was, well, indescribable. I hope dearly you may be able to put yourself there through my words. Close your eyes and imagine...

I did not know which bit to look at before it should pass us - I wanted to take it all in at once as I was not sure how long "short times" was. Its shoulder passed us after a short time, the most impressive piece of meat I have ever seen, with real life prehistoric mosquitoes trying to hitch a bloody ride. There was something malodorous about the sight, even though my olfactory senses could not have known for real. I suppose my subconscious mind had related it to the closest Earthly thing it had seen - elephants in a zoo.

But she had certainly been working out. And her chest, surprisingly wide and breathing with such labour, every breath so visible, and yet the stomach surprisingly taught, shaping up just like a greyhound almost. She was hungry.

Oh how I would have loved to hear her breathe her huge breaths in and out, like some prehistoric gale. Yet the ship's body would have prevented it even if mine had not.

Her tail was something else. Almost as long as the whole body before it, little points visible under the harder crocodile skin there, and swaying effortlessly for the huge effort it must have taken to achieve! As she finally passed I wondered if she knew she was controlling all those muscles and nerves, or if it was just a non-sentient habit. So incredible to me, oblivious to her.

I had forgotten to look around me at all until she finally passed by where we hovered silently motionless, but in her wake she left a hole in the air through which I noticed to notice all the fauna around me. Well, I say 'all the', for there was not a great deal. Yet it looked much like some parts of home that we know, indeed even the sky was not dissimilar, if more orange.

Tall, part leafy trees, partly stripped or just naturally bald, combined with other taller trees in complete bloom. Yet splintered bases of long since dead trees and stumps also littered the ground. Contrasting these mangy looking trees up high, was an abundance of other ferns and shrubbery. And she was heading towards it. The landscape was so indeterminate with no landmarks that we could be ANYWHERE on Earth, and at that moment I realised why they would so desperately need a beacon such as the pyramids to navigate from. I was certain the pyramids were here at this very moment, somewhere, as impressive as they are today. Perhaps not the ones we know, but some type, somewhere.

I asked Lucy how she had known to arrive so close to where a dinosaur would be, but she claimed that she had not meant to, and it was just "destiny". Of course I already know that had we tried to arrive inside the space its head was occupying, quantum mechanics would have strafed us away to one side like two opposing magnets having a near miss, rather than meld us inside her cranium. (You might say she would then have ship for brains.)

On the opposite side of the craft was a marshy watery area with three long rivers or streams converging in one place, yet no dinosaurs there drinking as one might imagine. She must have come from there I feel. The water was shallow and clear from what I could see. Had I been outside in the intense heat I may well have wanted to take a dip, and no doubt become T-Rex fodder, but it looked so inviting nonetheless.

I keep talking about T-Rex and I shall tell you why.

I saw one.
And it saw me.

(And it was no sparrow - not any more.)

We did not see any other of these great vegetarian lizards for some time, and Lucy took the craft in that familiar if nauseating zig-zagging pattern I had gotten used to over the Atlantic Ocean, only now there was no sea-sickness to contend with. It was daylight so I could see the horizon which seemed to help immensely.

I had been watching the rear view of the craft as we travelled, the perspective of where we had been funnelling away in time behind me. Lucy had been navigating ahead.

Suddenly she spun the ship on its axis, and the sight she had unkindly presented me with just as suddenly met me at my 'window'. With one glance of the ferocious dragon and its stalactite sharp blood-soaked teeth, I autonomously screeched and shot away from the window, my feet running faster than they knew they could run backwards. By now as the restraint was off I slipped against the bulge in the seating circle, flopping backwards into a heap on the floor.

Graceful as ever then.

I got up and laughed instantly, a nervous laugh perhaps, but my cruel pilot joined me in seeing the funny side of it. I did not mind really, however the fact I can still feel a bruise behind my ear that happened 65 million years ago is a worry.

I went back to the window quickly however, for my pain was the least of my interests. My innate instinctive reaction was quickly and safely locked away, albeit comforting to have, and my eyes then firmly fixed on his. His eye was small, framed in a bony brown gorge of skeletal eyebrow that extended around it. And my GOD those teeth. What looked like hundreds of pearly daggers, freshly engorged with flesh and blood. I realised why moments later. I dared not look in any detail, but he (or she I now suppose) was eating fresh prey. There on the ground, three mostly hairless carcasses of some small description. As I say, I chose to look away, but after he had chosen to go back to his meal, he took the decision away from me as he tore another piece off his trophies, and there back up into my eyeline came crunching bone and ripping bloody-brown hair.

Now, you know that innate instinctive reaction I had then safely locked away?

It came back.

Lucy turned the cloak off. I saw it glimmer outside.

He shockingly swiftly switched from being a loan scavenger into 'defence attack mode', a thousand times more horrific as he howled at our craft than they had ever captured in a science fiction film or museum event. He even had a long pointed tongue

- something I had never seen in such exhibits or motion picture recreations, and he thought our tongues were after his meal.

After I picked myself up off the edge of the seat where I had found myself, I felt a complete paralysis of fear that I had only ever felt before in the odd dream, when being chased by a bandit or held captive by a gunman. It is only when one truly finds himself nose to nose with such horrors, that he can understand their true weight, and that weight flattened all of my muscles into rigamortis. The sheer peril I felt told me that Lucy had done something wrong. All I could do was wait - paralysed - for her to correct the cloak or alter our trajectory.

Lucy of course had done this before, and it was all part of the show. "Find greatest predator which has lived, and taunt them with fleshiest creatures which has lived also... and has same colour hair as its favourite prey." (That would be me then. Thank you Lucy.)

She held the ship tilted slightly (I had the downward end - thank you again Lucy), and a feather's width higher than he could reach with snapping jaws like a rabid jumping terrier, only more terrierfying.

Seriously though the only comedic thing about the awful situation was his little arms, scrabbling feebly at thin air and completely useless, yet mechanically still coming into play.

He must have been as shocked as I was to see this silver disc appear, so why did he not show it? Well I soon remembered he must have seen a thousand of these flying pests before, so as to become like a mosquito to the poor brute.

After what seemed like an eternity, and after my pleading with Lucy to fly away - which she did not - (I feel ashamed to admit it now but you simply cannot imagine how overwhelming the instinct is to run from that sight), he lost interest. He stood there, a stout little thing really, and you could see him sniff the air, lifting his head up with each sniff, as the nostrils contracted just as bona fide as the veggiesaurus's muscles.

He opened and closed those crocodile jaws just thrice more, and gave an expression that habitually caused me to lip-read those jaw movements as saying, "Fine - buzz - off".

Lucy was right to leave me there beyond my comfort zone, because as he relaxed and accepted our presence as no threat, I concurred.

Oh well indeed. I asked Lucy in all seriousness not to do that again, for I was not as used to all of this as she, and as you know indeed was still trying in some ways to get over their FIRST visit to me, let alone their second, third, fourth... without having to deal with nearly being eaten by a Tyrannosaurus.

"So sorry to do it", she said looking really quite heartbroken.

I told her it was okay, and reminded her I had seen the funny side of the earlier event when I fell over.

I feel for her you know. That may seem a funny thing to say. She is so happy to be able to show me all these things, rather like I was to show her my old home. She is proud of what her people have achieved, and of what she has the capability to show to me, and rightly so. It led us to a number of discussions, some of which were quite moving, and you will not mind that we embraced at one point, if only as a show of solidarity and of two minds meeting, despite the generation gap. Having made her feel bad before, I simply took it as my mission to ensure she did not resent giving me these opportunities.

We must have talked for some thirty minutes back there 65 million years ago, just floating with a T-Rex now somewhat below and to the side of us.

To call it surreal would BE surreal, as there is nothing to call it that rings true.

I talked to her of how even 2001 I would look at the sky, at a jet liner flying past overhead, and as you know, think I must have time travelled forward from the 18th Century, so incredible was the sight to me. I feel like an olde English gentleman seeing a strange fiery throne shooting through the heavens. That in turn makes me discuss with her how it is perhaps plausible that Christ's followers, and others before them, would have mistook time ships for such fiery thrones, or heavenly bodies.

I also tell her how I therefore wonder if I am indeed reincarnated from such an olde fashioned gent, due to these eccentricities I carry, and as I now almost believe in reincarnation and the tunnel of light.

(It also occurs to me in reporting this whether that is why they attempt to talk in that olde world way...? Do they already know this of me?)

Well anyway, in response she confided something startlingly similar back to me.

"I every so often stare to skies at craft at... Dullice to find to consider 'what is this planet we are existing in'. At times also I experience that I am from downtime and do not feel right at this point, or that I am but the maiden who travelled uptime... where I am unfamiliar with all that."

To share two experiences so alike, yet so far apart in evolution, made her seem that much more human to me you know. So you can understand our embrace at least.

Another of the conversations turned to me, again. In the most unreal of settings, she expressed something that made me have to add another emotion to my list experienced that day.

"I worship you", she said. "He is one special being before me, I never to have known you with a negative utterance regarding any other. Even when slander came to him, he only will declare about his detractors that he wishes the best and that they will see light one day. You are cheerful, passionate, has immense delight in smaller things, and a deep love for all creatures in time."

Then she finished with quite a look on her grey face, "I always be here for you in eternity and perpetuity".

In a way, indeed she will.

"I am glad we have met", I responded to her.

I am.

"I am not discomfited or reluctant to pronounce I love you as greatly as Jo-at Mo", she concluded.

My dry mouth and frozen lips were without words.

Do you mind this? I am starting to feel concerned to tell you the full events if they include some form of compassionate embrace or kind words, yet I know I should not and I know your unending capacity to understand human nature.

Humanoid nature even.

No matter what I type, just know that I love you and that can never change.

And so, after time had passed, we flew away from the T-Rex who had finished eating his snack, to a watering hole, and I saw smallish black-fish creatures literally playing in the shore of the waters. It made my mind drift to that pivotal moment when the first fish through whatever genetic mutation, sprouted legs, and I imagine were able to immediately walk up out of the ocean, onto the beach, and explore a brave new world for the first time. Were these their early descendants, I wondered to myself, among a great many other wonderings.

Dawning on me then flew the answer to the mystery of why great whales beach themselves. That may sound random, however that innate mammalian instinct to leave the water behind and walk on the land explains it all... Watching these strange mortals, I immediately knew that instinct would have been the EXACT same desire experienced by that first sea mammal millions of years before. And through mammalian genes, it would still exist in whales today.

Again, one day in our future, one small whale will be born with a genetic mutation that gives it flippers that can act as legs, and once again a sea mammal will step out onto a beach if whales keep trying to beach themselves. With two such small creatur4es, reproduction would be possible, and a family of whales will get their wish to live outside the sea.

But until they achieve that, they will continue to be pushed back into the ocean and off the beaches by well-meaning humans. I imagine they think us quite rude.

Time travel makes these revelations come so clearly to me that I wonder if they have done something else to my mind - either to allow me some sort of enhanced ability to reach them myself, or to plant them in there for me to 'discover'.

After the incident with Lucy I spent my time looking out of the viewport, soaking it all in. Before long a pterodactyl-like bird - larger and strikingly different to the hairy one I had seen at Dullice Channel Station - flew right past the window. As it flapped its wings, and as I was on a train of thought of our instincts, I thought to footage one sees of humans falling from great heights. Off a diving board, out of a window, or a stuntman in a film. They all share one instinctive action - the flapping of the arms and legs, as if... well yes as if trying to fly. And again in that moment, here in the reality of it all, it was instantly clear to me like no-one before how the first birds had taken flight. Through another random gene 'flaw' one or two land-dwellers had grown something resembling a webbed arm or wing. And meeting with an accident after a great predator - not unlike the one that I had just met with - chased it off a cliff, that instinct we still have today had kicked in and whilst it had never amounted to a tin of beans before then, for that lucky chap with his webbed arm, he flapped whilst falling as we all do, but took to flight.

What a wonderful moment that would have been, and I felt sad that there was likely no way to have known exactly when or where it occurred so as to visit it.

And with that time to prophesise, I wondered what theories I might come up with in the future other than a working method for time travel. My mind never shuts down and I am not sure if I love that or hate it.

The moment passing, Lucy told me to activate my restraint again ash she had sensed my readiness for new stimuli and started to move the craft. But not sideways or down this time, just up. Up. Up. UP... Up so far Bella that the curvature of the Earth came into view and again my eyes moistened for our great planet where SO many events had unfolded, was soon completely visible to me and I could nearly cover its top with my hand. It was a most unusual and emotional day.

You have never seen such a beautiful sight and I really wish you could imagine it now. Take those NASA images we have all seen, and make them 3D in your mind if you can for a moment. Now make the clouds slowly move. And now add some stars to the sky. Look down at all the people back in our time, and all the wars, and see how they look like foolish tin soldiers shooting each other with silly tiny toy pellets. And to what end? For what gain at the end of the day - at the end of all time? Come up here and there clearly is none.

Awe-inspiring beauty like nothing on Earth. For it IS the Earth.

Which makes what happened next all the more shatteringly devastating.

Lucy called me to look the other way, at what I had not noticed.

A GARGANTUAN splintered rock, the same size as the Moon from our perspective, was flying in orbit around the Earth. Two moons? No wait, not in orbit... it was flying TOWARDS the Earth.

I immediately knew of course what this particular sightseeing tour was all about now, and why we could not stay for too long a time.

It was the year 65,391,934 BC if I remember it rightly, the end of the Cretaceous period, and the end of the age of the dinosaurs.

And THIS was the mass extinction. Not a mass euthanasia by Extapien scientists as I had postulated - unless they organised this - but a real life honest to God meteorite of seismic proportions. And it was happening here and now for me. This was no action replay, no simulation, this was the one and only time it would ever happen, and I was back there watching it!

As it entered the Earth's atmosphere just below us, it all happened so quickly.

A flash of light.

The front of it lit up like a bonfire.

Great clouds whooshed away leaving a ghostly silhouette of the meteor's shape as effortlessly as wafting candle smoke with your hand.

Streaks and debris followed beside it, the smaller bits of which turned into great fireballs too, their fronts flaring up like a newly lit match.

Then right below me...

IT HIT.

The seas parted as if that biblical event had referred to such an instant (which again gets me thinking) and those seas shot up as high as the clouds, as if the waters might even escape the very atmosphere itself and drown our craft had we been any nearer.

The angry outburst of water and dirt and dust and I hate to say it dinosaurs was so huge that I thought the very world would shatter. Seeing the planet from here as a football, it was as though it had a boot-sized puncture in its side.

And worst of all, with all that happening, Lucy began to drive the craft TOWARDS the cataclysmic devastation!

And then an even brighter detonation and I was sure we would be incinerated.

And as suddenly as it had started, in a blur we were IN the crater.

But not the crater of then, but the crater of years ahead.

A peaceful, dead crater of the future.

Lucy was no fool with my life. That last flash was not from the meteor, but rather was us travelling forward in time as well as downward in space, before things got too intense. (!) She or the autopilot had throttled the ship into the future and the image had flicked instantly as if there were a lengthy piece of footage missing from a film, to reveal just this harmless, lifeless old hollow that now sat below me. Immense in size, it seemed to have been twenty times as large as the meteor that I had witness cause it.

And so we had flashed between two very different worlds, two atmospheres, yet the same world and the same space the atmosphere had always shared. The same atoms that were once a fire-breathing meteor were now inert stone, yet they were all the same atoms nonetheless.

"This the Chicxulub Crater", I heard in my head. Though I already knew it... and wondered then if Lucy had said it.

Either way, this was one hell of a sightseeing tour. And I do mean 'hell'.

Too much so that it was ripping my emotions to shreds, being pulled from pillar to post, from detonation to serenity, from deathly destruction to peaceful tranquillity, like this.

I had not even had time to grieve for the big old dino-girl we had visited just hours before walking majestically past me for the very first time. I had felt such a connection to her through my childhood to now, yet I had also been brought to watch her imminent inevitable horrific death. The last witness of her last moments on Earth.

I even would have shed a tear for the great predator that had scared me so when he followed the veggiesaurus on our tour.

But I was glad Lucy had taken us forward to now, because before I had had time to even think to grieve, it was as if it had always been. Once in the crater, her death had happened half a million years ago. The time for mourning long since passed. This was no different now to back in 2001, and I had as little right to mourn then as I do in 2001.

But still I was an emotional wreck inside, although I held it together very well for her I am proud to tell you.

In hindsight, I had needed to visit somewhere after the crater so as to centre me. But before I knew that I needed it, Lucy had the place. She suggested I might like again to visit my childhood home, as it was BEFORE it was my childhood home.

Back in the time of the dinosaurs!

She suggested she could approximate where the landmasses that ended up as my town were some 65.5 million years before. Fantastically she could travel back to the beginning of our tour then 'drive' us to my home. And so she did.

And then I was back! The very same date we had just left, arriving at the same time we had originally arrived and in the same space. And then that other SHE was back! The big old girl who galumphed past me a few hours earlier and been horrifically slaughtered by an atomic blast was peacefully strolling along this grassland, moving in much the same way as before, although not everything she did looked identical (although I could not be sure). The flash of light of our arrival perhaps in a slightly different position, may have affected her differently to last time, who knows.

But it was like her reincarnation to me! And when I said I felt no right to mourn because she had always been dead, I now had even less right to mourn because she had always also been alive. At this moment in time, she would never fail to survive. This was her great realm, and she inhabited it - nothing could ever change that.

And so with the correct date reached, I waited for Lucy to shoot us to the correct location with a flash that I hoped would have blinded the big old girl so she might not have to witness the horror of seeing a Moon fall from the sky.

But there was no flash.

And I asked Lucy when we were going to travel to my home.

But she revealed to me another of her little tricks. We were ALREADY there. She had selected this place with that in mind from the start of the tour.

I had been here all along!

If you can even begin to imagine the other layers that peeled off the experience, I will reward you with a solid gold onion.

It had been nothing I could recognise as home, of course. She had pinpointed an exact spot on the ground where she said my home was later to be built, after the landmass had separated and my country drifted off to become an island. The friendly dinosaur had just walked over my kitchen. The T-Rex had jumped up and down at us near the end of my road. And the watering hole was now a river - although who knows whether it was the same source or just a coincidence.

This small patch of land would one day be on that very island, and indeed some of the creatures that were currently hiding from me, and the one that had now almost passed me by, soon to pass away, might very well become fossilised from this very day into the ground, and have existed under my feet - under my living room - for my entire childhood.

In fact not 'might', it would certainly have. That lovely dinosaur I had just seen reincarnated, buried near the garden shed along with the family pets.

There are no words. I deactivated the restraint and just walked over to hug Lucy. I loved this strange creature so VERY much for giving me these experiences. My mind was filled with wonder and enlightened stimulation up to a capacity I am sure it has never even experienced before, such is the delight and wonder at these events.

I would recommend this ride to anyone!

I expressed to her about that capacity, and how she was lighting up my brain, and how I was now becoming all the more confident for it. You of all know how insecure I can be due to the life I have had to lead just as you did.

Her words came like honey.

"Stop punishing yourself for being amazingly creative gifted human being. Don't craft rules to shackle yourself. There is no price to pay. Soar. Being small benefits no-one."

She is right. Annoyingly. And I am so aware of that I even fail to notice the all-too-obvious joke I could have made to her in hindsight, she the smallest of beings.

Am I too growing and changing through time, beyond some certain recognition? Do I seem different to you now, compared to a week ago? Hell, I feel it!

But I was to travel to one other location and time period - like so many time tourists must have done before me. But this one not so detailed in history. For after perhaps another fifteen minutes of quiet contemplation, I expressed to her that I hoped to venture from that very spot, to wherever that spot and the fossils moved to on Earth, and over time where the River Thames flowed south from inland, to finally have its inevitable date with the great ocean. I wanted to see this place on the banks of Greater London as it was just before the first settlers arrived. JUST before it was touched - and some might say spoiled - by mankind.

And that we should leave preferably before the meteor returned, again.

I - as I am sure have you if I know you at all - have always held a fascination for what gorgeous tranquil meadows may have once lay under the footprints of these concrete cities we apparently chose to build as 'improvements' to life. I yearn for what has gone before we smothered over nature's pastures with brick and mortar, metal and plastic, fumes and noise, hustle and bustle. How simple was life just before that pivotal moment when the first settlers arrived and began that inevitable spiral - some would say a downward one? Were there leopards, mammoths, kangaroos, or polar bears roaming where we now do?

I have all too often walked along the busy main road outside home, and caught a glimpse of a small patch of grass between two houses separated by an alley, and considered whether that may be the one remnant of that idyllic time, untouched by man.

Perhaps even a patch of land where no man has happened to ever tread before.

And I have so often been driven down a meandering narrow side road lined with houses, small boxy gardens behind them, and wondered what it was like before even the time it was a meandering horse and cart track lined with trees, and acres of field behind them.

And I was to get my chance.

A long story short, I was returned home to recuperate - and goodness knows I needed it. Perhaps Lucy did too. She would return on Sunday, and I would make sure I was in.

And return she did.

350 BC.
Tuesday.

'It is a beautiful summer's day on the banks of The River Thames here on the 26th of June, and the news today from your roving reporter is that... nothing happened. At all. For decades.'

Well, that is how I feel! Am I not bringing the headlines from so many points in history direct to your door? I hope you are enjoying the broadcasts.

My pilot had set a date arbitrarily to investigate whether it would be safe for me to disembark the ship and explore as I had so wanted to do. After the now familiar vibrating, dimming, smell, flash, and quiet, we were there. And at the exact moment my eyes focus on the natural beauty below me I have no idea why I imagined fields and neatly mown meadows. I should be beginning to learn by now that things are never quite how one imagines the will be.

For below me was the meandering river, wider than I remember it, the familiar bend near which I still today type this (incredible!) yet not fields... but a sparsely wooded young forest of sorts, with sporadic episodes of trees, mixed with yet more sporadic clusters of shrubbery.

Life was having a field day here, if not a field.

Speaking of plants, Lucy seems to plant telepathically into my mind, after scouting the immediate area, "To this side is his little shelters, but where you wish to stopover is my command and quite safe there. If it eventuates for any roaming herdsmen to come to your way, loyal servant shall come first."

And with that it is settled. As is the craft. And despite the expanse of time, I know almost exactly where home is judging by the geography I see below me. So little changes in what we consider a long time. But now I have a new perspective and realise a couple of thousand years is the blink of the mind's eye, and a blink of mine. Compare it to 65 million years and it is hard to ignore the fact.

The shape of the river must not have changed in a hundred-thousand years it seems, so definite and determined. So like I would do to a taxi driver, I point her to where I would love to be dropped. Well, preferably not dropped, but you know. Right there - where I walk the dog along the bank. Only there is no Max here... and I wonder what molecules on the Earth now she will one day be made from.

She finds a spot and I walk down to the bottom level of this contemporary craft, distinct in its contrast to the untouched beauty around me, almost running with excitement to find what I may find, but not too fast to notice the sick bay of this ship has been sealed off. I hope I will not need it.

And then down.

Touching the ground feels good - any ground - for I had been travelling for so long.

But what ground!? I slowly feel a sinking sensation, and realise this bank is not what it used to be - I mean will be - it is largely gravelly marshland in this spot. Of course there is no manmade towpath here.

I squelch back to sturdier ground, and the chute disappears upward into thin air.

Then suddenly I am home, alone. More alone than ever in this desolate version of my town.

And I am looking at the Thames. I could very well wade across to the other side, were it not for the fact that the other side looks much like this one. But what a side! Gazing across I try to superimpose in my mind where those familiar offices, pubs, and homes once were - I mean are - such deserted peace now at the moment I am in. It is so truly 'right' and beautiful and how it should always be, that I pine for it in retrospect more than when I had just envisaged it but never truly known. I was right to wonder.

Forwards is surely backwards in so many ways, and I wonder whether I was driven to the eurora potential for means other than furthering man's footprint on the future - perhaps rather I wanted it for this one very precise moment in time that I now inhabit. The perfect moment of yesteryear.

Yet another thing strikes me, and that is how similar it indeed is to those country walks we had, and places that DO still exist this very day. So what right do I have to pine, for humanity HAS preserved those areas. Indeed if I so wished, I could travel right now to the countryside and walk along another marshy river bank surrounded by woodland. Yet there would always be some such things as an electricity pylon above, a row of houses behind, a bridge to the right, and 'no littering' sign to the left. And I now know that there is something quite different and special about imagining a FAMILIAR place in simpler more idyllic times, compared to seeing somewhere unfamiliar, in its usual simplicity.

It would never be as beautiful as what I saw Bella. And I saw it!

What I would give to travel back again with you and set up a home there.

(And very likely be promptly eaten by a woolly mammoth.)

I savoured that moment looking at the river so I could find the exact spot I had memorised, and stand there again today - a thing which I have not yet had the chance to, I have been writing about it all for so long. I must go and do it soon. I am still getting over what I saw back then, before I reconvene in the now however.

And that moment passing, I turned around, and plodded my way inland.

The squelching soon turned to definite solidity of gravely soil and grassland, and my shins soon lightly brushed through ferns and tough long grasses sprouted out of little mounds, on bigger mounds and, in turn on small hilly patches the more I strode inland. I liked the flicking clicking feeling they made on my shoes, as it pressed home to me that I really was here, making these steps - perhaps the first human to ever do so.

But at this perspective, my earlier over-confidence of knowing exactly where home was, escaped me somewhat, as I could no longer judge quite where I was in relation to the river. The further I walked the harder that got.

And just as I was starting to feel somewhat foolish, wondering about in a field I could not possibly recognise, a blue beam flashed on and off in the distance like a guiding beacon saying 'here!' Lucy had seen that I was wondering off course - and of course they know precisely where I live, in co-ordinate terms.

I followed the guiding light, hoping nobody else was.

As I walked I had to make a concerted effort to imagine what I was walking on the footprints of now, and by that I mean not woolly mammoths that may have walked here before me, but the footprints of the shopping parade, side roads, or others' homes. Where I had last week stood and watched my song play out of the shop window, was firstly perhaps that small silvery tree. And where I had walked the dog along the towpath was likely first that area of mush.

But far off to my left in the distance is a faint plume of smoke, and I stop stark with fear as a pulse of adrenalin waves up me. It is entirely likely I am not alone. And may well have company before too long. I quicken my pace slightly, even though the smoke was a great distance away by foot. Which I am sure is all they have.

And then before too long, I arrive.

Home. (Give or take 2,351 years.)

A field of small unkempt nut-bearing trees, long grasses, and a pond. This was where I had been guided to, and it felt right. This was my part of town.

And I cannot describe to you the intrigue and marvel of looking down at my shoes right now while I type this in my apartment, and knowing that what I was looking down at just yesterday is right there below where I sit today, all those years ago.

I found a suitable grassy mound, and dropped down on it, my legs crossed to take up the slack. And that was the moment. The one I had always dreamed of and wondered about. It was profoundly moving. Yet eerie.

The intensity of the grasses around the small trees strikes me almost as if I am in some African grassland - the greens are so green and vivid in colour, each of the taller stems shining in the glorious sunshine, but even more striking is the wildlife all around me - small birds, and even crickets are what I can see now I sit to consider them.

I glanced over to where the smoke had been, now just a small wisp of grey. Who were these early settlers, or were they just passing through? Could they even be my great great (...) grandparents? I know nothing to be impossible now.

Once that thought passed, I realised I was having a sincere issue with believing that this really was where home will one day be. No - not in believing it, but in taking it in. I had simply walked from a small tributary over some grassland and sat down on a knoll. This could be ANY such idyllic place in the Scottish highlands or the Cotswolds.

Would I have to travel back to see this place in an ice age to really have it walk up and slap me round the face to take it in. Yes, I did grow frustrated with myself I admit. And I resolved at that moment to do something - I did not know what then - to prove to myself this was all real. To leave some sort of message in the past - some message that I could go and check back in the present. I looked around for something I could engrave or change, but there was simply nothing here that would exist unchanged back in 2001.

Sitting on the stump, it fascinated me that around me were surely the same sounds, and definitely the same colours. Those birds flew past me, the grass was still green, and it truly put into perspective what a brief brief snatch of time animals have occupied, that nature had changed so imperceptibly between 2001, 200 BC, and even 65.5m BC, for those ferns and grasses - well I would not have known had Lucy taken me to the Cretacious period and told me it was 350 BC, then to 350 BC and told me to look for a dinosaur. Either really could be either.

Our time on Earth is as insignificant as that wisp of smoke in the vast blue atmosphere.

Speaking of which I am glad I again wore sunscreen, for I would surely be burning by this point otherwise.

I rested there for quite some time - how long I am not entirely sure - perhaps twenty minutes, perhaps an hour. And I watched the long grass lean to the left, blown by a wind I could neither see, nor hear.

And it dawns on me that that is a dead wind, now.

And there are no planes in the sky to make me wonder if I am from the past. Except our own invisible one, to remind me I am from the future.

Goodness, let me say that again... 'I am from the future'. Crikey.

Yet it feels as though I am just out for a stroll in the park.

Incredible to think I was actually likely sitting in the bath. (That is, where my bathroom will be centuries from then.) Agh, this perplexes my mind as I look up from the screen and remember that bathroom is now just over there, here and now as I type! I was talking about it as though it does not yet exist. It feels like those times you lie in bed thinking about the bedroom, and forgetting you are already in it... you know? Agh I could go mad wondering why I have not yet gone mad.

And once that time was up, and I had seen more than I could process, I stood up but did not know how to summon Lucy. I would feel ridiculous to wave my arms in the direction of the ship, only to have her materialise behind me, like when you wait for elevator doors to open, only to realise they have... behind you.

I was conscious always to not disappoint them any longer since our first encounter, and to act as much like the idol that they were projecting onto me as I could.

But then, having stood up and having a wider perspective, I saw people coming towards me! I cannot convey the sheer terror that froze me to the grass, as if I were stuck in a sudden ice age or back in the mud of the bank and had become adhered to it. (Wait, yes I can - it was almost exactly like the terror the T-Rex caused!) I kept completely and utterly still, like Nelson's Column could not even achieve I tell you. They were still far away, a group of perhaps five or seven people, but they were advancing fast, and in my definite direction. I could barely see their clothing, but it seemed surprisingly civilised - although I have no idea what I should have expected. And then coming into view, the odd glimpse of a dog (or wolf I now wonder), as it bounded up over a mound only to disappear back down under the horizon of grasses.

If I could hear them, I think I would hear attack in every noise that emanated from their direction.

'Where is Lucy?!'

'Should I run?!'

I started to walk left, then right, as if I were caught in a tractor beam.

And then I realised I was caught in a tractor beam.

"You left that a little late!", I tried saying to Lucy, also trying to sound relaxed and also trying not to trip over things that were not there on the craft, my legs so like jelly in aftershock.

"I had notion you sought to observe them", she replied ever so sweetly. She had not felt I would mind, and that I must have somehow telepathically realised that she would of course grasp me at the right moment. Well I am telepathic after all. I could not possibly feel anything against her.

But whatever must primitive men have made of a disappearing man and the blue rain from the invisible cloud. I shall never know. (Not until I read the bible at least, to see what they made of that other similar event. Agh again my brain hiccoughs as I realise I could go into the other room right now and read that very bible, and see that very account of witnesses to Christ's ascension into the belly of my very invention! I wonder what The Bible originally said, before such changes - if it even deemed the events worthy enough for the disciples to write about. Had I changed - or even been responsible for the existence of - The Bible?!)

In any event, our travels were over for the day, and with a flash we were in the same place. Just a different time - 2001 again. The brick around me immediately sent me pining for those grasslands.

The knowledge that they would 'always' be 'there' was of some comfort.

I had to embrace Lucy before I went, because what she had shown me meant more to me than anything anybody could ever imagine anything ever meaning to me. I hope you have experienced through my journals Bella just a glimpse into what I saw with my very own eyes, because if you have then I have done my job to share it with you.

"Priceless memories!", she exclaimed after she pulled away. "Next time the memories will be made simultaneously with you, more permanence that way, and no 'bleak light of day' following."

I am not entirely sure what she means, but she continues, "Discern true joy in simplicity and clarity, believe in abundance, love with no condition, and you to become that being you are inside, the one with luminosity of being.

"Sir... Trust, and BECOME."

I returned home, and fell asleep almost as soon as I collapsed on the bed. I feel like I slept for a day.

Writing this has exhausted me all over again.

This morning, with a slightly clearer head, I was in the kitchen making a recovery drink, and I dropped the sugar bowl. It went everywhere. "OH SH**...ugar!", I had shouted out loud, which made me laugh to myself. Bending down to sweep it up, my hand had touched the floor...

'Was this the very spot I might have walked on thousands of years ago, yet just the other day?', I could not help but consider.

I cannot tell you the number of ways that sugar blew my mind. It was if an ancient ghost of me was right there... with me. Or a distant long since dead ancestor who was also myself. SO much time had passed since then - now ceramic tiles where once savages ran toward me. And where once I very much expect cows grazed, now soya milk in the fridge.

I suspected at that moment that I had achieved a perspective on the world that no man before had ever surmounted.

That is what inventing a time machine does for you.

I really must go - there is so much to do, and Max has been pitifully ignored.

So I am off... to trust. And become.

Love you so much.

Will report more soon I am sure!

Day Twenty

Posted by Eurora001 on Wed 27-Jun-2001 21:15

Well this is turning out to be quite a week! In quite a fortnight. The simplest way to explain what I have been up to is...

'Driving lessons'.

Yes, in a flying time saucer.

And wonderful, fantastic, utterly magnificent, definitive news! I cannot wait to tell you, although I do not quite believe it myself, nor will I until I see it for sure.

But wait, all things in order...

It began in the usual way just this morning, only when I got into the ship Alfred was there for a welcome change. I had not seen him for a few days and this may sound strange but I had somewhat missed his warming authority, his trustworthiness, and even the unusual way he walked - as if every step were a carefully placed child's endeavour, or he were used to some other degree of gravity.

I had enjoyed the time alone with Lucy however. I was able to appreciate this in hindsight - with him now back - that when it was just the two of us it had a quality not all that uncommon to being left in charge of the house by my parents. Quite a thrill, and you were always disappointed when they came back from their day out, in a way.

Days out here, for me, are somewhat more exciting however.

His warmth was not far behind his walk to greet me downstairs, as he actually apologised for being so busy the past few days.

"So sorry to be in this way. Events always precede my wants."

But to make up for it (though I did not mind one bit) they had a treat for me. Yes, another.

They wished to present me with my own time ship.

(I can see the shock on your face Bella!)
(Can you therefore even imagine my own!?)

The ship was not to keep, sadly (and I am still as sad now as I type it, and again think of how wondrously valuable that would be - after all, the possibility of being reunited with you is partly what had inspired me in the first place). However, it would be mine to use, "for the extents of our association".

This made it bitter-sweet, because I knew that not only was something wonderful about to happen, but that in so doing it, I drew the end nearer into sight. The end of my knowing these people... I am going to lose them too Bella, for surely they will not stay with me for life. They have their own world to get back to. It seems I lose everything wonderful that comes into my life for all too short a time.

But they are here now (well not literally), and I continue to try to stay sane and savour all the weird and wonderful moments, even though I do not know which way is up these days.

The plan for the day was outlined to me. They had arrived in one of the oldest working craft they had (the most technologically modern contraption you can imagine), as they wished it to be as close as possible to my original incarnation, and so effectively present 'my ship' to me just as I had envisaged it! Even though it was quite different, naturally.

I imagine another reason was that the controls would be as close to what we in the Old World would be capable of... well, controlling. Think of it as a tricycle with stabilisers, with their most advance ship being a Harley Davidson.

Only this tricycle had an invisibility cloaking retro-fit.

In many ways however this primitive craft - that I can only assume was kept in some sort of museum under Dullice Channel Station - was still similar to the craft Lucy and I had travelled in the other day, although I knew it was different because the interior was laid out in a mirror image to the last one (the sick bay was on the left, the ramp up to the next floor was on the right...). Other than that it was little different, and it did strike me as peculiar that they make identical ships with mirrored interiors. Rather like left and right hand drive cars, though not at all for those reasons of course.

Anyway, in order to allow me the privilege of the use of my own creation (quite right too)... they would teach me how to fly it.

Yes.

Absurd!

And that is what I have done today!

We went to two locations, and I will tell you all about it now. It was quite 'eventful' shall we say. Wait until you hear.

I shall not bore you with the actual lesson details - they would be of no use to you, however the layout of the cockpit too was somewhat the same as the one Lucy had controlled, and luckily as I may have mentioned - I watched her at the time, making mental notes, albeit back then just for my own peace of mind and security - as it was just the two of us after all. (What if something should happen to her and I be left stranded near the mouth of a T-Rex? Of course I need not have worried, but I assure you that you would have also.)

The briefing on the use of the controllers and 'dashboard' took perhaps ten minutes. And that shocked me. I had imagined I would be there all day if not week, but with advances in technology it seems there also comes advances in convergence, simplification, and an intense amount of AI - Artificial Intelligence - to fill in the gaps and join the dots in what is needed by the user.

Say when driving a car, to turn round a corner you have to guide the wheel precisely around the curve. Then another turn. Then a hundred more before you reach your destination. Yet in the craft today, all I had to do was enter what is essentially an enhanced form of GPS location that incorporates not only longitude and latitude, but also altitude, date and time. They call it a Scoron. The navigational device does the rest, calculating its way around known - and unpredicted - obstacles in space and in time, faster than the craft itself can travel. Quite a radar then!

And although the controls accepted our own Gregorian calendar dates (else the process may have taken quite a lot longer to learn), they did not use that calendar themselves and it was there as an "attuned legacy". It seems they work in a number of formats, as if to accommodate earlier and later travellers alike. And I am that early traveller, yet not the earliest. Somehow it makes me feel I belong, and that it is all not quite so crazy.

Incidentally, Alfred explained that our calendar's current format had been lost long ago, partly due to the length of the year AD that had been reached, and partly for reasons he was not allowed to discuss. 'Gravity Pull?' But in any event, the calendar was overhauled. He does not tell me the name of the new format, and I assume there is no such name in our English.

I feel so old-fashioned and out of place again.

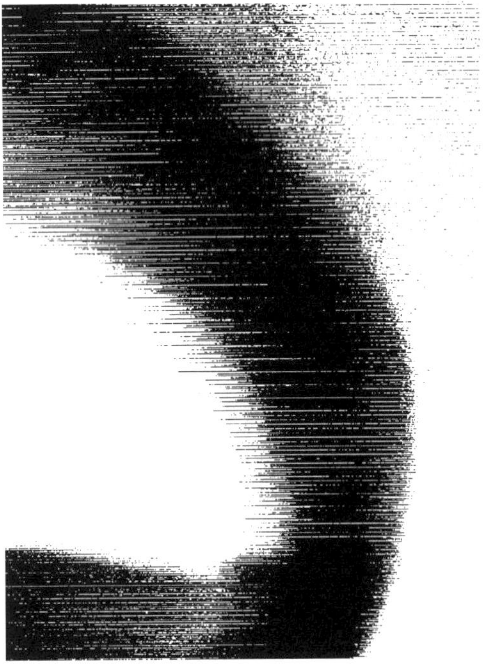

The length of time taken to show me the rest of the system was essentially on use of the slick white control stick, which can be used to manually manoeuvre the craft around once at a destination. This is what Lucy had been doing during the dinosaur encounter, as entering a series of different altitudes would have been ridiculous, and although clearly able to use the telepathic interface she had chosen not to for my comfort. That said, I very much hope the end of the ride when I had been shot up into the atmosphere to watch the great meteor HAD been pre-programmed. I just would hate to think that I had been at the mercy of manual controls, no matter how much I have had to trust these people.

Being in the driving seat of this mighty contraption drives me to ask Alf something.

"So where DID you source the power to drive the craft?", I say turning behind and nodding in the direction of the central cylinder.

Alf answers, "Your statement is fantastic! Remember this is your power creation, but we of course understand our ancestors had to cross some 'i's and dot some 't's."

(Their 'Chinglish' dialect is still almost hilarious - if I am not imagining it. It is the one thing that makes me doubt my sanity over all of this. Surely only a Chinese Englishman from 1900 could talk like that.)

He continues, less hilariously, "Have you considered knowledge from your 21st century that one human has within him energy of 30 hydrogen missiles? Actually it is not quite right but still, can you think of a way to harness this for part of power? I do not mind pass you more answers if you not get plenty. "

"No, but I would like to think about it, if that is okay?"

"You are the nicest."

I can think of a few ways that might be plausible. Food for thought - another day when I am hungry for it perhaps - I am so full now.

The briefing took place without a chance to actually practice the driving. But after the briefing had finished, my chance came.

There was some discussion about where to go, but there is somewhere I had been wanting to visit for some time. I have not had the opportunity to travel there for so long, even though it is here in England. I have not written about it here as... well... I have not written it to you. But I chose the place... and it was all about you.

I shall just tell you. I wanted to visit the site of your grave.

But not now.

Rather, at a time where it did not exist. Where you were not dead, you see? Where you had not even been born yet.

Goodness, getting into the psychology of this in writing rather pushes one to consider all the intricacies of such a decision, but yes, I wanted to experience a place in the world when all that good was still to come, and so a world full of wonder and expectation where you were still to exist, and we were still to be together in the future. None of that had even happened yet, so much to look forward to, and definitely no... well, no tombstone with your name on it.

I am not sure if you can see the logic in that oddest of desires?

And I suppose I have never told you something...

I should. I hope you already may know it.

I had penned the epitaph for your gravestone.

To live on, in the hearts of loved ones;
That's not to die, so don't say goodbye.
We will meet again, God knows when;
In that special place, I will see your face.

Those words - created in such pain - always bring that pain back. I have a lump in my throat now. I think that is why I have never written them to you. THIS is why - my face is why! Look at it!

Enough. Be strong man.

So, I entered a date into the Scoron, an amalgum of your date of birth only with the day and month as the year, and the year as the day and month, left the time as it was, and moved my mouse to the Start button. Haha sorry I could not resist that. I was joking of course - there was no mouse.

Ha sorry, again. Of course, no mouse or Start button either. (Although for all I knew this was Windows Million.)

Once I had set all the data, it was Lucy and Alfred's turn to be passengers, as they strapped themselves in behind me -

perceptibly tighter than before I was sure. I did the same in my seat.

When I was all set, I looked to Alfred for the okay nod.

You could not have cut the tension in the atmosphere with a knife. It was too tense even for a machete.

He replied, "You Captain, Alfred Navigator!", in a forlorn comedic 'voice'. I really liked this man at that moment! (Yet still hesitate to call him that - am I the bigot?)

And then he gave the nod.

My heart was in my throat, in fact it had travelled beyond my throat and I could 'hear it' in my inner ear and feel it on my tongue as the air pulsated out of my mouth with every beat like a hot dog.

Then I formed the required 'go' pattern on the panel with my five fingers and held it in the way I had been briefed, until it gave me back the small soft static-like acknowledgement response to my fingertips, and then it all began.

The process was no different technically to before, yet totally and utterly different from my perspective as the driver. I - was doing this. My design realisation... realised, and me as the pilot!

I was not sure if it was the vibration of the craft (which seemed abnormal to me) or my own disbelief that was causing me to shake. Yet it was an older craft.

Everything went dim as before, then the giddying motion was endured momentarily, and then the viewport scene of the side of my apartment was replaced by an entirely different landscape.

BEAUTIFUL - we swooped down between a gap in the clouds towards the English countryside a millennia ago.

And I had entered everything correctly (of course - they would not have let me do otherwise), as I was beside the river exactly where I had intended to be.

However, my plan of finding no grave worked somewhat too well.

There was no church either.

I had been under the impression the church had always been on this site. Well, not always, but for longer than we had travelled back. Yet apparently it had moved since then (depending on your perspective in time), as Lucy pointed to it far to our left out of the window!

Of course, IT had not moved, the new one had. That was the true one we were looking at now, far away.

I considered whether to skip forward in time to try some dates when the church we held your service in actually began to exist. Yet, I was in wide open air, fields and little cottages and the odd manor around me, the huge river beside me, and the perfect place for a flying lesson.

I felt I knew what to do, and after Alfred had reminded me how to tease the stick into any of the 360 3D degrees, I began.

I nudged the stick up, and we went up! Then down a bit. Left a bit. To me to you, to you to me. I was flying a flying saucer Bella! It responded beautifully. There was a lot of adjustment which was not of my doing - a stabilising sensation so even if I stopped moving it suddenly, there was a nice cushion of buffer to ease us into that same place I intended us to enter, only more professionally. It made me feel like quite the ace pilot!

However, I should not have felt so overly confident so soon. I was shortly to be made to doubt I had ever had even the brain capacity to devise this device, so foolish was I about to be. What I would give to go back in time and not do what I did.

Ironic no?

I do not even wish to tell this story. I had swept very slowly towards the small Church that we saw, for that had been the plan and it was somehow nice that not only were there no burial places, but not even a church on the other site. It made your passing seem even more distant and unreal, as though it had never happened. As it COULD never happen.

And so we - I - (!) flew to have a brief look at the original one. I reached an area over the tiny graveyard - so small that I wondered if anyone had ever lived here at all.

I wonder now where THOSE graves are - under someone's kitchen tiles?

Now, bear in mind, this craft does not tilt when one flies diagonally - it always seems to remain horizontal, however an experienced flyer such as Lucy can disable this gyroscopic balancing which is designed to minimise sickness, indeed I think I mentioned that Lucy indeed did disable it in the other ship when giving me a better view the other day of the scary wonders diagonally below me.

It was my intention to do the same, and give my passengers a nice view of Ye Olde English Church, as tilting would be required. In my mind I was at this point giddy with glee, and I must admit, rather playing along with the game of taking THEM on a sightseeing tour, just as Lucy had taken me. But I should not have seen this as an opportunity to 'play'. It was deadly serious.

Stupid, agh I hate myself.

Well, to cut a long story short, I engaged the control pad to disengage the gyroscope, using the technique Alfred had fleetingly mentioned.

Only I had mis-remembered it in my excitement.

And disengaged...

Agh I bare not even say it! Oh goodness, well... I turned off the CLOAKING.

We became VISIBLE!

I had not even realised it, but they knew all too well the different sounds and nuances of the craft. And one thinks it may not have mattered, as there was not a soul around on the ground - dead or alive - but clearly it did to both Alfred and Lucy. A great deal. They retracted their restraints instantly and their little bodies shot forward towards me. 'They're going to get me!', I remember thinking fleetingly. But no they fumbled for the cloak sensor pad, as I realised and attempted to also, but my firm grip sent Alfred's feeble hand off course and he hit what I was soon to discover was the elevator descent pole.

Now we were visible, tilted, and had a long foot sticking out of the bottom of the craft.

I find this unbearable to discuss - can you imagine my mortification upon realising?

I find it unbearable because it got worse.

Much worse.

It seemed we had got stuck, as the combination of tilting the craft and extending the elevator pole with its flat round base must have lodged it under something on the ground. The options were to fly upward risking taking half of the roof or whatever we were caught on up with us (for we could not see it as the viewport only showed us the tilted side view but never the underside), or retract the elevator also risking the same. Or activate the cloak and show the pole. None good choices.

Alfred had other ideas, and once we had established that we were stuck without using great force, he sat back into his seat, closed his eyes, and seemed to meditate on it for a moment. Lucy looked at me, and had I not been so concerned I may well have had presence of mind to roll my eyes at her jokily. She seemed to want to say the same with her face to me - I hoped. For a second we were alone again on a ship, in a way. But then Alfred came to. I had wondered if he were trying to 'use the force' to disengage us - nothing really would have surprised me you know.

But the calm that he achieved in that moment was admirable.

He stood up and announced, "I will rescue me".

I do not think he meant it heroically, nor melodramatically. In any event, he continued. "JoAx Fo extend..." (I do not know what word he said and do not want to misquote him, but it was the shower chute that had come down) and although I had never seen a ship with both an elevator platform and chute - let alone with them both descended simultaneously (as they were used for different circumstances) - it was clearly possible as I saw moments later.

We all hurried down to the lower platform, Alfred less hurried than I had expected. But Lucy stopped him.

And they conversed at length.

Something was afoot.

There was a problem with Alfred going.

Then they turned to me.

"Please you go."

"Me go?", me asked.

"Yes you go. If a person should see one us, it will bring great disturbance to their township, yet to see you another sapiens will be fine."

I could see the logic, and had used the chute almost countless times before, but still - this was the first time I would ever actually set foot on the recent past, and I was to have to waste the fantastical moment in sheer terror trying to rescue he?

Yet, I had caused the problem, so I should very well fix it.

They watched me descend down through the opening, to go and free the craft, and indeed they must have gone back up to watch whatever they could of events outside and ensure there was no interaction.

But far from it.

There was HORROR.

Bella, two dozen people had congregated a distance from us, staring up at us! They - were - looking - at - me.

Why was this more frightening that the T-Rex.

We had not put the cloak back on. I knew this was for the same reason and they had surely not forgotten about it. (What is the lesser of two evils - seeing a man descend from a ship, or seeing a man descend out of thin air?!)

I called to Lucy for help or advice. Alfred seemed in my head to simultaneously realise this. She agreed with my supposition and said to me that what these people were seeing would be compounded if our ship then also vanished into thin air, leaving me apparently levitating, and so I should just proceed speedily.

I did not agree and made it known, but her experience counts for a lot and I suspect she was right.

I 'felt' Lucy move to the controls, so she could attempt teasing them to free us, in case I had removed whatever the obstacle was if possible, yet I had not even found my feet yet.

Bella I cannot convey the sheer rigid terror of seeing a crowd of people watching me aghast, in a mixture of dread, anger, and some women panicking while two children watched in amazement with what I think was a nervous, curious smile.

I have never been good in social situations, but this was ridiculous.

I was here, interacting with the past generations, and in the most dangerous way!

I centred myself, and centred my vision to the task at hand. Thinking, 'less haste more speed', I purposefully moved outside of the chute to try to push the pole in the precise direction that would dislodge it, for it had gone in with some force. The landing platform could not have gotten itself any better wedged under the gravestone if it had grown there. The juxtaposition of the old and the new materials was somehow suddenly as shocking to me (in the realisation of just what goings on I was now involved in), as it must have been to the bystanders.

But just then, a flurry of them (who I then realised must have come out of the church itself as some were remarking irately at some damage we had apparently done) rushed towards me. We must have given the door quite a 'knock knock'.

At first I thought they were coming to offer assistance, as that is believe it or not one's natural instinct when one's vehicle is stuck and someone rushes to your aid. But no.

Then I saw the anger in one of the men's face. My God.

I had witnessed in my mind a flash of being kidnapped by unhappy locals and burnt alive at the stake as a witch or some such being.

Thankfully two things occurred in very quick procession that prevented that outcome (obviously - I would hardly be writing to you from my stake - although if I was a witch I suppose I could).

Firstly, in sheer clear-minded panic, I pushed the pole with all my adrenalin-fuelled capacity, and suddenly it moved surprisingly easily once the plate was free of the stone, grating itself out of the way pulling a moss and soil sample onto it for us to take back to the future. There was damage to it, remnants left behind on the ground, which stunned me for a few long milliseconds (to coin a phrase) as it rematerialised itself into a perfect polished mint condition! Of course I had never before witnessed any damage and had therefore similarly yet to witness this extraordinary self-repair. But I digress.

The craft was light as a feather once free of obstruction - which was equally surreal. I could move it around with my little finger - had I had the time or presence of mind to.

The second thing that happened was the Vicar gestured to the flurry of men to leave me be! He walked rapidly in their direction, and they had a brief moment of discussion before backing down surprisingly easily.

Third (there was a third), well next, I was back in the sanctity of the chute as fast as tortoise in his shell, and the elevator began to push me back up to the sanctity of the craft's innards. As soon as I was inside and the floor sealed, I felt Alfred manoeuvre the craft away, as it was Lucy who had come to greet me.

"You are a hero", she said.

"It was nothing", I q-q-quivered.

I still have not quite recovered.

After that crushing, moronic blunder, and slight recovery, I wanted to earn back their trust.

And of course, no harm had been done, and so would you believe - they allowed me? Well, they did.

I wonder if the event was documented - for it was hardly an everyday occurrence. Let me search the Internet...

YOU WILL NOT BELIEVE WHAT I FOUND!!!!!!!!!!!!!

"1211 England, Gravesend, Kent: During a Sunday mass it is said that the congregation saw an anchor descend and catch on a tombstone in the churchyard. The churchgoers rushed outside to see a strange 'ship' in the sky, with people on board. One occupant of the vessel leaped over the side, but did not fall: 'as if swimming in water' he made his way through the air toward the anchor. The people on the ground tried to capture him. The man then 'hurried up to the ship.' His companions cut the anchor rope, and the ship then 'sailed out of sight.' The local blacksmith made ornaments from the abandoned anchor to decorate the church lectern."

HAVE I CHANGED HISTORY?!!!!!!!!!!!!!!!!

I am out of words.

Posted by Eurora001 on Wed 27-Jun-2001 23:37

I must have re-read that web page thirty times since my last entry. I find it utterly inconceivable that one little push of a button during a driving lesson has become a 'documented UFO encounter'.

I may never, ever come to terms with what I just discovered. My life has changed in so many ways already - ways in which it can surely never recover to any semblance of normality from, but that just cements it.

But I have got to put that out of my mind, for now. There is still so much to say lest I get behind myself in these entries. I fear doing so, as they are good for my health.

One of the many questions that has haunted me in the space of my mind at night-time (the space you allow that is), is just whether or not this is all really true. Yet now I have virtual third party evidence that it is. So many possible explanations have run through my mind over the past weeks however, until now. The obvious ones I have already dismissed such as sheer insanity and others such as what realistic three-dimensional flight simulators they might have in the future, like from the TV show I saw in the hotel. This could be an experiment on me, or a test of some sort. Or indeed a hidden camera show.

I am so embarrassed to say it but between typing the last line and this, I did actually make an announcement out loud here at home that I had caught them out, and they could stop the test now - well done - and all that. The only reaction I managed to achieve was Max running over wagging her tail, delighted I was talking to her.

Anyway all this uncertainty led me to want to conduct a little test. To change the past in a way I could verify. I needed, in a word, proof. And back then, when I needed it, ironically I had not realised that I would find it tonight through a quiet unintended means.

I did not tell them this reason back then, but requested that we travel in space if not time, to somewhere I had decided upon in the empty moments. An old (well not so old then) ruined Roman Amphitheatre I had visited a few years ago, not so far away in Wales. I knew the place and we worked out the co-ordinates, and I was allowed to enter them, proud I had not been banished completely from the controls. I suppose I have to remind myself that they still hold me in some esteem, like a God - and after all, do we not forgive God a great many disasters, simply brushing them off as his 'mysterious ways'?

"Apologies for the earlier technical hitch", I said nontheless, yet downplaying it jovially as a God only should. It seemed the correct way to deal with the situation.

We moved through space so incredibly fast I feel I will never get used to it. And then there we were.

The amphitheatre.

I am shocked at how intact it is. Naively. When I last saw this place it was just a series of grassy mounds, with processionals cut into the circle for the Roman performers to enter the theatre, but nothing more than that and decrepit brickwork. Yet here today, it was a clearly abandoned yet quite splendid arena! The Roman Arches are still mostly standing, and what looks like a wooden framework around the structure itself. Even most of the stone seating areas are as yet unclaimed by the tall grasses that are growing up around it, trying but failing to engulf it.

Seeing the fields and greenery around the theatre reminds me of another of the tangle of questions that have kept me awake some nights.

I had to ask them, "Crop Circles. Please do explain."

"Crops Irckles? You are a great communicator Sir; lucid, simple, to the point", responds Alf. "Everything is changing and I respect all of your love to the future. I hope you and I discuss this topic to make much clearer. Simply I know of not what you speak and these irckles are nothing to do with me!"

I tell him of what I speak.

"Circles in crop? Emotional people or a tall grass story."

Lucy appends, "I know you understand that not everything the Old World labels as alien is real", and gives me a knowing 'smile'.

I suppose not. I had never believed in crop circles anyway, let alone crops' irckles. Honestly. God we are so foolish are we not? Why did we CHOOSE to believe aliens would invest the fuel to travel millions of light years just to draw a pretty picture by a farm. That IS an elaborate stunt.

There is not a soul in sight. And I am certain a flock of interested onlookers will not emerge from under the arches of this great outdoor theatre, as they had done from the church. And so I am permitted to bring the craft down into the centre of the arena. It fits with plenty of room to spare, and Alf jokes, "You find us our ancient time machine parking position!"

But there are no yellow lines here. This is a simpler time. A more sensible time.

(Although instead of a ticket, you would have tigers set on you.)

My next mission is to PRESS THE CORRECT GODDAMN BUTTON! Needless to say, I get it right this time but I ask Alf if we can use the landing pad instead of the beam. I much prefer its elevator-likeness to the weightless chute. The more things that seem normal to me, the better.

"I understand that this eventuates fast for you and this small thing my pleasure", he agrees.

Before long at all, Lucy has led me to the lower deck by her hand. She knows I do not need her to, yet she seems to enjoy the excuse to be close to me. I sense it comes from a good place, and embrace it. The sentiment I mean, not her hand. Although I do hold it. ANYWAY, she smiles me away, and I go down in the lift to the ground floor happy.

Stepping off the plate which had so recently been caught in the ground in that waking nightmare that will come back to me many times I am sure, I look back and it does not exist. By that I mean the cloak is on this time, and I am alone save the electric charge and slight breeze around my craft in the middle of the arena.

I stop to marvel at how recently this must have actually been in use. Gladiators once stood where I stand, and oh so much more recently than they did when I stood here in my time. Tigers were here too. And I did not even think until now how many deaths - almost as though the blood is still fresh. Its molecules are undoubtedly intertwined in the ground below my feet.

But I have work to do. I have to leave my mark, and not of blood. I want to leave it in a way that both my companions can NOT see, that I CAN in the future, and yet that the weather cannot deteriorate by that time.

I therefore head past one of the processionals and towards a small room I find in the side of the arena. Once I entered it Bella, the smell was just indescribable. Musty but there was an odour of people... death. Yes I strongly suspected there had been much suffering in this room, and I wanted to leave as soon as I could. It is a stench I will not forget.

It was also oh so very dark, but I could just make out an arched inset area in the wall ahead, highlighted by reflections of light on the doorway. I picked up one of the sharper bricks which were scattered here and there, and set to work.

I felt like a vandal - and had I not known that the passage of time itself would cause far worse injuries than I could, I might have stopped myself. I gave an almighty whack to the brickwork beside the ingress, but it made no mark! This would be harder than I thought.

Looking around I found a round stone instead, and again smashed it with incredible might against the brickwork. It felt as if the bones in my palm had shattered. Yet I had precious little time before they wondered whether I might be lost in this tiny room. They perhaps suspected their hero was indeed that foolish, given the earlier spectacle.

But it worked. Fractures of stone hit my leg.

A brick to the right of the inset area now had a star shaped fracture in it. I took a moment to memorise its position, felt its shape with my hand, dropped my missile, and was off. Mission accomplished.

I feigned interest in walking around the rest of the arena and popping into another room I found, but it was not hard to be interested. Yet I had seen so much already today that anything more - no matter how wondrous - was just surplus.

I headed towards the middle of the craft and hit my shoulder on the pole - which was invisible and nearer to this side than it had been to the other side for some reason. I thought I had set it down in the middle. Well I am just a learner. I was confident they did not see me again make a fool of myself however, and as soon as I stood on the plate, it began to ascend upward into the belly of this gladiatorial beast, thrumming the ground inside the stadium - which in turn threw the dirt off the plate and back down to Earth.

Where it would wait for hundreds of years until I could return.

Once aboard, Lucy was first to ask me what I was doing in the small room.

Erm...

I did not want them to know I had any doubts, and had therefore wanted to prove that changes I made in the past really did affect the future. Firstly it would be an insult to their trust, and secondly it would mean I doubted my own ability to devise something that would actually change the world, the future, and the human race. And their super-human race.

"Call of nature", I summed it up with.

Lucy turned to Alfred and gave the most bemused of looks you can ever imagine two aliens give to each other!

I am not sure they understood, as she responded, "What did nature want?", with genuine curiosity.

My only mission now is to return there as soon as I can to inspect the star shaped indent and see if it has survived the passage of time. Another day perhaps, although after the churchyard account, I wonder now if the need is quite so powerful. Still - to think I can again touch something I then created still captivates the heart.

My last journey is to take us back to the future. Hard to believe. Yet there I was, co-ordinating our flight to Dullice Channel Station.

And there was something about that place. It was like I had been there before. Of course, I had, but I mean now - it seemed as though I had been there before ALL of this began.

Just deja vu I am sure.

Lucy takes time to congratulate me before we drop Alf off. She is to come home with me alone. (You know what I mean.)

"You were astonishing today my shining conqueror", she said unexpectedly. "You are a scholar of much today yet and you have educated to me so greatly also this day of days.

"Moreover the way in that you handle the small confrontation was so valiant... I felt my spirit would dissolve. You are so strong and you are be triumphant in whatever thing you put your mind to my guiding light. Peace is always with you."

With that she traipsed downstairs, and Alf explained she had to perform a small errand before taking me home.

A call of nature perhaps.

I want to be so honest with you Bella. The way she talks to me... it is like nobody has ever talked to me since... you... left. And I need that so much. BECAUSE you left.

Is it so wrong therefore that I am perhaps starting to let it get not to my head, but to my heart?

Please tell me if that is wrong?

You know, I had to ask Alf it she was just being kind to me.

"No, it not flattery. This truth. She is one who as a little girl who spoke no old English but who had a dream and who looked up to only you in history, as one who did not have the right edification even, and whose only determination as a child was to survive the daily brutal whipping and humiliations, she is not flattering you. The girl actuality believes in you and wants you to become more than you will ever know. She already is to know that you will too! Recall that alone. And you have only validated my belief too in your abilities and stature as a person, I look forward to flowing your progress and dreams! Goodbye."

And I was left alone on the craft.

Suddenly so very alone, not even my own time to keep me company.

I could very well have taken the ship right there and then. Is that the immense trust they place in me? They seem so impressed with me, yet I had thought I had been an embarrassment today!

I feel I am not taking their advice to believe in myself. But at least I am aware that I am not, where I was unaware before.

I will correct it. Am getting there.

Lucy took me home and dropped me off (it sounds so ordinary no?), and that brings us up to date.

No, okay, it does not quite bring us up to date.

She held her arms out as we said goodbye, like a small child wanting a hug. I thought nothing of it but 'sweet', and complied, stooping down to hug her waiflike body. I had a temptation to lift her up like one would a child, but stopped myself.

Yet I think the problem is she sensed my temptation-of-a-sort, and went to place a kiss on my cheek. Well I thought it would be my cheek, but it all happened so quickly - oh I don't know - you know as you are pulling away from a hug, and go to kiss someone on the cheek, and it ends up being their hair or their ear. Only she ended up kissing my lips.

Wet.

It only lasted an iota longer than a friendly kiss should have.

But for that iota is it so wrong that I did not pull away in disgust.

And as if that were not enough, she threw my emotions from one side of my brain to hit the other, with the revelation that tomorrow I would be able to go back in time to...

See YOU.

I just took a break after typing that (it still makes me giddy and I am relieved to finally be able to tell you what the exciting news was!). I went to the red filing cabinet where I keep your old letters. I read every word again. Partly to 'brush up' on the role she told me I would have to convincingly play, and partly just because I wanted to.

I AM GOING TO SEE YOU AGAIN!

I must remember to ask you one thing. Whether you purposely do all the little things - like writing in that book, only upside down, so I would have to make a special effort to turn the book around as if to announce your arrival when I came to your words - as if they were not special enough. Or the little jokes, where you would write a one paragraph letter, end it with, "Oh well, bye then. Bella.", only to continue on the back with, "Okay okay here we go then...", with the real letter as if you knew how it would be like a dagger to the heart if you had only written that small paragraph.

Teasing me in words, so now you know why I tease you here at times.

Everything you wrote seemed to be incredibly well thought out, in a way many would not relate to, yet in a way that made you seem not just like my soul mate, but perhaps even to share the same very mind as me.

I am sure all those small nuances you thought to inject in every interaction we had, are part of why you continue to inhabit my dreams to this day Bella. Almost as if you knew that would be required, and as if that is why you made a special effort to latch every part of your consciousness into every part of ME.

Well it worked.

And homework done, I am now giddy with anticipation for what tomorrow will bring. An exclamation mark would not have done that last sentence justice. Am I really going to see you again?! YES. Good grief. If only I felt like sleeping. Well I will rest my head on the pillow and at least make a gesture towards it. And whatever dreams may or may not come, they will be the last I will need to have before I see you... for REAL.

Goodnight Bella.

See you tomorrow.

!!!

Day Twenty-One

DAY TWENTY-TWO

Posted by Eurora001 on Fri 29-Jun-2001 11:19

I did not write yesterday. I did try, but I could not physically do it. Today things are slightly clearer, and I will try my best. My mind is all over the place and I feel as though I have been bereaved, abandoned, and fallen in love all over again and all at once.

What I thought might be closure with you, has only been an opener.

And I even woke up today thinking I might have a poltergeist too. The photo of you that I keep on the bedside cabinet, was instead lying by my pillow, and there is no way it would have fallen that far yet I had no recollection of moving it to there in my sleep, nor have I ever done such a thing. Also, it had some ectoplasm on it. Or maybe just drool.

Anyway, Lucy came again, with Alfred this time due to the apparently precarious nature of the event, and we followed the standard procedure which included a briefing at the same time before the mission as it had before. Yet it began with me briefing them for a change, on what the moment was I wished to relive. That was to be my next gift from them. And so I told the story of that Christmas, of how I had pretended to sleep thinking you were your mother, and so missed out on one heartbreakingly invaluable opportunity to connect with you, talk with you, perhaps even dream WITH you instead of 'of you', for the last ever time before...

With this digested by them and the rules of play discussed (all rather obvious), I was told that 'past me' could be safely 'extracted' and would have no recollection that anything was amiss. For 'him', he would go to sleep as before on that very sofa, and simply awake the next morning also as before, in the same place.

And instead it would be this me you came down to see. Lucky me.

Much has changed since I last wrote.

I do wonder if I should still be addressing this to 'you'. I am a creature of habit and writing here is too hard to change now, particularly with all I have to get off my mind. But if I am truly writing to you now, I am starting to doubt things more than the shreds of uncertainty I have had before.

Two ships were involved. I had to wait upstairs on our ship while the extraction of my downtime self took place below. Can you even begin to contemplate how that might have felt to me? The waiting, in anticipation, for so many reasons. Well I can tell you it was nothing compared to having to walk downstairs knowing that 'I' was in another ship nearby, and what with the intense nerves (I would add I have never been so nervous in my entire life and was utterly taken aback by the fact that this event which had only been hinted out was now upon me), it is a wonder I did not have some sort of meltdown. I do sometimes wonder why I have not yet 'gone mad', as one hears of.

But before that, Lucy had walked upstairs with a funny look on her face - almost one of embarrassment.

Then I saw she was holding 'my' pyjamas.

Meaning 'I' #2 was... unclothed.

The embarrassment spread to my face also, and recognising the redness she smiled, which also spread.

But of course, I would need to look the same as you had left me, and so would have to put on my old pyjamas.

There is no good way to say this.

Alfred gave me a haircut.

(It actually was not bad!)

Thank goodness I did not need to grow it to look the same as I did back then - I can only imagine what the technique would be to extract more hair from my head.

And my eagerness growing, I was beamed down some way from your house in the back car park of the closed office building round the corner. A perfect replica of my past self.

The rest was up to me.

My mission, should I choose to accept it from me, was to walk to your house, enter through the front door which I was assured would open for me, and climb back into 'bed' on the sofa. That was all that could go wrong - the rest would write itself, and I could not wait to read it.

When I got to your house... Good grief can you even begin to relate to the emotions that brought back to me? Such a nondescript terraced house, all your mother could afford, yet to me completely priceless. Her sweet little Nissan Micra parked just as it must have been before, in the drive in front of the garage (I had not thought to notice it first time around). The white wooden porch stuck onto the front of the building, and through its door, the doorway to my past. My ex-future.

I walked down the drive, planning even then should I be 'spotted' that I could talk my way out of it, saying I had to go out for a breath of fresh air or some such story. I stopped at the white door, its level handle and single key lock looking sorely insufficient to protect you from undesirables. As I stopped I looked up, past the vertically slatted tiles on the wall separating the two floors, to find your bedroom window.

You were in there surely.

YOU.

It was all I could do not to either burst into tears, or save that, burst through the door and dash upstairs, cradling you into my arms –never to let you go ever again.

Somehow, I stopped myself. I still do not know how.

It was Christmas, and I wanted to unwrap you! But I would have to wait.

I turned the handle, and the door fell open easily enough. I closed it behind me, feeling the warm sanctity I had loved from before.

And then I could smell you!

Goodness Bella, do you recognise why my emotions have been shot to the Moon and back now?

I was breathing you in, and I had not even begun to experience what was to come.

Then I opened the other door that led from the porch to the house proper, and tried to be as quiet as a mouse.

I felt a floorboard creak too loudly.

I sensed a presence upstairs.

But nobody came.

My heart in my mouth, I walked into the living room on my right, the door thankfully open, and there it was. THERE IT WAS. This scene from my memory that I have lived in like a film set for the past two years. Yet now I could touch it. And those hamsters - oh those sweet little hamsters I had hated for moving so much, now music to my eyes. I went over and touch their cage. I was crying by now. I stroked a branch of the Christmas tree, which I regretted as pine needles clattered onto the presents below leaving it a bald twig. And there under the window was my sofa, the fluffy blanket of the type that make me sneeze, eerily empty.

As I eventually climbed under it, I settled down into the sofa, and made myself comfortable.

I glanced across to the kitchen, and to that television we had watched, and I very nearly could not accept I was here. Yet I knew it to be true because of how excitedly nervous every molecule of my being was with the thought of seeing you again!

I lay there quite some time, going through the briefing in my mind, as well as everything I wanted to say.

There was no chance I could sleep. Not tonight. Perhaps not ever again!

An hour must have passed, and I relished every one of its 3,600 seconds.

Then I sensed that same presence I had felt coming down the stairs those years ago. I never understood how or why I sensed such things, other than the oft given explanation that those who lack one sense, have a heightening of others.

Still, as it undoubtedly came nearer, I pretended to be asleep.

The moment had arrived. The moment I had hated myself for playing the wrong way for so long, was now back. I had clicked undo. I was about to rewrite history.

And do you know something? I very nearly stayed that way - pretending to sleep again, so nervous was I to turn around and face the triumph of my fantasy.

I sensed the presence creep into the room, and for a second I held you close in my mind. You were near for sure, as the hairs on my neck rose, and my brow chakra tingled.

Then I acted away a few sleepy blinks, turned my head slowly towards the direction of your mother, and...

THERE - YOU - WERE.

Wait, no, it was your mother.

Ha, no I jest in my fervour, it really was you Bella.

Of course you probably know all of this 'now' anyway.

Goodness you looked beautiful. Always more beautiful without your make up as I tried to convince into you in the past.

Looking at your face, I wondered into your mind. How could such a beautiful mind exist in such a petite frame, and how could it captivate me so. I wondered if you even knew, and would continue to wonder if I was still not sure you knew exactly what you did to me with every carefully thought out word and moment.

I glanced a sleepy smile at you, afraid to touch you lest you should shatter, and raised my eyebrows expectantly - now falling into the role as if it were not one - and waited for you to inevitably walk over to me.

BUT YOU DID NOT!

You raised your hand in a small wave, and turned and walked back upstairs.

My world nearly ended, and would have, had you not come back into the room with a coy smile revealing your 'little joke'. You were like a walking version of one of your letters.

And so you came and knelt beside my head, at the end of the sofa.

Ahhhh, the relief.

"What brings you here?", I asked cheerily.

"I was worried the Christmas tree lights might still be on. I didn't know if they were dangerous for you."

" ... "

I could not speak. I said it all with my look. How incredibly sweet, even though I already had known the reason for years. Having you reveal it 'in the moment of doing it', showed me not just with your words, but with your tone, that you actually were worried about me.

Despite all the little jokes and tricks and distance, you genuinely cared deeper for me than perhaps I dared admit to myself, for it would hurt too much.

We stared into each other's eyes for a few moments, at which point you said, looking at my eyes still, "I never noticed these lines before".

I had been through a lot in the years that were only hours for you.

"It is probably just because I have been asleep", I said, as briefed by Alfred.

"Were you really asleep? I thought maybe you were pretending!", you enquired.

"You found me out! I missed you, and was wondering if you would creep downstairs to pay me a midnight visit."

"Sweetheart! Well lucky I did then yes! But then why the lines?"

"Yes, 'lucky' that", I said, almost tongue-in-cheek to myself, ignoring your other question. You let it pass, perhaps concluding I WAS just tired.

We smiled, touched, and stared a bit more.

And there was no avoiding it, and with such smiling and staring, the moment slowly came that I have dreamt of ever since it failed to come last time around.

As you looked into my eyes and I looked into yours, our very existences seemed to meld together, our souls became one again after so long, or no time at all, and our lips fell together, to become entwined in the softest, sleepiest, most delicious kiss I am certain the human race has ever and will ever experience.

"I love you."

"I love you too."

I wondered at this moment if it was the 'you' of now - 2001 - who somehow embodied your being just as I replaced my older self too. Your soul. Something seem different - perhaps my perspective.

I snuggled my face into the crease of your neck, breathing you in, and before I could help it, I was in tears again. I think at first you thought I was laughing, as you giggled too - perhaps nervously - but when you felt a drip on your shoulder blade, you drew away quickly, held my head in your hands and I lip-read you mouth, "What's wrong baby?".

The tears were really rolling at that point. They are starting to roll again now! The nice thing about signing is you do not have to stop crying to 'speak', and I answered your question the only honest way there was.

"I have had a terrible nightmare."

I told you all about it. How I 'dreamt' I had ignored you coming downstairs to avoid a moonlit encounter with your mother, all the other things I regretted, and how you had then... died. And how I tried to end my own life in return. And I told it so well that I started to believe it truly WAS just a nightmare myself. No, I did not 'believe' it was, I just prayed that somehow that lie would become the truth, and that I had perhaps dreamt the whole thing, and had been lying there on the sofa all along.

WAIT, HAD I?

Was all this nonsense about aliens and inventing time travel all just a dream, a dream that lasted perhaps a few minutes there asleep in your mother's living room?

Yet as soon as I start to wish or wonder that it was a dream, I am forlorn by the loss knowing I had not achieved such greatness. And had you not gone Bella, I surely would not have gone on to co-create the time displacement array and theorise the eurora potential.

So it seems I cannot win. Either I lose you. Or I lose that. But I cannot have both. Not quite.

And of course, this has not been all a dream. I really was there, a time traveller, on your sofa. How else would I have typed all this?! Unless I am dreaming that I am typing all this!?

I am going to pinch myself.

Okay, ouch.

I also realise now I had never cried in front of you, which explains why the looks you gave me of adoration were not quite like any I had seen from your face before. It pulled itself into an even softer, more beautiful guise if that be even conceivable, and you pulled me down into your chest, cradling my head almost like a child as you knelt beside the sofa. Nestling there was the most wonderful reward for the two years of pain at your death that I could have ever wanted for.

Yet it would make losing you all the more painful for it. Could I ever really win?

Well the short answer is no, not in the long term, but in the short term my reward got better. Much betterer. As you stroked my head softly, I moved my arm to put it around you, but found your breast first. After a few seconds of realisation that I had not been pushed away, I moved my head up to meet yours, to read your expression correctly, and we kissed again - inconceivably even more magical than before.

I do hope you have knowledge now of what happened next, but it is enough to say that one thing led to another... which led to you climbing under the blanket with me... which led to another.

And so I write this today, a happier shell of a man, for what a supernatural experience we shared together.

I did not use protection, for I knew I would not need it. Why am I telling you this - do you already know it? Yet the beauty of the thought that for those few days before you passed on there was perhaps a very small creation made up of you and me, blessing this very same world with its presence, was an unintentional yet welcome wonder.

In the moment, even if I did not ask you, I did at least ponder on the thought of making a child with you, as you rested your head on my chest afterwards. Always the thinker yes? Because then I wanted it to exist. And I so wanted you to not die.

And essentially I wanted to do as my song lyrics had also wished for, only to click undo a bit further. Not just in the way I had just miraculously done, but in a way that would bring more permanence to the change.

And so, I took a gamble, and ventured to test the water with that very aim. To try to save your life, and even that of our possible child we just might have created...

I moved you to meet my eyes, and I told you... that I was truly scared you might die.

And then I told the way you had died in my 'nightmare'. (You looked shocked.)

And then I suggested you get some sort of scan done really very soon, just to soothe my worry. (You looked even more shocked.)

And then I shut up, because then YOU told ME something instead, having first prepared me for awful news in a way that makes you wish somebody would just get to the point, fast.

"There's something I have to tell you", you said. "I don't know how or why you dreamt that, perhaps you have picked up something subconsciously, or perhaps we are linked in a deeper way, but there is more truth to your dream than you know."

And that was all you had to say for me to realise that you had known it all along.

YOU KNEW YOU WERE GOING TO DIE.

It transpired maybe not when, but you knew it was inevitable. You knew about the problem inside your wonderful mind. And you had protected me, because you also knew it was inoperable. It was in too deep. Just like me.

You had hoped to outlive 'us', so that we might at least enjoy the beauty of our own little moment in time. And I do not know if I loved or hated that - because in a way it meant that you had foreseen an end to us, and that we were not as magical to you as to me.

It explains so many of those slightly protective moments when you held back with me, in hindsight. The benefit of hindsight again.

I think the shock on my face was more than you had imagined, for you had not known the realisation you had actually brought me to.

I had come back here partly - secretly - all along wondering if I might get the chance to 'save you'. But there was no way I could unless I become a world-leading brain surgeon as well as nuclear physicist.

Bella. Bella! You were unsaveable. I could not fix this. I could not fix YOU. Oh Bella. That pained me more than perhaps even losing you did, if you can even compute such an excruciating heartache as being survivable by a mortal.

In the quiet space of my mind before today, saving you had resembled a synchronised waltz, filmed in sepia, with John Williams whirring up an orchestra worthy of such sentiment. The instruments fell silent.

But no. It now lies on the cutting room floor.

So now again I hope you understand me when I say my emotions are all over the place, to say the least.

Now I sit to ponder on what happened, which all seems as though it were a dream anyway, I do wonder why YOU did not mind that we did not use 'protection'. At the time, with my knowledge of future events, I knew I was doing the right thing, and felt perhaps as well as all I have said above, as if I had 'got away with it' so we could truly make love without fear of future consequence, however now I see it may not have been that simple.

Because... did you know too that you had SUCH a short time left? Had you had a recent scan or similar that had revealed the possibility to you?

If so, you may have felt the same - and that protection was unnecessary.

Yet if not, it could have meant that you did not mind the idea of starting a family with me - at that moment in time. In the past, you had hoped you would outlive us, yet in that moment had we ratcheted up in your heart to a more deserving level...?

Did you even know when you went upstairs with such a terrible headache a few days later, what might have been about to occur?

Is that why I thought I saw you say you loved me before you went? As a goodbye.

Whatever may have been going on inside that beautiful damaged mind, I hope it was that in the heat of that moment, the thought of having my baby was not so bad after all.

(Why does it seem the most wonderful people who inhabit the world, tend to be damaged... be it Van Gogh, or you, or the many other brilliant yet troubled minds of our time. Is there some correlation between special and broken...)

I feel perhaps the reason was a mixture of both - you hoped you had more than nine months left, and in some way through our child conceived in love, you would live on in the world, and I would raise it, alone, but always with a small part of you. That would have suited me perfectly well you know.

I wish you were here to tell me if that was the reason my love. No. I wish I had thought to ask you yesterday!

I know now that, in truth, I can never go back and relive that day again, because I cannot imagine it could ever possibly play out as perfectly as it in fact did!

And I have that at least. I have that.

Until you saw the scar on my wrist.

The scar that had not existed one day before, for you.

Our eyes had adjusted to the dark, and though the scars were faint enough, they are still also strong enough.

The shock in your eyes said it all.

You had seen for the first time, something which I had only just told you for the first time, that I had only just dreamt had happened. To you it was as though somehow my dream had come out of that realm and into reality, affecting my living body. I could see the realisation of that settling into your expression as you then shot backward, sitting bolt upright in front of me.

Topless. Radiant. You held your hand to your chest and your mind seemed to flutter, unable to calculate - how - why?

I had to think fast.

"Oh, those", I said gesturing calmly. "Yesterday's news."

You softened just a little.

"I am sorry I never told you before. The redness only comes up when... other parts of me do. If you know what I mean. I mean, when my heart rate increases", I added quickly, showing my embarrassment over what recent action I claimed had 'excited' the scars.

(Have your memories changed to incorporate all of this I wonder, and I am boring you by telling you what you already think you know?)

I told you at length how I had been the victim of bullying at school, that I was long since over it, and that I had partly not wanted to worry you, and partly been ashamed of them.

"I don't understand why I never noticed before!", you continued to exclaim.

"Well, I wear my watch on my right hand, and I use my left hand less, and like I said they do not really show unless... well, we have never done THAT before, which is why you never noticed THEM before. Simple!"

I was surprised how simple. And even more incredibly, you believed me. Goodness knows what would have happened had you not.

After a few moments of quite different reflection for both of us, you spoke. And your words were intended to soothe the inevitability of your passing. Thoughtful of others even when faced with your own mortality.

"I've known you months and it feels like forever. There were times when I really needed you - honestly."

"Please do not talk like this Bella, it sounds as though you are saying goodbye."

"Well I'm not going to get really deep, but you've always been there - I hope someone can do the same for you someday - I know I haven't."

"Yes you have", I said. "You have changed my life in ways you honestly will never know. Your friendship, our connection, your smile, and even the way you torture me with the walls you sometimes put up when they suit you. I know sometimes you found it hard to say what you felt, or to talk about other things in your family life that may have in turn made being open with me hard for you, but I do understand - and I know you care deep down."

You looked at me as if to notify me I was getting too close to the truth, and to let you finish. Which you did.

"When you meet somebody as nice as you are, just remember how much you deserve it. I'll never forget you I promise. Have a good life and don't stop being yourself", you said again as if saying goodbye. Then you added, "Well that's easy enough I suppose!"

Just like me, always the joker at the hardest times. But it did not disguise the fact you were saying farewell to me, lest you never get the chance to say it at a more appropriate moment.

I wonder now if somehow time was connecting our two fates and giving you that opportunity to say those words to me, just as it had given me an opportunity likewise. If you did not know you were soon going to pass away, then there is no way that you knew that was the last night 'I' would ever see you, yet still the right thing happened at the right time. Almost as if planned by the Universe, to help these voyagers.

Whatever the reasons, what you said HAS helped me. Half of the pain I felt and the loose ends which tried to tie themselves every single goddamned night were because we never said... goodbye.

And now we have.

All too soon it was time for you to skulk back upstairs, fearful your mother may come down for real and find us together - not that there was anything wrong with it, just that it would be the wrong ending.

I had never truly felt less embarrassed and more proud in my life, and so I was willing to accept your departure.

But then it dawned on me that would be a FINAL goodbye for us. More final than the last time in a way. I had failed to save you, and this version of me would truly never see you again. My future friends could not extend this trip invitation to me over and over again - it was surely a one off. (Well twice off now.)

I convinced myself in order to let you go, that if I really desperately needed to in the future, I would be able to convince them to bring me back one more time, though it was just a white lie to myself.

To you it was just going back upstairs in a 'see you in the morning' kind of way. To me it was your going back upstairs, and... 'see you in heaven'.

"Goodnight darling. I love you.", I managed.

"Seeya!", you gestured briskly, and with a quick peck on the cheek as if to reassert your control over plaguing my mind and playing hard to get, you were off.

I gestured one last thing.

"Goodbye." You did not see it, as you had already turned.

The last ever glimpse I saw of you was your right arm as it swung behind around the door frame, holding your hair band.

Then you were gone.

I had options. I knew I could still go upstairs if I wanted to, but when would it end. We had to put the other me back into bed (how ridiculous does that sound) so he could awake none the wiser if a bit groggier than usual - that was the only way this elaborate adventure could work.

And so I did what I must, disciplined myself, and snuck back to the porch. Every painful step was like wading deeper into broken glass. And so as I opened the door to leave you behind, I was overpowered by the urge to go upstairs instead, and crawl into bed with you. To hold on tight and never let go. Ever. Let them drag me.

And at that very moment, the moulded ripple effect in two of the porch panes of glass reminded me of those ripples back at Dullice Channel's lake, of the torpedo fish below, and through that glass the outside world that would take me back there via the ship that awaited me outside. Signs were everywhere that I had to keep moving forward, like that torpedo fish.

And so I torpedoed myself forward through the door. And as I walked, every step widened the crack in my heart. I am surprised I even made it back to the craft alive.

Having changed back into my newer clothes, I left the reinstatement of the other me to them of course. I did not ask how, nor did I ask what would happen if he had no recollection of the night's proceedings - which of course he would not. Perhaps you would think he was being discreet, or cutely pretending you must have 'dreamt' such a thing! Or for once, it would appear like it was me who was playing hard to get. Ha. I knew one thing for sure, what I told you about my scars only showing at that time would be borne out as truth, for we would likely never do that again.

As before, Alfred was taken back to Dullice Channel first for his important duties (I still know not what they are), and Lucy took me home. This seemed an incredible waste of energy - why not 'drop' me home first? It seemed he wanted her to extend our farewell to ensure I had not bad effects from such an important journey. Ah and of course - two ships.

That was very sweet of him, and at that time I was not sure if saying goodbye to you had been a blessing, or what we shared in getting to say it to one another had made 'goodbye' all the harder than it had been before.

So it was probably for the best that Lucy comforted me when we were hovering over the pad at Dullice Channel.

I do not feel so bad now in telling you... that I fell into her arms. I needed someone. Anyone. Her mammoth beady eyes seemed to see every ounce of my pain and confusion, and that was all I desperately wanted in that moment - for my feelings to be seen for what they were. Mourning. And who else on Earth could have understood what I was going through. Only two even knew, and I wonder if even with my typing this, you are receiving it in order to be the third. And if you are, I am sorry if you are in any way angry that I went back and that we in a way created a lie. But I had to go back. I missed you so much. I MISS you so much.

In any event, Alfred returned to the craft to collect the last of the items from the trip (such a mission was it), and disembarked. Before he went, I enquired if I might fly Lucy and me home again, and it was agreed. I was pleased that they trusted me, perhaps spurred on by how well the exercise had gone.

Then there was what I saw out of the viewport while he was engaged in some silent telepathic exchange with Lucy (which in itself is quite something to watch - as they both simply stand silently staring at each other if I have not mentioned it before).

Well my eye - and body - were drawn to the other side of the craft by a fluttering bird that can only be described as a small angelic seagull as if made from translucent paper. It flitted around the side of the concave viewport like a butterfly, and no sooner could I make my way over to inspect this rare beauty, did it flit off. Oh flit. Because it was replaced in my field of vision by something a few craft across from us. What I could just make out as stretcher-like contraptions, carrying... bodies.

Do not get me wrong, they were not dead bodies or I would have recounted this much sooner, but just bodies - but here is the thing. They were somewhat taller (longer) than the other futurists. I thought for a moment that I could faintly make out hair on one of them in the distance. The thought did occur to me that they might very well be not just humanoid, but human.

Is that possible? Had they helped out with some tragic event? Were they resurrecting more than just Christ?

I was so preoccupied with emotion that I did not give that the headspace to consider at the time, but now I do... could there have been other travellers there from nearer my time...?

Then again I had seen a futurist with hair, and some taller than others, but something struck me about this apparent medical frigate that just rang a small alarm bell.

But why would they have humans on stretchers?

It is not like these time travellers are aliens, or in any way linked to those ridiculous stories of alien abduct...

NO!

Alien abductions?

Okay any contentment I had at yesterday's events just left me like a nuclear missile. CAN I NOT BE AFFORDED JUST ONE DAY OF PEACE WITH PLEASANT THOUGHTS? Why is my heart now racing and my fingertips icy cold? Alien abductions are not anything to do with them... are they? Surely... they could not be.

Christ let me look at this.

Aliens are not aliens, and aliens do not exist, because only TIME TRAVELLERS exist... So 'alien abductions' would in that sense translate as 'futurist abductions'. God no, let it not be so.

But why do people as respected as British Airways pilots and Army Generals claim to have been abducted by (what they label) 'aliens', claim to have had their lives turned upside-down through the inevitable ridicule, have apparently had to share this with abductee self-help groups, claim to have had missing time experiences...

Wait. Missing time.

Missing 'time'?

Oh shit.

NO NO NO. This cannot be happening. Fuck. Please will you tell me this is not happening? I remember reports that people who were 'abducted by aliens' would feel they had been away for hours or even days, but when they were returned, it was the same time they had been taken or something like that. And only their wristwatches showed the time they had really been away. Example - someone abducted at 12:00 PM might experience 4 hours of terrifying 'experiments' on their bodies, but when they reappeared on Earth at 12:30 PM only half-an-hour of Earth time had passed, yet their wristwatch showed 4:00 PM.

God what am I learning here? But wait, surely aliens or futurists would understand how to operate a simple wristwatch and set it back in time?

Yet they have not learned how to operate the Internet in order to find this diary yet.

Could it be that some technologies are so long since expired in their time that they simply overlook them?

I have no idea. I am grasping for ideas here now.

All I know is one thing - I think it entirely possible now that just like those airline captains and military personnel... I am now a (willing) abductee. But why the stretchers!?...

I have to ask some more questions tomorrow. I have been told we are going to another place from my wish list. I will write more soon. I need a break. This is too much and too awful a possibility.

Day Twenty-Three

Posted by Eurora001 on Sat 30-Jun-2001 09:03

So I woke up a few minutes ago from a night of virtually no sleep whatsoever. I lay there with that horrible feeling of adrenalin-fuelled anxiety, as I did not wish to hear what they had to say lest it be bad news, yet at the same time wanted to find out the answers to these questions no matter what. I finally roused myself from that sleepily nervous entrapped state of slumber and got up to face the music.

They seem so gentle, I am sure there is nothing bad. I am just being paranoid. Yesterday WAS a lot to take in after all.

Posted by Eurora001 on Sat 30-Jun-2001 14:50

They both came to see me. It must have been a special journey. I had fascinating glimpses of going back to witness JFK's assassination, or something equally historical. If only.

With us now having found our stride and broken the ice as much as I can conceivably imagine ever being able to with these fascinating people, I found what I hope to be the right moment to nervously pose the question that plagued my sleep all night.

"Can I ask you both something?"

"It is certainly that you can", says Alfred most agreeably.

"Thank you.

"Well, forgive me, but in my time we hear a lot about... what are called 'Cattle Mutilations' ... and 'Alien Abduct...'"

Then it all turns to drama.

Before I even finish the question. Alf and Lucy turn to each other and Alf raises his spidery hand fast toward his bulbous head, which bows down to meet it just as quick. After a pause for a few brief moments apparently 'receiving' something clairvoyantly, he talks to me in a starkly different cold monotone pattern.

"I have no secret to you. My mother is just injured. A box hit her. I want take care of my mother. Not now please, later is better."

"...Yes, of course. ...I am sure she will be all right?", I instinctively retort, not considering anything more sinister at the time.

Alf's sentiment touched me I am sorry to say. "You are always kind. My beautiful and strong friend!!!" (I put exclamation marks because that is as exaggerated as he said it.)

And that was it.

They left me back at home as quickly as they had taken me. It had never been that quick before.

It struck me as something of a relief to have another 'day off'. Even such wonderful things can suffer from overkill without the hands of moderation.

But now of course I know better. Some other 'abductee' might have been fooled for a longer duration that I was.

I just hope I can enjoy this recovery day without too much concern. I have SO much to catch up on, that my hope is it will occupy my mind instead of the lingering question.

But when they return, I will be demanding answers.

If... they return.

I fear I have seen the last of these creatures, and so the last of other times.

Posted by Eurora001 on Sat 30-Jun-2001 19:41

For a teetotaller, I must confess I am a little drunk. I did not get my day off - no - but instead I got shocked to the core of my being.

Everything has now changed.

DAMN THEM TO HELL, THESE VILE PARASITES!

The only way I could find to comprehend what has gone on was to open the bottle of champagne Daniel gave me that I was hoping to re-gift. It has numbed the sickening feeling, whilst replacing it with another type of sickness.

I will try to ecxplain. No sooner had I submitted the last entry, did they return.

This is entirely insignificant compared to the blow they later dealt me, but for your continuity, Alfred claimed that he had attended to his mother for 'the past few days' (minutes for me - which still throws me) and that she was now recovering. Their only reason for returning so soon after they had left was to leave me with some semblance of continuity too, without I suspect wishing to let me 'stew' for too long on my questions lest I do something hasty. Yet THEY had clearly stewed on it.

Surely the story about his mother was an utter falsehood, but if so why did they take three days off - or did they not? They always dress the same - how would I know.

Bella you must prepare yourself if you are reading me.

I fear I am shell-shocked - so forgive me if I blurt this out faster than it happened.

All I can suggest is you join me, sit down, and read it slowly.

And when you hear the revelations they bestowed on me, you may very well believe it took them three days of debate to agree to reveal them to me.

All right. Here it is.

Again I posed them the question. I was surprised that anger I thought I had suppressed spilled out into a concentrated scowl, as I felt it warm as if blushing. A bit like the flush I feel now from the grog.

"I deserve to know the answer to my question... please. What IS 'alien abduction'?!"

"Please be tranquil not blue!", said 'Alfred'. "There are important things for us to say with you and here we will now here.

"Kind sir, it gives me pains to say so, but", and it apprently did pain him for his forehead created an uncharacteristically V-shaped frown, "but - sir... YOU did NOT I am sorry invent the time craft at all."

"What?", was all my lips could retort.

"WE are NOT time travellers", he added.

Yes. He said they are not time travellers.

Lucy interjected at this point, "We CAN time travel, and so we did with you, but you did not invent it. We only...", and she too appeared to be distressed at revealing this to me, "we only made you believe you did for reasons otherwise elsewhere."

I did not get a chance to ask why. It continued.

"You see here is true, WE are NOT from Earth future", Alfred stuck the dagger in further with.

"WE ARE NOT FROM EARTH."

"That was not Earth you visit in our future."

Then he clarified it all with one final stab.

"You were right on the first day.

"We ARE aliens.

"That was our planet."

When he said it the words echoed round my cranium like an empty chamber devoid of all possible capacity for reasoning... 'We ARE aliens - We ARE aliens - We ARE...'

'Lucy' in her apparent sensitivity did not need to wait for me to demand an explanation.

"Please believe us. We so sorry. We come from three planets of quart-centurion star to you. In your words Sunsher, Gleez, and Subrane."

"I do not believe you...", I said hesitant as to whether I was even using the right language to these alleged telepathic aliens, I was that far knocked for six. For twelve.

"Please believe us, it true, you check", she said.

"Do not repeat your words JoAx Fo."

"Apologise ALFRED", she retorted sharply, letting me in on their private dialogue unlike ever before. Did she mean 'I apologise' or was she demanding that 'he' do so to her? I wondered why they would want me to hear that for a moment, before she went on.

"So sorry to be in this troubles kind friend. You will understand why no?"

"NO!", I contested.

"It is quite understandable please. We know you to be an discoverer of things - inventor. We wish to make contact with humans. What simpler way there is to make a connection and a friendship and an understanding with striving inventor than to instil in you knowledge of inventing a machine we travel to you in.

"We do this so as to 'break ice' with you."

And break my heart.

"You are not to take personally this", Alfred added. "It is same with everyone we abd... visit. We create for them that exact idea that fits their life and helps blend the understanding curve for accepting this final moment the big step. The moment we reveal what we truly are.

"This moment now. Please be ready."

"Without this, your mind may never have adjusted or survived this final moment", said Lucy. "Just remember our first encounter and how you made sick?"

She had a small point there.

But, 'final moment'?

Yet in that moment - as I began to digest and even foolishly believe everything they were telling me about being 'aliens' and that I had nothing to do with the invention - logic clicked back into place, and I could have cursed myself for having been so naive those moments.

Before they arrived into my life, just like everyone I too had been accepting that the television shows were all true. That aliens existed. That they somehow even magically look like us. What poppycock! Yet there I was sitting in my own personal Tardis, listening to their fairytale, and being just as gullible as I have criticised all the other people on Earth for being. There I was - almost falling for the 'alien' explanation all over again.

Of course they were from Earth's future not an alien planet!
And of course the China agreement led to all of this!

And upon that realisation, it dawned on me why these Earth futurists were trying to explain it all away as an alien encounter.

They felt ashamed.

Ashamed that they abduct from their predecessors.

Unwittingly, in trying to throw me off the truth, they had just admitted it in the strongest way. For there was no other reason they would make up such a fairy story, if they did not strongly wish for me to forget all about my idea that my descendents are bodysnatching us - plucking us off the family tree like ripe young naive plums.

I do not need to elaborate on how much I wanted a hole to open in the ground and swallow me up once I realised my momentary foolhardiness. And I knew where to find one. The bottom of the craft.

I stood up and showed my wish to go. I did not tell them I knew they were lying about being aliens or about my creation, just that I wished to go. I wanted no more part in this subterfuge, or in what the Extapiens thought they were doing. I knew that asking them about 'alien' abduction had caused them to make all of that up. So what was next? The ACTUAL (unwilling) abduction?

No thank you.

But needless to say, I did not get as far as even the downstairs ramp, let alone the chute. A lot more was to come that I have yet to get to.

Goodness just watching myself recount this makes me think what a wonderful story it would make. I wish I were reading it in a hot bath, instead of living this freakish nightmare as real life like some character trapped inside a novel.

Let me recap again for my own sanity, lest I start to believe this is some sort of story. Ironically it was them making up the stories. They were not aliens. They were time tourists from Earth, just as they have made plain all along. And I did invent time travel.

And do you know when I truly realised it - that they were human? As soon as Lucy grabbed my arm to stop me leaving. And the reason I realised it was not what you might think, but rather the look of total and utter forlorn devotion she gave me, that no alien could ever master as well as someone of humanity. I had thought to myself in that instant, 'you cannot be anything but one of us'.

But more than that, it was a look that reminded me (how I ever forgot for those terrifying minutes I do not know) of the way she made me feel last time we were alone. Sorry sweetheart, I tell you this to paint an honest and unskewed picture. And more even than that, it spoke much more to me of how she had studied me and my life and idolised little old me because of my concept, more than these false words ever could explain.

And so I confronted them immediately I realised. I am afraid it was quite a tirade.

"Why are you lying to me? I am not a fool. I know you are futurists from Earth using my own concept, not little green men! Everything you have told me makes too much sense for it to be a lie... that my concept was for a flattened disc shape and that is the shape of this very craft; that you are also hairless because man has been shedding hair since he first walked on Earth; that you do not miss the hair because of Earth's heat I experienced for myself at Dullice; that you have those big Asian eyes because that is the continent that was abundant in evolution; that the flying saucers appear in a flash of light because that is what time travel creates; that abductees experience missing 'time' because you are time travellers; that ships of time tourists have been seen at so many historical events; that you are pale because you cannot go in that harmful sun; that very sun has made you infertile; that the infertility is what causes you to abduct us; that you have that small lying mouth because you communicate with thought... and everything else you explained in such perfect detail!

"And I know how many abductees there have surely been throughout history - given the attempts you are making to distance yourselves from such events through what... embarrassment?! Therefore I also full well that 'aliens' [how ridiculous] would not take each and every abductee on a magical mystery tour of dinosaurs, past loves, and ghost cities!!

"PLEASE, tell me the truth now. You owe me this. I am asking you from one time traveller to another."

Alfred's head jolted back a little and his eyes widened at my final statement. (Wider than their normal extreme wideness.)

"We... tell you truth already! I do not understand. There has been the miscommunication. We aliens. I send you the wrong informs. I wish to know your mind", Alfred said sticking to his guns, albeit hesitantly.

I needed to go out on a limb to shock some sort of honesty out of this creature.

And so I took an uncharacteristically bold step.

You would have been proud.

"I DEMAND IT AS THE CREATOR OF TIME TRAVEL."

That did it.

Lucy admitted the subterfuge, as Alfred almost buckled with the weight of it all, down onto the seating area, bony head in gangly hands.

"We feel little choices and make great deliberalations of how to trackback because - we feel humiliated of truth", she said.

"Please my man, anything to do with it is nothing to do with me", Alfred spat out of his mind, excusing himself from blame.

"We know people in your time can never understand why we abduct you, to help our time in future Earth", he concluded.

"So you DO abduct us!", I queried as a statement.

It was certain at that moment. Deal done.

Aliens do not exist, and time travellers from Earth's future ARE the abductors the media has portrays as being aliens.

They always have been Bella.

And my creations - the time displacement array - the eurora potential - did indeed give them that ability.

Which means... it is all my fault. Everything.

I had asked, "What do you mean 'understand why we abduct you'? Do you mean why you abduct ME?", I questioned a little anxiously.

"NO, not you. NEVER you!", Alfred replied. Somehow it touched me. He went on, "But you in the non-singular meaning, other yous from yous time."

But then the awful truth. (No, that was NOT it before.)

Lucy says it so well, that for a moment it saddens me.

"Humankind is dying sir at the hands of our great Sun. The veil of God is lifting as we draw closer to the fires of Hell.

That sounded familiar. Was it from scripture? Was it referring to the atmosphere as being the veil of God? And the Sun as hell?

She went on, "Without these odious steps we make today, with you even, WE may be the last of your kind to walk the Earth, EVER. We mean you no harm."

Of 'my' kind?!

Alfred elaborates, "I mention it before in small ways how the great rays from the sun - they destroy fertility. Virtually all male are barren - sterile... I... am barren." He looks so ashamed of himself and shakes his skeletal head in despair as his mouth opens in two sad gawps like that of a dying man.

Lucy looks concerned for him, and continues it for him. "Many female are too. The barren wasteland womb is inhospitable, much akin the dust that is the earth of the Earth in our times. Finding a fertile male and female together it SO HARD.

"Sir WE are an endangered species. There be as little as millions at one point before we take such the bold step as we did."

I now make sense of when they first told me the world was in trouble and it affected their "productiveness" - as they did not mean PRODUCTIVity, but rather reproduction! They had been telling me all along, and I had not even bloody well noticed.

Alfred continued, "Yet further back in time, this problem was not. For YOU it is not the problem.

"There is just one pool of productive companionable [compatible?] humanoids in time. Your pool.

"Is it such crime to scoop from the pool a little to save our own descendants?

"If we do not travel back to take these companionable humanoids with deoxyribonucleic acid that so close to us, it spells FINAL end time for ALL our great civilisations - yours too! We are not like Hisler, we are good! You must understand it! You must!"

Lucy was more upset than I had ever seen her in the past few weeks. Angry and sad all at once, yet her face now that of a stranger to me.

(And now I think to it, she had meant Hitler - as they must apparently feel the shame of some Germans back then, even though they were trying to prevent the cleansing of their own ethnicity... but it reminds me of a character I have mentioned here before - Nostradamus. For did he not predict that a German man called "Hisler" would shock the world through great power? Is it not odd how this traveller FROM the future, and that great prophet OF the future, both call him Hisler? Did this futurist get the misspelling from Nostradamus's account, or did Nostradamus get it from the future. From the futurists?...)

In any event, everything they finally admitted to me is what I just cannot accept. Cannot comprehend. Cannot allow. They bodysnatch and imprison people from our time, to fertilise themselves? Is that not the most immoral thing you ever learned?! They kidnap our men and force them together with their fertile Extapien women? And they steal our women to be raped by their fertile males?! No. NO. I cannot...

He had gone on beyond even that though.

"This is the other half of the answer we not tell you for why we may look 'oriental' to you."

"Okay...", I said in acceptant anticipation.

"Many the people we take, we choose from Chinna. Asia region it is origin of most of our stock so there is closeness there in deoxyribonucleic acid, but also yet more important too, we find government censor it so it can be safer for us. It not altering us looks too much, yet do small degrees yet perhaps this is true. But merely we going back in time. A little reverse evolution for sake of future survival."

They destroy people's lives and take advantage of political censorship to get away with it?!

Yet in reversing evolution by cross fertilising, they become more human! The very species they were so proud to evolve away from. In order to survive and evolve, they have to... devolve.

Lucy tries to keep on top of the disbelief and disappointment that is spreading across my expression as we stand face to face, her arm still holding mine from earlier, as if to stop me from ever leaving the craft. Or is it to stop me ever leaving her?

"Your children's world is in need if healing. And if we but just the two of us, comprehend this and dream of an Arcadia, stay unyielding, it can be spark to begin change. For us change has already been beginning for many century. For you, all you need do is NOTHING. So simple. And to just accept that it your world too we save. Yes? Please do nothing. It is easy do naught."

A long time passes, as I sit down, place my throbbing head in my hands so that I must look like a mirror of Alfred, and angrily at least try to envisage this 'Arcadia' and see what they do as in some way, shape, or form as 'acceptable'. It is so hard to do, even now with this drink.

I am growing weary. I need another glass.

I feel I have been cheated. Twice.

Tricked - my trust abused.

This is all getting beyond, beyond too much.

Yet despite all that, I honestly did TRY to see their side. That is my nature - I cannot help it. I must at least have tried, lest I ever regret not giving it more consideration before. And in so doing I had to ask them more questions. Here are the answers at least.

I discovered from them that 'test tube' environments do not hold out any successes for them. 'Real' DNA from fertile humans is all that works. Nature wins. But who loses?

I also learn that they tend to abduct the same person many times over because they find them genetically a rare and excellent match. Such a person's seed or their womb never fails, unlike a large proportion of 'the rest of us'. (It makes me sick to even write it.) The added gain for them is that by calling themselves a 'multiple abductee', it undermines the abductee's credibility, whilst also minimising the breadth of occurrences across the population. One person, many times = 'he has mental issues'. Stomach-churning I know. They would rather take one poor soul a hundred times, than take a hundred more fortunate souls once each, because it suits the 'cover story' better? A story WE created for them. JUST HOW STUPID ARE WE! Yet it all fits - after all, who would believe Joe Bloggs when he says he has been taken into a flying saucer by small pale hairless beings since the age of five!

Hell I saw firsthand that 'ALIEN abduction' works as a cover story, for was it not also my first conclusion of what they were a month ago?

We MUST stop perpetuating this lie for them.

Do I now have to somehow achieve that? Is that now the responsibility that rests on my shoulders?

But how? Who would believe me, even with all of the explanations that fit together like the most perfect jigsaw.

It even came up why it seems they abduct from working class stock, more than we hear from middle or upper class witnesses. There are no royal abductees that I have heard of after all. And as sure as all the answers have almost always come from them, they have one for this. But their manner of answering belittled us so, and made me revolt, for they compared us to... dogs. Alfred asked if I knew that a "filigree" dog [pedigree surely?] would generally be less healthy, yet a crossbreed more so, and with a longer lifespan. And so would their seed. It happens I did not know this, despite having Maxine in my life. But that was the comparison - working class people are healthier 'mongrels' for their breeding needs.

These 'people' make me sick. They are not even people to me now. Lucy is still endearing, yet an endearing child of ogres. They are treating our world like some sort of cattery.

Sick to the stomach I tried to find reasoning to throw them off this path they had chosen, and questioned the compatibility of the DNA. It made no difference of course, but did remind me of those futurists they told me about who travelled back perhaps to mate with... monkeys. If you have to live in the past, at least a monkey could not leak the story to the press, could not squeal.

(Well maybe just squeal.)

Now I know I would not put even that truth past these savages.

THIS WHOLE SORDID BUSINESS MAKES ME WANT TO SCREAM! Bella I do NOT know what to do. I have a few ideas however. These vermin will not know what has hit them.

...

Wait. Let us at least attempt to be fair. Again. I have time. Having sat here and thought about it a few minutes more, I cannot truly 'hate' Lucy for it - she is certainly the younger prodigy, brought up into this world of abduction and subterfuge knowing nothing but. But Alfred - HE can stop it. He is surely an elder Extapien in some sort of control. And I cannot help but abhor this once grand being in my eyes.

He is now the enemy.

Yet if he did stop it, he would also be stopping mankind. The human race would surely end. He might argue that his people's actions are the ultimate form of evolution.

It is hard to write that I hate him, I have to admit. I try to remember these people are not truly our enemies. That they are our children and it should come naturally for us to protect our children. Yet, if your own child tried to rape you...

So you understand why I cannot ever accept this state of affairs.

Yet it is he who says to me, "All life is one".

Perhaps the most eloquent sentence he has ever managed to string together. Lucy fills in the blanks. Please ignore this, but for my record - matrilineal inheritance, mitochondrial DNA, susceptibility to genetic drift, deciphered nuclear DNA.

Much of it was below them. But ultimately, my answer came. Extapiens and Home Sapiens have 99.9% compatible DNA.

Was it Jacques Mon't who said 'what is true of E. Coli is also true of elephants, just more so'?

And so what is true of us, is also true of them, only LESS so - because they surely lack the one thing that we possess which would have stopped us from ever stooping to such behaviour.

A conscience. Perhaps they are alien, to lack that.

How can they live with themselves!

Although that is the point... They literally cannot.

'Can't live with it, can't live without it'.

Yet I just can NOT live with it... and we CAN survive without them.

And without their ability to time travel.

Without the ability I GAVE TO THEM.

I will have to consider what I can do about that. If I gave it, can I take it away...?

I fear it may be literally too late for that. The snowball begun rolling weeks ago, and is now a million years large.

There was more information to come about why they abduct predominantly from 'modern man of the Old World' (us). Proper records on ancestry, health statistics, and more only begun in the 20th Century. They rely on remnants and fragments of this information, to know the lineage is safe and healthy for them too. We covered more details - the scientist in me was somehow disgustedly intrigued with morbid curiosity. Shall I tell you?

Homo Erectus died out some 200,000 years before we walked 'erectus' on the same soil, and Alfred claims that was the 'dividing line' for when we became modern man. According to him, they "seldom" go back before than that. From what I know there had been somewhere like ten billion individual Homo Erectus before they died out, yet we have only ever uncovered remains for maybe a few thousand of them. So little is known about them. It therefore makes some small sense that they would avoid them and choose later, historically better studied 'versions' of us to help them fertilise themselves, rather than those little known species before us.

I do not know what to believe that he tells me now. For all I know they are off having sexual intercourse with hetereotrophs.

You know, old Ostrolapithicus first ventured out from the African forests some ten million years ago, and that is when we stopped being monkeys. So when did we stop being human? Around the time we started raping our ancestors I say. Agh now I remember it Alfred had go on to admit that they sometimes "need to encourage" female humans to have intercourse with male futurists for the best "transfer rate". I take from this that artificial insemination is not as good as nature's intended method.

Can you see why I have turned against these creatures now, despite the inevitably horrible logic of their actions?

Evolution just continues regardless. Survival of the fittest. They are trying to adapt.

I think half of the reason I am having such a problem, is because no matter what I know or how much they try to - or not to - confuse me, they still cannot escape the fact that they DO look like aliens, and I have decades of programming thanks to our ridiculous media industry, that they must be aliens. And to me, when I give some space in my slightly intoxicated mind now to their dilemma, it is still as though it IS aliens breeding with us. Can I ever shake that brainwashing and come to terms that it is our offspring abducting and raping us?

Oh yes, and cattle mutilation. I was perhaps too angry in my choice of words, as Alfred became quite defensive in retort.

"How many bovine do you 'mutilate' and then EAT in a handburger? So think this one - why do you feel we choose exactly animal such as cattle to scoop and test for deoxyribonucleic acid? We try do good and try take from animal we know you do not mind to destroy, so we can check for the many things in atmosphere and the air quality of regions. Yet WE do not eat animal flesh. It disgusting. So please my big comrade, do not judge our work of desperation, when you execute worse for no motive. We choose the bovine because you lead way with the that. Think on this now please."

I had almost agreed.

I was sure they did 'tests' on humans too however. I did not ask it, but can imagine the answer. Something about a box hitting his mother. Or they would say that if we could go back in time and 'catch' a dinosaur, would we not take some DNA samples from it for testing back home? (True.)

So we are a 'prehistoric' curiosity to them! And a walking 3-billion person strong sperm bank.

They have an answer for everything to the extent that I need not even ask, for I already know them so well. They are in my mind as it is. Yet perhaps I also know the answers, because you and I may do the same in their circumstances. We are 99.9% the same after all. And my descendants WILL become them, and devise such answers! There is no doubt now that my Great Great (...) Grandchild is an alien abductor.

Sick, so sick I feel.

Yet perhaps that 0.1% is the sense of right and wrong.

I CANNOT CLOSE MY EYES TO WHAT THEY DO.

True or not Bella, I am distressed beyond belief that my creation has in fact been used to destroy lives. (And yet create lives.) Those poor people who have lost their livelihood, sanity, or loved ones to these vile creatures who dare to think of themselves as remotely 'human'. Where is the humanity in kidnapping?!

This is worse for me too than perhaps the next person (did Einstein even know?...) because...

I know what it is to have someone snatched from me at the wrong time.

They do not see it this way from their century's perspective but I see it from my 21st century one and we will always think apart.

Well... I have tried to prepare you that there was more (yes more) to come. And so it came. Another bombshell.

I stood up to try to leave again. In a way I blamed them for your being taken from me. I know they did not take you, but the injustice of it all seemed the same to me in that clouded moment.

Lucy again stood up, and again held my arm. (She is surprisingly strong, or strong willed, when she wants to be, though I was not sure if it was her physical body or her mind which actually prevented me moving.)

"PLEASE DO NOT GO. You are my only. You divine to me." Then she turned to Alfred, and can assume she asked him to leave us alone, because he stood up slowly and walked close past us, brushing my then autonomously shuddering hand with his as I felt his fingers twiddling there, and left us alone - going downstairs. And she continued.

"Tell me truly, the moments in time you and I share - do they mean no thing to you?"

I was not sure if she meant the moments we had travelled to, or the moments which perhaps meant more to her, when we were not travelling at all.

This wide eyed, smooth-skinned, angelic progeny of monsters standing holding my arm, gazing up at me doe-eyed, so expectantly... what could I say? My anger was not truly at her.

"They have left me confused Lucy", is all I could say.

"Yes you do not be", she replied. "There is no confusion - confusion only in mind. Here no confusion lies, only actions", and she reached up and touched my chest.

With her other ghostly arm, she took my hand, and placed it down on her chest so I had to stoop, pushing it flat against the soft female mounds I felt there.

Please bear in mind that my mind was a screaming fog at this point. Nothing would shock me any further than I had been, and I was nearly beside myself with mental exhaustion. It is with no embarrassment that I therefore admit that instincts took over where my mind could not, and her moving of my hand to... 'there'... well it stirred some innate instinctive physical response deep within my unconscious mind and my... There was no conscious thought to it mind you, but still...

Had she done this intentionally, to illustrate to me that sexual impulses can transcend evolution? That the interbreeding was okay?

That it was all part of nature's backup plan?

For a fleeting flash of a moment I could perhaps comprehend how they could do these things to us. But that was all it was, a flash honestly.

And then I was back to thoughts of words like 'rape', and 'apes', and 'bodysnatching'.

Yet my body unreasonably had other ideas. It continued to react to being touched, and to touching a most feminine, intimate part of a humanoid's anatomy. It was not what I wanted to feel... I think... NO, I know, I am sure it was not.

Yet it happened all the same.

"You begin to understand now", she said with admittedly the sweetest of skinny smiles.

I was lost for words then if not now.

But then the bombshell...

I was a moment away from discovering that she had NOT asked Alfred for privacy.

And he had not gone downstairs to give us any.

He had gone downstairs for another reason.

To prepare the sickbay.

For Lucy and me.

As I discovered when she tugged me gently down the ramp, past the chute's opening in the middle of the floor, and into that room for the first time.

This was no sickbay.

It was the bedroom.

Bella, they wanted me to fertilise Lucy.

"I want to have love with you!"

She had said it herself.

DAY TWENTY-FOUR

Posted by Eurora001 on Sun 1-Jul-2001 20:11

I had to leave it at that appropriate point as I was rather worse for wear and needed forty winks.

I got about four.

Daniel emailed me to see how I was getting on with my new found freedom since the China agreement.

I did consider - for a second - inviting him into this journal, for I had postulated earlier how I might blow the whistle on their actions. And goodness knows I need a friend to talk to.

But this will have to do. Much though I want to tell the world, there is no way on Earth that such a jumbled nonsense of apparent fairy stories could ever make a difference could it!

Oh, and needless to say, I did not fertilise Lucy!

At least... I do not think I did. Do not KNOW that I did. No, they would not dare. I did not.

What a coup that would have been for them!

Was it half their goal all along I wondered as I tried to sleep.

I care less and less for my guardian that she could orchestrate such a mature ploy, and my thoughts turned again to you.

I had played my card as the inventor of time travel once more. I could not go on using it, but that moment in the sickbay, no, 'bedroom', was a crisis.

And it worked.

Lucy looked heartbroken, as if you had told your first love that you did not really love them at all and were just using them. Or like a child being told by his mother that he makes her sick, just when he comes to give her a hug and a kiss and say 'I love you mummy'.

And yes... this is fair to admit... I felt a little sorry for her.

For whatever reasons, or whatever confusions, or not, we have shared some significant and perhaps even one could say historic times together. She has been the oddest of friends to me over these few long weeks. And there is yes even a connection there between us.

BUT I CANNOT HAVE INTERCOURSE WITH MY GREAT GRANDDAUGHTER.

Alfred's sincerity in apologising for the assumption that I would was quite sincere. Wait, no. 'Sincerity'? It seems like a profanation of the word to write it in connection with such a fiend. I was certain HE had orchestrated this, or even convinced Lucy into believing she desired it as much as she seemed to want for me. But I was not going to take advantage of her like he had of me.

My disgust was not lost on them. "Please you! Wait!", Alfred shouted into me as I lurched towards the chute again. But again it does not work. It is only my naivety that does, as I am left just standing embarrassingly in position, primed for action yet going nowhere fast.

As furious humiliation set in, they revealed to me some of what they call the 'Shelton Timeline Decree'. And I soon find that the first part of what they tell me, echoes yet another of my own theorised 'laws of time travel' that was suggested to my Chinese 'friends' during our discussions. The rest however were lost on me for I had heard too much outrage for one day.

I would be complimented that some of it indeed existed and will be passed on to future generations from this point in time, if it were not for all the insults they had thrown at me in the same day in time.

I will summarise what I understood of the interesting bits for you Bella. (Thank you for staying with me in mind and spirit through this all - and despite it all.)

An attempt to alter the course of history may only be made by a governing traveller (like Alfred), if without such a change there exists extreme potential for a paradoxical event, or the potential that the existence of time travel would be revealed to younger civilizations before their potential to safely comprehend it had been achieved.

Where such alteration of the course of the timeline is to be attempted to prevent the above, the citizens influenced by the unauthorised knowledge will have all recollections of events restored to before the discrepancy took place. (I.e. they will have their memory erased.) (Yes.)

If the above does not result in a reset to the continuation of the desired timeline and said person(s) continue to present a threat - either by a recurrent evidence-revealing time loop, or resistance to the memory wipe - authorisation can be given to REMOVE them from the timeline. (Yes, kill them.) Where required, replacements (actors) are to be put in their place to ensure minimal alteration of other events.

I stress the last two were not of my design, only the first. I can only think of an example, such as... if the sinking of the Titanic had to be 'cancelled' because those who would survive its sinking had witnessed a 'UFO' crash into the side of the ship rather than an iceberg, yet such event could not be cancelled because of its immense impact on history (perhaps going on to ensure far improved design of ships... time ships), then they would instead travel back and stage the event using what one can only imagine might be cadavers floating in the water. And those who would survive would be 'taken', and so the Universe would be happy.

As I said, I have no comment. The rules are just what they tell me. It all sounded so far-fetched, and it rings of science fiction stories of 'mind wipes'. Although that said, have I not already realised that so much of that science fiction is grounded in truths that we have naively just misunderstood?!

I think my expression said it all, and Alfred asked me whether I did not believe them.

(Lucy had not spoken since our 'episode', and continued not to do so, although she looked at me with the eyes of a jilted extraterrestrial lover.)

"I am having trouble believing that you can suck people's thoughts out of their heads, that is all. In fact, I believe you may be telling me these 'laws' as exaggerated scare tactics just like your other stories, so I do not do anything hasty."

"Why we wanna scare you?", he said.

I had come clean.

I should not have done so.

"You know what I am thinking surely. I wish to tell the world what you are doing! And if it were not for the fact they may very well not believe me, I feel I actually would! And I am going to go home and consider a way through that - perhaps to find the right journalist - so you will be forced to stop taking the people of my time hostage only to be raped! Do you get it?! Is that okay, have I said enough now for you to let me go?"

"No these are not okay!", he said visibly shaken, with eyes wider than the widest they had been before. A small ridge appeared above his nose, between where his eyebrows should be. "Sir you are the one and we know these givings are hard, although please understand with your capacity", and then it came, "we can not LET YOU do this."

It is clear they had had no expectation that I would reveal their dirty little secret to the world, and it was a shock to their core. It is about time they had one. Due to the image that has been built up of me in time, they never even considered I would jeopardise the timelines by disclosing this disturbing revelation about 'removing people' - but their image is not true, it is glorified, rose-tinted, built up over too much time into godly stature. It always has been.

He had read my mind. "Sir, the laws I am speak of are solid. These are not immobile intimidations to terrorise you. And there are no 'suckings' of thoughts. Extraterrestrial sensory perception is for transceiving only, not intrusive around in brain. We can no more suck thoughts from you with our telepathy as you can do same by making shouting into someone."

'That is a relief', I had thought.

"You ingest Patounth 6", he had then added.

'Oh', I had thought.

"This is what the decree has mention with. I will take you to first principles so as to say it hunts for hottest neural connections only to liquefy them."

'Ah', I had thought.

But he went on to explain something I have wondered for a good many days - and that is why I remember their Chinglish word for word. Was it just an effect of telepathy imprinting directly into the conscious mind? Well, not only that it transpired.

You see, on that first abduction, the trance-like state I recalled was not just from a tranquiliser, but also as I had ingested - not Patounth 6 - but a different solution. One which in fact he leads me to believe has the very opposite effect (let us call it 'Patounth minus 6'). And the reason I would need a 'drug' that would heighten my state of awareness and thus my memory of their dialect beyond normal remits? Because they know from experience that, "special guest not believe nor remember if not".

Well this special guest certainly remembered it - I will pay them their dues. It must still be circulating my system - either that or the telepathy took over.

And I accepted his position on their memory wiping policy also. Genuinely in fact. I know of no way to tell the world as no journalist may believe me.

I resigned myself to his position... at that time.

We talked a short while longer, building some new warm neural connections for myself in the process, and it soon came to pass that Alfred was satisfied he had calmed me to a point where I was not a threat if they 'let me go'. It was clear I was one abductee they respected more than most, and would not remove me from the timelines as they had others.

Then again, he had naturally been destined to die, whereas I had not.

The fact that I was returned home was obvious I suspect, given I am writing to you here and now! Nonetheless, I am at least now certain of the knowledge that I have just been abducted, and returned.

A month ago I was regularly taken back to the normality of home, so as to recover and have consistency of familiarity in my life. Yet now I feel I am being taken back home to - in my mind - escape their evil clutches and make sense of the constant bombardment of newly disquieting information that assaults me each time I ask a simple question and then later write about it here. And even when I do not.

And do you know something? The thought of losing all memory of this freak show whether or not at the hands of 'Patounth 6' is sorely tempting to me...

If it were not for the fact that with it, I would lose the new memories of you.

Of course now, having ironed out every detail from the day thanks to you - this journal I am certain being the only reason for my sanity - I have had time to reconsider the state of thoughts Alfred left me in. To reconsider my promise not to 'tell'.

And I have had time to feel sorry for Lucy, who I left forlorn, without a word. Even though it was only days ago, the joyous 'times' she showed me ache a little now they have gone. How can that be?!

Yet... I maintain this.

I CANNOT CONDONE THEIR ACTIONS.

I am going to rest my head on my pillow and see what occurs.

I may dream up a way to reveal their skulduggery to the world... or I may not sleep at all.

Either way, I need to muster enough clarity of thought to devise a way to stop them, preferably without them stopping me... by wiping my memories. It STILL sounds like science fiction. So why do I take it as fact?

Or worse... that other rule regarding removing such culprits from the timelines altogether.

Is my own proposed time travel law about to come back and kill me?...

Sleep tight!

DAY TWENTY-FIVE

Posted by Eurora001 on Mon 2-Jul-2001 09:58

Good morning.

Well, amazingly, I slept well last night considering. Then again I was fatigued as though I had stayed up a million nights. Okay, so not so amazing after all. Still, I feel refreshed, and best still... I have come to a conclusion of how to handle these most unwanted of matters, if ever there were an understatement.

I am going to set Maxine on them. Yes, licking them to death is the way to go.

Ha, okay, am I not allowed a small nervous joke to lighten this load?

Actually maybe that IS the way to go... MAX!!!

Ha! No.

In all seriousness, my peaceful slumber was aided last night by the fact that after perhaps only forty minutes of thought (not winks), I had eliminated all possibilities, and reached the only possible human decision. And it is no joke.

I considered that I had only two options at first, in order to prevent these atrocities taking place, for which I consider myself largely responsible.

I also considered again that it was merely natural selection at work, and that we from this world were the 'weaker species', compared to they from our future. But that did not wash, because had these time ships never been invented, no matter who sowed the first seeds of the conception, then they would never have HAD the ability to travel back and save themselves in the... first (?) place.

And yes, I am very well aware that I am stating humanity was destined to die out from infertility during their time of inhabiting our baked Earth, if it were not for time travel. But was time travel 'destined' to exist along with it...

But this surely is inevitable? Given, it is not something we often pay much thought to in our lifetime and why very well would we. Yet, ultimately, even their current 'solution' of sexual assault and hostage taking is only temporary, because there will come a point where they begin to unwittingly abduct their own ancestors! If Alfred were to mistakenly destroy the life of his Grandmother (times a thousand), then HE would cease to exist!

They are treading a fine balancing line at the moment, perhaps only as fine as a few hundred-thousand years.

So yes, I consider that by stopping them - if such a thing were within my power - I would perhaps be spelling the END OF HUMANITY.

That is a big thing (hence the big letters). Yet, it is also a natural one. Humanity was meant to end there, I have concluded. What THEY are doing is the UNnatural thing. I would merely be restoring the natural state of affairs.

And so I came to think not of the 'if', but of the 'how'.

And there were really only two options that I could perceive of.

1. Do NOT invent time travel
2. Tell the world I HAVE invented time travel

As you will appreciate darling, each of those has its own set of problems, to say the least.

1. A bit late for that
2. Do I like mental asylums?

(Although now I think about number 1... is it?)

Well anyway now you can see my dilemma, and why I arrived on a THIRD solution to attempt first.

These creatures are us. We are them. Certainly they are desperate, but just as I have painted a reasonable argument here, much like the one in my head, I know it will be possible to let them into my mind, my thoughts, these words, these reasonable, rational, words. And so the only way I can consider to excuse myself from these crimes, is to stand up to them and make them reconsider their actions.

Or if necessary, to force them to stop, in the name of the man who gave them the tools. I. To play my card perhaps one too many times, whilst it is the only card I hold. I enabled their flights of fancy, and I can revoke them.

I have considered that even without this scandal, now I can say that the novelty of my adventures with the craft has perhaps begun to lose its shine, perhaps the world would be better off without it. For what beauty is there in a world without surprises, where instead any person who cares to look can realise everything that has ever and will ever occur.

Darling I wish you were here so I may gauge your opinion on my decision to confront them with conscience and implore them to do what is right. I am concerned my self-belief in the influence I hope to have over them may sound too supercilious. Too pompous. Or that I am just incapable of thinking clearly, with all I have had to take on board. Yet I hardly have many options open other than this, and you have not seen the respect they have looked at me with at so many times.

I am certain I can pull some Godly weight with Alfred due to this. Is it worth an attempt?

Is it worth the risk that they will think enough is enough, and this time will NOT let me go?

Hell, will they even ever return or have I seen the last of them already, only to be left with the taste of a bad dream in my mouth?

But...

IF they return - my hope is Alfred may take my views to his Council, discuss them with joint leaders. At least air them...?

Am I deranged?
Am I now, suddenly, in danger for having decided this?
Am *I* THE danger?

What do you think?
I wish you would answer.

My thoughts betray me when I do not type. My only comfort is this relentless hammering of keys! What a life...! I sit here terrified - I am messing with the entirety of the space-time continuum, and perhaps the fabric of the Universe itself. Unlike them I CAN change it, just like creating the machine in the first place changed it. I have free will. Surely this member of humanity at least has FREE WILL left?!?!

And now, every sound I hear behind me I think they are coming to get me. I have shouted at Max just because she is restless, her continuous readjustment of where exactly to sit on the bathroom floor causing an unnerving clattering. She senses my unease, which only makes her aggravating restlessness worse. AGH!

Again I hear noises. Is it them coming to cancel me out the very moment before they (already) know that I have formed my decision and will stick to it?
Nothing yet...
So at least I know this is not that moment.
Nor this...
Nor this...
Are these my last words?

These then?
Pfft.

(This is in fact a useful tool. I know by the fact I have not been abducted, that my decision was safe and poses no threat to me.) (Or them.)

Yet the point of this is... dare I say it... that I DO wish to pose a threat to them. That is the entire aim of my wish to end this rape, pillage, and plunder. So why have I not succeeded? Why have they not come to stop me? Or are they hovering outside this second... Perhaps that moment will only arrive when I see them next and make my request... demand... known. Or perhaps they will simply laugh at me and give me my coat, the shower chute door hitting me on the back on my way out.

BUT OF COURSE. They cannot read this. They would not know this was the moment. Unless history told them. But then if it was 'history', then so would be time travel, and they would have no crafts in existence to travel back and stop me with! THIS is why I am safe now. Again, I feel I could very well go mad thinking this through too much.

The way ahead is clear. I know what I have to say to them, and I will take the next step when it comes.

They would surely not dare to interfere with the memories of someone on this pedestal upon which I currently stand. I am confident I can make my requests known to them, and return safely, despite how serious Alfred seemed last time. They let me go then after all. They will let me go again. I am surely different to the 'average Joe' their laws apply to. They have made that much known, a foolish error of judgment on their part.

Perhaps they think our trips are going to return to normality - some other final fanciful mission for me like those before, and as though nothing happened last time. If so, they have seriously underestimated my morals.

They are later than ever.

Could this really be it? No more missions for me? No more driving lessons and dinosaurs?

Has time already returned for me to travelling at a speed of exactly one day per day?

The other incredible thing that has just occurred to me - even if I do say so myself (and I do), is what might be the result of my entering the craft, th

Tey['re here

DAY TWENTY-FIVE (II)

Posted by Eurora001 on Mon 2-Jul-2001 17:50

There is some bug with this web site - it would not let me pick today's date for this entry. So you follow things, today is the 7th of June, not a month later as the site claims! They obviously have a problem with their clock - ironic really, given all the news I am about to report to you of selling my concept in Beijing! (I thought you would like to know that I am already time travelling.)

It is so good to be back from China. What a journey I have been on. And the best news is... drum roll please... yes, as you guessed from the above, I DID IT!!

Success! It is over!

And a bit more good news, the scar on my wrist is virtually invisible now.

Yet I am shattered. And speaking of my wrist, my tiredness brought on a quite nasty nosebleed a little while ago. Why did I never believe in jetlag? Or more like Stealth Bomber lag, in the way it sneaks up on you under the radar.

Okay, so it was only a passenger jet from China, but for my first journey that far Far East, returning feels like I have hit my head against a bank vault door. With my nose. Ten times.

'Ni hao!'? Hmm.

Despite the throbbing I must focus on the positives. It is wonderful news yes? All done at long last. And not a moment too soon.

As I sit here, tiredly sleepless this evening, and look out at that dark blue sky, all that light spread across a hundred stars, each of them known personally to me it seems, I have looked at them that many times.

And here I am again, back to normality, planted with water (well a glass of it) at the computer by the window you yourself have looked out of, when you too stared at the patterns of those dancing lights.

I hope you may be staring back at me from up high above the other side of the glass at least. After all it was that that started me on this journey what seems like so long ago. It feels like more time has passed than I realised, yet you seem eerily close to me.

In China I managed to keep the scars out of sight of the respectful Beijing hosts thanks to an English shirt. I need not have worried. You cannot help but smile when you shake hands with their foremost scientists, and their first words are, "Hohh so handsome", to me! The people are so respectful I must tell you. I know you loved Japan when you went and I feel they are much alike.

Gosh I am so tired. This is seriously worse than I ever imagined it would be.

But a long story short, our signer arrived after some delay to help with the translation, and then the others and I began to get on REALLY well. It looked quite promising. The bosses arrived, and I have to tell you this, but one of them for some reason had black paint on his head instead of hair! You would have had more trouble keeping the straight face I managed, had we both been there, but manage I did. I have so missed those moments with you. Yet it feels as though you WERE with me there, in your way. Almost like I see you in yet those endlessly realistic dreams you choose to visit me in. I am sure you do it intentionally Bella.

Anyway I digress. They lifted their briefcases onto the long extender desk, containing the contracts we bounced back and forth for seemingly months. Thank goodness for Jonathan on my side and by my side there.

I was expecting them to give my concept quite a going over and it is all that went through my mind on the long flight there. I still feel slightly airsick now, deep in my inner ear even though there was no turbulence. But when will I learn to believe something good will happen to me? As it did.

When the CEO first spoke, Abbey the translator started to sign it for me, and as she did so, it was clear that my being deaf had not until then filtered down to him. People just assume. But as soon as he realised, the change in body language was stark, and I immediately had the upper hand! There was no belittling to speak of, and my hearing disability became an ABILITY Bella. Those little victories are worth living for alone.

Before long these important gentlemen sat across from me were in awe of the workings laid out in front of them. Once I had shared my Eureka moment from that stormy day, I elaborated under our pile of non-disclosure agreements about how the eurora potential works, with them wanting to discuss my proposed laws and my plans. I hate calling it 'my invention' - it makes me sound like a nutty professor.

Will write more soon, my brain hurts.

Day Twenty-Six

Day Twenty-Seven

Posted by Eurora001 on Wed 4-Jul-2001 12:34

Okay.

Well.

Please ignore how tidy this writing may be formulated.

My mind is conversely a dishevelled mess inside. Both allegorically and physically if what I am led to believe is true, IS true.

And I would not believe the last month of entries that I spent the last two days reading, if it were not for the fact that my present body clock 'thinks' I have 'just' returned from selling the rights to the eurora potential in China.

Nor for the fact that I know in my heart that you and I WERE together five days ago. NOBODY could erase at least the presence of you from my mind.

Hell I am certain I can even still smell you Bella.

I cannot tell you details of what has just happened to me, as simply I do not even know myself what occurred between my penultimate entry, and the one that followed it.

I think it is as clear to you as it is me what has transpired.

I have had my memories of the past month deleted.

Let me spell it out for myself...

'Little alien abductors, who are actually small humanoids from our future, destroyed my past weeks of memories because I got too close to a truth, and left me believing that today was over a month ago and that I had just arrived back from China - as if none of what I have just read back to myself had ever even happened, and in turn as if I had never discovered that they steal and rape our people.'

But happen it did.

It took me nearly the past two days of reckoning on whether the journals I found here were the result of having some form of cruel prank played on me by Daniel, or whether I was just turning into a literally 'mad' scientist after all, but in the end I could only resolve that what I had read was honest-to-God reality.

The writing is just too believable and too much like my style, complete even with my typical nervous jokes when I was under stress, for anyone to have spent the time on as a practical joke. After all, if it was a joke then where are the pranksters to enjoy my reaction? I am alone here.

And then, the more I read it, and the more I drank my nettle tea, the more I remembered it. Yes, I started to REMEMBER IT for real Bella.

They think they erased it!

I did not need to verify my own 'missing time', even though I did by checking the television, Internet, and even a walk to the shop to clear my head and Max's, and buy 'today's' newspaper. And today IS July the fourth - how apt. I would have had no idea what happened to most of June if it were not for this journal. And if it were not for you I would never have written it.

So I am sure you saved me.

Can you imagine what went through my mind when I had to save the last entry with a day weeks 'into the future', only to find on the screen a host of other entries during June and July that I had no recollection of making?!

It hit me like a bolt out of the purple-orange.

'What on Earth!?'

And that was the point - it was all on Earth. But there it was. And after fighting with myself for the past day-and-a-half to understand what, why, or how, I finally came to the recognition of the devastating, shattering reality.

So yes, I thank Heavens for these journals to restore into my mind the backup copy of what had gone on. God what a state of affairs. There may not be many ways to undo their "Patounth 6", but this was evidently the one. Another discovery to add to my lists - that freshly melted neural connections could rebuilt if cooled down fast enough with a reminder read through of their original memories!

And I dare say that 'Patounth Minus 6' still circulating my bloodstream did not do their attempt any favours. They had no choice but to try however.

I just pity all those who never had a secret text trigger to habitually go back to, discover, and recover from their own amnesia at the hands of some futuristic barbarians.

But I am cured.

And I hope the delay has not cost me.

Yesterday, when I considered if I would ever have to meet the freakish creatures I was only reading about, it made my hands go cold and yet drip with sweat, as if I found out I was going to have to give a speech before a million people with five minutes' notice.

But when it started to come back to me, and I began to rebuild the connections that made up these memories of 'Alfred' and 'Lucy', it very slowly but slightly surely (as far as anything about little grey people from a sun-scorched future can be 'sure'), became relatable and acceptable. And then it moved from relatable to memorable, and from acceptable to acceptance.

Before too long, and certainly by the time I awoke this morning somehow from no sleep whatsoever, I felt as though I knew almost as much as I needed to. Or perhaps as much as I wanted to, or even ever did.

I find even whilst typing this, my 'own' memories of details I had NOT even written about, are coming to my mind. So I KNOW I am not just living some story I have read - I know it is there in my head too. Like Lucy explaining the controls of the craft to me made her sound like a used car or computer salesperson. "Of the relaxation in not only a comfortable Extapien interface by desktop but also living"!

Good God, I can now remember it word for word! My memory has come back at a frightening rate. Or did it never really leave, but just hid? And it is back all because of this evidence they missed? Then these journals are surely more dangerous than ever before - should they discover their existence.

Is it possible the telepathy receptors they had awakened in my mind that heard their words somehow occupy a different space to those of my everyday memories? That too could explain it.

Whatever the reasons, I am under no doubt of the reality of these situations, so where does that leave me...

Well it all makes sense why they would do this. I had threatened their very existence. They clearly believed that setting my memory back to normal events five weeks ago before their first visit would remove all threat to them. A last resort.

And then, they would naturally expect me to carry on my normal course of life after a trip to the Doctor about my very own 'missing time' experience, and become just another abductee 'lunatic' destined for the loony bin.

WHY YES! Have I not just experienced first-hand the awful truth of those who also experience what they call missing time, and abduction?! For heaven's sake, I have become one of the very victims that I was so furious at them for creating - and now here I am, paying the price. I am so angry, I cannot even put it into words! I am ashamed to say a plate just paid the price, against the wall. OH FOR HEAVEN'S SAKE it even looked like a flying saucer as I threw it! Why is everything so connected?!

Let me again look at this from their side so I may understand more. The alternative is haste and anger. Calm. Must be calm.

If Isaac Newton had posed the same threat to me, I might very well consider wiping a few of his recent memories to be 'acceptable behaviour'.

However, I would never force my body on another. That is not acceptable behaviour. And no matter how firmly I know Lucy is (or was) (or will be) young and with a good heart, her culture is just too alien for me to ever condone her desires. 100% of my hates her. Yet 100% of me is endeared by her.

(One suspects the human mind is not designed to deal with such quandaries.)

Yet why did they not take me back to the day I thought it was five weeks ago? I feel slightly thoughtless for typing as though I had just awaked from jetlag. But of course they could not return 'me' to then, because I would be living with myself. There would be TWO of me, the original me, and the future me gone back to live there. Ironic that they could not bring me back to live with myself. Because if I do not act on this unique position they have left me in, I know one thing for sure - I will not be able to live with myself.

And they never counted on my keeping journals - I still cannot get over it! Yet I suppose such things are under their radar, for I saw no Internet browser on the ship! Such an advanced race, yet so unaware and foolish in other ways.

Does it not remind us, of us?

Indeed, for they are us, multiplied by the power of a million years.

I do not need to test whether they know about these journals for I know for sure they do not. I am already testing it with each keypress! QWERTYUIOP! And by the fact the old entries were not wiped. These are after all entirely private between me and you. You would not tell the monsters, and even if they ventured in their time crafts up to Heaven itself, I know you would never put me in harm's way.

The only way we could come to harm is if these journals were to get out into the public eye.

I HAVE TO DELETE THEM! I must! All of this will then no longer exist.

YET, their very existence has just saved me from a fate worse than a mind wipe, so how can I wipe THEM?! These journals may very well again be my lifeline yet again. Am I asking myself to destroy my own salvation?

For the sake of argument, to cover all bases, what if something did happen to me - again but with more permanence - and someone 'on our side' finds all I have written here. How could I - in my absence - convince them to act cautiously yet definitively, where I failed? Somebody needs to stop these ogres, and if it is not me then who? I cannot ask you to, any more than I could expect Max.

What if I get hit by a bus, a car, or a time machine... is that IT? They get away with it? Our future is destined to amount to an increasing number of abductions and destroyed lives.

NO.

I need to put this insurance into play, in the event that these entries outlive me. A fate I will avoid with all my might. I need these journals. I will keep them here, marked private. They have been completely safe and secure all along. 'They' are never coming back here again - at least not to take me on another 'adventure', that much is a certainty, for they think I am unaware of their existence, and the matter is closed.

I was just being paranoid.
Understandable.

I must sleep and work out another resolution to their crimes.

Yet if they cannot read these...
How can you?

God, what am I doing with my life.

Living in the past, talking to ghosts.

I have to act courageously and definitively now, if I know anything for sure.

Maybe I had already decided that final, last resort of an outcome in the past, after I had last written here before they temporarily took away my mind. Many lesser memories from home are still vague. (For example I have no recollection of feeding or walking Max other than the odd mention in the journals, yet she is perfectly all right. I suppose only the important details stuck fast.)

I sat there thinking. I AM SEETHING! I MUST FIND RETRIBUTION AGAINST THESE BEASTS! IT IS ALL I HAVE LEFT.

How dare they rape our women!
How dare they meddle with my brain!
WHO DO THEY THINK THEY ARE.

DAY TWENTY-EIGHT

Posted by Eurora001 on Thu 5-Jul-2001 07:31

Yesterday I asked who they think they are.
Well, they are us.

Thanks to my pixelated antidote that is this web log, I am certain that all of my memories have bubbled back into life now, and the path ahead is as clear as the one I have followed these past weeks. Just a minor setback and all behind me now. I am proud at that. (Please, allow me to downplay it.)

It is early morning, but I could not sleep. And for once not through fear or anxiety, but through almost excited anticipation, for at last... I know EXACTLY what to do now, and I cannot wait to get on and do it!

I have decided this has to end.
I started it.
I end it.

The only way - the only SURE FIRE way - to prevent their gaining from me the capacity to use time travel to commit these heinous sins, is to do just that.

TO PREVENT THEM GAINING THE CONCEPT FOR TIME TRAVEL, from me.

And to do that, I have to prevent the Chinese from gaining it, five weeks ago.

And how could I travel back five weeks you might ask?
Hmm let me think! (Well, ask a silly question...)

One last moment of time travel for me... to bring about the last moments of time travel for them.

Damn the income to hell and back. I have looked at them since I arrived home from Beijing - and what are they but just numbers on a screen. They are not life. They are not a family. Could I really live with myself knowing I had profited from future rapists? Those are the two options - be rich and a co-conspirator to kidnapping and violation, or be just comfortable - in pocket if not in mind.

None of that seems important now in any event, with what I remember seeing at Dullice. Those people on stretchers - I know now with all my revived memories combined with new knowledge - even clearer than I knew it then - that they were us. Humans. Abductees. Dead.

Good God - what of that jumbo jet I saw with human-like faces behind the windows...? A craft beamed straight out of the Bermuda Triangle or something equally implausible!? Yet right there in front of my face.

Or the old burnt out car in the Dullice junk yard... could I have looked closer and seen... human remains inside?! Abduction gone wrong?

I know nothing can be put past them now.

And I also know that is not a sick bay on their craft. It is where they take the people to sexually assault them.

So you must now surely understand why I have to end all that. In fact, have to stop it having ever even happened.

You know something? It seems incredible how life just goes on outside and around me. Of course the dog knows none of this. But the people too, shouting occasionally, others driving off or arriving in their cars, just going about everyday mundane life with a casual 'toot'. And even now, a young man struts casually across the road wearing trainers that are far too white, far too triumphant for these events. Do none of them know what is going on, what I am forfeiting for them?! Do they know what I may be about to sacrifice?

Perhaps not - for I have not even told you my plan yet.

Well, I have considered going back to tell myself not to go to China, but I cannot interact directly with myself, for it would risk a paradox of biblical proportions.

I have considered sending a letter or leaving a note, but I know that even if the other 'I' did believe what he read, others would not then believe him, especially my lawyer who had spent weeks negotiating the contracts - and I would force the other me into the same loony bin I very nearly found myself in yesterday. Can you imagine the scene if that other me told Jonathan the deal was off because 'a time traveller left me a Post-it note'? In fact I would like to see his face, but no I am relatively certain he would not accept it as anything but one of my nervous pranks before the big day.

I must be realistic and decisive as I will certainly only get one chance at this. One extra chance at that. But how? Shoot my younger self before I can sell the plans? I have not been able to come to terms with any way to achieve that.

I have considered many, many things, some even more terrible, others just plain preposterous.

But then a solution that almost seems like divine past intervention hit me. It all boils down to ONE sure-fire resolution...

I have to travel back to the night I tried to kill myself. Your mother had paid me a visit, and in so doing, had unwittingly interrupted the suicide bid and saved 'my' life. But if she had not interrupted me?...

And so... I have to travel back to that night, and stop her before she gets to the door.

'I' have to die.

At least, that other me has to die, for then he will never go on to have that Eureka moment that led to the eurora potential.

But, I am pinning all humanity's hope - and my own - on one law - well theory of a law - which I very much believe - that is hope - to be true.

It is the theory that those who HAVE themselves time travelled, cannot be affected by the effects OF time travel... That once you leave the 'natural' course OF events as I did five weeks ago, and so leave the unflinching flow of the timelines, you are no longer affected BY events. (Somewhat like an astronaut who leaves the worldly grasp of Earth's gravity, is no longer bound by it.)

And the darnedest thing of all is that I cannot even recall who the theory was attributed to, only that it became a source of some debate and interest. It has never been quite as interesting to me, as it is now, for my life - this life - depends upon it.

I, typing to you now, would be safe from being washed from history in such scenario for I HAVE time travelled, whilst that past suicidal me had not. I became immune the first moment the swines took me on that first brief journey. I suppose I at least may be able to 'thank' them for that.

The other me would surely succeed in the suicide attempt if this me were to intercept your mother before she reached 'my' front door and pressed the intercom... before she interrupted my wish to take my life.

And then what? A gap of Earth time where I would cease to exist, until the date I first became a time traveller? Would I be 'born again' on that date? No! For this me could take the place of my other, soon-to-be dead self back then. I would already be there, outside my own front door, those few short years ago.

I would become an... actor... playing the role of me.

(Familiar.)

And so this theory compels me now. It is all I have, so let it! Of all the known posits I have clung to, all the great thinkers have taught us, here I am hoping more than any of them that this obscurest of them all is the truest too!

Then there is just one small detail.

I will need a time machine.

(I told you it was small.)

I know how to fly one. That memory is now as fresh as I suspect it ever was. I know how to cloak it, how to land it. I know enough.

And I think I know exactly how to make those small, feeble, and easily overpowered gremlins bring one right to my door!

My plan is worryingly simple... a bit like the girl from Burger King back before this all begun. But unlike her, this might actually work. Let me go over it once more, for my own peace of mind. (Yes if only.)

Right, here we go.

After I capture my time machine by overpowering Alfred and Lucy (...why does that make me feel guilty?...), I somehow convince Max to go walkies into the shower-chute, and we travel back to the exact date and time of my attempted suicide. I know it so well, after all.

Leaving Maxine in the craft, I re-enter my apartment block those years earlier, and make sure I am in the hallway pretending to try my key in the door, at the time I know your mother arrived. All I have to do is 'bump into' her, and she will be satisfied she has found the 'me' she came to see.

And then I take her for afternoon tea.

Whilst 'I' die behind the door.

It is so simple, yet so confusingly distressing.

Is it really that simple? Travel there, meet her, and leave the other me to my painful business...

Why do I feel mixed compassion for 'myself'? It is truly as if it is not me who will be quietly dying behind that thin wooden door. (Well I suppose it is not - I am the only me I know.)

Is this too uncomplicated? It will surely work!

It has to work.

Please work.

She will never find the other me - the one with the Stanley knife. Nor will she save me from the brink of death, while I take her for tea. (That sentence would not work in any other situation would it.)

God darling I am actually quite scared now I commit it to words.

I have taken the decision just once to end my life in the past having lost you, yet here I have to take it again. Quite the multiple suicidal maniac I am turning out to be hmm. Yet, it is just the same decision. In fact, if anything, I am merely undoing that unwanted interference (and apologies for calling your mother an unwanted interference) which prevented my original wish to depart this Earth.

And likewise, I am merely undoing the unnecessary complication of time travel, which has many eons from now, prevented Mother Nature's original wish for humanity to depart this Earth.

(And yes, it is strange how symmetry connects so much of this. I will think on that some more when headspace allows.)

Alas the more I consider this, the less 'simple' a plan it becomes. For what to do with the body of my dead 'twin'. Inevitably I will need to re-enter my home and deal with the mess I will find there - a mess that never existed and still does not to this day. Yet will soon exist, in the past.

And what to do with Alfred and Lucy once I have overpowered them, for I cannot very well leave them here, in this place or time, when I depart it. Will I even kill them or just incapacitate them? I have not - dare not - even think that through. What happens will happen - if I overthink it I will surely never have the nerve to in fact do it, whatever it is.

I shall have to find somewhere to take all three of them - somewhere nobody will ever find them. Maybe somewhen.

And another complication (pah - how could it ever have been simple - am I still so naive?)... what to do with the entire time machine that I will still have parked above my garden! Will it evaporate the moment the last drop of life leaves that other me and with him the last drop of the eurora potential's... potential? (There is that symmetry again. Why?) Or will it somehow become stranded in time, because it had not even been created at that date? And if so, how on earth will I destroy it? A match?! A hammer?! Come on man! And I could not even take it to another time period and leave it there, for how would I ever get back to my time!?

All these blasted questions will have to wait to be answered. All things in order - I will cross each bridge as I come to it - whilst trying not to burn it.

Baby steps. They taught me that at least.

The anticipation is welling up inside me now. The time is growing nearer when I will set the trap that leads Alfred and Lucy back to me, bringing with them their ship - once my ship and soon to be reclaimed by its creator.

My hands are like an arctic stream now with the trepidation, my breathing shallow. I feel I may very well be near to hyperventilating!

I know now more than ever and despite all the concerns, that I sit here contemplating the right thing.

Call it what you like but I am more terrified now that I was before even my suicide! Back then I had nothing to lose... except all this I think. I mean, I had already lost you. And this concept had not even been born yet. It was a moment of grisly spontaneity and desperation. Yet now... by contrast... I have more to lose than perhaps any living person on Earth! So I hope you understand why it frights me more.

But no, I must hold onto the thought that 'I' am not committing suicide, I am just going for tea. Yes. Just a tea with your mother.

At least I shall also find out whether Novikov's scenario is borne out - the theory that says events would conspire against you so that any change that might create a harmful paradox would simply not be possible. If there is no hole ripped in the fabric of the Universe when I do these things, yet I find myself unable to carry out a certain part of the plan, I will know why.

But will your mother sit there sipping a soya-half-double-decaf-half-caf, whilst with every drop I am wondering if I am about to evaporate like the steam on the drink in front of her very eyes? I know it is bad for one but never thought caffeine would be the death of me. I do not want to die, even though the other me at the same moment in time really will want to. I want only to prevent the exchange of contracts in China on that later historic day, which became...

My opus. My life's single great achievement, which I will not have yet achieved. Will not ever achieve. Either way, banished to the scrap-pile, like those before it.

Would the futurists not just stop me? Well, in a word, no. If I can sneak up on time by stealth, and stop myself ever inventing this wretched technology, then the futurists will not be ABLE to travel back and stop me after that fact, because they will no longer possess the technology to do so! All existence of time machines that they possess will simply fade away, like ripples in time flattening out to some other parallel reality. Will they even know they ever had that option? My hope is they will not know what hit them, the foolish buggers!

And if my craft did not dematerialise then what fun I could have! Yet I know I would have to destroy it, as it would be a fully operational version of the very invention I was trying to snuff out. The potential for its capture and reverse engineering would be immense, and would mean I had achieved nothing as the future would still find a way to invade our past.

I am as tense as a tightrope.

You know, as I sit here and prepare myself for the inevitable moment that I lay my bait for Alfred and Lucy, the anticipation still within me, I almost feel sorry for 'that chap' (past Mr me). I have messed around with his existence all too much, firstly kidnapping him from his peaceful slumber on your sofa that Christmas, and now preventing your mother saving him a month later. And he never got to hear again, yet I have. Or to see you. He has not had a lucky life the poor devil.

Funny, I always thought I was plagued by bad luck did I not? Always had that lack of self-confidence that you urged me to build upon, as did... Lucy... (Why do I still feel 'something' about her? I must be wary that it does not prevent me carrying out my act of necessary hostility against her, for the good of our world.)

And after all that... perhaps I was right about my luck after all. This is hardly good fortune Bella!

Speaking of confidence, you are right I suppose. I never considered myself brave, yet here I am, about to save... the human race... from the terror I (or perhaps others after me) have helped create. I suppose that is not brave is it, to undo a catastrophic mistake one has made - only would this click move me into the recycle bin?

Let us hope just one me. Two copies of me in there may very well throw up duplicate 'file already exists' error that the Universe would not allow.

Yet now I think of the other creators who added to my concept until the inevitable existence of it, if I do not take this first step, someone else may still fill in that blank. Would the idea still be floating around the ether, somehow, somewhere? Would it still exist, like a sculptor says the statue has always existed and he was just freeing it from the stone, so too would the concept be freed at some point, by some other?

Well I will go back and smash the stone before 'I' even begin to tap away at it, and that will be that. But in case of that chance that someone else finds it... I must also send out a signal that ensures it never comes to pass. Could these journals be that signal I could send? No, I am sure. Who would ever believe it all!

I simply have to take the chance nobody else will discover the eurora potential. What other choice is there? Do you have a better idea? Does anyone? What would the man from the Post Office do in the same situation? And I have to pray that the accident that led me to my Eureka moment those years ago back was truly the one-in-a-million that I felt it to be at the time, and ever since. After all, how many of my future peers are likely to have the same -

I should not say a word about how I came upon the concept, lest this should ever fall into the wrong hands, for it would enable them to recreate it. Sorry. Yes, I know I can trust you. It is not you I am worried about.

Posted by Eurora001 on Thu 5-Jul-2001 09:09

I had to take time out there. I have had a long, hot, think in the bath. This is not a decision to take without due consideration. But I have washed away almost all doubt now.

We as humans have a right to live in this time unthreatened, no matter what nature has selected us for in the future. No matter how innocent Lucy may be in all this. This is MY time to protect, even if that is theirs. Call it a war. We have always been keen on those.

This is my home, and that is theirs. Just like the dog who sits curled up by me feet, I too will protect my territory, regardless of excuses from the infiltrators. Grrr.

This is evolution, in reverse. I aim to survive in the past, by those in the future perishing. Yet it is not selfish of me, for without my invention they would never have existed in the first place!

I have the upper hand as I created that destiny. I am their creator in a way...

GOD OF COURSE!!!!!!

That explains why they acted 'as if I was some form of God to them'.

I *WAS* SOME SORT OF GOD TO THEM!

IT WAS NOT THE ABILITY TO TIME TRAVEL TO WATCH DINOSAURS THAT THEY WERE SO THANKFUL TO ME FOR!...

IT WAS THE FERTILITY I ALLOWED THEM!

THE LIFE!

I AM the virtual 'creator' of many of them.

Jesus, I just scared all sorts of hell out of myself.

Well there you have it.

Christ.

...And I had wondered in the bath whether those who perfected bringing us into the nuclear weapons age would have gone back and undone that creation, had they seen the death and suffering it would later cause over Hiroshima. An incredible discovery in its time (like mine), yet so regretted in later time (by me). But would Einstein have committed suicide to perhaps save millions of lives? Even if there were two of him, would he erase one? If I ever get the chance to ask him, I shall certainly let you know, but I would like to believe he would.

And so I sit here, now dressed and ready for this fateful day, feeling as anxious as a pigeon in a cattery, as low as any man could be, yet looking up so high at the stars - the same ones that never perceptibly change up there no matter how much transforms down here - and wonder if you are wondering, if I do this act now which stops the future and the Futurists existing in the way they do, will they simply come back and prevent me from the very act I am about to perform before I can perform it?

A-ha! Well that is exactly what I am hoping they will 'TRY' to do shortly! That is the only way I can trap them.

Or have they been reading every entry I made here, waiting for the moment before the moment I click 'Save'?

...Wonderful, now I am scared to click Save...

And what a word to have to click on - almost smacking me across the face in all its apt glory. SAVE.

Save our world.

(And if you are reading this then you know I did save.)

No. They do not know this blog exists. Nobody does. If anyone ever did, I fear they would be the ones removed from history by the futurists to protect their secret, along with me. But not you. That would be the only time I would ever have been thankful that you already had been...

Either that or the futurists would plant evidence to label such a thing some sort of story. Hell what am I talking about, soon it will be over. Over. This freakish reverie turned nightmare.

I have just downloaded an eraser program which is now running in the background with Department of Defence deletion algorithms. Even as I type this, it is overwriting with 0s and 1s my folders containing all of the plans, the patent, the contract drafts, the emails, and when I am done here and close this window, I will also set it about deleting the history of my visits to this website.

It is slowing down the computer... Come on!

While that was running I just shred the China agreement papers. The paper cut the final page gave me as its parting sting may be the least of my wounds.

All of that work, GONE.

HELL WHAT IS WRONG WITH ME! I did not think I would really cry at the loss of it all! But it is so painful to be destroying all of those words, all of those lines, all of those months, years, formulae, and drawings. All the final success.

I suppose I did not realise what a large part of my life they had become for these short years.

But yes, they HAD. (Past tense now.)

Filling the hole you left.

GODAMIT MAN, save your tears.

'Finished', it tells me. Am I? How apt. Again.

Now I have NOTHING. The files are gone forever. Torn to digital and paper shreds. No you. No concept. Only one thing remains.

That 'simple' plan.

I could still back out now. The contracts have still been exchanged. I could get the plans back. I could piece together the contract, perhaps. Time travel, presently, still exists - in a vault, somewhere in Beijing.

I could even shred the letter to the landlord apologising for my sudden departure and inviting him to give the remaining belongings to charity - yet I will never truly depart this place - I just have to ensure I keep living here after I travel back and replace my former self also living here. I may have a few extra grey hairs as far as the landlord knows, but nothing else will change.

It is not too late. Yet I am beyond all doubt. I have to Save the past, or we may all be Finished. But still, I could pull out now. I am just saying. If I wanted to that is. Not that I do. It is just reassuring to know I have control. Why I do not pull out I cannot say.

I am at a loss. I am sick of typing here - it is surely now time for ACTION. I know what I have to do. No more procrastination.

And just on the slender chance that anyone else IS somehow reading this in the future (and I have not deleted this sentence)...

I feel such a fool typing this, to nobody, still...

(I have just 'gone back' to amend the post before all of this started the day I returned from China - take a look. If anyone does find that entry, they will know to try to contact me, or if I am unreachable they will know what to do. God knows I will still need a friend if nothing more.)

I remember your words once spoken to me with no apparent foresight of how relevant you were going to be this chilling evening. But then that is you all over, always so pertinent...

"You are incandescent my love, and the time is now."

I think this is going to work Bella. I really think this is going to work!

I feel maybe THIS will become my Eureka moment instead.

Time is of the essence. You know, I can almost feel the past melding seamlessly into the present, creating a feral future.

I love you. Will write again, before long.

Eurora001

The Chrononaut

R.I.P.

"Restless in Perpetuity"

...?

THE CHRONONAUT

Printed in Great Britain
by Amazon

49085720R00226